*The Living
and the Lost*

The Living
and the Lost

Ellen Feldman

ST. MARTIN'S
GRIFFIN
NEW YORK

First published in the United States by St. Martin's Griffin, an imprint of St. Martin's Publishing Group

THE LIVING AND THE LOST. Copyright © 2021 by Ellen Feldman. All rights reserved. Printed in the United States of America. For information, address St. Martin's Press, 120 Broadway, New York, NY 10271.

www.stmartins.com

Design by Meryl Sussman Levavi

The Library of Congress Cataloging-in-Publication Data is available upon request.

ISBN 978-1-250-78082-9 (trade paperback)
ISBN 978-1-250-82181-2 (hardcover)
ISBN 978-1-250-78083-6 (ebook)

Our books may be purchased in bulk for promotional, educational, or business use. Please contact your local bookseller or the Macmillan Corporate and Premium Sales Department at 1-800-221-7945, extension 5442, or by email at MacmillanSpecialMarkets@macmillan.com.

First Edition: 2021

1   3   5   7   9   10   8   6   4   2

In memory of
Meredith Kay

And for
Stephen Reibel
again and always

God, I hate the Germans.

—General Dwight D. Eisenhower
in a letter to his wife, September 1944

*I can hate Germany and all things German
with a passion, but I can't hate individuals.*

—Gerda Weissmann Klein,
survivor of a Nazi slave labor camp
and a 350-mile forced march

One

❧

BERLIN HAD NEVER BEEN SO QUIET. CARS AND TRUCKS lay in useless pieces. Even bicycles were scarce. There was a rumor that a Soviet soldier had shot a woman who'd refused to yield hers. Smart-stepping boots no longer echoed on the pavements. People trudged the streets dour and mute. The city had been cowed into silence. The hush was as unsettling as the physical devastation. The rest of Germany had been bombed. Berlin had been obliterated.

She'd been in the city for only forty-eight hours, and the shock of the destruction, wreaked first by Allied planes, then by fierce fighting between the Wehrmacht and the Red Army, and most recently by Soviet rape and pillage, was still raw. Some neighborhoods looked like moonscapes, all dirt and craters and dusty shadows that when she got closer turned out to be *Trümmerfrauen*, the sullen, silent women who picked up broken bricks, pieces of pipe, and other debris and passed the wreckage along from hand to hand in a weary assembly line of forced labor, forced if the women wanted ration cards to eat. But what amazed her even more than the ruin was the Russian roulette aspect. Here and there, parts of buildings still stood, though walls or roofs had been blown away, exposing to cold and rain and prying eyes old bed-steads, broken toilets, and desperate inhabitants still clinging to what was left, because where else could they go? Sometimes one side of the street was nothing more than a pile of rubble while a building across the way stood untouched, the architectural details still handsome, or garish, the glass of the windows unshattered, the Biedermeier breakfronts like this one in the parlor of the flat gleaming in the setting winter sun that spilled into the room. The breakfront had caught her attention as soon as she'd stepped through the sliding doors to the parlor. It was standing between two tall French windows that opened onto Riemeisterstrasse. She told herself Berlin was full of Biedermeier chairs and tables, secretaries and breakfronts. There was no reason to think this was a piece from her own past. But reason had nothing to do with it.

She started across the room. The woman in the rusty black dress that hung on her scrawny frame as if on a scarecrow— Millie was willing to bet that in happier times she had liked her schnitzel and *kuchen*—dogged her steps. A girl, about four or five Millie guessed, though these days with all the malnutrition it was hard to tell, clung to her mother's dragging skirt. The child's eyes, when she stole a glance up at Millie, were saucers of fear in her thin washed-out face. Don't be afraid, Millie wanted to say. I won't hurt you. Then she caught herself. Who was she kidding? Of course she was about to hurt the child. She was about to devastate the entire family.

The woman moved to step in front of the breakfront, as if to protect it from Millie, and the stench of sour body odor grew stronger. These days soap was as hard to find in Berlin as food, and what little there was crumbled into hard gray pebbles the instant it met water. Breathing through her mouth to avoid inhaling the smell, a trick a medical student back in the States had taught her, Millie ran her fingers over the birch and ebony inlays. The wood felt smooth and familiar beneath her touch. Berlin might be full of Biedermeier breakfronts, but how many had elaborate geometric inlays and ebony columns with brass capitals? The piece was too elegant for this solidly *kleinbürgerlich* flat. Middle-class, she corrected herself. She was here to speak German to the Germans, not to wander down her own linguistic memory lane.

"It is, how do you say in English, a fake," the woman said.

Millie took a step away. Even breathing through her mouth, she couldn't escape the smell. She reminded herself it wasn't the woman's fault, but that didn't make the odor, or the woman, any less offensive. Whose fault was it that there was no soap in Berlin?

"*Fälschung.*"

"You speak German?" the woman asked as if she'd been tricked.

"Apparently. But *fälschung* or *authentisch*, it's part of the inventory."

"It is a family piece," the woman insisted. "Of sentimental value only," she added in an unsentimental voice.

A family piece. Of sentimental value. Millie knew something about that. She turned from the breakfront, crossed the sitting room, and started down the hall. The woman tried to bustle ahead, but Millie blocked her way. She did not want to be shown the apartment, as if she were a prospective renter or boarder, as if she were a supplicant. We come as conquerors, not as oppressors, General Eisenhower had announced, and though Millie was officially sworn to the second part of that sentence, she wasn't about to forget the first. More to the point, she was determined not to let any German she came in contact with forget it.

She made her way down the hall. The dining room was crowded with a heavy carved table and too many chairs. No

Biedermeier elegance here. The kitchen was primitive, but she didn't intend to do much cooking. She wasn't in the military, only attached to it, but she would still have access to various messes and officers' clubs, requisitioned restaurants, and that wondrous outpost of American prosperity, the envy of the world or at least of the inhabitants of Berlin, the PX. So would the roommate she'd been told to expect.

In the first bedroom, a massive four-poster was piled high with eiderdowns. Again, the woman tried to run interference, but Millie took a step around her, put her hand on the eiderdowns, and pressed down several times, testing the mattress. She knew she was taunting the woman, and she felt a small flash of shame, but not enough to stop. The woman's hand lifted, as if she wanted to slap Millie, then fell to her side. The child moved closer and wound her arms around her mother's leg. Now Millie was ashamed. Goading a grown woman, a grown German woman, was fair play, or at least justified. Intimidating a child, even a German child, was unconscionable. Except that the German child was likely to grow up to be a German adult.

She moved on to the bathroom. It was spartan but immaculate. The woman was a good housekeeper. That couldn't be easy with all the dust the *Trümmerfrauen* kicked up collecting the rubble and wheeling it along the broken roads.

She entered the next room. The woman followed with the child still clinging to her thigh. The bed here was smaller but still piled high with eiderdowns. She didn't bother to test the mattress. She'd made her point. She moved on to the last room. The small chest of drawers and narrow bed were painted white with pink and blue flowers. A stuffed bear, the cross stitches of his mouth set in an eternally winsome smile, was propped up against the pillow. Is that your teddy? The words were almost out of her mouth before she swallowed them. The child really was testing her resolve. She didn't want to taunt her, but she was determined not to be seduced by her. Giving a wide berth to a dollhouse that stood in a corner, she walked to the window, looked out into the bare alley where a few weeds sprouted among the rubble, then turned, left the bedroom, and made her way back down the hall. She was not going to look at the breakfront again, not so much as a glance, but her eyes had a will of their own. As she passed the doorway, her head turned to take it in one more time. The piece was so handsome it was almost an affront to the city, and the times.

She and the woman stood facing each other in the entrance hall. The fear she'd read in the woman's faded blue eyes when she'd opened the door and seen Millie's uniform had hardened into hatred. Millie could feel the rage coming off her, acrid as the smell of her unwashed flesh and greasy hair. That was all right. That made it easier. The woman's hatred was like a stick poking her own to life.

"Three o'clock tomorrow," she said in German. "You, your family, and your personal effects must be out by three o'clock tomorrow."

"But the child . . ." the woman began.

"Three o'clock tomorrow," Millie repeated and was out the door before the woman could protest any further. If she was going to worry about a child, she had better candidates for her pity than that little girl, who, even after all these years, even after everything that had happened, still had a teddy bear to cling to.

She made her way down the stairs slowly. She told herself

she was being careful because there was no light in the stairwell, but she knew it was more than that. The shadow of the child followed her all the way.

Pulling open the door to the street, she stepped into the falling dusk. The winter solstice was still a month away, but the shortening days made the ruined streets feel even more ominous. The rubble wasn't as bad here as in some parts of the city. Zehlendorf, a borough of handsome villas, cobblestone streets, lakes, parks, and upstanding German citizens, had been of no strategic value, except perhaps for those upstanding citizens. It had been spared the worst of the bombing. But it still felt broken.

She crossed the street and stood looking up at the French windows of the flat she'd just requisitioned. The woman appeared in one of them and stood staring down at her. Even at this distance, Millie could feel the rage. Again, she told herself that was all right. That was welcome. The woman's hatred banished the shadow of the child that had stalked her down the stairs.

She'd been in Berlin only two days, but in Germany for a week. The experience was not what she'd expected. She didn't mean the hardship. She'd been warned of that. The unwanted sympathy, her own, not the Germans', was the problem. It was easy to hate from a distance. She was surprised to find how much energy it took close up.

As she went on staring up at the window, two GIs turned the corner onto Riemeisterstrasse. One of them took a last drag of a cigarette and flicked the butt to the street.

Suddenly four small boys appeared out of nowhere. Three were wearing torn trousers that were too thin for the winter weather. The fourth was in shorts. All four of them dove for the cigarette butt. The scuffle didn't go on for long, a few punches, some wild kicks, violent curses. The boy in shorts pulled away from them, ran halfway down the block, and turned back to look at the others. They stood watching him but made no move. Honor among thieves, or at least a code of behavior among scavengers. The winner took a small tin box from the pocket of his shorts, opened it, and placed the cigarette butt inside. The incident was something else she'd been in Germany long enough to understand. *Kippensammlung*, or butt collecting. Children, and sometimes able-bodied men, if any were left, and the elderly as well, collected cigarette butts, removed the remaining tobacco, rolled it into new cigarettes, and sold them on the black market. They weren't as valuable as American cigarettes—four cents a pack at the PX, ten dollars on the black market, fifteen for Pall Malls, which were longer—but they were profitable.

She looked from the boys back up at the windows of the flat. The woman was gone, leaving only the memory of the encounter. She hadn't found requisitioning the flat as painful as people had told her it would be, but neither had she found it as satisfying as she'd expected.

Two

⌒

"WHAT THE FUC—PARDON MY FRENCH, CAPTAIN, WHAT
the hell are the Krauts up to now?" Private Meer muttered
as he turned the jeep onto Riemeisterstrasse and slowed to a
stop.

Millie hadn't yet met Major Sutton, who would be her
boss, but he'd given her his jeep and driver for the move into
the flat. Private Meer had been trying to watch his language.
She was an American girl, clearly off-limits because she held
the equivalent of officer rank, but still a welcome sight in Berlin in late 1945, or so she had been told repeatedly. Not that
the city wasn't full of eager Frauleins. They were off-limits
too, technically. The Army's rule against fraternization—no
socializing with Germans, no visiting their homes, no shaking hands with them even—had been one more article in
the conquerors' creed. It had also been a sop to wives and
girlfriends back home. Unfortunately, or fortunately for
those involved, the rule had turned out to be totally unen-
forceable. GIs wandered the streets arm in arm with German girls. Often the girls were wearing nylon stockings and
munching chocolate bars or smoking cigarettes. It was as if
they were acting out the worst clichés of the Occupation.
The first afternoon she'd been in Germany, she'd passed an
enlisted man snapping a photo of his buddy, grinning to

beat the band as he stood with two Frauleins, an arm around the shoulders of each and his big hands palming a breast of each. She bet that was one photo that wasn't going home to mother. The officers were no better, or so she'd heard. Every one of them had a "frat" stashed away somewhere. She'd been in Germany only a week, but she'd already heard the story of the young officer who'd wanted to bring his wife over. "You must be nuts," his superior had said. "You don't bring a sandwich to a banquet." Millie qualified as a sandwich—barely that, she supposed, since she wasn't anyone's wife—but if that made her less desirable, or at least less accommodating, it also made her more respectable. Private Meer was doing his best to watch his language around her. "What the hell are the Krauts up to now," he said again, as if repeating the bland word would wipe out the more vivid expletive.

Halfway down the street, a crowd of twenty or thirty men and women, some of the women with children, was gathered in front of a building. They weren't shouting or jostling or even milling. They were simply watching, almost respectfully, as if at a funeral. One of the men was even holding his cap in his hands.

Meer put the jeep in gear, cruised to the edge of the group, and stopped again, but he left the engine idling and glanced behind them. She knew he was checking for an escape route. The crowd was calm, but situations could turn on a dime. The Soviets were more volatile than the Germans. That had to do with the vodka. Skirmishes between the Ivans and the Amis or the Tommies—there was no German slang for the French occupiers, whom they clearly saw as also-rans—were not unheard of. But the Germans were sullen and self-pitying. Under the right circumstances, those traits could be incendiary too.

As she and Meer sat watching, a man came out of the building where she'd requisitioned the flat the day before carrying an armful of pots, pans, and kitchen utensils. A woman in the crowd crossed herself. A man muttered, more in despair than anger. You didn't have to speak the language to understand the tone. Every man and woman in the crowd, even some of the children, knew the same fate could befall them. Tomorrow or next week or next month they could be carrying their own kitchen utensils out of their own houses. And it was likely to get worse before it got better, if it ever did get better. The rumor was that the Amis were going to bring over their families. All those women and children would need places to live, though the houses and apartments wouldn't all be requisitioned space. In Frankfurt, the headquarters of the American sector, German POWs were already at work building an all-American suburb behind barbed wire, complete with schools, movie theaters, bowling alleys, hair dressing salons, and other aspects of American culture. But until that was complete, a lot of Germans would be giving up their *Lebensraum*.

The man carrying the kitchen utensils began making his way through the mob. Several American soldiers started to push the crowd back to make a path for him, but there was no need. The bystanders separated on their own.

"Like the Red Sea," Millie muttered.

Meer turned to her and grinned. "You nailed it, Captain. That's the Krauts for you. Like Churchill said, either at your throat or at your feet. Even with each other. Especially with each other these days."

The man reached the street where a wagon stood, the shafts for harnessing a horse resting on the ground, black paint peeling from the sides, a scrap of black fabric fluttering in one of the broken windows. In an earlier life the vehicle must have been a hearse. The man bent to put the utensils inside it, but he was carrying too many, and they clattered out of his hands, shattering the reverential hush. Somewhere in the crowd, a woman let out a single sob. The man collected the fallen items from the street, put them in the wagon, and started back to the house. The crowd went on watching. They were respectful and sympathetic, but they were curious too. Was the wife a good housekeeper or a slattern? Was the family better off than they pretended or living beyond their means?

Meer shook his head. "Damn Krauts. I'm not saying it ain't what they deserve, but they sure do know how to pull at your heartstrings."

Millie didn't answer.

A moment later the man came out of the house again. This time he was trailed by a helper. The first man was carrying a pile of folded linens and eiderdowns, the second some clothing and a pair of beat-up military boots. A subdued murmur rustled through the crowd. She couldn't tell whether it was admiration for the quilts and linens, which even at this distance she could see were snowy, or shame for the depths to which the boots had sunk.

The men went back into the house and came out several more times. Finally, the second man emerged empty-handed, strode to the wagon, and stood waiting. A few onlookers around the edge of the crowd began to drift away. The show was over. Others hung on doggedly for the last act.

The door to the house opened again and the woman Millie had gone through the flat with the day before emerged. She was wearing the same rusty black dress, and the child was clinging to the skirt with one hand while she clutched the stuffed bear with the other. Chin lifted, eyes straight ahead, immune to her neighbors and their pity or perhaps schadenfreude—the two sentiments are rarely far apart—the woman started toward the wagon. As she did, the first man came out the doorway again. He was balancing the dollhouse Millie had noticed in the child's room against his chest. Another murmur, a little louder this time, went through the throng. A handful of women surged closer to get a better look. These days a beautifully preserved house, even a miniature one, was clearly an object of wonder. Some of the people who had started to leave turned back.

The man was halfway to the wagon when one of the soldiers stepped in front of him. The man started to move around him. The soldier stepped sideways to block his path again.

The soldier said something in English. The man responded in German. Millie was too far away to make out the words.

"*Nein*," the soldier's voice was louder now. "*Ist* on the inventory."

"It belongs to the child," the man shouted back in German.

They stood that way for a moment. Without letting go of the dollhouse, the man managed to raise his elbow to mop the sweat from his face, though the morning was cold. The soldier, who couldn't have been older than eighteen or nineteen, worked a wad of gum around in his mouth.

"*Nein*," he said again. This time he reached for the dollhouse. The man twisted his body away.

They stood that way, facing off over the miniature slate roof. The soldier's jaw was moving faster now. The man was still sweating, but he didn't try to mop his face.

A moment passed, then another. The soldier's eyes were

ricocheting around the crowd. He knew he'd made a mistake, first in stopping the man, then in reaching for the dollhouse, but he didn't know how to get out of the corner he'd backed himself into. Besides, as he kept insisting in what he seemed to think was pidgin German, the dollhouse was on the inventory of the furniture that must stay, though heaven knew why. Perhaps the sergeant who'd compiled the list had a daughter back in the States. It wouldn't be the largest spoil shipped home, or the most valuable, not by a long shot.

The woman took the few steps back from the wagon to where the man and the soldier were standing. She seemed unaware that the child was still hanging on to her skirt. Millie couldn't make out her words, but she recognized the snarl on her face. The soldier went on working his jaw around the wad of gum. "*Nein*," he repeated to the woman. "*Ist* on the inventory."

"*Räuber*," she shouted. "*Dieb*." She took a step closer to the soldier. He stood his ground but couldn't keep from leaning his upper body away from her. That was all she needed. She raised her hand and began poking him in the chest with her index finger as she repeated the words. "*Räuber. Dieb. Schwein*."

The soldier's jaw and eyes were going faster now. The mob began taking up the woman's cries. "*Räuber. Dieb. Schwein*," they howled.

Beside Millie, Meer turned and glanced behind them. "Maybe we better get out of here, Captain. The major wouldn't want you mixed up in this."

"I'm fine," she said. She wasn't fine—the shouted viciousness was taking her back to a place she didn't want to go—but she would not let them drive her out again.

The crowd was still shouting, but now they'd taken up

a new word. "*Schande*," they howled. "*Schande, Schande, Schande.*"

"I got *Räuber* and *Schwein*, Captain," Meer said, "and I think *Dieb* is thief, but what does *Schande* mean?"

It took her a minute to translate for him, though she knew the word. "Shame," she said finally.

"They got a point. Don't get me wrong. They deserve everything they got coming to them," he repeated. "But a kid's dollhouse?"

"If I'd noticed it on the list, I'd have taken it off," she said, though she wondered if she would have. Maybe the dollhouse had been bought for the child. Maybe her father had made it for her. Or maybe in an earlier life it had belonged to a little girl with the last name of Cohn or Levi or Lowenstein. She thought of the Biedermeier breakfront again.

The shouting was getting louder, and she noticed something else. The throng was closing in more tightly around the soldier. The three other GIs were trying to keep it back, but as they pushed one way, the mob pushed against them. A man in a cap and a torn Wehrmacht jacket dyed an uneven orange—Germans were forbidden to wear proper military garb—came up behind the woman and began shouting, not the words the crowd was chanting but a harangue. He was yelling, and people were screaming, and the woman was poking the soldier's chest while he stood frozen to the spot. Only his jaw and eyes were moving. Then slowly, almost imperceptibly, or the gesture would have been imperceptible if Millie and Meer hadn't been watching so closely, his right hand moved toward his thigh and hovered above the pistol in its holster.

Millie felt her breath catch in her chest.

"Don't do it, kid," Meer muttered.

The soldier's hand kept going until it found the handle of the revolver, then rested there.

The woman dropped her hand. The man in the dyed Wehrmacht jacket stopped shouting. A murmur, soft and nervous as a tremor, ran through the mob. No one moved.

Suddenly an American officer was cutting through the far side of the crowd, and bystanders were stepping aside to make way for him.

"I think the cavalry just rode in," Meer said.

The peak of the officer's cap cast a shadow over his face, but Millie didn't have to see his features to recognize him. She knew that long-legged stride, more lope than walk, and the thrust of those shoulders that he'd learned to use as a weapon precisely because they were not broad or powerful. As a boy, he'd fought a lot of skirmishes in a variety of places.

He elbowed through the last few people and reached the quartet at the center of the dispute. The soldier took his hand from his gun and executed a snappy salute.

"Who ever thought a fucking salute would save the day?" This time Meer didn't even try to apologize.

The woman and the man in the dyed Wehrmacht jacket both took a step back from the soldier. The other man didn't move, but simply went on standing there, holding the doll-house against his chest.

The officer said something to the soldier, then stood listening. After a moment, he beckoned to another soldier who was holding a clipboard. The second soldier handed the clipboard to the officer. He stood studying it, then shook his head slowly as if in wonder. She recognized that gesture too. It was his response to the world's insanity. He turned to the man with the dollhouse. He was speaking quietly, and the mob couldn't hear what he was saying, but the man stood with his head down, as if to catch every word. The officer stopped talking. The man nodded and, still carrying the dollhouse, started for the wagon. The woman opened her mouth to say something. The officer cut her off and glanced down at the child for a long moment. Millie waited for him to pat her head. She didn't know if she'd be able to forgive that. She'd fought the instinct the day before. Surely he would too. He moved aside so the two of them, mother and child, could make their way to the former hearse where the man was placing the dollhouse. He wedged it in among the other possessions, then helped the woman up onto the seat and lifted the child to sit in her lap. He walked to the front of the carriage and bent to pick up one of the shafts. His helper picked up the other. They began hauling the wagon. It rode low and heavy on its wheels down Riemeister-strasse.

"Well, I'll be damned," Meer said as he sat watching the gathering disperse. He threw the jeep into gear and started toward the building where the officer was still standing. As they got closer, the smile on the officer's face grew wider.

Meer pulled up in front of the building and killed the engine.

The officer looked up at them. "I hear you're in the market for a roommate, Mil."

She climbed out of the jeep and stood staring up at him.

"That is if your kid brother won't cramp your style."

She threw her arms around him and turned her face away so he wouldn't see that she was crying, though he'd know anyway.

"I think I can work around you," she said.

"It isn't a coincidence," David explained as he lifted her suitcase out of the jeep and they started toward the house. "Though these days the world is lousy with coincidences. A guy in my outfit—we were at Camp Ritchie together and got citizenship the same day—managed to get permission to take a jeep back to his hometown near Mainz. He just happened to hit the local railroad station as a slow-moving freight was pulling in. His twin brother was sitting on a flatbed. Fresh out of Dachau." As soon as the words were out, he cursed himself. He knew what her next sentence would be.

"Did any of the rest of the family survive?"

"I didn't want to ruin the party by asking. The point is, it's not a coincidence I'm here." He pushed open the door to the building, then followed her in. "When you wrote that Russ had wrangled you a job with the denazification office in Berlin, I managed to pull a few strings of my own. I'd already volunteered for the Control Council. Camps and displaced persons." He was damned if he'd call them DPs. The survivors had already lost so much. It didn't seem fair to abbreviate even their miserable status. "I didn't need to pull too many. There aren't a lot of men who want to stay over here to work with these people. For one thing, they find the survivors distasteful." He drew out the last word to milk the irony. "All that lice and TB and other communicable diseases. Not like the nice clean, blond, blue-eyed Germans—"

"Look who's talking."

He grinned. Years ago a teacher, new to the school, had singled him out as a perfect specimen of Aryan superiority. The class had snickered, but no one had corrected the teacher. In German schools, no one did.

"For another," he went on as he followed her up the stairs, "they're all hot to get back home. At least the ones who did the fighting are. The armchair officers are another story. They can't wait to get over here. But they want cushy jobs pushing papers around an office, living in formerly Aryanized, formerly Jewish mansions, and driving confiscated Mercedes-Benzes and BMWs. They aren't about to get their hands dirty with those dirty Jews. Or in Patton's words, and I quote the general, those animals."

"You did the fighting. Aren't you hot to get home? The GI Bill is waiting."

"It will still be there in a year or two." They'd reached the door to the flat, and he turned to her. "In the meantime, I am home. And I'm not talking about this damn city."

They stood staring at each other. Except for the oval shape of their faces, there wasn't much of a resemblance. They had the same wide mouth, but on him it was firm and determined, on her mobile and vulnerable. His shock of corn silk hair that had misled the teacher so many years ago was always falling over the blue eyes that had also fooled the teacher. Her dark hair grew back from a widow's peak that made a neat v in her high forehead. Nonetheless, to each of them it felt like looking in a mirror.

He turned away. "Come on, show me my new digs."

She led the way inside, and he followed her through the rooms. They argued about who would take the master bedroom with the carved four-poster.

"You're older," he said.

"I haven't been sleeping in foxholes for the past year and a half."

"That just means I'm used to hardship. Which this isn't by a long shot. Besides, a girl needs her beauty sleep."

"I resent that."

"Don't. You look good, Meike." The name had slipped out. He waited to see how she'd take it.

They'd been standing in the doorway, staring at the huge carved bed, and now she turned to him.

"No one's called me that in years. Not even you."

He stood staring down at her. "How does it feel?"

She thought for a minute. "I wish I knew."

She'd saved the sitting room for last. When he followed her into it, he understood why. She led him to the breakfront, and they stood side by side staring at it. He knew what she was thinking. She was wrong, but he didn't want to argue with her, not about this, not about anything.

Three

⁓

SHE LAY IN BED STARING THROUGH THE DARKNESS AT the faint outline of the ceiling moldings. Every now and then, headlights swept through the room like searchlights, then passed, leaving it in shadows again. There wasn't much traffic, but she'd been lying there for long enough to distinguish what little there was. An army truck lumbered by. A jeep rattled. Once a horse clopped over the cobblestones.

She turned on her side, but it was no good. The mattress she'd pretended to test in order to irk the woman was too soft. Only she knew her insomnia had nothing to do with the mattress. She didn't understand it. She'd been sure she'd sleep tonight. She'd sleep tonight as she hadn't for the past two years. David wasn't parachuting out of a plane or storming a beach or—and this was the image she'd tried again and again to banish, but had never been able to—lying dead in a ditch. He was safe in the next room. And she was exhausted from the incidents of the day, from the events of the past week. Everything was new and difficult, or familiar and more difficult. So why couldn't she get to sleep?

Another pair of headlights swept through the room, then the world went dark again. She wasn't going to be able to do this. Even with David in the next room, with the two of them together again, she wasn't going to be able to do this. She'd thought once she was back in Berlin she'd be able to see the world more clearly. In Berlin, she'd find certainty. All she'd found so far was turmoil. Nothing felt as she'd expected it to.

She turned on one side, drew her knees up in a fetal position, stretched out, turned on her other side. It was no good. She sat up, swung her feet over the side of the bed, and slid down until they were touching the floor. Even that motion brought it all back. The beds she'd slept in back in the States—the Danish modern twin in the house where she'd lived when she'd arrived, the narrow cot in her dormitory room at Bryn Mawr, the single bed in the apartment she'd shared in Philadelphia with two other girls—had all been lower slung. This bed was straight out of her childhood, high enough to have to climb up to rather than sit down on, made higher still by the thick mattress and eiderdowns. There had been enough of those in the household to requisition some and let the woman take the rest.

She pulled on her robe, slid into her slippers, and started down the hall. Outside David's door, she stopped and stood listening. In the old days, when they were on holiday from school in their adopted home in the States, she would have opened the door, crept in, and stood looking down at him, reassuring herself that he was there, that he was safe, that they had each other. She wondered if he still slept on his stomach, arms and legs flung out. Her hand hovered over the doorknob. She wouldn't disturb him. She just wanted to see him. Her hand gripped the knob, then let go of it as if it were hot. He was a grown man. He'd seen more of the world than she ever would. The days when she could slip into his room in the dead of night to reassure herself he was all right were long gone.

She reached into her pocket, took out a handkerchief,

and blew her nose, then started down the hall toward the kitchen. They'd brought wine home from dinner. Surely that would help her sleep. But when she reached the kitchen, she kept going, past it and the dining room, into the parlor.

The night had been cloudy when they'd come home, but now the sky had cleared and the light of a full moon streamed through the French windows and illuminated the breakfront.

"How did you know?" her mother had asked as the two men, one brawny, the other seemingly too frail to make a living moving furniture, set the breakfront down between another pair of French windows, opening onto a different street where no bombs had fallen and, they were all sure, none ever would. That was how unimaginable the future had been.

"How did I know?" her father repeated after the two moving men had left. "Every time you passed the store you stopped in front of the window. Like a kid in front of Kranzler's. Worse than that. It was easier to pry the children away from the strudels and pfeffernüsse in Kranzler's display than it was to get you past that breakfront in the shop. Now you don't have to go out to enjoy it."

"It's beautiful," her mother said.

"Beauty should live with beauty," her father answered, and her mother opened her amethyst eyes wider. That was how you knew she was really smiling, not just curling her mouth. David and Sarah had both inherited their mother's eyes. Meike had got her father's more pedestrian brown. Brown, but of a most interesting almond shape, her mother always insisted.

Millie crossed the room and stepped into the pool of moonlight. She was back there. She was Meike. She was safe and happy with the whole world ahead of her. Her biggest worry, her monumental worry, was her rapidly changing body and whether she'd emerge from the transformation pretty like her mother and cousin Anna or ugly like the girl she sometimes squared off with in the mirror.

She ran her fingers over the inlaid pattern, as her mother had that last day. How many years after the moving men had delivered the breakfront? Four? Five? All she remembered for certain was that she had just turned sixteen. It was early November, and they were wearing coats, her mother in her Persian lamb with the frog closings, her father in his Mannheim Berliner, she and David and Sarah in their navy blue chesterfields with velvet collars. She was supposed to have gotten a new coat that winter. She was too old to be dressing identically to her younger brother and little sister. But more pressing matters had intervened. Five suitcases were lined up beside the door, one for each of them, though they were all packed so full that Sarah wouldn't be able to manage hers, and her father would have to carry it. In the end that made a difference.

Their father was urging their mother to hurry. "The train, Gerda. All this time you've been begging me to leave. Now the time comes, and you can't tear yourself away."

"I'm coming," her mother said, but she wasn't. She was standing with her hand on the breakfront, looking around and memorizing the room. The paintings on the walls, which she hadn't liked at first, but now that the government had pronounced them decadent, she'd become a fan of modern art. The glass-fronted cases crowded with volumes, many of them editions of books that were being burned in the streets. The silver frames, standing empty on the tables. She had taken out the photographs and packed them in the suitcases the night before, distributing them among all five as she had the few pieces of jewelry she hadn't sold, the little cash they had left, and two Leica lenses her father had bought for their flight, all secreted in jars of cold cream, tubs of Vaseline, and tins of talcum powder. The frames were empty, but the photographs were so familiar they could still see them. A young couple in bathing costumes on the beach at Wannsee; the same man and woman, only a little older, pushing a child in a stroller in the Tiergarten; the child, taller now, holding the hand of a small boy in the botanical garden; the two children, older still, with a third squinting blindly into the sunshine, again on the beach at Wannsee; the man alone, younger again, in the uniform of the Imperial German Army of the Great War with an Iron Cross Second Class pinned to his tunic. Her mother hadn't wanted to take that, but her father had insisted.

She wasn't going to be able to do this. She really wasn't. She stepped out of the circle of moonlight and made her way into the hall. She wouldn't disturb him. He was a sound sleeper. At least he used to be. He wouldn't even know she'd looked in. But she had to see him with her own eyes. She had to hear his breathing and sense the heat he gave off. He was her connection, the one being who could keep her from floating off into the darkness, untethered as a helium balloon. Especially now that she was back in Berlin.

Her slippers made no sound on the floorboards as she went down the hall. Her hand moved to the doorknob again. This time she turned it. She started to push the door open, but she hadn't bargained on the unoiled hinge. She stopped and waited for some sound or movement in the room. There was none. Slowly, carefully, she pushed the door open.

The room was dark. No moonlight filtered through this window. She stepped inside, then stopped and waited. Again she sensed no movement. She took another step. The room wasn't large but her journey across it seemed endless. Finally she reached the bed and stood beside it looking down. It was hard to tell in the darkness, but there didn't seem to be a body beneath the eiderdown. Certainly no David sprawled across it, arms and legs hanging over the side. She fumbled for the lamp, hit it at the wrong angle, grabbed it before it went over, righted it, and pulled the cord. The bulb didn't give off much light, but it gave off enough to see that the bed was empty. It hadn't even been mussed.

She went through the flat, turning on all the lights. She even looked in the closets. Then she went through again and looked under the beds. The idea wasn't as farfetched as it seemed. Before she'd left the States, the magazine where she'd worked had published an article warning the women of America what to expect when their fighting men came home. They might be moody or angry or jumpy. A sudden noise could startle. A backfiring car could make them take cover. But David wasn't under any of the beds. He wasn't anywhere in the apartment. She couldn't imagine how he'd left without her hearing him go, but he'd managed to.

She went back to the parlor and sat on the ugly red plush love seat across from the Biedermeier breakfront. It was still bathed in moonlight, but now she barely noticed it. There was no reason to panic, she told herself. He could be anywhere, doing anything. The city was full of GIs out drinking and gambling and sleeping in the wrong beds. Still, he could have told her he was going out. But that was ridiculous. He was a grown man, she reminded herself as she'd been doing ever since he'd come home in uniform. He didn't have to ask her permission to go out. He didn't have to confide in her. She'd never told him about the weekend with the medical officer who was shipping out. Family ties didn't necessitate full disclosure. Full disclosure could fray family ties.

She just hoped he wasn't out with a Fraulein. Only a few hours ago, the idea would have seemed impossible. Not her own brother. Not after what they'd been through. But she'd seen the way his eyes had followed the girls on the street. He was a grown man, she warned herself again. He'd been trained for battle and groomed for intelligence work. She hadn't known about the latter back in the States. Camp Ritchie, set up to instruct foreign-speaking men, many of them still boys, most of them Jewish, had been top secret. But now the war was over, and she didn't think he was as well prepared for peace, at least this particular peace. What was an Army manual about prisoner interrogation or instruction in photo interpretation against the hundreds of Frauleins in the city, hungry for chocolates and nylons and cigarettes? He'd fought a war and experienced a thousand horrors and terrors she'd never know. He must have lost countless buddies. He didn't talk about that. He didn't talk about anything he'd gone through in the war, though when he'd unpacked his things this afternoon, he'd taken out a snapshot and tucked it in the frame of the mirror over his dresser. In it, he and two other GIs were perched on a jeep, smiling into the camera. "The Ritchie Musketeers take Aachen" was written across the bottom. She'd asked who the other two were.

"Buddies," was all he said.

She didn't press it.

The point was she had no right to sit in judgment on his actions. Nonetheless, there were some things you didn't do. Sleeping with the enemy was one of them. More than the enemy, his own personal nemesis. She was no prig. She didn't care whom the rest of those lonely, sex-starved, far-from-home men went to bed with. She found it distasteful, in view of what these people had done, but it was none of her business. David was her business. He knew what these people had done as well as she did. He'd suffered what they'd done along with her. The more she thought about it, the more impossible she knew it was. She had no idea where he was or with whom, but she did know one thing. He could not be sleeping with the enemy.

She heard a key scraping in the lock, jumped up, and started toward the front door. Then she stopped, turned, walked quickly down the hall to her bedroom, and closed the door behind her. She'd caught herself in time.

Since the war had ended, she'd lived with two recurrent fantasies. In one, David came home from the Army, got his degree, perhaps a medical degree—their father would like that—and married. She married too. She was no heroine out of a nineteenth-century English novel, sacrificing herself for a brother or father. In that blissful fantasy, David and his wife and she and her husband and their children—there would be lots of children—lived near one another, perhaps on different floors in the same apartment building or neighboring houses in the suburbs. One of the children would be a little girl named Sarah. Maybe they'd each have a girl named Sarah. She saw the children flying in and out of one another's homes, entwined in one another's lives, David's Sarah and Millie's Sarah, the joy of them, the beauty of them, the sheer Sarahness of them doubled. And if they found Sarah, when they found Sarah, the delight would be tripled. They were not a superstitious family. They did not believe, as did many Jews, that naming a child after a living relative was inviting trouble. This would not be tempting fate; it would be celebrating it.

In the other fantasy, David married and pulled away from her. What man, or woman for that matter, wouldn't strain against the possessiveness of an overbearing older sister? And as he disappeared from her life, his visits growing fewer and farther between, his phone calls clearly matters of duty, she grew more bitter, a lone woman, even if she was married, an alienated familyless woman.

She stood behind the closed door of her bedroom, listening to his steps going down the hall. She had caught herself in time. She refused to become that unloved woman. Where he'd been, what he'd been doing, was none of her business.

Four

~⌒~

She didn't say a word to him about his being out the night before. She made coffee for them, and toast, and they joked about the indignity of eating Wonder Bread from the PX in Berlin because the handful of bakeries that were functioning again couldn't get ingredients for good German rye or pumpernickel. She even managed to keep it up until he left for the displaced persons center. A few minutes later, she stepped out of the building into a chill November morning. The clear moonlit sky of the previous night had disappeared behind a scrim of dirty clouds that pressed down on the city like a lid. The wind made her turn up the collar of her Balkan bunny. That was what the girls on the ship coming over had called the Army-issue trench coats lined with fake fur. The joke had been that they came in two sizes, huge and gargantuan. Some of the smaller girls had almost disappeared inside all that fabric, the hems dragging along the floor, the shoulders making them look like professional football players. She was lucky. She'd got one of the merely huge ones and was tall enough to carry it off. No one would call the coat fashionable, but it was warm, and if she cinched the belt tight enough, she didn't look like a sack of potatoes.

She started down the street in the direction of Kronprinzenallee. Despite the lack of familiar landmarks—many houses

and shops and public edifices were no more than unidentifi-
able rubble—here and there a still-standing building brought
the city back to her. Perhaps that was why it happened. The
familiarity in the midst of all that destruction was unnerving, as if she was moving through two worlds at once.

The girls must have been on their way to school. Classes
had resumed only a few months earlier. The delay hadn't
been due entirely to the fact that buildings were in ruins.
The more significant problem was a shortage of teachers. An
alarming number of them had Nazi pasts. You could give a
street sweeper back his broom or let a clerk return to his desk,
but you couldn't entrust the nation's youth to the men and
women who had led, or followed, it down the recent path
in the first place. The lack of text books was another difficulty. All the old ones had to be pulped and new ones written. She hadn't thought it possible to inject propaganda into a
math book until she'd seen some of the examples. "A usurer
charged an honest farmer 12% interest on a loan of 400 marks
for 4 years. How much did the Jew swindler get?"

The three little girls were swinging along ahead of her
holding hands. Their heavily mended cotton stockings were
nothing more than patchworks of darns. One of them wore
a coat with the unmistakable mark of a hem that had been
let down; the second's coat had a wide band of another fabric
around the bottom; the third had no coat, only a sweater.
But despite the cold and their lack of protection from it, they
seemed to be having a good time, impervious to the weather
as children often are. The one with the strip of different fabric
at the bottom was in the middle, and as she turned back and
forth from one friend to the other, her dark braids swung in
the cold morning air. Millie quickened her step to catch up
with them.

The closer she got, the surer she was. The girl with the braids dropped her friends' hands, skipped forward a few steps, then without turning danced back. Millie would know that high-stepping caper anywhere. She was almost running now to catch up. The closer she got, the more certain she was. The thick dark braids, the narrow shoulders, the coltish legs. The girl shouted a few words back at her friends. The sound of her voice, like a bell in the icy morning air, shattered something inside Millie. These girls couldn't be older than seven or eight. But that was the age she still was in Millie's mind.

As she came abreast of the three, she couldn't help glancing over at them, though she had already realized her mistake. They stared back at her, taking in her government-issue trench coat, half curious because they were children, half suspicious because they were their parents' children.

At the same moment, two MPs caught up with her.

"You okay, Captain?" one of them asked.

"Fine."

"We saw you running after those girls. They swipe something?"

"No, I was just . . ." She let her voice trail off.

"Don't let them put one over on you."

"Put one over on me? They're children."

The MP shook his head. "Sure. And they'd slit your throat for a pack of cigarettes."

She stood staring at him for a moment, wondering how she'd slipped down this rabbit hole.

"I'm fine," she managed to insist again and started walking.

Turning the corner onto Kronprinzenallee, she kept going, though suddenly she had no idea where she was. It took her several blocks to regulate her breathing and get her bearings.

She never should have run after the girls. One thing she knew for sure. She wasn't going to tell David about the incident.

❧

The building that housed the press and publishing clearance office was a heavy, soulless example of fascist brutal architecture at its best, or worst. It didn't invite. It wasn't satisfied with impressing. It was determined to intimidate. She climbed the steps and made her way through the massive doors.

The entrance hall was large, bare, and perfectly proportioned to make an individual feel insignificant. Long hallways extended from both sides. Men in uniform and women, some in uniform, some in civilian clothing, hurried back and forth, carrying brown manila envelopes, thick folders, and sheaves of papers. She started down the hall to the right. Even if she'd been inclined to ask for help, she doubted anyone would pause to answer her. She passed a few doors, realized the numbers were going in the wrong direction, turned, went through the entrance hall again, and started down the hall on the left. The numerals 113 were painted in black on the frosted glass window of the fourth door. She pushed it open.

A low slatted wooden divider ran the length of the room. On one side of it, benches lined the walls. Men and a handful of women were crowded on them. Others stood. A man was squatting on his haunches. They were a motley lot, some in well-cut if worn, patched, and too-big suits, others in even shabbier outfits. On the far side of the barrier, a thin young woman with hollow cheeks and an unhealthy pallor sat behind one desk, a buxom girl with yellow braids wound tightly around her head behind another. The nameplate on the desk of the dour one said Fraulein Weber. The *Mädchen* with the braids was Fraulein Schmidt.

A few of the people in the waiting area looked up as Millie entered. She tugged the belt of her Army coat tighter, as if girding for battle, and approached the secretary with the crown of braids. She didn't seem friendly, merely less hostile than her hungry-looking colleague.

The secretary lifted her Dresden blue eyes. They registered the Army uniform. A slight frown tugged at the side of her rosebud mouth. Millie was willing to bet the response would have been warmer if the person in the U.S. Army uniform had been a man. Nonetheless, the frown did nothing to detract from the girl's looks. She wondered whether her new boss, Major Sutton, had hired the girl or some personnel officer had succumbed. She hoped it was the latter. She didn't like to think the head of the denazification office would be susceptible to Fraulein charm, though from the little she'd already seen, there was no reason he should be any different.

She gave her name to the girl, who was even better-looking when she smiled, though the expression wasn't genuine. The girl said Major Sutton was expecting her, stood, and led Millie to another door with a frosted glass window. MAJOR HARRY SUTTON was painted in black letters on this one.

She stepped through the door the girl held open, and Major Sutton looked up from the papers he was studying. Beneath a high forehead, which the receding light brown hair made higher, his face was long and narrow, bisected by a Roman nose that was a little off-center, as if it had been broken and not properly set. He swung his feet off the big, ornately carved desk, righted his chair, and stood. The tall, wiry body went with the long face, but when he came around the desk to meet her, he moved on the balls of his feet, like a tennis player, and seemed suddenly younger. She wondered how old he was. The war had been fought largely by young men.

She'd been surprised when she'd found the commanding officer David had referred to as "the old man" was twenty-six,
only two years older than she was now. Sutton held out his
hand, though he kept the other one in his pocket, and smiled.
His smile was easy, too easy she thought, but his eyes, almost
green behind steel-rimmed military glasses, were watchful
and, she was sure she wasn't imagining it, speculative, if not
downright suspicious. Perhaps he knew about all the good
words Russ Bennett had put in to land her here.

"Welcome to the Occupation, Captain." His voice was
a deep smoker's baritone, and his accent was British rather
than American. She wondered if he'd gone to school in England or had an English nanny as a child. She should have
known the government might staff the denazification office
with German-speaking Jews who'd fled the country, but they
wouldn't let one of those suspect characters run it.

"Flat requisitioned and all squared away?" he asked.

"Yes, sir."

"You don't have to sir me, Captain. You're attached to the
Army, not in it." He flashed the too-easy smile again, then
went back around the desk, sat in the swivel chair, and indicated one of the straight chairs on the other side of the desk.
"And while we're on the subject, I'm curious to know why
you're attached to the Army. I'm not suggesting I'm not delighted to have you, but not too many Bryn Mawrtyrs—"

She was surprised. "You know the term?"

"Doesn't everyone?"

So that was the way it was going to be. He thought she
was a pampered girl from a family who'd had the foresight to
get out early and had connections to people like Russ Bennett. He thought she was here on a lark, a kind of grand tour
of postwar misery.

"But my point is not too many Bryn Mawrtyrs want to leave jobs at swanky magazines to come to this bombed-out hellhole to look for needles in a haystack. Or to put it another way, to find Germans with sufficiently clean hands to run the press and publishing operations of the supposedly new Germany. What attracted you?"

"I didn't leave the swanky magazine. It left me. Now that the men are coming home, the girls are being sent back where they belong. Only I don't really belong anywhere, so when I heard the Occupation had several million *Fragebogen* to sort through and not enough personnel who read German, I decided to sign on."

He looked across the desk at her. "So you're inspired by patriotism?"

She smiled, though she had a feeling her expression didn't look any more genuine than his. "I'm not about to break into an imitation of Kate Smith singing 'God Bless America,' but I am grateful to the country for taking me in, my brother and me both."

"And what about the country of your birth? No residual fondness for Germany before it became the Thousand-Year Reich?"

"Not an iota. Not even before it became the Thousand-Year Reich. I hate Germany, past as well as present, and all things German."

He leaned back in his swivel chair and shook his head. "That's what I was afraid of. Let me tell you something about our operation here. Some of our best denazifiers—an absurd term too close to fumigators, if you ask me—are German Jews. Chaps who got out of Germany before the war and became American citizens. They not only know the language, they have a sense of the psyche. They can read expressions and equivocations and evasions better than the Yanks who are fluent in the language but didn't grow up in the culture. Needless to say, the Germans hate them. There's even a rumor that during the war they guided American bombers to pinpoint their old hometowns. Rubbish, of course, but let's not forget these are people who have been buying the big lie, the bigger-the-better lie, for thirteen years. The problem is we've had complaints, and not only from the Germans. Overzealousness is the way our people phrase it, and I don't have to tell you that some of them have their own, shall we say, preconceived ideas about certain groups of people. So a word of caution is in order. We strive for fairness. I don't want to lose some of my best people because one of them gets carried away and word comes down from the brass no more German Jews in the denazification business. Now let's get to work." He leaned forward, picked up a fat handbook bound in gray cardboard, and held it out to her. "Military Manual for Control of the German Press and Publishing Industry" was written on the cover.

"Take a look at it. Not that it's likely to be much use. Pure military gobbledygook. Sometimes I wonder if the people who write these things speak English," he said in his own King's version of it. "But it will give you an idea of what we're supposed to be up to here. The idea is that you can't build a democratic state without a free press and publishing industry. Simple premise, right? Except that neither is likely to be free if they're run by Nazis. So part of our job, the part you're going to be working on, is to weed out the undesirables. How we manage to do that is where it gets dicey. We interview people. We go over their *Fragebogen*, though often as not their answers on those questionnaires are pure fiction. 'Were you ever a member of the Nazi Party?' 'What's the

Nazi Party?' One of these days a customer is going to walk through that door and say, 'I voted for the National Socialists in 1932 and was an enthusiastic member of the party right up to the moment the dear Fuhrer did himself in.' That's the day the entire office gets snookered on my dime. But until that halcyon moment, it's our job to hand out various clearances to fill certain jobs in the newspapers and magazines we're supposed to be helping them establish. Or not." He leaned forward with his elbows on the desk and his hands in the air. That was when she saw it. The pinky and ring finger of his left hand were missing. She glanced away, then back, then away again. In the hospital in Philadelphia where she'd volunteered during the war, she'd seen worse mutilations, far worse, but for some reason his threw her. She supposed that was because she hadn't expected it. He was an officer sitting behind a desk, not a boy who'd come home on crutches or a stretcher, though he must have seen his share of field hospitals and surgeries during the war. If he noticed her reaction now, however, and she had a feeling he did, he gave no sign of it.

"There are five categories."

With the thumb and index finger of his left hand he grasped his right pinky. Again her eyes veered away, then back. Now she wondered if he was trying to make her uncomfortable.

"Exonerated or non-incriminated," he went on. "They all claim that, of course." He moved on to his next finger. "Followers or fellow-travelers. Then less incriminated." He continued to work his way through the fingers of his good hand. "Activists, militants, profiteers, and incriminated." He reached his thumb. "Major offenders. The problem is a lot of these Krauts who rate pretty high on the infamy scale were upstanding members of the community, more's the pity for Germany, and even worse for us. They're also the ones who know how to run a newspaper or magazine or publishing house, because they've been doing it for the past thirteen years. And if they wanted to keep doing it during those thirteen years, they became members in good standing of the Nazi Party. The others, the ones who managed to keep their skirts clean, were either small beer no one cared about or are dead."

"So what do we do?"

"Improvise. Use your judgment. Maybe even, God forgive me, your intuition. You'll get the hang of it soon enough. You can sit in on my interrogations today. But come along, I'll show you your office first. And introduce you to the others." He started for the door, then hesitated. "You said America saved you and your brother both. Your brother isn't by any chance the David Mosbach who works with the DPs and survivors?"

"Do you know him?"

"I've heard of him."

She thought about that for a moment. "You mean the business with the dollhouse yesterday?"

"Meer told me about it. According to him, your brother rode in like the cavalry."

She didn't like the tone of his voice. It was one thing to be suspicious of her. Russ Bennett and those strings again. But he had no right to be sarcastic about David.

"He's doing good work over here," she insisted.

"I never suggested he wasn't."

He opened the door and they stepped into the waiting area. Several dozen supplicants sprang to their feet and strained toward them, as inexorable as the tide to the moon.

Sutton didn't seem to notice the reaction. Head up, eyes straight ahead, he cut past them. She followed but couldn't help glancing around. The anger was palpable. So were the misery and despair. Without intending them to, her hands clenched into fists. She would not be taken in by the suffering. They had brought it upon themselves.

"I couldn't have done that a few months ago," he said when he'd led her into another office and closed the door behind them.

"Done what?"

He took a cigarette from the breast pocket of his jacket, put it between his lips, took out his lighter, and lit it, all with his right hand. "Ignored them. Behaved as if they weren't human."

"What makes you think they are?"

He shook his head. "Nice to know you took my little sermon about fairness to heart."

The office held a desk with a chair behind it, two in front of it, and a leather club chair wedged into the corner. It was a lot like his, only smaller.

"The club chair is for when you have doubts about someone and want one of the others to sit in on the interrogation. The others being Theo Wallach from Hamburg, Werner Kahn from a village near Stuttgart, and Jack Craig, who learned his German at Yale. Needless to say, they don't always agree, and when they don't, I get to play referee."

He walked around the desk. "Come here." He waited until she was standing beside him, then leaned over to show her a button fixed to the inside of the well of the desk. "That rings in the guardroom. If you have any trouble, even a suspicion of trouble, press it and the MPs will be here on the double." He started toward the door, then stopped and turned back.

"One more thing I should mention. If you get a scientist or expert technician who wants permission to start publishing again, send him straight to me. It's our job to expedite those chaps before the Russkies can get their hands on them. Understood?"

"Perfectly."

He stood looking at her for a moment. "I can't tell if you're going to turn out to have a sixth sense about the Krauts, Captain, or if you're in over your head."

That made two of them.

She spent the day sitting in the club chair in the corner of Major Sutton's office as Germans filed in and out. Few of them noticed her. They were too busy sizing up the officer behind the desk who would determine whether they were destined to run a newspaper or edit a magazine or clear rubble. That gave her plenty of opportunity to scrutinize them. She studied their expressions and watched their movements, subtracted years from their faces and added weight to their bodies, ignored their shabby civilian clothes and imagined them in uniform: not the ubiquitous gray-green Wehrmacht uniform but the more ominous black of the SS. She'd made a mistake with the girls on the way to school that morning. Longing had clouded her vision. But from now on, she was going to be clear-eyed. Besides, those two faces from the railroad station were as sharp as a photograph in her mind's eye, especially the younger one. She'd know those sizzling electric blue eyes anywhere, and she'd seen the perfect classical features on statues in the Greek and Roman galleries of the Philadelphia Museum of Art. In the railroad station, she'd been horrified that she'd noticed how handsome he was.

Over the years she'd tried to put the blame on the God she no longer believed in. Only a practical joker would paste a face like that on evil.

She hadn't come to Berlin to track down those two. She knew the odds of that were unlikely. Still, it would be an added bonus if she happened to. As she sat in the corner of Major Sutton's office, she imagined sitting behind the desk in her own as one of them walked in, frightened, groveling, lying through his teeth. And she imagined herself catching him in his lies, exposing his crimes, meting out his punishment. She had to keep tugging her mind back from the fantasy to the business at hand.

Some of the customers, as Major Sutton called them, came in bowing and scraping, others strutted; some waited to be invited to sit, others took a chair as if they were throwing down a challenge; some leaned forward eager and ingratiating, others sat erect, their faces arranged in masks of disdain for these barbaric Americans; some glanced nervously at the questionnaire on the desk as if it held a nasty surprise, as if they hadn't filled it out themselves, others ignored it ostentatiously.

The fifth or sixth customer—she'd lost count—came bowing into the office. He was short and carried a walking stick in one hand and a Tyrolean hat with a feather in the crown in the other. The walking stick was missing its knob and the hat was battered, but he was keeping up appearances.

He stood waiting for Major Sutton to indicate a chair. When he did, the man bowed again to her, then to Sutton, and taking the fabric of his trouser legs between thumb and forefinger, hitched them up as he sat. It was hard to imagine that they could get more wrinkled than they were, but he was making it clear to them that he had his standards.

Sutton glanced at the *Fragebogen* on his desk, then at the man.

"You're a printer, Herr Moller?"

Herr Moller admitted that he was.

"A member of the union?"

Herr Moller shrugged. "One had to be to work."

"A member of the Nazi Party as well?"

"I never joined the Party."

"Are you certain? We have ways of checking."

"I have no interest in politics, Colonel."

"Please don't inflate my rank, Herr Moller. I'm a Major, as I think you know."

"Forgive me, Major. I have no interest in politics."

"Wasn't that perhaps irresponsible, in view of what was going on?"

Herr Moller nodded eagerly. "*Ach*, I can see that now, Major, but at the time I was a young man. And I was in love. Engaged to be married."

"I see."

Herr Moller leaned forward in his chair. "May I tell you about my fiancée, Major? She was Jewish."

The eagerness of the confession, even the way he pronounced the word *Jewish*, as if, like medicine, it tasted bitter but possessed healing qualities, made her want to slap him, but Sutton leaned back in his chair with his left hand in his pocket, crossed one leg over the other knee, and sat listening with that easy insincere smile.

"She was a beauty. And so cultured. I'm no philistine, Major, but this lady, this angel, put me to shame."

"So your wife is Jewish," Major Sutton said.

The man looked startled. "Oh, no. No, Major. We never married."

"Why not? How could you let a girl like that get away?"

The man shrugged. "The Law for the Protection of German Blood and German Honor. It forbade relations between Germans and Jews. I was opposed to the law of course. But what could one do?"

"I've been at this for three months," Sutton said after the man had backed out of the office thanking him, "and I don't think a week has gone by without at least one of these customers bringing up his beautiful, cultured Jewish girlfriend or fiancée. Before the war the Fatherland must have been crawling with comely museum- and concert-going girls of the Jewish persuasion."

"You think that's impossible?" she asked.

He closed the folder and swiveled his chair to face her. "I was questioning the veracity of the Krauts, Captain, not the likelihood of comely, cultured Jewish girls."

"Yet you gave him a fellow-traveler classification. Despite that ridiculous story about the Jewish fiancée."

"We can get them for party membership or lying on their *Fragebogen*," he said turning back to the desk, "but not for toadying."

It went on that way all morning and well into the afternoon. One after another, they told their tales of what Sutton called the three I's—innocence, ignorance, and impotence. They had been listed as members of the Nazi Party without their knowledge. They had sent their children to an elite boarding school run by the SS only because there was no room in the public schools. They hadn't really published an article in the *Völkischer Beobachter*, the Nazi Party rag, at least not knowingly. It had been lifted from another, more respectable newspaper. Through it all Sutton sat listening, trying to distinguish, he admitted to her when she questioned him between customers, the outright liars from the mere equivocators, the people who had made off with Jewish property from those who really had intended to store it for safekeeping, those who had avidly hounded Jews from those who had merely averted their eyes. And through it all he remained cool, distant, infuriatingly polite. Only once did he lose his temper. No, not lose his temper, merely permit himself to become engaged.

The applicant wore a tweed hunting jacket that must have been fashionable in its day, and expensive, but the fabric was fraying and the empty right sleeve was pinned to the shoulder. He took one of the chairs in front of the desk without being invited to and launched into a chronicle of what he, what the entire nation, had suffered under the Allied bombings. Family and friends killed, the beloved home he—and his father before him—had been born in destroyed, his priceless stamp collection lost, his body, as they could see, maimed. He shrugged his right shoulder in case they hadn't noticed the pinned empty sleeve. She saw Sutton begin to take his hand out of his pocket, then change his mind. Poor Germany, the man repeated again and again, poor Berlin, poor Herr Lang. He referred to himself in the third person.

Calmly, as if he were looking for a pencil or a fresh pack of cigarettes, Sutton opened a drawer, but instead of a pencil or a pack of cigarettes, he took out a photograph. She caught a glimpse of it as he handed it across the desk to Herr Lang. It was one of the pictures taken when the troops had liberated the camps. Bodies stacked like cordwood was the phrase everyone used, but she refused to. The inanimate analogy was another kind of murder. The fact that those people were dead did not mean they had never lived.

"If you want to talk about loss," Harry Sutton said quietly, "perhaps you'd like to discuss Dachau."

The man glanced down at the photo. "That, as you must know, Major, is a photograph of victims from your bombings of Dresden."

Sutton sat staring, his jaw tight as if he was locking in words. He held it that way for a moment, then relaxed, marked something on a card, and handed it over.

"What did you rate him?" she asked after the man had left.

He swiveled his chair to face her again. "Follower or fellow-traveler."

"After that comment about Dresden?" She was incredulous.

"We can't get them for self-pity or stupidity or recalcitrance any more than we can for toadying. Sometimes I think it would make just as much sense to flip a coin. And be twice as fast."

"Or perhaps it might make more sense to remember what these people did."

"All of them?"

"Nobody ever voted for the National Socialists, but somehow they won elections. No one ever went to a rally, but in the newsreels those stands looked pretty full and the roar of the crowd was pretty loud."

"Collective guilt?"

"More credible than collective innocence."

"I suppose you have a point. But then again so did our friend with the Jewish fiancée. '*Was könnten wir denn tun?*' Forget 'Deutschland über Alles.' That's the new German national anthem. 'What could we have done?' And maybe they have a point." He leaned back in the chair and studied her. "What did you do?"

"What?" Her voice was startled. She knew the question was rhetorical, but she still didn't like it.

"All I'm saying," he went on, "is maybe the ones who stayed—not the sycophant with his fictional Jewish fiancée but some of the others who really didn't join the party or stop talking to their Jewish friends, but who also didn't flee, even if they had the chance—deserve the benefit of an open mind."

It was a nice theory, she supposed, if your name was Sutton, you spoke the King's English, and you had witnessed things from across an ocean. But if your name was Meike Mosbach—Meike Sarah Mosbach, because when the Nazis came to power they added "Sarah" to every Jewish girl's name and "Israel" to every Jewish boy's—and you had the chance to leave, you grabbed it. No matter what the cost. She had to keep reminding herself of that.

"The *you* in my question was hypothetical," he went on. "I was talking about Germans, not German Jews. If they had the chance to leave, they would have been fools not to grab it."

❧

She was putting on her coat to leave the office at the end of the day when Theo Wallach appeared in the doorway. Before Major Sutton had started the interrogations that morning, he'd taken her around the office to introduce her to the other three interviewers in this part of the department. She'd expected hostility, or at least skepticism: What was a woman doing in a man's job? During her years at a women's college she'd been spared the question, but in her job at the magazine she'd kept coming up against it, or rather against the assumption that once the war was over she'd step aside to let a deserving man take her place, and go back where she belonged, wherever that was. To her surprise this morning, she'd been welcomed. All three of them—Theo Wallach, Werner Kahn, and Jack Craig—assured her they were drowning in *Fragebogen* and needed all the help they could get. Theo Wallach added that it would be nice to have a girl on the team.

She wasn't entirely surprised by the comment. As Private Meer and any number of other GIs had made clear, American girls were rare birds in Occupied Berlin. But she hadn't expected it from this particular GI. Theo Wallach had the appearance of a tough guy straight out of central casting. She had the feeling that wasn't entirely an accident. He looked as if he worked at it, though the physical features helped. His eyes were dark beneath brows that met in a rage over a surprisingly snub nose. The only feature that softened the effect was the thick fringe of lashes most girls would sell their souls for. He wasn't tall, barely an inch or two taller than she was in her regulation low-heeled oxfords, but he was compact and quick on his feet. Even standing still, he gave the impression of being ready to spring.

"We have Schmidt and Weber," Jack Craig had said.

"I said girl, not Kraut gold digger," Theo had answered.

He stood now with his hands in the pockets of his trousers leaning against the doorjamb. No German would lounge against a doorjamb like that, especially in an office, especially in uniform. He was showing off his Americanization, but it was a masquerade. He wasn't relaxed. She had the feeling he never relaxed.

"How did your first day go?"

"I'm not sure I'm cut out for this."

"Sensibilities too tender?"

"Mind too closed."

"That's our gallant leader speaking. The trouble with Sutton is he thinks he's back on the playing fields of Harvard. Nice shot, old boy, and all that crap."

"I take it you don't agree with his stand."

"Eighteen."

"Excuse me?"

"The number of family members I lost in the camps. And I'm talking immediate consanguinity, not distant relatives. Nice irony, don't you think? Eighteen is *chai* in Hebrew. Life."

She didn't say anything.

"Do you smoke?" he asked.

"Occasionally, but no thanks, not now."

He shook his head. "I wasn't offering you a cigarette. I was giving you advice. Take up the habit more seriously. I chain-smoke through every interview. It unmans the customers completely. They're so busy looking at the cigarette, inhaling the aroma, remembering the taste, salivating over the damn thing that they can't remember the lies they told on their *Fragebogen*. That's how I catch them out."

"A whole new form of psychological warfare."

"It works. I'll let you sit in on one of my interrogations sometime. They're a far cry from Major Fair Play's."

"I suppose he has a point."

"Don't you believe it."

Five

❧

MEIKE LAY ON THE FLOOR WITH HER EAR AGAINST THE register. Below her in the parlor her parents were whispering, as they did far into the night these days. Whispering, because they didn't dare speak in English or French. David and Meike knew those languages. Even Sarah could recognize a few words and phrases. Yiddish, which many older people used to keep things from the children, was no alternative. Her mother barely knew it, and it was too close to German anyway. So since other languages were not a possibility, night after night they went into the parlor, pulled closed the sliding doors, and whispered in their own. They thought they were protecting the children. They didn't realize that the heat register carried sounds up to Meike's room. If they had, they would have locked themselves in a closet or stood out on the street. Anything to shield the children.

The funny thing was that it started with the children. Or at least the children brought it home to them.

One day shortly before her fifteenth birthday Meike returned from the *Lyzeum* with a peculiar story. The teacher had told the students to take out their German history books. Then he passed out a single-edged razor blade to each of them. A murmur ran through the class, part excitement, part apprehension. When had they ever been handed such dangerous objects? The teacher turned to the blackboard and began writing numbers on it. "These are the pages you are to cut out of your books," he explained as the chalk screeched against the blackboard. He was excited too, or perhaps merely fearful. That was why the chalk broke. He bent to retrieve the two pieces and went on writing with one of them. "Be sure to leave the margin of the old pages so you can paste in the new pages," he told them as he scrawled a long line of numbers.

The exercise was peculiar, and Meike couldn't make sense of it, until she began reading the pages she was supposed to discard. Every one of them mentioned a Jew who had made some contribution to German history or culture.

She saw the look that passed between her parents when she told them about the class that night.

The second incident occurred a few weeks later. David was late returning from school. When he arrived home, the sleeve of his *Gymnasium* uniform had been torn off, his shirt was bloodied, and his nose was beginning to swell. Their mother chipped a piece of ice from the block at the bottom of the icebox, wrapped it in a towel, and told him to hold it to his nose. Then she took him into the bathroom to clean his wounds. Meike and Sarah stood in the doorway to the bathroom watching until their mother noticed Sarah and gestured to Meike to take her away. But later that night after their mother had washed and iodined his cuts and bruises and their father had returned from his clinic and made sure she'd done a thorough job, David told Meike what had happened, though she knew her mother had told him not to. They had to protect the children, even from each other, or at least from each other's knowledge.

Three boys had chased him down an alley. He was fast

on his feet and sure he'd escaped until he saw two more boys coming at him from the other direction. He knew them all. Three were in his class, two in the class ahead. One had been his best friend until a year or so ago. They'd taken turns, four of them holding him down while the fifth punched and kicked him. The worst part, he told her, and she could tell how hard he was fighting the tears, was the end. He'd thought it was over. He'd wanted to stand up and walk out of the alley. He'd even started to. But then one of the boys had pushed him back again, and he hurt too much to fight. He curled on his side with his hands over his head, waiting for them to leave. But they were not quite finished. One of the boys taunted his former best friend for being a Jew-lover. He hadn't punched and kicked hard enough. The others took up the cry. The former best friend had to prove his mettle. He unbuttoned his pants, took out his penis, and peed on David.

"And I took it." Now he was crying. He hadn't in front of his mother, and especially not in front of his father, but he did now in front of her.

"It would have been worse if you'd tried to fight back. There were five of them and one of you."

"I still should have tried," he said, and his thirteen-year-old voice cracked, not with growing pains but with shame.

That was the night the whispering began.

"I've had enough," her mother said. "We leave."

"They're isolated incidents," her father insisted.

"Isolated incidents! You call boycotts of all Jewish shops and businesses isolated incidents? You call boys and grown men too scrawling ugly words and Stars of David on the doors and windows isolated incidents?"

"They're riffraff. Not the real Germany."

"Riffraff is the real Germany now, Max. Maybe it always was."

"Don't say that, Gerda. I fought for this country. I was wounded for it. I was awarded the Iron Cross."

"Did your precious Iron Cross save David this afternoon? Did it excuse you from the law forbidding Jewish doctors to treat anyone but Jews? Does it help you when gentile patients, former gentile patients, tell you they don't have to pay you what they owe because you're a Jew and all debts to Jews have been canceled? Your precious Iron Cross is worthless. It doesn't exist. When the history books list the men who won it, Max Mosbach's name will have been sliced out with a razor."

The whispering went on that way. Sometimes her father persuaded her mother things would get better. They only had to be patient. Sometimes her mother convinced her father they should start writing anyone they knew in America and England and applying for visas.

Then one night changed everything, or perhaps Millie only saw it that way because she associated the incident not with her parents' whispering or David's beating, but with Sarah. Hindsight always paints a different picture.

She was sitting at the desk in her room, in her nightdress. She'd already gone to bed, but a realization that she'd mistranslated a word in her Cicero assignment had propelled her out from under the eiderdown back to her book. She made the correction and was about to turn out the light and return to bed when she heard the sound. It was coming from the direction of the Tiergarten. At first all she could make out was a low murmur. Gradually it grew louder and closer. The volume of voices was building. The noise of shuffling on the street was mounting. Then it was right beneath her window, a thunderous roar of voices and pounding of boots. The room, in shadows except for the circle of light cast by the lamp on her desk, flamed with a rosy glow. She got up from her desk, moved to the window, and opened the curtains a crack. Dozens of torches were snaking down the street. Dozens and dozens, maybe hundreds and hundreds, of men were marching beneath them. Their footfalls made the street tremble. Their voices, no, their single voice, roared. The words, half shouted, half sung, echoed off the stone and brick and wood of the buildings and soared up into the heavens. "When the blood of the Jews flows from the knife, all is great."

As she stood watching them go by, she felt something pulling at her nightdress. She looked down. Sarah was looking up at her.

"Can I get in bed with you?"

She closed the curtains, helped Sarah up onto the bed, climbed in after her, and pulled the eiderdown over both of them.

"Go to sleep," she whispered.

"I'm scared."

"There's nothing to be scared of," she lied. "I'm here. Big sisters don't let anything bad happen to little sisters. Now go to sleep."

Sarah, her face pink with the light that was still flaming from the street below, lay looking up at her. Meike scrunched her features into a monkey face that always made Sarah giggle. She didn't giggle, but she did look less frightened.

"I'll go to sleep if you scratch my back."

"You're incorrigible."

"What's incorrigible?"

"Little sisters who will use any trick in the book to get their backs scratched."

Sarah grinned. The gap in her front teeth showed. The *Zahnfee* had come only the night before to leave a coin under the pillow. She turned over with her back to Meike.

"You're too close," Meike said. "I can't move my arm."

Sarah scuttled a few inches away. "Is that better?"

"Perfect."

Meike began to scratch. Her hand worked its way up and down the skinny back, from one side to the other. Beneath the flannel nightgown and warm skin, the shoulder blades felt fragile as twigs.

Six

MAJOR SUTTON WAS SITTING BEHIND HIS DESK, smiling. The expression was genuine, as if he was actually amused and not merely out to disarm.

"Fraulein Schmidt said you wanted to see me." Millie took the chair on the other side of his desk.

"Why does your voice always take on an edge when you mention her name?"

"Is that what you wanted to see me about?"

"No, I'm just curious."

"I guess because she looks as if she just stepped out of a prewar ad for a *Volksfest* in Bavaria. And we know how those turned out."

"She's actually from Frankfurt, but I get your point. What about Fraulein Weber? Is she more to your liking?"

"She looks as if she's getting ready to audition for Lola in *The Blue Angel*. Not the Dietrich glamour, but the air of disrepute."

"Fraulein Weber—" he started, then stopped. "You don't take any prisoners, do you?" he said instead.

She decided not to answer that.

"But our Frauleins, as you intuited, are not what I wanted to talk to you about. Do you remember a Jürgen Steeber?"

She thought for a minute. "You gave him the highest clearance."

"Oh, yes. He was in a concentration camp."

"Do you know what he was in the camp for?"

"Did they need a reason?"

"True, but there was usually an official one listed in the records."

She thought for another moment. "The magazine he published. Subversive contents, if I remember correctly."

"Subversive is one way of putting it."

She waited, trying to figure out where this was going.

"Herr Steeber's magazine was a Wehrmacht favorite, passed from hand to hand among officers and enlisted men alike. Even at the front. You know, Eros and Thanatos. Or didn't they teach that at Bryn Mawr?"

She was beginning to catch on. "Are you kidding? It was the most popular major."

"The magazine was pornography. They didn't lock him up for his political opinions. They locked him up for undermining the morale of the troops, or perhaps only enervating them. Don't misunderstand me. I have nothing against either literature of a certain hue or debilitating enemy troops. I just don't think Herr Steeber is qualified to run a major newspaper or magazine in our new fumigated Germany."

"I'm sorry."

He tipped his chair back and put his feet on the desk. It wasn't the first time she wondered how an officer in the U.S. Army got by with such scuffed shoes. "Don't be. We get few enough laughs around here. My only regret is that I can't dine out on the story."

"Why not?"

"I protect my people. Even the ones who pulled strings to get here. Maybe especially the ones who pulled strings to get here."

Until now, he'd never mentioned the letters Russell Bennett had written on her behalf.

"The only question is why."

"Why what?"

"Why you were so eager to get over here."

"I thought we went through that."

"Ah, yes, all those *Fragebogen* that need translating." He leaned forward and handed her the pornographer's file. "Just downgrade him a little. He was no Nazi, but we still don't want him using American taxpayers' hard-earned dollars to put out a girlie magazine.

"Oh, and going from titillation to outrage or heartbreak or whatever the bloody hell you want to call it, take a look at this." He handed her a newspaper. She glanced down at it. *Der Weg*. "The Jewish community organization is already getting out a paper. Of course, they don't have to worry about old Nazis popping up in their midst the way we do, though I wouldn't rule out some of them trying. A year ago, a card identifying you as Jewish was the kiss of death. Now it's the hottest ticket in town. Jumps you up a notch in the food ration and housing sweepstakes. Might even let you keep your stolen flat or filched paintings. I wouldn't be surprised if those cards start showing up on the black market. One more irony of the demise of the Thousand-Year Reich."

"I'm glad you can joke about it."

He stopped smiling. "Mind if I give you a piece of advice, Millie? Mind, for that matter, if I call you Millie?"

She shrugged.

"Take it easy. You keep going at this boil, and you're going to flame out in one or two months' time. To mix my heat metaphors."

"If you say so, sir."

He shook his head. "As I said, no prisoners. But take a look at the newspaper. We don't have to worry about this one the way we do the propaganda sheets the Soviets are turning out, but we ought to know what's going on."

She knew what was going on. At least, she could imagine the stories in that paper. David came home with them every night, or the nights he came home. "You wouldn't like to give it to Jack or Werner or Theo?" she asked.

"Jack can barely keep his mind on his work during office hours. After seventeen hundred hours he's too besotted with his Fraulein to see straight. Werner's busy with the Russkies, trying to untangle some mess about a screenwriter they won't clear. And I'm not about to give this to Theo. The anti-German chip on his shoulder makes yours look like a splinter. My only consolation is that you're immune to his passes. At least you seem to be. I shudder to think what would happen if you two got together. Just take a look at the paper so we know what's going on," he repeated.

She left Harry's office and went straight to Theo's. The air was thick with smoke and the place reeked of cigarettes, though he wasn't interrogating anyone at the moment. He looked up from the papers he was studying.

"You know that dinner you keep suggesting," she said.

The angry eyebrows lifted in surprise.

"I'm free tonight."

Before Millie had left the States, she'd been cautioned about the hardship of the posting. Despite the requisitioned living quarters, officers' clubs, and bargain PX luxuries, Berlin was the reputed crime center of the world, a bombed-out Wild West where drunken soldiers brawled; thieves, murderers, and rapists preyed on the unsuspecting and one another; spies plied their trade; and werewolves, as unrepentant Nazis were called, schemed to rise again. It was a black market free-for-all where heirlooms, weapons, drugs, title deeds to property, and every kind of sex was for sale. She'd been warned of all that, but no one had told her about the hedonism. Perhaps it was the euphoria of peace, or the distance from home, or human nature, but whatever the cause, all of Berlin, at least all the American and British forces in Berlin, were on a spree. Many of them worked hard during the day. Most of them played harder after hours. The Occupation was an ongoing binge, fueled by alcohol, oiled by sex. So far she'd avoided the latter. She knew her emotions were too raw, her nerves too jangled by walking this tightrope between past and present to risk it. She feared an intimate touch would unravel her, an explosion of pleasure unhinge her. She could not risk losing control. But evenings out, if she remained on her guard, were harmless. And Harry Sutton's comment about what would happen if she and Theo got together was almost a dare.

The officers club that Theo Wallach took her to was an art deco fantasy of carved mahogany and etched glass, once a popular Weimar restaurant, then a favorite Nazi haunt, despite, or perhaps because of, its luxurious decadence. An impossibly lithe couple in evening clothes danced the tango across a mural on one wall; opposite it, two women in revealing diaphanous gowns did the same. Below the dancers sat men, boys really, and a few women from America's small towns and farms, cities and suburbs, offices and gas stations, assembly lines and Ivy League colleges, leveled now by the rough cloth of their uniforms, half homesick, half dazed by this softly lit pleasure palace from another era. A German oompah band played Cole Porter's "Night and Day" again and again, badly.

Somewhere between the martinis before dinner and the wine with it, she found herself wondering why she'd resisted Theo's invitations until now. Conversation between them was easy. She felt as if they'd known each other for years. In a way, they had. They'd both had German childhoods and German-Jewish adolescences. They'd both experienced the hope and terror and guilt of stepping off a ship into a new land. She and David had arrived in New York in 1938. Theo had come to the States alone in 1935, if you could call arriving on a ship with ninety-nine other children alone. Sitting across from each other in that out-of-time restaurant where no one belonged, it was almost as if they did, for a moment.

As the evening wore on, she discovered they had one more thing in common. They were both appalled at the rampant fraternization.

"Yesterday they were bombing them," Theo said. "Today they're bedding them." And he was even more critical of Harry Sutton than she was. "Every time he starts to go on about guiltless Germans, I think of that Hemingway line." English and American literature, it turned out, was one more shared interest. "Isn't it pretty to think so?"

They said good night in front of her building on Riemeisterstrasse. He joked about her inviting him up, but he didn't press the point. He merely kissed her a few times—for an

angry man he had an extremely soft mouth—and said good
night. She stood watching the beam of his flashlight slice
through the darkness as he made his way down the street.
An elderly German hobbling on one crutch was coming the
other way. Theo veered toward him, forcing the man into
the gutter to pass. The ploy was familiar. The Nazis had
done the same thing to Jews for years, until there were no more
Jews on the sidewalks to force off them.

David wasn't in the flat when she got upstairs. She reminded
herself again that he was a grown man. He didn't have to account to her for his comings and goings. She couldn't even
fault him for a lack of consideration. When he planned to
be around for the evening, he always left a note suggesting
dinner at an officers' mess or club or together at home.

She took *Der Weg*, the newspaper Harry Sutton had asked
her to look at, out of her briefcase. There was a reason she'd
tried to persuade him to give it to one of the others.

The war was over. The camps had been liberated. The
forced laborers were free. But existence in the Jewish community was still a tale, thousands of tales, of suffering and
loss and heartbreak. Every night, or at least the nights he came
home, David returned overwhelmed by the vastness of the
misery and his helplessness to ameliorate it. The loneliness
was unspeakable. Old people, children, and everyone between left without a single child, parent, sibling, aunt, uncle,
cousin, or relative several times removed. The physical toll was
appalling. Bodies maimed and broken by disease, hard labor,
and starvation. The lawlessness and violence were terrifying.
Survivors hadn't survived by following the rules. They'd lived
by stealth and theft, lies and betrayal. Individuals who had

spent the past two or four or eight years being brutalized had learned brutality from the masters. The destruction and filth were sickening. Men and women and children who'd forgotten what sanitation was urinated and defecated in hallways and courtyards and wherever the urge moved them. And underlying the acquired bad habits was rage. The fury filled them from the stumps of their frozen toes to the roots of their deloused hair. Perhaps the fury explained David's nightly disappearances. Sex was a means of amnesia, even oblivion. She didn't begrudge him girls, only Frauleins. According to stories she'd heard, some Jewish GIs used sex with Frauleins as an instrument of revenge. She didn't think the boy she'd grown up with was capable of such cruelty. But she had to admit she was barely acquainted with the man the war had made him. Still, not David. Not with a Fraulein.

She sat on the sofa in the parlor, switched on the lamp beside it, began skimming, then turned from the first page to the inner two. The broadsheet was only four pages. Paper was hard to get. Type was impossible. The result was ugly and amateurish, black letters swimming blurrily on the rough yellow stock. But she knew, even as she widened and narrowed her eyes to focus, that her inability to read had less to do with the quality of the publication than the pace of her heartbeat. She hadn't expected the list, though she supposed she should have. Name after name looking for name after name.

Her finger trembled as it raced down the column, then returned to the top and moved down it more slowly. Stranger things had been known to happen. She thought of David's buddy from the Army who had driven into town at the same time his twin rolled in on a freight train from Dachau. She couldn't stop thinking of that story.

She ran down the list a third time. Some of the names

seemed to ring a bell, but then some of the names were
scarcely unusual. How many Sophie Rosenbergs and Her-
mann Steins had there been in Berlin, in all of Germany, in
all of Europe, because millions of people were on the move,
before the war? Now there was only one of each. At least there
was only one of each in Berlin looking for someone else in
Berlin. She went through the names a fourth time. Finally,
she gave up. No, she gave up for the night. No one was calling out to her on this list, but there would be other lists. And
she could be on them. Tomorrow was Saturday. No Jewish
paper would be open on Saturday. But first thing Monday
morning she'd place an ad of her own.

David was sitting at the heavy carved table drinking coffee
and eating tasteless PX white bread when she came into the
dining room carrying the copy of *Der Weg* the next morning.

"Have you seen this?" She put the paper down beside his
place.

He made a noncommittal sound. He'd seen a copy at work
but had been hoping she hadn't.

"It's amazing. All these people searching for one another.
I bet lots of them find whom they're looking for. Like your
friend whose twin rolled in on the freight train. It gives you
hope."

"You call it hope. I call it an obsession that makes you
chase little girls down the street."

"I never should have told you about that."

"They're gone, Meike."

"We don't know that for sure."

"Mr. Streit who was with Papa in the camp said so. One
of Mama's friends told us the same thing."

"They could be wrong. Crowds of people. Mistaken identity. And who knows where anyone was being sent. People shunted from camp to factories to other camps. Forced marches. Prisoners driven east and ending up with the Soviets." She was silent for a moment. "And we didn't find anyone who knew anything about Sarah."

"Please, Mil, you have to stop this."

"It's easier for you. You fought them. You killed them. You did something."

He put down his coffee cup and sat staring at her. They both knew it had nothing to do with what he'd done in the war. It had to do with what he hadn't done before the war, and what she had, and the gulf between the two that he felt bound them and she was sure separated them.

He picked up the paper, carried it to the kitchen, and dropped it in the trash.

"What are you up to on this frigid Saturday morning?" he asked as he came back to the dining room.

"I don't know. What are you?"

"Feel like going to a bar mitzvah?"

"What?"

"You know. The coming-of-age ritual when a Jewish boy turns thirteen and is considered responsible for his actions."

"No one likes a smart aleck. I meant since when did you become observant? I thought you believed religion was the opiate of the masses."

"No, you believe religion is the *opiate* of the masses. I know the accurate translation. *Die Religion ist das Opium des Volkes.* But I promised the kid I'd go."

"The kid?"

"One of the kids from the displaced persons center. Actually, I've gone to a few since I've been here. Some of us who were in Camp Ritchie together usually try to. There aren't a lot of fathers left to do the honors."

"How can you do the honors? You can't read Hebrew. And you haven't set foot in a synagogue since . . ." She let her voice trail off. It hadn't been a deprivation. He hadn't wanted a bar mitzvah. The family wasn't observant, as her father had repeated again and again during those whispered discussions she'd eavesdropped on through the heat register. But choosing not to participate in the ritual of your own volition was one thing; deciding not to do it out of fear of having everyone involved beaten, or worse, was another.

"Mostly I lend moral support. And a little glamour to the proceedings."

"Glamour? You've got to stop hiding your light under a bushel."

"Haven't you heard? A guy in a U.S. Army uniform is sexy."

"So I gather from your nightly disappearances. But to a teenage boy?"

"Especially to a teenage boy. Especially to a Jewish teenage boy. I fought a war. I beat the hell out of his Nazi tormentors. I did to the Nazis what those poor boys in the camps dreamed of doing. I'm a hero."

"What about a girl in a U.S. Army uniform? Will she be as welcome?"

"That's a different kind of sex appeal. Pure pinup. Come on, it'll be good for you."

"Okay, I'm game. Where is it?"

"A cemetery in the Soviet sector."

"A cemetery? I know there are no synagogues left, but doesn't a cemetery seem a little ghoulish for a coming-of-age ritual?"

"Where else can you find family and community these days?"

She sat looking at him. How could she ever have suspected he was sleeping with the enemy?

❦

They came out of the building into a dazzling winter morning. Beneath a cloudless sky, the air felt sharp as glass. The snow that had turned to slush the day before had frozen again. She turned up the collar of her Balkan bunny and pulled the belt tighter, though the fabric bulked around her hips. He'd stuffed her pockets with the packs of cigarettes he couldn't fit in his own. When she'd gone into his room to see if he was ready, she'd been amazed to find stacks and stacks of cigarette cartons.

"Where did those come from?"

"The PX of course."

"You're dabbling in the black market now? Or from the look of it, more than dabbling."

"I'm not selling them, I'm giving them as gifts."

"To a thirteen-year-old boy?"

"To the guests. And some other people I know. Just don't let them show on the U-Bahn or we'll have a riot on our hands."

They had to elbow their way into the U-Bahn car, which stank from too many unwashed bodies packed too close together. Some of the riders scowled at their uniforms, others made way for them, several did both.

They came up into the same grim bombed-out world, except for one difference. Everywhere she turned, red flags and red streamers and red banners with Soviet slogans she couldn't read whipped in the wind. There were also red-bordered posters of Stalin.

"This remind you of anything?" she asked.

"The mustache is bushier this time around."

The snow in the cemetery, a few days old but still pristine, lay like a shroud over the toppled and vandalized gravestones. As they made their way through the gate, she noticed one headstone that had been brushed clean. At first she thought someone had visited it to pay respects. Then they came around the other side and she saw it. A swastika was scrawled on the granite surface. The marking was fresh. She was sure of it. She hurried her steps to catch up with David.

Off to one side of the grounds, a crowd of thirty or so people were milling around. A few of the men had gotten their hands on white prayer shawls, but with the exception of three other GIs in uniform, most of the men and all the women wore dark threadbare suits and coats. They stood out against the white landscape like a murder of weather-beaten crows. Even the movement of some of the men who were already praying, dipping forward and back, made them look like birds pecking. The unforgiving landscape, the smashed monuments, the broken beings struck her as heartbreaking, but as she got closer, she saw something else. These people did not see themselves as a heartbreaking murder of crows. They saw themselves as celebrants. Standing in that desecrated graveyard, with hunger in their bellies and mourning in their hearts and scars that would never heal on their souls, they were celebrating this one child who had survived, one among millions who had not, but still one, and a cause for joy.

Two of the men carried a scroll to a wobbly wooden table

and opened it. Another man began to read from the parchment. Some bowed their heads, others watched carefully, bearing witness. Beside her, a small girl in a thin wool coat stood shivering. She was looking up at Millie. No, not at Millie, at her trench coat with the collar turned up over her ears. Millie smiled down at the child, a rictus admission of guilt. The girl smiled back. Only two teeth were visible in her small mouth. Suddenly it came back to her. Berlin was having that effect. Every corner she turned, every face she saw, every figure she followed was taking her back. The night before she'd lain in bed scratching Sarah's back and telling her lies of safety, Sarah had lost her own front tooth and collected a coin from the *Zahnfee* for it. This child shivering in a snow-covered cemetery had received no gifts from the tooth fairy. And who knew if the teeth had fallen out from natural causes, or malnutrition, or violence? She was still smiling up at Millie and still shivering. Millie unbelted her coat, undid the buttons, and held it open. The girl looked up at her quizzically. She smiled down and nodded. The girl moved into the depths of the coat and Millie folded it around both of them, leaving only the child's face exposed to the brittle air.

Now the boy was summoned to the open scroll on the table. His face was red, but whether from the cold or embarrassment was impossible to tell. With the man standing at his side, pointing to words in the scroll, he began to chant. His voice was high and reedy and cracked occasionally, but as he went on, he grew more confident and his voice stronger. He chanted the sounds and sang the cadence, and the sacred words beat like wings out over the silent snow-covered cemetery. They couldn't right the toppled stones or recarve the defaced names or erase the fresh swastika, but they did defy all that.

When it was over, they filed out of the cemetery in small groups and made their way to a displaced persons center a block away. The girl stayed inside Millie's coat all the way, bumping Millie's hip with each step. She knew it was ridiculous. Her Lady Bountiful complex, she told herself when she caught herself at it. But more extraordinary things had happened. She'd been taken in by strangers, she and David both. They'd been saved. Why shouldn't this child? Why shouldn't Millie pass on the good deed? She wasn't foolish enough to think it would absolve her, but it would be a way to do some good.

Only when they went through the doors into the damaged building, held up on one side by wooden struts, did the girl break away. Bent over, hugging herself, she fled down a hall and skidded around a corner. Millie stood looking after her.

"What did you expect?" David asked. "Lifelong gratitude?"

"I just wanted to know something about her."

"You just wanted to take her home with you," he said. "Give it up, Mil. Stop chasing little girls on the street—"

"Could you please drop that?"

". . . and taking them to your heart, or at least wrapping them in your coat."

"She was freezing."

"And you were kind. But don't expect anything in return. They don't have anything to give. They lost it all in the camps."

"I know," she said, but he could tell from the way she said it that she didn't know.

He held both hands out to her, palms up. "Okay, fork them over."

She reached into her pockets, then stopped. She didn't know whether to laugh or cry.

"What is it?" he asked, but he already knew.

She handed him the packs of cigarettes from her left pocket, then pulled out the lining of the right one to show him it was empty.

"Nimble little thing, isn't she?" she said.

"You get that way learning to survive."

Seven

HARRY SUTTON HAD WORRIED ABOUT WHAT MIGHT happen if Millie and Theo Wallach got together. He was sure each would stoke the other's rage. It didn't happen quite that way. At least it didn't always happen that way. They often found solace in each other's company.

They began having dinner together several times a week. On weekends that were clear and not achingly cold, they walked the city, roaming the wasteland of rubble and weeds that the Tiergarten had become, wandering past the burnt-out hulk of the Reichstag, crossing to the Soviet sector in the shadow of the Brandenburg Gate, which rose from the ruins more like a charred caution against hubris than a triumphal arch. Though they should have been used to the scene by now, they still couldn't quite believe it. The destruction filled them with horror, and another emotion they were too ashamed to admit to each other or even themselves. Neither of them could escape a longing for what had been. Though they hated Germany and Germans, they could not hate their happy childhoods. Separately, silently, they ached with the memory of them.

Some aspects of the city, however, were coming back to life. The Russians were vying with the Americans and the British for cultural as well as political ascendancy. There were concerts and plays, operas and cabarets. The cabarets tended to be raucous and raunchy, but even the more staid events could turn into tinderboxes. One night at a chamber music concert, a handful of music-loving GIs burst into shouts and whistles at the conclusion of Mendelssohn's String Quartet No. 6. The Germans in the makeshift hall were on their feet in fury. They knew the Americans were barbarians, but to boo a Mendelssohn piece was beyond the pale. The air, so recently vibrating with the sound of strings, was suddenly pulsating with rage. A shoving match had already erupted when an American officer went running up the aisle and climbed to the stage. Only when he turned around to hold up his hands to silence the audience did Millie recognize Harry Sutton. His presence wasn't particularly commanding, but his uniform was. Germans respected a uniform. Some former Wehrmacht soldiers saluted it on the street, though the Americans were forbidden to return the salute. The shoving match stopped. The shouting subsided. Switching back and forth between German and English so both sides could understand, Sutton explained that in America shouts and whistles were an expression of extreme appreciation.

"Perhaps not the best mannered," he added in a German aside he didn't bother to translate, "but well-meaning and heartfelt."

The hostility simmering in the air gave way to suspicion, then evaporated into smiles and handshakes and even a few back slaps.

"That was a close call," Millie said as they filed out of the hall.

"Maybe," Theo said, "but while he was apologizing for those rude Americans, he should have reminded all those civilized Krauts what they thought of Mendelssohn and his music a little more than a year ago."

"You take even fewer prisoners than I do."

"Did they take prisoners? I'd like to line the whole damn nation up against a wall and mow them down. No, on second thought, I'd like to make them dig their own graves first, the way they did, and then mow them down."

Sometimes she wondered how he could live with so much hate. Other times she knew.

The incident at the officers' club happened a week or two later when they were having a drink in the bar with Werner Kahn. They'd invited Jack Craig, the fourth interrogator in their department, to join them, but Frauleins were not permitted in officers' clubs, and Jack couldn't bear to spend even a few hours of an evening away from his. Though some men tried to sneak in their Frauleins as Poles or Ukrainians, Jack said he was perfectly happy spending nights alone in his Fraulein's room.

"Doesn't the mother mind?" Theo asked.

"Mind? I gave her a turkey from the PX for Christmas. For a turkey, the old girl would get in bed with us."

Giving food to Germans was against the rules too, but somehow that infraction didn't seem quite so offensive, especially if children were involved, though Jack's Fraulein wasn't exactly a child.

That night in the club only one unoccupied stool was left at the bar when a baby-faced lieutenant came in with a girl in a red sweater that turned every male head. The stool happened to be on Theo's left. Millie was on his right. Werner was on her other side. The lieutenant pulled the stool out for the girl. She slid onto it and crossed her legs. Millie noticed the nylons. They might as well have had the PX tag still dangling from them.

Theo lifted his drink, took a long swallow, put it back on the bar, and turned to stare at the girl. "This is an American facility, Lieutenant," he said without taking his eyes from the girl. "No Krauts permitted."

"She's Polish, sir," the lieutenant said.

"If she's Polish," Theo answered, "I'm Hedy Lamarr."

"She is, sir," the lieutenant insisted.

"Say something in Polish," Theo said.

The girl sat with her head bowed and her eyes on her lap. Millie put her hand on Theo's arm. He shook it off.

"Say something in Polish," he repeated, but louder this time. By now half the bar was staring not at the girl but at Theo.

"She's not hurting anyone, sir," the lieutenant said.

"Not hurting anyone?" Theo was off his bar stool now, his face inches away from the lieutenant's. "Not hurting anyone!" he repeated. "Auschwitz, Bergen-Belsen, Buchenwald. Do I have to run through the whole fucking alphabet for you, Lieutenant?"

"It's not her fault, sir."

"Chelmno, Dachau. Should I keep going or will you get the Kraut out of here?"

The lieutenant stood staring at Theo. He was an inch or two taller, but had the look of a chubby boy. And unlike Theo, he'd come out for a good time, not a fight.

"Why don't you just take her and go," Werner said quietly.

"It will be better if you go," Millie said to the girl in German.

The girl slid off the stool. The lieutenant stood staring at Theo for another moment, then took her arm and started for the door.

The others at the bar went back to their own conversations.

"What if she really was Polish?" Werner asked.

Theo shrugged and signaled the bartender for another round. "You think they're any better than the Krauts? There's a reason Ike had to separate the Jews from the Poles in the DP camps, and it wasn't to protect the Poles."

※

But there was another side to Theo, and it came out on the evenings when instead of going to an officers' club or concert or cabaret, she cooked dinner for him in the flat. Those were the times she thought she might be falling in love with him, if she were capable of falling in love, or if he were. The data on both those questions wasn't in yet.

One of those nights changed everything between them. She knew his fury. It was hard to miss. His kindness was less obvious, but she'd caught glimpses. Sometimes she told herself she was the only one who had. But that night with the Berlin winter assaulting pedestrians and sleet streaking the windows of the flat outside, and domesticity simmering inside, he let her in on his vulnerability.

They'd finished dinner and moved, with coffee and the bottle of brandy he'd brought, to opposite ends of the parlor sofa. Maybe it was the brandy that made him tell her the story, though she thought it was more than that. He'd taken off his jacket and tie and opened the top button of his khaki shirt. She'd kicked off her shoes and put her feet up on the cushion between them. As he began to talk, his hand caressed her toes. The gesture was more affectionate than sexual. That was what she meant about his being a different man when they were alone in her flat. He was certainly different that night. Two or three times before, she'd asked him the story of his arrival in America. She was interested. She was also guilty. She knew she'd had a shockingly easy time of it. In the past he'd managed to slip the question, but now he began to talk.

"The first day in New York was fine," he said. "Hell, it was a lark. They took a bunch of us to the Automat. I was thirteen, not exactly a kid, but young enough to get a kick out of slipping those nickels into the slots, opening the little glass doors, and taking out a tuna fish sandwich or a piece of pie or whatever you wanted. I wanted four slices of coconut custard pie. It was a wonder I didn't throw up.

"After the Automat, they put us on a bus to a barracks upstate. The place was pretty spartan. Long rooms lined with double-decker beds along both walls. I thought it was just fine, but the woman in charge kept telling us it was only temporary until some foster family agreed to take us in. They were lining up to do it, supposedly, Jewish families with a conscience, Jewish couples who had no children of their own, Jews who needed the forty-eight dollars a month they'd get for their trouble. We being the trouble." He stopped and shook his head. "Apologies for the self-pity. A thirteen-year-old stranger who barely speaks English probably is trouble, though God knows I didn't plan to be.

"Sure enough, the couples began turning up. Usually on weekends. They drove up to the barracks, walked through, took their pick of the litter, and off the lucky kid went, sometimes half a dozen in one day, sometimes only one or two. But never me. No one was interested in taking home a boy who could barely communicate. Not like our friend Sutton with his Oxbridge drawl. They'd stand there, right in front of me, and go back and forth about God knows what. I felt like an animal in a pet shop. It can't understand what's being said either, but it sure can pick up on the emotional weather. I know now part of it must have been I was just too old. Who wants an awkward thirteen year old when you can have an adorable five year old? Small is cute. Small is lovable. A displaced boy on the edge of manhood is a lout. And I was a lout who barely spoke the language. At the end of two months, I was the only kid left from that first transport. I thought about running away. I even tried it. A policeman from the nearby town took me back. I'm not sure if he was worried about me or a small town in upstate New York with a German Jew on the loose. About a week later, a new shipment of kids came in. This time around I got chosen—next to the last. By then I'd learned English. And the couple who took me in spoke Yiddish most of the time. They were also old and needed help around the house. I'm not complaining. I was damn lucky they chose me, and I know it. But every once in a while, even now, I see that thirteen-year-old kid, standing at the foot of his perfectly made bed—I knew how to tighten a blanket so a coin bounced on it long before I went into the Army—with his hair slicked down, his tie pulled straight, and a smarmy please-take-me-home smile on his face, and it makes me sick to my stomach. God, I was disgusting."

"That's not the way you sound to me."

He shook his head. "Yeah, but you didn't know me then."

She sat up and moved closer to him. "I do now."

"That's just pity talking. I never should have told you the story."

"I'm glad you did." She put her hand on his arm and felt the muscle tighten. He always did that. He wasn't the only one. It was a universal male trait. But his reaction now was extreme. He was trying to compensate for the story. He was slipping back into his tough-guy persona. She reached her arms around his neck and pressed her body to his. He responded as she knew he would.

They rode out the night in that big four-poster bed as if they were riding a ship in a storm, and in a sense they were. There was sympathy, which is a kinder word for pity. There was passion. There was certainly lust. But mostly there was desperation. Each of them was after oblivion. And lost in their own bodies, drowning in sensation, they found it, for a time.

After she walked him to the door and they said a properly ardent good night, or good morning, she lay in bed thinking about the evening. He hadn't been entirely wrong about the pity. But pity is not a despicable emotion. And there had been more than that, much more. She should be euphoric, or at least happy. And she was. Nonetheless, something continued to nag at her. She didn't realize what it was until she came suddenly awake at three a.m. Their bodies had enjoyed each other. Her flesh still felt tender with the aftermath of pleasure. The physical closeness had been intense. But there had been no intimacy. With his eighteen relatives, several million strangers, and three others whom she'd tried not to think of, the bed had been too crowded for intimacy.

Eight

‹∽›

FRAULEIN SCHMIDT KNOCKED ON THE OFFICE DOOR
and opened it without waiting. Millie always had the feeling
the secretary was trying to catch her at something, though
she couldn't imagine what. Fraulein Weber, on the other hand,
avoided her at all costs. Millie wasn't the only one. Weber
kept her distance from the entire staff. She wasn't any more
cordial to the Germans who crowded the office on the other
side of the slatted wooden divider. Weber was so sour, Millie and Theo agreed, just looking at her made your mouth
pucker.

"There's a woman here to see you," Fraulein Schmidt said.

"Put her name on the list and tell her she has to wait her
turn."

"She says she wants to see you especially."

Millie wasn't surprised. Fewer women than men applied
for clearance, but the ones who did, especially the older or
less attractive ones, often wanted to see her rather than a male
officer. They thought a woman would be more sympathetic.
"If they only knew," Harry Sutton said when he heard that.

"She still has to wait her turn. Has she filled out a *Fragebogen*?"

"She says she doesn't have to."

"Everyone has to. You know that, Fraulein Schmidt."

"She says she doesn't. She says she's"—Schmidt hesitated for only a second, long enough to give offense without seeming to mean to—"a Jew."

"Are you sure?"

Fraulein Schmidt shrugged, as if to say who would pretend to be a Jew if she wasn't. "She has a card to prove it."

Millie thought of the little girl who'd lifted the cigarettes. She didn't blame her. At least she tried not to. A child isn't likely to come out of a concentration camp with a well-boxed moral compass. Still, she wasn't going to be played again.

"Tell her to come in. The others can wait."

Fraulein Schmidt's rosebud mouth shriveled into a frown. Clearly she didn't approve of favoritism, but it was not her place to say so.

A moment later a woman appeared in the open doorway and stood for a moment, as if debating whether to go through with this or bolt.

"Come in, please."

The woman took a few steps into the room. She had a slight limp. Half the people who walked through that door limped, and Millie felt sure at least some of them were faking it, but this infirmity looked real to her. She thought of the filched cigarettes again.

The woman took another step, then stood waiting. She was gaunt, with a tight, nervous mouth and dark eyes sunk in darker circles that gave her the appearance of a raccoon. Her white hair, so thin her scalp showed through, made the sooty eyes more striking. She took the last few steps to the other side of the desk, and Millie inhaled the pungent reek of unbathed flesh. These days it was the scent of Berlin, just as the smell of fresh bread and silver lindens had once been. Still, it was better than the stench of rotting corpses, which,

she'd been told, had been the bouquet of the city in the first
weeks after its fall.

"Meike?"

A charge, jolting as an electric current, went through
Millie.

"You don't recognize me?"

"Of course I recognize you," Millie lied.

The woman shook her head. "I have a mirror in the room
where I stay. Even I do not recognize myself. I am Anna. Your
cousin Anna Altschul."

Millie was holding on to the desk now. This wraith could
not be Anna, the glamorous older cousin who had taught her
to ski and swim and navigate the world. Even her voice was
different, thinner, less resonant, more tentative. She thought
again of the gap-toothed child who had stolen the cigarettes.
This broken vessel was an impostor, out to beat the system
and bilk Millie. But the impostor smiled, and something in
the knowing curve of the mouth opened the floodgates. Millie saw herself, Meike, streaking down the mountain in Anna's
wake, blinded by the sun glinting off her silky red hair. Anna
had refused to wear a ski cap—she was vain about her hair,
with good reason—so Meike hadn't worn one either. She saw
herself treading water as Anna carved a perfect arc from the
diving board into the lake with every pair of male eyes on
her as hot as the sun. Meike perfected her dive that summer,
but no scorching eyes followed the arc of her movement. She
remembered the sly knowingness of Anna's smile, that same
expression that had crept through a moment ago, as she in-
structed Meike about boys and sex and other forbidden top-
ics long into the night in the rooms they'd shared on family
holidays. One night Meike had covered for Anna when she
returned to the room long after she was supposed to. She'd

been out walking along the lake, in the moonlight she said, though as Meike had sat nervously waiting she had noticed the night was hot and overcast, without a moon. She'd been out walking in the moonlight with a man named Sigmund.

"Guess what happened," Anna said.

"He kissed you."

"Of course, he kissed me." She flopped back on the bed and stretched her body as if she were basking in the memory of the kiss. "And when he did, he put his tongue in my mouth."

Meike was shocked, and repulsed, but she didn't say anything. She was waiting for Anna to instruct her in the proper response.

"It was wonderful," Anna sighed.

Millie went on staring at her, still gripping the desk from the dizziness, but persuaded now by her own memories. This woman was no impostor.

She was around the desk in seconds, embracing the emaciated body. She didn't even try to breathe through her mouth. That was a trick for strangers.

Anna didn't resist the embrace, but she didn't return it. Beneath the threadbare coat, no protection against the Berlin winter, her bones felt as if they might break from the slightest pressure. Still, Millie could not let go. She wasn't sure how long they stood that way, her clinging to a hope fulfilled, Anna enduring. Finally, Millie released her and led her to one of the chairs.

"Tell me. Tell me everything."

Anna told her, not everything, not what she'd been through certainly, but enough. It was an inventory of family names and an itinerary through hell. Aunt Ida at Bergen-Belsen,

Uncle Josef at Dachau, Anna's parents at Auschwitz. And Sigmund . . . , she started, then stopped.

Millie waited. Had Anna saved her husband for last, or almost last, out of guilt for her good fortune of still having a husband or the need to put off the pain?

"He came so close, Meike. So close. Two days before liberation." She stopped again. "On the forced march from Buchenwald. His friend who made it told me."

They sat in silence for a moment, the week-long prescribed period of mourning compressed into an instant, observed in a government building where uniformed officers and enlisted men came and went, and Frauleins Schmidt and Weber typed and filed, and Germans sat on benches waiting their turn to be absolved.

Finally, Millie worked up the courage to ask the next question, the most important question. "And Elke?" She could barely get out the name.

"She's safe."

Millie let out the breath she hadn't known she'd been holding.

"I'm sure of it," Anna went on.

"What do you mean, you're sure of it? Isn't she with you?"

Anna shook her head.

"I don't understand."

"Do you remember Frau Kneff? She lived downstairs."

Millie shook her head. Too many names and faces, closer than a passing neighbor, were swimming in her mind.

"She was crazy about Elke. Always picking her up and petting her. Always offering to help me on the stairs with the carriage. She knitted her first pair of booties. I was never any good at that sort of thing. You know that. And hats and mittens and sweaters. Frau Kneff just couldn't stop. She didn't have any children of her own. One day she tried to tell me why. Something about a damaged uterus. I admit I didn't want to listen. I was head-over-heels in love with my new baby. Why would I want to listen to the sad story of a woman who couldn't have one of her own? Now this is the punishment I get for my heartlessness."

"What punishment? I don't understand."

"As things got worse, Frau Kneff kept offering to take Elke. 'I can keep her safe,' she kept saying. 'People will think she's mine. I'm a good Catholic. They'll never suspect her of being Jewish. I can do it. I'm not afraid.' I knew she meant well. And she was right that it could have been dangerous for her. Harboring a Jewish child was forbidden. You know that. But I couldn't bring myself to do it. Sigmund agreed. We stay together, he insisted. But as things got worse, I began to have second thoughts. Sigmund was trying to make plans to go into hiding. But people were afraid to take in a baby. You can secrete a family in an attic or basement or storage closet, but you can't secrete a crying baby. I was terrified, but I understood. Maybe the stories were apocryphal, but everyone had heard about people who were given away by a crying child, or even worse, mothers who had accidentally smothered their babies while trying to keep them quiet." The gaunt body shivered. "But what would happen if we were rounded up? I was going crazy trying to think what to do. Sigmund was too, but it's worse for a mother. I'd be giving her a bath or putting her to bed and thinking how could I give away this child. Then the next day I'd watch her taking in the world—I remember one afternoon when she was trying to grab a stream of sunlight coming through the window—and think she's so young. I'd had my life. Maybe not all I'd expected, but I'd had a happy childhood and married Sigmund and had Elke. How could I deprive her of the same joys? And all the time Frau Kneff kept after me.

"One day a man turned up at the apartment. He had official papers saying the flat belonged to him. This was after your father got the visas. We thought you were all on the ship by that time. Anyway, Sigmund said the papers were legal according to the new anti-Jewish laws and we had no choice but to move into a *Judenhaus*. There were eight or ten of us to a room. People can get ugly in circumstances like that. They aren't so nice to a fretting baby. But Frau Kneff still was. She'd linger outside the *Judenhaus* for me to bring Elke out. She took Elke to the park where I wasn't allowed anymore. Elke would come home laughing. She never laughed in the filthy overcrowded room in the *Judenhaus* where people begrudged any morsel of food I could find for her. Frau Kneff had no trouble finding food. Her husband was an officer on the Russian front. When Elke came home from outings with Frau Kneff, her sweet baby breath smelled of chocolate.

"Little by little it wasn't so crowded in the *Judenhaus*. Every day they took more people away. Sigmund said it was only a matter of days, hours maybe. By this time he'd made up his mind, and he kept at me. Just like Frau Kneff. 'What chance will a child that young have in a camp? At least this way one of us will survive.' Finally, I gave in. As it turned out, I was just in time. Frau Kneff came to take Elke away at two-twenty-five in the afternoon. I know because, and you probably won't believe me, my watch stopped. Do you think, Meike, the force of a heart breaking can stop a watch? They came for us that evening."

Now a different silence hung over the room, not of grieving but of suspense. Millie had a feeling she knew what was coming. That was why Anna was here, to see her, of course, but also for help.

"Where is Frau Kneff now?"

"That's the problem. I can't find her. The first thing I did when I got back was go to her flat. The building had been bombed, but a neighbor was still living in one of the rooms. A wall gone, rain and cold coming in everywhere. You've seen what it's like. The neighbor said Frau Kneff and Elke had both survived the bombing. I almost fainted from the relief. Where are they, I asked. I was ready to run all the way. The neighbor didn't know. I was disappointed, but I thought, all right, others are bound to know where they went. Neighbors. And Frau Kneff had a sister I'd met once or twice. I even remembered her name. Frau Klempner. There was her church too. I used to see her going to mass every Sunday and confession every Saturday. When her husband was sent to Russia, she began going to mass during the week too. So I started to make the rounds. No one knew where they'd gone. I went to offices and authorities. There was no record of a Teresa Kneff. I thought maybe she'd be listed under her husband's name, but there was no Frau Axel Kneff either. I went to her church. The priest hadn't seen her since last April. She'd stopped going to mass and confession a few weeks before the surrender. Everyone knew Germany was defeated. She must have known that if I were alive, I'd be back. The point is no one had any idea where she was. Frau Kneff had disappeared. No, that's not entirely true. I did run into one woman from the old building. She said she'd seen Frau Kneff in the Soviet sector. I asked if she had Elke with her. The woman said she didn't know the child's name but Frau Kneff's daughter was a beautiful little girl. 'I don't know where she got that lovely red hair,' she said, 'but she's an angel. And so well behaved.'

I should have been proud. I was sick with the news. I knew then she had kidnapped her. Frau Kneff has kidnapped my baby."

"We don't know that," Millie said, though they did. "Is there still a Herr Kneff?"

"He was killed in Russia."

They both knew, though neither of them said it, that Frau Kneff's widowhood made the situation worse. Now Elke was all she had in the world. She'd never give her up of her own volition.

"She can't have disappeared into thin air," Millie said, though she was afraid she had. Frau Kneff could have left Berlin, gone to another sector, changed her name. Everyone was on the move. No one had papers. "I'm sure we can find her," she lied.

Anna reached across the desk and took Meike's hand. "Yes, please, Meike, please to God, you can help. I thought you were in America, but when I found out you were working here—"

"How did you find out?"

"I saw David. He was just a boy when you left, but I still recognized him."

"Where? He didn't tell me."

Anna hesitated. "I forget where."

"Anna!"

"Potsdamer Platz."

"The black market?"

"I go to all of them. Pariser Platz. Alexanderplatz. Platz der Republik. I'm not trading. I have nothing to trade. I'm looking. A woman who'd kidnap a child would know her way around the black market."

"I wouldn't care if you were trading. You must be hungry."

She didn't add that David had no such excuse, but she refused to think about that. He spent his days trying to save people. Perhaps the stacks of cigarette cartons had something to do with that.

"He told me you were working here," Anna went on. "That's when I said to myself Meike will know how to find her. She has access to records. She knows people. She will help me find Elke."

"If I can't," Millie said, because she wasn't as certain of her abilities and connections as Anna was, "I'm sure others here can. Let me see if Major Sutton is free now."

She started out of the office, then stopped in the door and turned.

"Anna?"

"Yes."

"You haven't had word of my parents or Sarah?"

Anna shook her head. "I would have told you. I would have told you right off. You know that."

Millie started out of her office again and went down the hall to Harry Sutton's. Fortunately he was alone. She started to tell him about Anna and Elke and the missing Frau Kneff.

"Slow down, Millie. Remember what I told you about flaming out."

"Damn it, this is serious."

"I know you're not actually in the military, Captain, but it's generally considered bad form to swear at the commanding officer."

"I'm sorry. It's just that it's been quite an afternoon. First she walked into my office, and I had no idea who she was. Then all the other relatives dead." She stopped for a moment. Not all the other relatives. "And now this awful story about the woman disappearing with her child."

"The woman can't just have disappeared. Old Nazis disappear, and I'd put money on their turning up in Argentina or Uruguay or God knows where one of these days. Spies disappear and surface in Moscow. But German hausfraus with little girls do not disappear into thin air."

"Then you have some ideas?"

"We have records. So do the Brits. Neither as good as the Nazis', but useful."

"Would you talk to her?"

"I'll be there as soon as I take care of the Russkies. It seems they're up in arms because a scientist chap they had their eye on is already on a plane to American headquarters in Frankfurt."

She was on her way back to her office when she thought of it. There was plenty of room in the flat. Not in the child's room painted with pink and blue flowers. That would be too cruel. Everywhere Anna looked, Elke would be lurking. Millie would give Anna her room and move into the child's room.

"Where are you living?" she asked Anna when she returned to her office.

"Near the Tiergarten. Not far from where you lived before. A room in a cellar. It's fairly safe, or as safe as you can be in Berlin these days, and it has the furnace, so if there's any heat at all, I get it."

"I have a better idea. There's an extra room in our flat. You can stay with us."

Anna shook her head. "That's generous, and I'm grateful, but I can't."

"Why not? You'll be a lot more comfortable there than in a cellar."

"I must stay where I am."

"I don't see why."

"To find Elke. Everywhere I have gone, everyone I have spoken to, I have told them where I live. If anyone sees her, if anyone hears a word, they'll come to me there."

"Of course. I'm sorry. I didn't think. But there must be something else I can do. Food. You must need food." She thought of the closet at the end of the hall. That was where they kept the care packages that mothers and wives and girlfriends were still sending, despite the fact that sons and husbands and boyfriends no longer needed them. Most of the packages ended up in displaced persons centers, but some were stored here.

She took the key from her desk drawer, hurried down the hall, and returned with several boxes. Anna wouldn't be able to carry them all, but if Millie took out the shaving cream and chewing gum and magazines, she could fit plenty of food in one of them.

She put the boxes on her desk and began opening them. "I'll get more from the PX, but this should tide you over in the meantime."

As she took the unnecessary items out of one box and moved the tins of tuna fish and fruit cup and vegetables into the spaces, she avoided Anna's eyes. She didn't want to see the eagerness. She'd be even more embarrassed to see the shame.

She was about to close the box when she thought of it. She'd found the cake of soap the day before in a store that had almost nothing else to sell. It was Naumann Caressa. Her mother had sworn by Naumann Caressa. There had always been a stockpile of cakes in the bathroom closet. Millie had forgotten to take this particular cake she'd bought out of the pocket of her coat when she'd gotten home last night. She crossed to the coat tree in the corner, took the bar of soap from the pocket, and put it in the box with the tins of food.

Anna's eyes grew wider as she watched, but she didn't say anything. Millie only hoped she hadn't offended her. Did people sense their own smell?

She was just closing the box when Major Sutton came striding into the office and introduced himself to Anna before Millie could.

"Should we call in one of the Frauleins, Millie, or do you want to take down the information?"

Millie said she'd do it. She didn't want to let Schmidt or Weber near Anna.

He began firing questions. Where exactly in the Soviet sector were Frau Kneff and Elke spotted? What about the woman who spotted them? How long ago was that? He went on that way for a while, asking for lists of names from before the war, places she'd searched now, fragments of anything else Anna might remember about Frau Kneff. Where had she been born? Where had her husband been born? What was her maiden name? And what about the churches? She said she'd asked the priest, but had she thought of lurking in other churches during confession? "This Frau Kneff doesn't sound like the kind of woman who could go for too long without confession, especially with this particular sin blackening her soul."

It was after five by the time they finished. Millie said she'd walk Anna out of the building. She didn't want to take the chance of having the guards stop her because of the package.

Harry Sutton was still in her office when she returned. The cake of Naumann Caressa soap she'd put in the care package was on her desk.

"She forgot the soap," she said when she saw it. She picked it up and started for the door. "I bet I can catch her."

He put a hand on her arm. "Don't."

"But it's so hard to get."

"She doesn't want it."

"What do you mean she doesn't want it? People are paying packs of cigarettes for a cake of soap like this."

"Maybe, but she doesn't want that particular cake of soap. Give her Ivory or Camay or something from the PX, but not that."

"This is better. My mother swore by this soap." She stopped. She hadn't intended to bring her mother into it. The less he knew about her past, the better.

"Frau Altschul was in a camp, right?"

"More than one."

"Some, not all, but some of the survivors from the camps refuse to use German soap."

"I don't understand."

He stood staring at her. "Think about it."

She did think about it. That was when it happened. She was sweating and shivering at the same time, as if she was coming down with a sudden flu. The room lurched around her. Her body jackknifed over the metal wastebasket. Her lunch went spewing into it.

Then the strangest thing happened, stranger even than her violent reaction, which when you came to think of it wasn't strange at all. Everyone had heard the stories about the Germans making soap from the fat of dead Jews. As she bent over the wastebasket, vomiting up the repulsion, Harry Sutton came around the desk to where she was standing, reached out, and put his hand on her forehead, the way one does with a child, to support her head during the violent spasms, to ameliorate the horror.

Nine

〜

THEY WERE SILENT ON THE TRAIN. AT FIRST THEY WERE unable to speak. The race down the platform, David sprinting ahead to find a compartment with two seats—they had to stay together—turning every few steps to make sure Meike was behind him, Meike's suitcase banging against her leg as she ran to keep up, left them breathless. He spotted a compartment with two empty seats, skidded to a stop, yanked open the door, flung his suitcase inside, pushed Meike up the steps, and followed her in. The three men and one woman already inside glanced at them, then away. Perhaps they were being polite. The two young people looked distraught. Or perhaps they simply had no interest in them. These days minding your own business was the safest course of action, unless you wanted to make trouble for someone. David heaved Meike's suitcase, then his own, into the overhead rack. Still panting from the run, they sat, Meike in the middle, David beside the door to the corridor. The window seats were already taken by the woman and one of the men.

Gradually, their breathing became more even, but they still didn't speak. Through Hanover and Bielefeld and Munster, they didn't say a word, not to each other, certainly not to the others in the first-class compartment. Her father had decided that since they couldn't take money with them, they ought to spend it on getting out. He was also betting that they'd be treated with more respect traveling first class. He'd been wrong, but it was too late to worry about that.

Through lowered lashes Meike glanced at the others. She didn't want to meet anyone's eyes. She didn't want to call attention to herself. But she was trying to stay alert. She was trying to keep her wits about her.

A motherly looking woman—though motherly was a peculiar term under the circumstances; the woman, plump and deep-bosomed, looked nothing like their own svelte, chic mother—held a box of chocolates on her ample lap. The man beside her was nothing more than two large hands with dark hair at the knuckles holding open a large broadsheet. Next to him and across from David, a man in a dark double-breasted business suit sat erect, his shoulders barely touching the back of the seat, his feet planted several inches apart on the compartment floor. Though he was sitting, he gave the impression of standing at attention. She couldn't turn her head to see the face of the man beside her in the window seat, but she managed to take in his short body and elegant clothes. The pale camel hair coat was immaculate. The pigskin gloves miraculously free of the soot of the railway car. His shoes were shined to a dazzling glow. Every now and then he reached inside his coat, drew out a spotless handkerchief, and mopped his brow. The car wasn't that warm. He must be as nervous as she was.

Beyond the window, the fields lay hard and brown in the unforgiving winter sunshine. The train didn't slow for the smaller stations but sped through in a whoosh of noisy vibration. The shudder of the car was jarring. The slowing of the train for no apparent reason was even more unsettling.

Each time it did, she stiffened with fear, imagining every kind of trouble. David must have too, because once he took her hand. She squeezed his in what was supposed to be reassurance but was closer to shared terror. Then the train picked up speed again, and they let go of each other. She looked past the man in the polo coat to the quickly moving landscape. Each mile, each minute, was taking them closer to the border, nearer to safety. But not fast enough. The trip was supposed to take nine or ten hours. It felt like months. The sun set. Dusk closed in. Night fell.

The train was slowing again. She looked out the window into the darkness. Everyone in the compartment looked out the window as they glided into a blaze of illumination and came to a full stop. The platform was lit up like daylight. Men in uniform were swarming up and down, shouting orders, swinging up into the cars. She would have known they were at the border even without the signs. The Netherlands was so close they could sprint to it. But that was the one thing they couldn't do. She felt the weight of the months of waiting, the more than a year of effort leading up to this moment pressing at her back, propelling her forward, and forced herself to remain still.

During the past year the whispered conversations she'd eavesdropped on through the grating in the floor had changed. Her parents no longer debated if they should leave, only how. Germany was tightening its stranglehold on those who wanted to emigrate. Other countries were finding ways to keep out those who wanted to immigrate. The Third Reich kept reducing the amount of money an individual could take out of the country until it was down to ten Reichsmarks, which amounted to four U.S. dollars. Other countries insisted on financial proof that the new arrivals would not become wards of the state. Sponsors were necessary. The list of obstacles grew and grew.

Her parents wracked their brains for relatives, no matter how distant, friends, no matter how tenuous, professional acquaintances. They wrote and rewrote, collaborating on the phrasing, fine-tuning every word. "Make sure they understand we won't be a financial burden," her father told her mother. "I'll get work immediately. Any kind of work. I'm not proud."

By this time the discussions were out in the open, and Meike saw her mother flinch at the last sentence. What was a man without pride?

"Do you think this sounds as if we're begging?" her mother asked about another letter.

"We are begging," her father replied.

The answers began to come back. Distant relatives had closer nephews and nieces, aunts and uncles to save. Friends described other demands and obligations. "The door is closing in our face," her mother said. "Not as long as I have my foot in it," her father insisted. Meike wondered if he was really that optimistic or merely keeping up a façade for the rest of them. Whichever it was, he refused to stop trying. That was how he came up with the idea of Russell and Lydia Bennett, though he admitted they were a long shot.

He'd met the Bennetts a decade earlier in Switzerland at a conference of the International Birth Control League. Lydia Bennett had gone to jail for the cause more than once. Russell Bennett was a magazine publisher who had bailed her out when necessary and run pieces supporting the movement and railing against a government that imprisoned women for trying to save the lives of other women and children. The

Bennetts flexed their social consciences every chance they got, so perhaps they weren't such a long shot after all.

Her father wrote the letter. Now there was a new twist. Meike had to put her ear to the register to discover it. The conversation had turned secret again, with good reason. If the Bennetts felt they couldn't sponsor the entire family, her father had written, perhaps they could take one of them. Late into the night, Meike listened to the debate. If only one could go, her mother insisted, it should be her father. He would stand the best chance of finding work and bringing the rest of them over. Who knew how long that would take, her father argued. Hope lay in the next generation. They should save one of the children. Finally, her mother agreed. Meike did not have to hang over the hot grate to know which of them it would be. She was the eldest, but David was the boy. A boy carried on the family name. A boy was by definition more important. A boy was a boy. The flash of fury she felt was more scorching than the heat rising through the register. Then she told herself she didn't have the nerve to start life in a new country on her own anyway.

As it turned out, her parents did not have to pit one child against another and she did not have to bank her rage and envy. The Bennetts, who had no children of their own, would sponsor all of them. The Mosbachs were a family again, not a Darwinian jungle.

Now all they needed were visas. Every weekday morning her father left the house so early that the milk wagons had not yet rolled through the darkness to break the nighttime silence. He was determined to be first in line at the consulate. He had a theory about that, two theories actually. Being first in line showed you were serious, energetic, hardworking, a potential good citizen. And the officials in charge were fresher in the morning, not yet exhausted by the folders full of financial statements proving the applicants would not become public charges, foreign letters pledging sponsorship, certificates attesting to good health; not yet jaded by hard-luck stories and tales of terror and appeals to their conscience, if they had a conscience. That was another variable. Some officials went by the rules, some bent them, and some tightened them like a noose around the applicants' necks, insisting on the optional papers, which were really farcical demands. What Jew in his right mind would willingly walk into a Nazi police station to request a certificate of good character, or anything else? There was a rumor mill about the various visa offices. Some said Hamburg was the most sympathetic, others warned against the vicious anti-Semite in Stuttgart. Berlin was anyone's guess. Getting a visa was like playing the roulette wheel in Monte Carlo, only for higher stakes. Yet somehow her father managed to get five of them. Only then did he take their savings and the funds that could be realized on what was left of her mother's jewelry and purchase five tickets on the S.S. *Statendam.*

Now the waiting really began. Day by day, their number inched up. A hundred were ahead of them, then eighty-five, then thirty. The list moved in fits and starts. The still-unannounced but constantly rumored slamming of the gates loomed. What if their name didn't reach the top in time? They didn't speak of the possibility, but it stalked the house, sitting down to meals with them, following them about their daily comings and goings, haunting their sleep. Finally, they were only ten from the top, but ten was no better than a hundred if the Nazis closed off the escape routes. Then suddenly Mosbach was only three from the top. They were going to make it. They really were.

Her mother covered the long dining room table with a quilt—they couldn't take the table with them, but that didn't mean she wanted to scratch or chip it—and lined up the suitcases on it. She went back and forth, upstairs and down, gathering clothes and mementos and photographs, the Leica lenses their father had bought and the few pieces of jewelry she had left. She secreted those valuables in jars of creams and tins of talcum powder. Day after day, she put things in the suitcases, stood staring at them, took them out, weighing practical value against sentiment, a warm sweater or pair of boots against the lace she and her mother had worn to walk down the aisle. The choices were excruciating. The emotion was so overwhelming that sometimes she had to hold on to a chair or table to steady herself.

There were moments of contention. She couldn't stop her husband from taking his Iron Cross, but she put her foot down when Sarah wanted to pack her teddy bear.

"It takes up too much room," she said. "And you're too big for a teddy bear."

"But I can't leave him here all alone," Sarah pleaded, close to tears. What she meant was that she couldn't go to a strange new home in a strange new country all alone.

Meike listened to the back-and-forth. Her mother was right. The bear would take up too much space in a suitcase. But Sarah was right too. She'd need something to hold on to.

"I have an idea," she whispered to Sarah when their mother went off to decide which of their father's suits he should take. "Can you keep a secret?"

Sarah nodded.

"I'll sneak one of your hand puppets into my suitcase. But just one. You'll have to choose."

It took Sarah the better part of an afternoon to make up

her mind. Did she want the schoolteacher or the ballerina, the clown or the puppy? In the end she decided on the puppy.

"Good choice," Meike said. "We'll need a pet in America."

Finally their number crested. Her mother closed the suitcases. The click of the ten metal fasteners echoed through the stripped-down rooms. Her father handed out the passports, each bearing a large J for *Juden*, each stamped with the words *Gut nur für Auswanderung*. Good for emigration only. That was all right, her mother observed. Who would want to return? Her father said nothing, though Meike noticed he'd slipped his Iron Cross Second Class into his breast pocket. A few months earlier she'd had a crush on a boy who hadn't known she existed. It occurred to her watching her father with his Iron Cross that her unrequited love for that boy had been nothing compared to her father's for Germany.

She sat in the chill railroad compartment now, clutching the passport in her gloved hand. Meike Sarah Mosbach. J. *Gut nur für Auswanderung*. Beside her, David held his at the ready. David Israel Mosbach. J. *Gut nur für Auswanderung*. They each must carry their own, her father had insisted.

The opening and closing of compartment doors, the gruff demands for papers, the confident booming or terrified mewling replies were coming closer. The door to the next compartment slammed shut. The boots pounded the corridor. Did they have to march even on a train? The door opened. An officer stepped inside. Another remained in the corridor. The interior lights glinted off the oiled black surfaces of their weapons.

Meike kept her eyes on the floor, but she watched them, again through lowered lashes. The officer who'd entered the compartment took another step until he was standing over the woman sitting next to the window. He held out his hand.

"Papers," he demanded. His eyes cut to his colleague in the corridor, then back to the woman. His voice was reedy, his cheeks dotted with angry red pimples. He couldn't be much older than David. Perhaps that would make him more sympathetic, or perhaps he'd be more desperate to prove himself. She'd noticed the glance toward his colleague when he'd demanded the woman's papers.

Balancing the box of chocolates on her lap with one hand, the woman held her passport out to the officer with the other. He stood studying the document. Did he really think a plump middle-aged woman with a sweet tooth was a threat to the Thousand-Year Reich? Finally, he handed the passport back. The woman smiled, opened the box of chocolates, and offered it to him. He bent a little to get a better view of the assortment in the box. He really was a child. Then he must have remembered the officer in the corridor. "No, thank you," he said and pivoted to the man in the middle seat.

The man had folded the newspaper and was holding his passport out in one of his hairy hands. Again the officer studied it for some time before handing it back. The man at the end, the one who managed to stand at attention while sitting, handed over his papers. This time the officer did not spend time studying it. He snapped to attention and thanked the man as he handed back the passport. Later she'd wonder if the presence of the man, whoever he was, had provoked the incident. Had both officers been showing off for his benefit?

The officer stepped toward the window again and loomed over the man beside Meike. He not only had his passport out, he'd opened it to the appropriate page. As he handed it over, she glimpsed the large J.

Again, the officer stood studying the passport. "*Juden*," he said.

The man shrugged as if the condition couldn't be helped. The officer asked his line of work.

The man said he was a jeweler. This time he didn't shrug.

The officer asked which piece of luggage was his. The man pointed to a worn but still handsome calfskin portmanteau in the rack directly over his head.

"Take it down," the officer ordered.

The man stood and turned, but he couldn't reach the rack. She hadn't realized how short he was when he was sitting. A porter must have put it up for him. The man lifted his arms and jumped, but it was no good. The officer stood grinning as the man struggled. The other men in the compartment were watching, but none offered to help. Meike sensed David beside her watching too. He'd already had a growth spurt and could have reached the rack easily. She took his hand to keep him from moving.

The officer ordered the man to take off his coat. The man undid the buttons, slipped out of it, and held it out to the officer. He rolled it into a pillow and put it on the plush upholstery. "Now you can reach it," he said, and half pushed, half lifted the man onto the seat. As he reached for the suitcase, Meike could see the sooty black prints his well-shined shoes left on the pale cloth of the coat.

The man wrestled the portmanteau, which he could still barely reach, out of the rack and, struggling not to drop it on the officer who was standing beneath him, climbed back down. He put it on top of the soiled coat. The officer snapped open the brass fittings, unfolded the mouth of the case, reached inside, and began pulling out the contents, a silk dressing gown, a pair of trousers, several shirts. One after another, he flung them to the floor of the compartment. Through downcast lashes, Meike saw the man flinch as each garment landed.

The officer reached in again, lifted out a traveling chess set, and tried to open it, but he couldn't work the clasp. Meike noticed the flush creeping up his skinny pimpled neck. He held it in front of the man's face and ordered him to open it. The man did. The officer took out a bishop and shook it. The only noise was the jeweler's heavy breathing. He sounded asthmatic. By now the second officer had stepped into the compartment. He took the bishop from his colleague and shook it beside his ear. Still no sound. One by one, they began taking out the chess pieces, shaking them, handing them back and forth, and shaking them again. The silence in the compartment grew more ominous. The asthmatic breathing heavier. A flush had crept up the younger officer's neck to his ravaged face. Now and then the older officer glanced at the straight-backed man in the corner. Meike thought of her mother's bracelet in the tub of cold cream in her suitcase, the Leica lens in the Vaseline jar in David's. Her insides felt as viscous as those sticky substances.

The senior officer threw a pawn to the floor and brought his boot down on it. Perhaps he thought the jeweler would hide his most valuable items in the least valuable pieces. The younger officer bent to pick up the shards. He handed them to his colleague and together they stood examining them. They clearly did not like what they saw. The older one threw another piece to the floor and stomped on it. Again, the younger one stooped to pick it up. They went on that way through the pawns, rooks, knights, bishops, queens, and kings. With each piece they flung more violently and stomped harder. They were glancing at the important official more often now. They'd boxed themselves into a corner. Everyone in the compartment knew it. The jeweler knew it better than any of them. Meike could smell the sweat and fear coming off him.

The senior officer muttered something to the younger one. Meike couldn't make out the words, but she recognized the tone. They weren't going to let some Jew outsmart them.

It took both officers to subdue the man. He was short and portly but desperate. As they frog-marched him out of the compartment and down the corridor, he continued to struggle. Meike glanced out the window to the platform. The man was still flailing. Then the blow from the butt of a rifle made him double over.

Meike waited for the officers to return. Surely she and David couldn't be this lucky. But the minutes passed, and no one entered their compartment. Doors were slamming. Officers were swinging down to the platform from other cars. The train lurched, then began to inch forward. The motherly looking woman stood, put the candy box on her seat, and began picking up the jeweler's clothes, folding them, and putting them back in the portmanteau. She was just brushing off the soiled camel hair coat when Meike saw a sign glide past the compartment window. YOU ARE ENTERING THE NETHERLANDS.

Ten

❧

THE DAY AFTER MILLIE'S VIOLENT REACTION TO THE realization of why Anna had refused the soap, she stepped into Harry Sutton's office on a minor matter and noticed something. He was leaning back in the swivel chair with his feet on the desk in his usual document-reading position, but there was one difference. His shoes had been newly shined. Their gleaming cordovan surface took her by surprise. Then she realized that the fallout from her regurgitated lunch had driven him to do what Army regulations had never managed to. Perhaps he saw the color rise in her cheeks, because he swung his feet off the desk, as if to hide the evidence.

On her way out she asked if there had been any progress on the search for Frau Kneff. They both knew it was the real reason she'd come to his office.

"No leads yet," he said, "but I had another thought last night. Wehrmacht records. She probably applied for her widow's pension. Even if there are no payments now, she won't want to lose her eligibility."

"Can I tell Anna that? I'm planning to take her some things from the PX tomorrow."

"You don't seriously think I'd tell you something I didn't want you to pass on? I saw you two together."

The joke among the American military in Berlin, and for all
Millie knew everywhere in Germany where there was a PX,
was that you stood a good chance of getting the bends going from the ravaged world outside to the smug abundance
inside. On one side of the armed guards and barbed wire
were hunger, misery, and danger; on the other, aisle after
aisle of shelves filled with breakfast cereals and peanut butter, ketchup and mayonnaise, Kraft and Kellogg, Campbell
and Heinz. Refrigerated cases overflowed with porterhouse
steaks and rib roasts, salamis and cheeses, gallons of milk and
pounds of butter. Stacks of Lucky Strikes and Camels and
Chesterfields stood like fortresses.

Shoppers pushed carts filled with American bounty. German staff in long white cotton coats bowed and scraped and
whispered of the men they'd once been. Millie found the experience disorienting in more personal terms as well. On the
streets of the city, in her U.S. Army uniform with the special
chevron indicating that she was not regular Army but still
cloaked in its power, she felt more American than she ever had
in the States. In the PX, she felt strangely German. Or to put
it another way, on both sides of the barbed wire she was an
impostor. She usually felt guilty as well, but this afternoon,
shopping for Anna, the plenty induced no self-reproach.

She pushed her basket up and down the aisles, tossing in
tins of fish and packages of sausages, fresh fruit and vegetables, coffee, a Lister bag of water purified by the Army for
brushing teeth, and half a dozen cakes of Ivory soap. Harry
had assured her Anna wouldn't mind Ivory. "Ninety-nine and
44/100% pure; it floats," the ads said. More to the point, it
was made in America.

At the end of the toiletries aisle, an elderly man in a regulation white PX coat had stopped stocking shelves and was talking intently to a girl in an Army uniform with a nurse's insignia whom he'd boxed in between two displays. Her light brown hair was pulled back in a regulation bun beneath her cap, the sprinkling of freckles across her nose made her look very young, and when she glanced over the man's shoulder at Millie, her large hazel eyes had a desperate cast to them.

"You don't happen to know German, do you?" she asked Millie. "He's been going on like this for a while, but the only word I can make out is Brooklyn."

The man turned his attention from the girl to Millie. She listened for a moment, said something in German, and maneuvered him aside to let the girl out.

"What did you say to him?" the girl asked as the man made his way up the aisle.

"I told him you couldn't help him."

"What did he want me to help him with?"

"Getting to Brooklyn where he has a cousin."

"Is he serious?"

"Dead serious. You know you can't get him to Brooklyn, and I know, but hope springs eternal in the German heart. I take it you haven't been here for long."

"Two weeks. I guess it shows."

"You'll get used to it. They tend to approach us more than the men. They think we have softer hearts."

"Don't we?"

"Not this cookie."

The girl looked surprised. "Anyway, thanks for saving me. I was beginning to think I'd never get away. I wish I could speak German. You're really good. I guess you've been here for a while."

"A few months."

"You got that good in a few months? Do you mind if I ask how? I mean did you take lessons or learn it in school back in the States or what?"

Millie hesitated. "I was born in Germany."

The girl's hazel eyes widened. "But you're wearing an American uniform. And you don't have a German accent when you speak English."

"It's a long story."

The girl blushed, and the freckles on her nose deepened. The effect was vivid, and very pretty. "My mother is always telling me I'm nosy."

"Let's say curious."

"It's just that I don't know many people here except the other nurses in the hospital. They're nice. They're swell, really, but . . ." She let her voice trail off.

"But what?"

"You'll think I'm silly. Or at least naïve."

"No more so than the rest of us mixed up in whatever we're trying to do here."

"I was so excited when I heard I was being sent to Berlin. I was in a veterans' hospital in Alabama for the past year and a half. I might as well have been back in Friendship. That's in Indiana, in case you didn't know, and I bet you didn't. So when I heard I was being assigned to the 279th Station Hospital on the Unter den Eichen, I thought, finally, I'm going to see the world. I only have six more months, but I was ready to re-up. That's how great I thought it was going to be." She shook her head. "Rubble and other Americans, that's all the world I've seen so far. You're the first person I've met who even speaks German. If you don't count the man who wanted me to get him to Brooklyn and the staff who mop the floors and stuff in the hospital."

"That's me. An exotic bird."

"I didn't mean . . . I keep putting my foot in it."

"It's okay. I was joking. And I'll take it as a compliment."

"You wouldn't have time for a cup of coffee, would you?" the girl asked.

Millie glanced at her watch. Her shopping had taken less time than she'd expected. Anna wouldn't be in her room for another hour at least. She'd told Millie she was going to make the rounds of some churches. They'd agreed that Major Sutton had a point about Frau Kneff not being able to stay away from confession.

"It just so happens I do have time for a coffee," Millie said.

"See what I mean? You say *a* coffee. People in Friendship, the nurses, everyone I know says a cup of coffee. Or coffee."

"It's the same thing."

"Only it sounds more glamorous the way you say it. Let's have *a* coffee." She held out her hand. "I'm Mary Jo Johnson."

As it turned out, Mary Jo Johnson wasn't as naïve as she claimed or as Millie assumed, at least in one area. On the streets of the city and in her office, Millie managed to keep the suffering at arm's length. In the hospital, Mary Jo met it up close. More than that, she had her nose rubbed in it. Nursing the GIs was hard enough. Men learning to walk with a prosthesis, to breathe with one lung, to shave a strange face in the mirror thanks to the advances of plastic surgery. Then there were the wounds that didn't show. At night, Mary Jo said, the ward sounded like a battlefield with GIs shouting warnings to absent buddies and cursing and pleading for their mothers.

The GIs broke your heart. The German children proved the world didn't have one.

"They just keep dying," Mary Jo said. "Newborns from dysentery. Infants from starvation. Kids of every age from all sorts of disease. And the mothers have to take them away. Last week one mother came with a cardboard suitcase. Can you imagine carrying your dead child in a cardboard suitcase?"

Millie couldn't. And she didn't want to.

"I'm sorry," Mary Jo said. "I didn't mean to go on like this. I thought I'd get away from it here. But all I did was let down my guard." Two tears ran down her freckled cheeks, but she managed a smile. "That's your fault. You've been so swell. Kind of like a big sister."

In front of Anna's building, two children were climbing a small mountain of rubble and sliding down it. They couldn't have been more than four or five, but again it was hard to tell with so much malnutrition. She thought of Mary Jo's stories about the children's ward, then reminded herself if she was going to worry about children, she had more immediate candidates. She wished she had some news for Anna.

Nearby, a *Trümmerfrau* was picking up bricks and stacking them in neat rows. As Millie approached, she looked up from her work, gave Millie a filthy look, and called to the children to stop that right now. The children went on climbing and sliding.

Millie made her way through the clouds of dust they were stirring up toward the building, or what was left of it. The windows were glassless holes in what remained of the wall. There was no door, merely an opening into a long, dark corridor that ended in a dusty cloud of light pouring in from the litter-strewn courtyard on the other side.

She stepped through the exposed steel and cement of the opening and started down the hall. On the first door on the left, a scrap of paper printed with Anna's name and attached by a rusty nail fluttered in the wind. "Anna Altschul" was scrawled on the wood of the door as well. She wasn't taking any chances on not being found.

Millie knocked.

"Come," Anna called.

"Don't you even ask who it is?" Millie said as she stepped into the room.

"I can't afford to be choosy. Who knows who might have word of Elke. Besides, there are no locks."

"You said the place was safe."

"As safe as anything in Berlin is these days. At night I wedge a chair against the door under the knob."

Millie glanced around the room. A narrow cot stood against one wall, the furnace Anna had said sometimes gave off heat, though it wasn't giving off any at the moment, took up most of another. A light bulb hung from the ceiling by a wire. Anna followed her eyes. "See, I even have electricity. When there is any. All the comforts of home." The single window was boarded up. Again Anna followed her eyes. "The only thing you can see from down here is the rubble and people's feet anyway. I'm fine, Meike, really I am."

"Where should I put these?" She held the bags out to her.

Anna took them, thanked her, and placed them on the cot. Millie was glad she didn't start to go through them. Anna's embarrassment for having so little was nothing compared to Millie's shame at having so much.

Anna straightened from putting down the bags and turned

back to Millie. She didn't have to say a word. Her upper body, skeletal in the thin coat, curved toward Millie as if it were a question mark.

"We have a list of Kneffs in the various sectors. No Teresas or Frau Axels yet, but she might be with family members. We're tracking down Klempners too. You said that was her sister's name. Most of the information comes from applications for ration cards. She'd need one for her and one for Elke. And Major Sutton had another idea." She told her about the Wehrmacht widow's pension. "We're making progress." She heard the fatuousness of her own voice. "At least we're trying. Really we are."

Anna stood staring at her, her big eyes, bigger now than ever in her emaciated face, hard with anger. "Trying? The Americans don't try, Meike. They do. When they want to. They bomb. They win the war. They liberate the camps. But they can't find one little girl? With time running out. Like sand in an hourglass. Every minute she's growing older. Every minute she's growing further away from me. She won't even know me."

"She'll know you," Millie lied. They both knew twenty months of infancy were no match for almost five years of care and love, but Millie told herself, if not Anna, that they'd worry about that when they found Elke. If they found Elke.

"Are you still combing the black markets?" Millie asked.

"I go wherever there's hope."

"There's no hope there, Anna, only danger."

Anna didn't answer. She knew Millie was right about the danger. But she was right about the hope.

"They're jungles," Millie went on. "Filled with pickpockets and thieves and"—she remembered the MP's warning the day she'd followed the girls on the way to school—"people who'd slit your throat for a pack of cigarettes. And if they don't get you, the military roundups will."

Anna shook her head. "They don't bother with me. I'm not buying or selling. I'm just looking."

"That doesn't mean you can't get hurt."

"You don't understand, Millie. You walk the streets in an American uniform, and everyone notices. Some hate, some fear, a few are grateful, but all of them notice. An old woman like me—"

"You're five years older than I am."

"I'm a lifetime older than you are. And I have the camps written all over me. No one wants to be reminded of them. So I'm invisible. The operators know I have nothing to trade. The cutthroats know I have nothing to steal. Sex? Don't make me laugh. And the upstanding German citizens selling their jewelry and furniture and whatever they have left blame me for the war. You know the saying. Another bad Jewish joke. The Germans will never forgive us for what they did to us. As for being rounded up, why would they bother with me when they have people with pockets full of jewelry and forged identity papers and penicillin and morphine to sell?"

Millie admitted she had a point, but she still worried. That was why she decided to go with Anna the following Saturday. When Theo heard about the plan, he insisted on accompanying them. "Two women alone are just double the quarry, even if one of them is in uniform," he said.

They started in the Alexanderplatz. The vast square was a landscape out of a nightmare. The imposing shops and office buildings, the famous Manoli cigarette ad with the ring of neon tubes circling endlessly that had intrigued them as children, lay in rubble. Here and there the remains of the

U-Bahn tunnels that had first served as air-raid shelters, then been flooded by the Wehrmacht in a last ditch effort to slow the advance of the Red Army were barricaded to keep people from tumbling into the holes. And everywhere crowds of people shoved and jostled, hawked and haggled. Arms shot out from coat sleeves to display half a dozen watches, everything from valuable Luftwaffe Ondas to inexpensive Mickey Mouse models, the favorites of the Ivans, for which they'd pay obscene prices. Private Meer swore he'd sold one for four hundred dollars. Fists opened to show a handful of diamonds. Young men peddled Wehrmacht ribbons, Hitler Youth badges, and knives with swastikas on the sheaths for GIs to take home to show the folks where they'd been. Old women and an occasional man hovered silent and watchful beside chairs and bedsteads and—Millie stopped—a handsome inlaid breakfront with ebony columns. She crossed the space and stood looking down at it. The geometric pattern was similar to the design on the one in the flat, but the drawers of this one had brass keyholes.

The woman standing beside it took a step toward Millie. "*Zehn* cartons," she muttered.

Millie went on staring at it. She reached out and touched one of the brass keyholes. She couldn't remember. It was so long ago. Did the one her father had given her mother have brass keyholes?

She traced the pattern of the inlays on the surface. If only she could be sure.

The woman was still watching her. "*Neun* cartons."

Theo and Anna were suddenly beside her. She hadn't realized they'd kept going when she'd stopped to look at the breakfront. "We thought we'd lost you," he said.

She turned away from the breakfront. The woman muttered something under her breath. Millie wasn't sure if it was the word *acht* or a curse.

They made their way through the crowd, Anna's head constantly turning, searching for women in the hordes of buyers and sellers, examining faces, lingering every now and then to study one more closely. She stopped suddenly and stood staring at a man who was holding out a camera for a GI to inspect.

"Is that someone you know?" Millie asked.

Anna didn't answer.

"I thought we were looking for a woman," Theo said.

Anna still didn't answer.

"What is it, Anna?" Millie asked.

Anna lifted her arm and pointed at the man with the camera.

"Herr Kneff?" Millie asked. "I thought he was dead."

"The Butcher," Anna said.

"From your old neighborhood?" Millie asked.

"From the camp. A guard. That was what they called him. The Butcher."

"Are you sure?" Theo asked.

"You don't forget someone like that," Anna muttered.

"We should find MPs," Millie said.

But Theo was already moving toward the man. He looked up from the camera, saw an American uniform bearing down on him—this was no potential buyer, this was a pursuer—grabbed the camera out of the GI's hands, and started to run. Only when he did, did they realize that he had only one leg and a crutch. His gait was so hobbled that it seemed with each step he would topple over. Theo caught up with him in a few strides. He staggered back with Theo's first punch to his face, doubled over and collapsed with the second thrust to his stomach. The crowd backed off in a circle around them, staring in silent fear and anger as Theo's right boot collided with the man's head. He took a step back. Millie thought he was finished. He was only positioning himself to exert more force. His boot swung back, then forward against the man's head. The man's body bounced with the blow. His blood spurted. Theo swung his boot back, then forward again. He kept at it, his mouth shouting curses while he kicked, until two MPs pulled him away, two others bent over the man on the ground, and suddenly a squad of officers and enlisted men was swarming through the market. People were grabbing their wares and running while others were being pushed into trucks. There was chaos, but there was no panic. Everyone knew they'd be released immediately and back within an hour.

Getting Theo out of custody took longer. Millie called Harry Sutton, and he came quickly, but it was almost ten that night by the time Sutton's jeep dropped Theo at his quarters with orders not to budge until further notice. Theo thanked Harry grudgingly, then came around the vehicle to cross the street to his flat and stepped into the beams of the headlights. The bloodstains on his trousers bloomed in the light like deadly flowers. She turned away from the sight, but she couldn't block out the image of Theo's boot connecting with the man's head again and again and again. It had been running in her mind all day, like a newsreel that wouldn't stop. She saw Theo's foot swinging back, coming forward, the man's body jolting with the force of the blow, blood spurting, and Theo's mouth snarling curses.

"I need a drink," Sutton said when the jeep started away from Theo's building, "and if you don't, there's something wrong with you."

She said she did and didn't tell him about the looping

newsreel. He'd heard enough details of Theo's assault from the MPs.

They went to the officers' club with the art deco murals where Theo had taken her the first time they'd had dinner. It had survived the decadence of the Weimar Republic and the deceptively scrubbed depravity of the Third Reich, but it was beginning to show wear under the Occupation. Someone, unloosed by alcohol or homesickness or both, had scrawled "Kilroy Was Here" in a bottom corner of one of the murals.

"The man was a guard in Sachsenhausen," she said when they were settled across from each other at a table beneath the two tangoing women in diaphanous gowns. "Anna recognized him."

"So you all kept saying. But there are protocols for that sort of thing, and beating the hell out of a man in a public square that just happens to be the biggest black market in town is not one of them."

"What's going to happen to him?"

"The camp guard or Wallach?"

She'd meant Theo, but Harry's mention of the camp guard started the newsreel looping in her head again. Now there was a soundtrack. She could hear Theo as well as see him. He hadn't been shouting curses. He'd been howling numbers. Kick. One. Kick. Two. Kick. Three. She wasn't sure how high he'd gotten, but she knew that if the MPs hadn't pulled him away, he would have kept going until he'd reached eighteen.

"I meant what's going to happen to Theo. I assume the guard will get what he deserves."

"He'll go on trial, if that's what you mean. But I wouldn't be so sure of just deserts. For every sadist like that guard, there are probably two or a couple of dozen garden-variety opportunists. They survived under the Nazis and they'll figure out how to survive in a new regime. All they have to do is stop singing 'Deutschland über Alles' and start whistling Dixie. And that goes for this guard too, if you wait a few more years. The new Germany we're supposedly building on the foundations of democracy isn't likely to be too different from the old one built on Nazism or fascism or totalitarianism or whatever the hell you want to call it. I'll put money on the same cast of characters running the show."

"That's encouraging. What about Theo?"

"With any luck, I can call in some favors and head off a court-martial, but Theo's days in the denazification business are over. He's a good man, when he doesn't let his anger get the better of him, but I can't afford him here. Especially now."

"Why especially now?"

He hesitated.

"My lips are sealed."

He still hesitated.

"Look at it this way. If you tell me, each of us will have something on the other."

"What do I have on you?"

"You can tell people how I disgraced myself all over your shoes."

"There are some who'd say the disgrace would have been in not getting sick at the realization. Besides, if nothing else, you got me to shine my shoes."

"So I noticed. What were you about to tell me?"

He glanced around the room.

"Nobody can hear you above that damn oompah band. I can barely hear you. Besides, no one cares. They're all too drunk or amorous or calculating their poker or bridge hands."

He leaned toward her. "Do you remember the first morning you walked into my office, and I warned you about what is known in official channels as excessive zeal? Or behind closed doors by the Krauts and more than a few of our own people as too many returning German Jews out for a pound of flesh?"

"I haven't taken a knife to anyone yet."

"Except the Frauleins, but I wasn't talking about you. There's an order kicking around headquarters." He glanced around again.

"You can't stop now."

"General Clay's office," he said finally, and his voice had dropped again. "That's how high up it is. Don't ask me how I know, but I do."

"I wasn't going to ask you."

"New directives about who qualifies to work in denazification. It's all stated in properly oblique terms. 'All officers must have been citizens for at least ten years.' 'No renewal of contracts of anyone who was not a citizen prior to 1933.' And my favorite, 'In carrying out these orders, officers must refrain from discussion of the subject.' In other words, the Krauts have got through to the brass. No more dirty Jews sitting in judgment of the still-master race. But don't let the word get out."

"I guess the only thing that surprises me is that I can still be surprised."

"Look on the bright side. This time they're just firing people, not hauling them off to camps."

"When should I start packing?"

"You shouldn't."

"My contract isn't up for another nine months, but I'm sure the Army can find a way around that."

He drained his drink and signaled the waiter for another. "You're not going anywhere. First of all, the order hasn't come down officially. Yet. It's there, but it hasn't been issued. The brass knows it's a bombshell. Secondly, if and when it does, we'll find a way around it. For starters, I'll point out that they won't have much of a department with only our good gentile Yalie, Jack Craig, in place."

"Jack and you to run the show and train the new people."

"Pardon me?"

"Surely they wouldn't reassign you. Even the anti-Semitic brass can't believe in guilt by association."

"Try guilt by birth."

"Are you telling me Harry Sutton is a Jew?"

"I just assumed you knew. Or guessed, given our preponderance in the department. Harry Sutton started life as Hans Sutheim. And before you get on your high moral horse, Meike Mosbach, I wasn't trying to buy gentile. I just didn't like being German. Any more than you did apparently, though I always wondered why you didn't change the last name as well. Figured your future husband would do the trick?"

"I figured it would hurt my father too much."

He sat looking at her for a moment. "The Nazis took care of that particular problem for me in '33," he said finally. "One of the first casualties at Dachau. Quite an honor, don't you think?"

"Yet you turn yourself inside out trying to be fair to them."

He polished off his second drink. "Sometime I'll tell you about that too. Maybe. But I've done enough undressing in public for one night. Not to mention spilling military secrets." He signaled for the check. "I just thought I ought to warn you about the order."

"Thanks. From now on, I'll be on my best behavior. But there's one thing I don't understand," she said as he paid for the drinks. "Where did Hans Sutheim pick up such a posh English accent?"

"From Victoria Sutheim. Nee Victoria Ayer."

It was the first time she'd thought of his being married. He didn't wear a ring, but then few men over here did. They weren't eager to broadcast their marital status. Besides, wedding bands were worn on the third finger of the left hand. Then again, people didn't usually acquire accents from spouses, though she'd known a secretary at the magazine who had sounded like a cross between Maurice Chevalier and Edith Piaf. When Millie had asked where in France she'd grown up, she'd said Northeast Philadelphia, but her husband came from Rouen, and she'd rolled the r like a growl.

"Your wife?"

"My mother. She was an English nanny to a German family. Until they found out she was a Jew as well as a Brit and tossed her out. That was before the First War. It wasn't as bad then, but being a Jew in Germany has never been all beer and skittles. She had to find a new job so she answered my grandfather's ad for a secretary. He hired her. My father fell in love." He stood. "And the rest is my history."

On their way out of the club, she couldn't help stopping and turning her head to look at him again.

"What's wrong?"

"Nothing. I'm just trying to get used to you as Hans Sutheim."

"You mean as a Jew?"

"Awful as that sounds, yes."

"Why? Because I don't practice? Neither do you. Because I don't believe? Do you? But even with all that, or rather without all that, I'm still a Jew."

"Because the world forces you to be?"

"Yes, but not the way you mean. Because the world forces me to choose to be. As long as it's a crime or a shame or even a disadvantage to be a Jew, I'll be one."

She went on looking up at him in surprise. "I never thought of you as quixotic."

"I'm not. Just stubborn."

They came out of the club into the Berlin winter. Snow had begun to fall again. Big wet flakes swirled around them. She turned up the collar of her coat. He switched on his flashlight. The beam caught a GI and a girl huddled in a doorway.

"It never stops," she said as they started down the street. "Even in the snow."

"Can you think of a better way to keep warm?"

She hated the fact that he could joke about it, but she didn't want to fight with him, not now, not after their conversation in the club, not after what he'd done for Theo. The thought of Theo started the newsreel in her mind again. The boot against the head. The body jolting from the force. Theo spitting out the numbers. How could similar experiences twist two men into such different shapes?

Eleven

SHE WAS SURPRISED WHEN HARRY CAME STRIDING INTO her office the next morning. He usually sent Fraulein Schmidt with a summons. It wasn't a matter of pulling rank. At least, it wasn't only a matter of that. He hated running the gauntlet of Germans who snapped to attention every time he stepped into the outer office. She wondered if last night's drink was going to change their working relationship.

He took a piece of paper from the folder he was holding, leaned over, and put it on her desk. "Take a look at this."

"Something to do with Theo?"

"Take a look," he repeated.

She picked the piece of paper up off her desk and skimmed the first few paragraphs. It was a character reference. She hadn't seen one before, though she'd heard about them. They were known as Persil letters after the popular cleaning agent because the intent was to whitewash the German petitioning for clearance. They were usually written by an individual's priest or minister, attesting to an immaculate soul as well as an unflagging dedication to the church and a long history of good deeds. Occasionally they came from Jews, citing kindness and protection offered during the Nazi years. Whether the letters were true was anyone's guess. The ones written by clergy might have been well-intentioned, even sincere, or merely opportunistic. The ones written by Jews were more puzzling. Perhaps some were true. There must have been Germans who tried to help their Jewish countrymen. But many must have been put-up jobs. So the real question was what would make a Jew fabricate a letter like that?

She looked up from her desk. "You think this is bogus?"

"Look at the signature."

She glanced down at the letter again. "Respectfully submitted, Frau Sigmund Altschul." Her head snapped up.

"Did she ever mention a Herr Huber to you?"

"I don't think so."

He took another piece of paper from the file and handed it to her. "Herr Huber's address before the war and during it was the building where Frau Kneff and your cousin lived, until your cousin was dispossessed. The timing is just suspicious enough to suggest that he was the one who took over her flat."

"Then why would she write the letter for him?"

"That's what I'm trying to figure out."

"I was planning to take her some things from the PX tonight. I'll ask her."

"Don't."

"She's still in need. Whether the letter is true or not. Maybe more so if it isn't. Maybe that's why she wrote it."

"I didn't mean don't take her things. I meant don't ask her. It'll only scare her. Falsifying information like this is as serious as lying on a *Fragebogen*. We'll take care of it ourselves. Once we've defused the situation, whatever it is, we'll talk to her."

She sat staring at him.

"Don't look so surprised, Millie. I'm not the s.o.b. you think."

"I never thought you were an s.o.b."

"Only a German-lover, which sounds suspiciously like that reviled figure from the last regime, Jew-lover. But back to Herr Huber. How would you like to pay a visit to the Documents Center, which just happens to hold the *Zentralkartei* of the NSDAP?"

"The what?"

"The central membership register of the entire Nazi Party."

"I can translate, thanks, but what exactly is it?"

"A Who's Who of infamy. Every member of the party, no matter how high up or how minor, signed a card. Two actually. When someone joined, duplicate cards were made, the member signed both, the first was kept in the local registry, and the second was sent to the central office in Munich. So those song and dances we get about I never joined, someone else signed me up are pure bollocks. Every last Jack of them, and Jill, had to fill out the application and sign the card in person."

"You'd think the officials would have destroyed them when they knew the Allies were getting close."

"They tried to. That's the best part of the story. Hitler didn't believe he was losing the war but plenty of his officers did. Needless to say, they didn't want their meticulously kept records falling into Allied hands. So some prudent soon-to-be-ex-Nazi arranged for a convoy of trucks to transport them under armed guard to a paper mill in the Bavarian boondocks. The orders were to pulp every last record immediately. Unfortunately, or fortunately for us, the owner of the mill dithered. Maybe he was anti-Nazi. Maybe he, unlike the Fuhrer, knew the Allies were on the way and wanted some leverage. Whatever his motives, he kept coming up with excuses. First he pleaded he had no fuel. The authorities sent some. Then his machines kept breaking down. He was playing a dangerous game, but it paid off the day the Seventh Army rolled into town. When the men came across all those sacks with official Nazi labels, they were over the moon. Gold bullion. Stolen loot. Even German schnapps and French champagne would have been a boon. Instead out came eight and a half million index cards. Every one of them ended up here in the Documents Center. So I think our first order of business is to head over there—it's not far—and find out if there's a membership card for Herr Gerhart Huber."

She had expected a forbidding concrete barracks. The jeep, driven by Private Meer, who had no trouble watching his language in front of Major Sutton, pulled up in front of a half-timbered villa not unlike dozens of others in Zehlendorf. The only difference was the barbed wire double fence, the klieg lights, which were just going on in the gathering dusk, and the heavy military guard. Inside the building, they had to show passes at several checkpoints before they were led down a narrow winding staircase to the basement vaults. She pulled her coat closer. The air in the vaults was as frigid as outdoors, and clammier.

"How many you looking for, Major?" the sergeant who was leading the way asked.

"Just one. Herr Gerhart Huber. Date of birth 8/19/01. Place of birth Oranienburg."

"Site of one of the first, if not the first concentration camp, eh?" the sergeant said as he guided them through a labyrinth of metal filing cabinets.

"True," Harry said, "but that's not what we're looking for."

"Sure he was a party member, sir?"

"Let's just say I have my suspicions."

The sergeant stopped in front of a filing cabinet, bent, and pulled out a drawer near the bottom. Millie stood watching as he walked his fingers through the files, hesitated, and pulled one out. He glanced at the contents, then shook his head. Gerhart Huber all right, but wrong d.o.b." He bent again, replaced the file, pulled out another, and opened it. "Here's your boy, sir. Dyed-in-the-wool. Member in good standing since '32." He handed the file to Harry, who studied it, then passed it to Millie. As she stood staring at it, she felt as if she were going down another rabbit hole. What had Anna done to survive? What did this man have on her? But then who was she to ask that question?

"Can we get a copy of this?" Harry said.

"I can have one of the girls snap a photo. While she's at it, would you like a tour of our other treasures from the glory days of the Thousand-Year Reich? The SS files starring Heinrich Himmler and his band of merry murderers are something to see. Then there's the Fuhrer's very own card. We keep that in a special safe."

"Thanks, Sergeant, perhaps another time. All we need now is proof of Herr Huber's membership."

"This doesn't make sense," Millie said when they were back in Harry's office. It had been too noisy to talk in the jeep. And neither of them wanted to discuss the matter in front of Private Meer. "I suppose he could have done some kindness for her at one time or another, even if he was a party member. She was a beauty in those days, hard as it is to believe now."

"I believe the beauty part. You can still see the bones. But I don't buy the milk of human kindness on Huber's side. It's more complicated than that."

Sitting across the desk from him, she felt herself stiffen.

"If you're suggesting there's something between her and Huber—"

"No, I think Huber is up to a different kind of blackmail."

"If you mean that she sold out others to save herself, you're even more wrong. I know Anna. She never would have done that. Never." She heard the vehemence in her voice mounting and went silent.

"Nobody knows what anyone would do under the circumstances. Hell, we don't know what we'd do. The only thing we know for sure is what we did do." He stopped for a moment, as if surprised at his own words, then shook his head. "But I wasn't talking about saving herself either. This is a different kind of desperation."

She sat staring at him. "You're talking about finding Elke. You think Herr Huber knows where Frau Kneff is but won't tell Anna unless she writes a letter for him?"

"Bingo. She writes the letter, he gets his clearance, and Frau Kneff's whereabouts suddenly become common knowledge."

The thought had been hovering since she'd heard about the Documents Center, but it didn't take shape until she was back in her own office. She retraced her steps to Harry's and stood leaning against the doorjamb, elaborately casual, as if she'd just now thought of it, as if it were an aimless question, not a matter of life and death.

"Those files at the Center were pretty impressive."

"That's the Krauts for you."

"Are they all like that?"

"What do you mean all?"

She shrugged. "I don't know. The files of all the different branches. Civil servants. Wehrmacht. The camps."

"Don't ever take up intelligence work, Millie."

"What do you mean?"

"You're as easy to see through as a newly washed window. At least about this. Yes, the camp records are meticulous too. At least that's what I hear. Nobody has access yet."

The next evening, Harry Sutton turned up in her office again just as she was putting on her coat to leave.

"Can I interest you in a trip to the Russian sector?"

"You found Frau Kneff?"

"Herr Huber wasn't exactly a hard case. It took about ten minutes to get the address out of him."

Millie pulled the belt of her coat tighter. "Should we pick up Anna on the way?"

"Let's get Elke first. In case Frau Kneff isn't there. Or puts up a fuss. Or any number of snafus."

Frau Kneff's building was a little better than Anna's, but not much. Though her flat was on the second floor and had all four walls, part of the stairwell had been bombed out. Harry heaved himself up, then turned and reached down to help Millie.

"You're a regular mountain goat, Mosbach," he said as he pulled her level with him.

"How does a child make that leap?" she asked.

"Resourcefully. And with her mother's help."

"With her kidnapper's help," she corrected him.

There was no name on the door of the apartment. Unlike Anna, Frau Kneff was not eager to be found.

"How do we know this is the right flat?" Millie asked.

"Huber gave me this address and said the second floor front. If it's not this one, we'll try all the others."

"Maybe we should have brought Huber with us."

"That would have meant MPs as well, which would have scared the living daylights out of a seven-year-old child. It's going to be bad enough when two strangers in uniform turn up to tell her they're taking her to her mother. As far as she's concerned, she's with her mother. But just to be safe, Herr Huber is spending the night in the guard room with those MPs."

He knocked on the door. There was no answer. He knocked again, louder and longer. "Frau Kneff," he called. Still no answer. "Frau Kneff, I have word from Herr Huber."

They heard footsteps inside the apartment. Berlin was still that silent. The door opened a crack. Harry's scuffed shoe was between it and the doorframe in an instant. He pushed his way in. Millie followed. Then she saw something she would never forget, though neither would she ever mention it to Anna. Elke—for who else could she be, this wraith-thin child with silky red hair that even malnutrition couldn't dull?—moved to Frau Kneff's side, wound her arms around her mother's torso, and hid her face in her mother's shoulder. The gesture rang a bell, more specific than the generic sight of a child clinging to a mother in fear. The day Millie had requisitioned the flat, the somewhat younger girl had clung to her mother the same way.

❧

The jeep was crowded on the return to the American zone. Private Meer was driving, with Harry beside him, and Millie, Frau Kneff, and Elke between them in the back. They'd decided not to tear Elke from one mother until they could replace her with another, as if mothers were interchangeable parts in a child's puzzle of life.

Meer pulled up the jeep in front of Anna's bombed-out building and killed the engine. Harry turned around to Millie. "How do you want to do this?"

"You wait here. I'll take Elke in."

Harry climbed out of the jeep to let Millie get out, then reached into the back for Elke. She clung to Frau Kneff.

"There's nothing to be afraid of," Millie said, though she knew she was lying, just as she would have if she'd spoken the rote words the day she'd requisitioned the flat.

Elke's arms tightened around Frau Kneff's middle.

"I want you to meet someone," Millie said. "Someone you knew a long time ago."

Elke still clung.

"Go, *Schatzi*," Frau Kneff said, "go." She gave the child a gentle nudge, and for a moment the fury that had been churning in Millie since before she'd laid eyes on the woman succumbed to a terrible pity.

Harry lifted Elke out, and Millie took her hand. It felt small and icy in her own, but at least the child didn't pull it away. They started over the rubble-strewn plot of ground. Clouds raced across the thin sliver of moon, throwing shadows in and out of their path. Every few steps, Elke stopped and turned back toward the jeep. It was hard to tell in the darkness, but Millie thought Frau Kneff waved. When Elke stopped the third or fourth time, Frau Kneff called out again. "Go, *Schatzi*." This time her voice broke on the words.

They descended into the damp basement hall. Now Elke was holding her hand tightly. In this black cave, even a stranger was better than no one at all.

Millie walked slowly, trying to avoid the worst of the rubble and broken glass that crunched beneath their feet. When they reached the door of Anna's flat, she stopped and hunched down until her face was on a level with Elke's. The child's eyes, too big in her emaciated face, glinted with fear.

"Do you remember another lady, Elke, from when you were very small? A baby, really. She had hair just like yours, red and silky and beautiful. You used to wrap it around your hands and put it in your mouth and tug so she laughed and laughed." Elke went on staring at her with those huge, terrified eyes.

Then it came to Millie. Music. You never forgot the lullabies of your childhood. She racked her brain for what Anna used to sing to Elke. All she could remember was what her own mother had sung to her, and then Sarah. Her unmusical mother had frequently been off-key, but she hadn't minded. Neither had Sarah. "She used to sing to you, Elke." She began to hum "Schlaf Kindlein Schlaf."

Elke's hand relaxed in hers. That was better.

"Mama," Elke said and began to pull toward the road where the jeep waited. Millie cursed her own stupidity. What German mother didn't sing that lullaby to her child?

She straightened, turned to the door, and lifted her hand to knock. Nothing was going to prepare Elke. No song, no explanation, no reassurance was going to mitigate the destruction of the only world she knew.

Millie knocked. "It's me, Meike," she called.

She stood listening to the silence on the other side of the door. A mattress does not creak like a bed when you rise from it. Cloth slippers make no sound on a cement floor. But the rusty hinges of a door creak as it's pulled open.

Just as Millie would always remember the way Elke had clung to Frau Kneff, so her reaction to her real mother, though

who was to say what constituted real and counterfeit under the circumstances, would sear itself in Millie's memory.
Anna's response was predictable. Her eyes went straight to
her daughter. She fell to her knees with a scream and clutched
Elke's thin body to her so tightly that Millie feared the child
would break. But as violent as Anna's reaction was, it was
the image of Elke that Millie would be incapable of expung-
ing. As Anna clutched her daughter, and cried, and laughed
hysterically, and thanked God, and pushed her away to look
at her, and drew her close again, and cried and laughed some
more, Elke stood stiff and stoical, barely present in her own
body. This was a child who had learned to weather hardship
and terror, hunger and cold, bombs from the sky, invading
forces on the ground, and a line of filthy-booted soldiers forcing her mother onto the bed, one after the other. Unlike
Anna, she didn't cry. She didn't try to pull away. She just went
on staring over Anna's shoulder into the darkness, her hands,
Millie noticed, balled into small fists of willful forbearance.

This time Anna accepted the offer of the flat. She had insisted
on staying in the room because she'd been waiting for word,
but now word, no, now a miracle had arrived. She and Elke
went home with Millie that night.

Even before they entered the apartment, Millie could feel
the tension, as if distant bombs or an earthquake were making the air around them vibrate. Anna could not stop touching Elke, holding her hand, stroking her hair, hugging her
shoulders. Elke put up with it. That was the only way to describe it. But the fear in those big eyes was giving way to anger.
Millie could read it, and it was making her angry in return.

She was trying to put herself in Elke's place, snatched from one mother, suddenly told she had another, but her heart beat with Anna in the pain of her loss and the thrill of her reunion.

She gave Anna and Elke the big bedroom with the high four-poster bed and carried her things into the small room that had belonged to that other child. Then she went into the kitchen and began taking tins and packages of food from the cupboard and a bottle of milk, a stick of butter, and a carton of eggs from the refrigerator. Fortunately, she'd been to the PX the day before.

"Elke must be starving," she said when Anna came in a little later, still holding Elke's hand, as if the minute she let go of it the child would bolt.

"Are you hungry?" Millie heard the singsong patronizing tone people use with children in her voice and hated herself for it. Elke must have recognized it too, because her small mouth shriveled with disdain.

Anna led Elke to the chair in the corner. "Sit, *Schatzi*, sit." Her voice was even more off-key than Millie's. It came out as half plea, half command, an order to a dog that might obey or might just as easily lunge at your throat. They were two grown women in terror of this twenty-five-pound tyrant.

She heard Harry moving around the parlor. He'd said he'd hang around for a while in case they needed anything. He meant in case there was trouble, though she couldn't imagine what that might be. Frau Kneff wouldn't dare return. Furious as Elke was, she was still a child. Nonetheless, something about the way he was prowling the premises reminded her of the bomb disposal experts who were dispatched to defuse an explosive device, or at least contain the damage.

Anna crossed to the counter and nudged Millie aside. "Let me do it. Please."

Millie relinquished her place. She could imagine how long Anna had been dreaming of preparing this meal. She went back to the big bedroom, put another eiderdown on the bed, plumped the pillows, arranged Elke's thin coat and extra sweater in the armoire, straightened Anna's comb and brush on the dresser. That was when it came to her. She should have thought of it before. Anna was already unhinged. She didn't want anything else to set her off.

She hurried down the hall and pushed open the door to the bathroom. The bar of Naumann Caressa soap sat on the sink next to the cake of Ivory. She'd brought it home that night she'd been sick, unwrapped it, and put it on the sink, but she'd never been able to make herself use it. She didn't know if David had. Now, wasteful as it seemed, she wrapped it in toilet paper, dropped it in the trash basket, and went back to the kitchen.

Elke was still sitting in the chair, her head bent, her face now hidden by the cascade of hair. At the counter, Anna was stirring soup, whisking eggs, and buttering bread in a frenzy of eagerness. Surely filling a child's stomach accounts for something. Surely that is one way to motherhood. Every few seconds she turned her head to make sure Elke was there. The gesture reminded Millie of Elke's turning back to the jeep to make sure Frau Kneff was there. But Frau Kneff was gone now, back to her own bare, unheated flat.

Anna turned again. "Supper's almost ready, *Schatzi*."

"I want to go home." Elke didn't raise her eyes from the floor, and the words were so quiet that at first Millie wasn't sure the child had spoken them. Then she saw the look on Anna's face.

"You are home, Elke. This is your home, yours and your mama's for as long as you like."

"I want my real mama." Again, the words were almost a whisper, but again Anna must have heard them, because her hand froze above the pot she'd been about to stir and her thin shoulders stiffened.

"Anna is your real mama," Millie said in that saccharine tone she hated. "The other lady was just taking care of you until your real mama came back."

The silence in that shabby scoured kitchen was brittle as glass. Then Elke shattered it.

"No!" The word was a howl. She was out of the chair, hurling herself across the room, butting Millie in the stomach with her small head, a demon determined to break free.

Millie caught her and tried to quiet her, but Elke struggled and pummeled and kicked. Her shoes struck Millie's shins; her fists hammered her face. Then Harry was prying Elke off. He wrenched her free and wound his arms around her to keep her in place. She struggled for another moment, then went limp in his arms. Maybe she knew she was no match for his strength. Or maybe she didn't have the same animus against someone who was not a candidate for motherhood.

He carried her into the parlor. Anna and Millie followed. He was still holding her, and she'd buried her face in his shoulder. Anna started across the room to them, then stopped a little distance away.

"Elke," she said. Not *Schatzi*, Millie noticed, but Elke. "Would you like to invite Frau Kneff for supper?"

Elke lifted her head from Harry's shoulder and stared at her.

"The other . . ." she hesitated, ". . . mama. Would you like her to have supper with us?"

Elke went on staring. She was clearly expecting a trick.

"Would you like that?"

She nodded.

Harry said he'd send Meer and the jeep to get Frau Kneff.

Twelve

⌒

DURING THE CROSSING ON THE *STATENDAM*, MEIKE and David never once mentioned their close call in that crowded railway compartment. They never brought up the jeweler. They didn't say, Can you imagine if they hadn't arrested him, what might have happened to us? They didn't speculate on whether the officers would have found Mama's diamond bracelet or the Leica lenses. They were still too afraid. They were also superstitious. Celebrating their close call would be tempting fate.

"You'll see. They'll get out," Meike reassured David.

"Of course they will," David agreed. "Papa's smart. He knows his way around. Remember the time in Switzerland when the hotel didn't have our reservation and he talked them into giving us a suite?"

"Look how he managed to get the visas," Meike said. "It took him a year, going from consulate to consulate, being first in line before the offices even opened, but he pulled it off."

"The visas are still good," David said.

"We just have to be patient," Meike agreed.

Nonetheless, they decided to wire the Bennetts from the ship to tell them what had happened. No, not what had happened, but to alert them to expect only two of them. For now.

"The others have been detained," Meike wrote. She started

to slide the form across the counter to the wireless officer on duty, then pulled it back and penciled in a ^ sign between the words *been* and *detained*. Carefully, so the officer could read it, she wrote the word *temporarily* above the caret.

The ship was packed with Americans fleeing the war that everyone was sure was coming, Jews escaping the Nazis, several Dutch families and businessmen, and an Austrian student who strode the decks spouting Nazi dogma. He must not have realized that Meike was Jewish, because one night in the tourist-class lounge he asked her to dance. She refused and, in case her distaste wasn't sufficiently clear, accepted an invitation from another student immediately after. This one was an American, returning from medical studies in Vienna.

As they were dancing to, ironically, the ship's orchestra's rendition of the Andrews Sisters' "Bei Mir Bist Du Schoen," an American woman who had taken Meike and David under her wing, or at least tried to, drew David aside. "In America"— she leaned close, because she didn't want to shout, and the orchestra was loud—"we don't do that kind of thing."

At first he thought she meant they didn't dance to a song with a Yiddish title, but that didn't make sense. Others were dancing to it, and most of them were Americans. Then she went on.

"In America white girls don't dance with *schvartzes*."

His head swiveled to her in surprise. "But isn't that the kind of thing we're running away from?"

"It's not the same."

"What kind of a country are we going to?" he asked Meike when he repeated the woman's comment.

Neither of them had the least idea.

❦

Years later they'd argue about whether they saw the Statue of Liberty that morning. David would describe the way she had loomed out of the mist, her upraised arm promising them shelter beneath it, her torch flaming freedom. Meike would assure him that if he'd seen the statue at all, it had been a glimpse of only part of her through a porthole in the ship's dining saloon, where immigration officials who'd come aboard in the harbor had set up tables to thumb through papers, fire questions, and bring the stamp down with a thunderous thud, or not. As they inched closer to the table, Meike grew more worried. She didn't admit it to David—she didn't want to frighten him—but she kept going over it in her head. Their visas were in order, they'd passed their physical exams, their sponsors would be waiting on the dock. But things could always go wrong. They already had.

Then suddenly they were leaving the dining saloon, properly stamped papers in hand, and going up on deck to stand side by side as the steel towers of the city sailed down to meet them.

The arrival hall was a vast metal shed of people searching for one another, shouting at porters, embracing, and going from one letter of the alphabet to the next hunting for trunks and suitcases. Luggage was supposed to be arranged by the first initial of the last name of the owner, but often wasn't. Meike and David didn't have to search. Each of them carried a single suitcase, carefully packed by their mother, down the gangway and into the deafening chaos.

Mr. and Mrs. Bennett were waiting. The four of them recognized one another from photographs that had been exchanged, Mr. Bennett big and bearlike, Mrs. Bennett wiry with a long upper lip that suggested unexpected reserves of strength. They snaked through the crush and din with wide anxious smiles. Then they were standing face-to-face, David and Meike on one side, the Bennetts on the other. Between them three other people loomed like pale images in a half-developed negative of the photo that was supposed to be.

Meike held out her hand to Mrs. Bennett. Lydia Bennett took it, drew her close, and folded her in an embrace. Russell Bennett hesitated only a moment longer, then decided David was more boy than man, put his hands on his narrow shoulders, and drew him near.

Later that night in the big master bedroom of the Tudor house in Ardmore on Philadelphia's Main Line, after they'd shown the children, as they called them, though both Meike and David seemed to have been through too much to warrant the term, to their rooms, the Bennetts discussed that moment on the pier.

"I wasn't sure if I should shake hands," Russ Bennett said, "but then I decided he was still a boy and a little more affection wouldn't be out of order." He stopped to take a cigarette from the case on the night table and light it. "And I'm glad I did. When I let him go, I saw the tears in his eyes."

Lydia Bennett reached for her husband's cigarette and took a puff. "I noticed." She handed the cigarette back. "I also noticed that her eyes were dry."

"That doesn't mean she doesn't feel."

She shook her head. "Of course it doesn't. That's what worries me."

Within a week of their arrival, David went off to boarding school. It was, Mr. Bennett explained when Millie protested at their being separated, what their father wanted. "When we were making arrangements, one of the first things he asked about was schools for David. For all of you, but especially for David. He's already lost part of the first semester. We can't wait till your father arrives to make decisions. He'll never forgive us. You know that, Millie."

She did know it, but the knowledge didn't make David's leaving hurt any less.

The night before Mr. Bennett was to drive David to school, she and David sat up in his room until almost dawn, reassuring each other that Massachusetts wasn't that far away, and he'd be home for something called Thanksgiving, which was just around the corner, and Christmas soon after that, and most important, this was what Papa wanted, insisted upon.

The next morning, she stood on the gravel of the Bennetts' driveway, clutching her coat against the November cold, with the muffled disoriented feeling that a sleepless night leaves behind, waving goodbye. Mr. Bennett wouldn't even let her go along for the ride.

"I know boys," he told her. "I was one myself. The only thing they'll razz a new boy about more than a big sister saying a weepy goodbye is a tearful mother doing the same thing. David and I are going to perform a manly handshake. Maybe even a slap on the back. Right, David?"

David smiled. It was hard not to like Russell Bennett. Both Bennetts. Their intentions were so good, and they were trying so hard. Nonetheless, as Millie stood watching the station wagon with the wood-paneled sides move off down the street, she couldn't get over the feeling that a part of her was being amputated.

Once David was gone, she had no excuse for resisting the rest of the Bennetts' plan. Mrs. Bennett was brimming with enthusiasm.

In the wake of Kristallnacht, while Meike and David were crossing the Atlantic and Meike was transforming herself into Millie, the student body, faculty, and administration of Bryn Mawr College took up a collection to establish scholarships for two non-Aryan German girls. Mrs. Bennett, an alumna of Bryn Mawr, had immediately put Millie up for one of them.

"There's nothing to be nervous about," Lydia Bennett said as she pulled the station wagon up in front of a stone arch that opened on the other side to an expanse of lawn crisscrossed by gravel paths and lined by handsome sheltering trees. A few flamboyantly colored leaves still clung to the branches.

Millie didn't say anything. The idea that an interview with the dean of a college could strike fear in her was ludicrous, but telling Mrs. Bennett that would be a slap in the face of her kindness and generosity and naïveté. That was why she played the model child to the Bennetts' uneasy assumption of in loco parentis roles. But she could never get over the feeling that the Bennetts were the juveniles in the equation. For all their experience and worldliness, their admirable achievements and considerable success, they were two cosseted babes in the wood, unacquainted with terror, innocent of horror, strangers to guilt, except the generic kind common to well-intentioned people of their class.

Mrs. Bennett turned off the ignition. "Do you want me to go in with you?"

"There's no need," Millie said. "Really."

"When you're finished, I'll be in the Deanery. Anyone can tell you where it is. We'll have tea. Celebratory tea. I'm sure they're going to give you the scholarship. The interview is only a formality. If anything, your German education has overqualified you."

Millie wished she'd stop talking. She wasn't nervous about the interview, but neither was she as giddy about the opportunity as Lydia Bennett seemed to be. She would have been if her parents and Sarah were here. She would be when they arrived. But until then, it was heartless, it was unconscionable to think about school or scholarships or anything except how they were and where they were and how soon they'd be here. She repeated the mantra to herself over and over. Their visas were still valid.

She won the scholarship. She never knew for sure, but she doubted there was much competition. How many academically prepared non-Aryan German girls with an alumna sponsor knew about the opportunity or were even in the States?

On the Sunday after Thanksgiving, a strange holiday built around even more peculiar food, but one that brought David home from school for a long weekend and Millie gave thanks for that, she joined the class of 1942 of Bryn Mawr College. Though the semester was half through, the urgency of the situation and Millie's solid grounding in a variety of subjects permitted her to start immediately. This time both Bennetts drove her to the campus. Mr. Bennett said they'd need a man to carry things and added he had no intention of missing the fun. When they arrived, he helped his wife and Millie out of the station wagon, then went around to the big drop-down door at the rear and began unloading the two suitcases—one with the things she'd brought from Germany, the other with the new clothes Mrs. Bennett had bought her—a box of books that were also new, and a lantern. The last was another gift from Mrs. Bennett. At first, Millie hadn't understood why she had to take a lantern to school. Surely there would be electric lights.

Mr. Bennett had laughed. "We Americans may be cultural barbarians, Millie, but we do have creature comforts. The lantern is a tradition."

"There's a ceremony at the beginning of the first semester," Mrs. Bennett explained. "It's called Lantern Night. Each freshman is given a lantern by a sophomore. It symbolizes learning and enlightenment. Since you weren't here at the start of your freshman year to get yours, I want you to have mine."

For the first time since Millie had heard about the scholarship, she felt a flash of real enthusiasm. Her parents wanted her to be educated because that was an aspect of refinement. No one had ever worried about her being enlightened. The thought was followed by a backlash of guilt. Criticizing her parents, even in her own mind, was another betrayal.

"You're in luck as far as dormitory assignments," Mr. Bennett said as they made their way through a fine drizzle toward a turreted gray stone building. "Most of the dorms were built in the last century, but Rhoads wasn't even here back when I came courting my bride. It was finished just last year. You'll be living in luxury, or at least modernity."

Her room was on the first floor at the end of a long hallway. As they carried her things down it, the few girls who passed smiled and nodded and tried to hide their curiosity.

Mr. Bennett put down the box of books and opened the door. Millie stepped into a sitting room with a sofa, two club chairs, and a cushioned window seat beneath casement windows. Mrs. Bennett crossed to another door, opened that, and stood aside for Millie to go in. The room held a narrow bed, a chest of drawers, a desk and chair, and a bookcase. Outside the window, a maidenhair tree glowed like gold. Even the rain couldn't dim its brilliance. It seemed impossible that such beauty could still exist in the world. She couldn't wait to write her parents about the tree and the campus and her room and enlightenment. Then she remembered. She had no address. That was when she decided to keep a diary. She'd record everything that happened during this time so Mama and Papa and Sarah, especially Sarah, could share her experiences when they arrived.

As they stood in the small bedroom, Mrs. Bennett told her that on the other side of the sitting room was an identical, except for what each of them added to it, room where her suitemate lived. "She'll be able to show you the ropes."

An hour later, after Millie had put away her clothes, organized her books, and placed Mrs. Bennett's lantern on top of the bookcase, she was standing in the middle of the room trying to decide where to put Sarah's floppy dog hand puppet—she wanted to keep it where she could see it, but she didn't want anyone asking about it—when a girl knocked on the open door, stepped into the room, and sat on the bed. Millie was surprised. She didn't mind the girl sitting on her bed. She just hadn't expected her to without being invited. She reminded herself she had a lot to learn about America.

"Thank heavens, a suitemate at last. The one I was supposed to have decided she didn't want to go to college after all. The little fool. I'm Barbara Gross." She leaned forward and held out her hand. That was when Millie saw it. She had to blink to make sure she wasn't imagining it. Around Barbara Gross's neck hung a gold chain, and suspended from it was a Star of David, clear as daylight, as blinding in its own way as the maidenhair tree outside the window. And Barbara didn't even seem to be aware that she was wearing it. What a school, what a country, where you could wear a Star of David right out in the open! It would be a few years before the star would become not a choice but a compulsion, not a piece of jewelry but a sign of shame in Germany and the countries it conquered. It would be only a month or two before Millie put another interpretation on the fact that she and the girl who wore the star were suitemates. In America, being Jewish wasn't a crime as it had become in Germany, but it was still a stigma. In the middle of this bucolic campus, of this halcyon world where young women gave one another lanterns to symbolize enlightenment, she and Barbara Gross had landed in their own little ghetto. The handful of other Jewish girls in other dorms were similarly paired off.

Their classmates didn't treat her and Barbara badly, or even differently. She was touched by their kindness and skittish concern. No one knew what she'd been through and of course no one dared ask, but most of them suspected something. Despite that, or perhaps because of it, they were quick to take her in. Sprawled in the smoking room, lounging on the stone patio of the dormitory overlooking a sweep of lawn called Rhoads Beach, gathering in a housemate's sitting room in their flannel pajamas and plaid bathrobes, they'd call to her to join them.

There were, nonetheless, occasional moments of awkwardness. No, awkwardness was the wrong word. That implied discomfort, and it never occurred to Kiki Newton as she chattered on about her coming-out party that those who not only would not celebrate that particular rite of passage but would not be invited to enjoy her commemoration of it might not want to hear endlessly about the orchestra and the flowers and the dress with yards and yards of white tulle she'd be wearing. When Grace Sommers quoted daddy on the fact that though Hitler was a madman, you had to admit the Jews really did control international banking, she didn't seem to notice that the Jew sitting across the table at dinner, who just happened to be on scholarship, might not take daddy's word as revealed truth.

But those infrequent incidents were no match for the joys. The sound of girls' voices echoing across the campus aflame with color in autumn, dozing under a silent snowfall in winter, greening in spring, drenched in innocence the year round. The cavernous Gothic hall of the library, where students in the sacred solitude of carrels, each illuminated by a green-shaded lamp casting circles of light on glossy hair, bent over pages that promised to unlock the meaning of life or the nature of matter or the workings of the human heart. The sheer ease of daily existence where maids made their beds and cleaned their rooms and waiters served their meals because these girls were supposed to devote themselves not to tidying the world but to opening their minds. The halls bubbling with anticipation as girls flew up and down in satin and velvet, tulle and organdy, hair curled, wrists and earlobes perfumed, cheeks so bright they didn't need rouge, while across the campus the starched white fronts of dress shirts that had come from Haverford and Swarthmore, Princeton and farther afield flickered like moths in the moonlight. Then suddenly, at odd moments, in the midst of all that joy, the thought of her parents and Sarah would shoot through her like a bolt of lightning, revealing her unspeakable selfishness in its unforgiving glare. What right did she have to all this? What kind of a monster was she to enjoy it? The mantra about their visas was no match for her self-loathing.

Occasionally she lost hope. On those days, she slipped

in and out of class like a cat burglar, hid behind the closed door of her room, and existed on fruit and crackers because she couldn't bear to sit in the dining room among all those blameless girls whose conversations were spiked with mother says and father thinks and mummy still believes and daddy insists. Then there were the stories about older brothers and kid sisters. She didn't begrudge those girls their vibrant present families. At least she tried not to. She was on her guard against her resentment the evening her suitemate Barbara, who lived in Philadelphia, took her home for Friday night dinner.

"Get ready for a cast of thousands," Barbara warned. "My two older sisters, Helene and Linda, their husbands, Eddie H. and Eddie B., my brother, Bobby, Aunt Esther, Uncle Sol, three cousins, my grandmother, and of course my parents. It's been like that every Friday night of my life for as long as I can remember. Don't even think about a movie or a date or anything else. I'm excused if I'm studying for exams or have a paper due, but otherwise it's a command performance. Occasionally I complain, but I bet if they ever stopped, I'd miss them."

"I bet you would," Millie agreed.

The living room was filled with men and boys, the kitchen and dining room were crowded with women and girls, and the entire house was redolent of roasting chicken, steaming vegetables, and freshly baked pies. Mr. Gross took her coat and welcomed her to the family, and Mrs. Gross hugged her and said it was about time she joined them for Shabbat dinner, and everyone tried to make her feel at home, though she sensed a certain walking on eggs. They wanted to know how she liked America and Bryn Mawr and her courses. Had she been to the Philadelphia Orchestra and Wanamaker's and

an Eagles game? No one dared inquire about her parents or
Germany or any of the other questions she could read behind their smiles. The only exception was Barbara's father,
who wanted to know which synagogue her family had wor-
shipped at in Berlin. Fortunately, he didn't give her time to
answer, but launched into the founding of their own temple
by German Jews who had conducted services in German
until the end of the last century. By the time he finished recounting the history of the synagogue, they were seated at
the long table covered with a white damask cloth, set with
what was surely the family's good china and silver and crys-
tal, and lit by, in addition to the overhead chandelier, flickering candles. The story of the synagogue set off the kind
of debate that can be waged only by people who have spent
their lifetimes bound by shared joys and setbacks, love and
grudges. With the exception of Millie, everyone at that table
knew everyone else's convictions, follies, and foibles. The
subject under discussion was whether women as well as men
should be counted among the ten heads necessary to make
up a minyan, or quorum for prayer. Mr. Gross thought so.
Mrs. Gross was sure of it. Uncle Sol and Helene's husband,
Eddie B., were vehemently opposed.

"Ten *men* are required for prayer," Eddie insisted. "The law
says men."

"Which law?" Barbara asked.

There were a variety of answers to that.

"What do you think, Millie?" Mrs. Gross asked.

"Of course, she'll be in favor of it," Helene said. "She and
Barbara, two peas, two Bryn Mawrtyrs, in a pod."

"Let her answer," Mr. Gross said.

"I don't know much about Jewish law," Millie began.

"See," Uncle Sol said. "That's young girls today. They know

all kinds of things they shouldn't know and not what they should."

"What shouldn't we know, Uncle Sol?" Barbara asked.

"Let Millie finish," Mrs. Gross insisted.

"I can't see why if women worship in the temple, they can't be included in the number necessary to make up the quo— the minyan."

"You see," Uncle Sol said. "She doesn't even know how to pronounce it. That's what will come of letting women in sacred places."

Mr. Gross laughed, slapped his brother-in-law on the back, and told him he was full of hot air; Mrs. Gross asked if anyone wanted seconds or thirds; Bobby and both Eddies began to talk about the Eagles; and Millie sat wondering at them. They were an unruly, argumentative bunch, nothing like her own family. Meals in the Mosbach house had been exercises in civility. Politics, art, and social issues had been discussed rather than disputed. Voices had never been raised. Even when the extended family gathered for holidays or went on vacation together, politesse reigned. But Millie wasn't fooled by all the noise and bickering. These people were clearly in love with one another. She was happy for Barbara. Really she was. But it hurt.

A few weeks later, Rosalind Diamond asked her home for the weekend. Rosalind, who planned to major in Greek and Latin and hoped to go on to graduate school, was, by popular consensus, one of the smartest girls on campus. She looked the part, with wire-rimmed glasses, lank hair she never even tried to curl, and baggy sweaters that camouflaged her body, which, when spied dashing in and out of the showers, was quite lovely. Millie couldn't get over the feeling that Rosalind worked at being drab. The weekend she went home to Scarsdale with Rosalind she realized why.

A chauffeur met them at the station with a long black Cadillac. A uniformed maid opened the door for them, took their coats, and when she saw Rosalind's bulky sweater and shapeless skirt, shook her head, less in disapproval than in sorrow.

"Your mother's waiting for you in the living room," she said. "She's going to love that," she added, indicating Rosalind's outfit.

Millie followed Rosalind across a large foyer and stepped down into a sunken living room. Two things struck her immediately. The first was that Mrs. Diamond, dressed in a black silk suit with a huge diamond brooch at the throat, must have been a beauty in her day. Seeing Rosalind beside her, Millie recognized the resemblance. Now she was sure that her friend worked at being dowdy.

The second was that there wasn't a single book or painting in view. There were bookshelves. They supported various china and glass knickknacks. The framed pictures on the walls were photographs of Mrs. Diamond dressed in fashionable suits and gowns at various lunches and dinners, a man Millie supposed was Mr. Diamond holding a golf club and waving from the deck of a boat and posing with other men—the pictures with other men were signed—and two boys playing tennis and riding horses and perched on the hoods or behind the wheels of expensive cars. There were photographs of Rosalind too, looking as if she'd wandered into the frame by mistake.

To give Mrs. Diamond credit, she waited until she thought

Millie was out of hearing to ask Rosalind what on earth she'd been thinking when she put on that outfit.

Mr. Diamond's approach was more affectionate, if totally oblivious of who his daughter was. Rosalind's mother knew the girl she was dealing with. Her father hadn't a clue. He called her Princess, teased her about how the phone had been ringing off the hook all week with her brothers' friends who'd heard she was coming home, and bragged to Millie about how many awards she'd won in school. He didn't seem to know what they were for, but he did take pride in them.

After dinner, Mr. Diamond left for his regular Friday night poker game and Mrs. Diamond brought out the big guns. First she talked about a friend of Rosalind's from school, her own friend's daughter, and a cousin of Rosalind's, all of whom had gotten engaged since Rosalind had last been home.

"How nice." Rosalind's voice sounded like a recording of an announcer trying to reassure the public that the fire was under control and there was no reason to panic.

"How do you think I feel?" Mrs. Diamond asked.

"Happy for them?"

"Don't be impertinent, Rosalind. You know what I mean. I can barely hold up my head."

"Because your daughter's a failure?"

"That's not what they say to my face, but that's what they think. I will not be pitied. The rest of my life is in order. More than in order. Everyone envies my home, my clothes, my successful husband, my two handsome, popular sons."

"Everything but your unhandsome, unpopular daughter."

"You wouldn't be either if you just made an effort." She turned to Millie. The woman had an uncanny ability to point with her chin.

"You live with her, Millie."

"Actually, we're in different dorms."

"Can't you do something?" Mrs. Diamond went on as if Millie hadn't spoken. "Can't you help her with her clothes?" Her eyes wandered up and down Millie. "That's a perfectly acceptable sweater set. Can't you get her to wear makeup?"

"No, Mother, she can't."

"And that school doesn't help. I know the motto. 'Only our failures marry.'"

"It isn't a motto," Rosalind said. "It's a joke. Kind of. And the line is our failures *only* marry."

"It's the same thing."

"It's not the same thing at all," Rosalind said, but her mother turned to Millie again.

"What about you, Millie? Are you planning to stay all four years? Like my impossible daughter?"

"If I can."

"What do your—" Mrs. Diamond stopped abruptly. She didn't put her hand over her mouth, but she looked as if she'd like to.

"Millie's parents are still in Germany, Mother. I told you that.

"I hope it wasn't too awful for you," Rosalind said when she walked Millie to her room that night.

"It wasn't awful for me. I was just an innocent bystander."

"That didn't stop you from getting caught in the crossfire. But thanks for being here. Impossible as it is to imagine, she runs at me even harder when we're alone. Tonight she was on good behavior." She started to turn away, then pivoted back to Millie. "The worst part is sometimes I think she's right. Maybe I'm tilting at windmills. Maybe I ought to give up and marry the next candidate she comes up with. I don't fool myself that I'm so desirable, but my father's money is. Does the world really need another classics scholar? And even if it does, I'm not sure I'm equal to the job. Even if I'm smart enough, and I'm not sure I am, I don't think I'm strong enough to withstand her."

"The entire school knows you're smart enough. And if you weren't strong enough, you wouldn't have made it this far. How did you manage to get your application past her in the first place?"

Rosalind smiled. "You're right. She goes through all my drawers. I kept it hidden at school."

Millie felt sorry for Rosalind, whose brilliance, she admitted, she'd always envied a little. But something else about the weekend troubled her more than Rosalind's plight. She didn't realize what it was until she was back on campus in her own world, away from the big house and the ostentatious furnishings and the servants. It had to do with all those things, and Rosalind's mother's obsession with appearance, and her father's weekly poker game, and her brothers who spent their time riding horses and playing tennis and driving fast cars. The world didn't care. Even other Jews didn't care. Her mother and father and little sister were enduring unimaginable hardship, if they were alive, and no one gave a damn.

Then several weeks later, on a warm evening in May, the world righted itself, almost. She was in the library studying for her anthropology exam when she looked up and saw Russell Bennett striding down the line of carrels toward her. The white envelope in his hand glowed like a pale moon in the dimly lit

Gothic expanse. It couldn't be anything else. She jumped up and began running to meet him. Heads turned as she went. No one ran in the library.

When she reached him, he held the envelope out to her.

Mr. David Mosbach
Miss Meike Mosbach
c/o Mr. Russell Bennett

She'd know that handwriting anywhere. She tore open the envelope and took out the single sheet of paper. Her hands were shaking as her eye raced over the words. She could barely make them out in this gloom, or rather could barely believe them. She glanced around for an empty carrel where she could read the letter in the light. They were all taken. She hurried back down the line to the one where she'd been sitting, shoved her books and notes aside, spread the letter out in the circle of light cast by the lamp, and bent over it. Her eyes raced through the words again, then returned to the top and read more slowly.

My dearest children,
Just a line to let you know we are safe, so there is no need to worry. We are living in a small town in the east.

She noticed he didn't say the name of the town. He didn't even say the east of Germany or farther east.

I am employed in a factory. Your dear mother is too. You would be proud to see what a game she makes of it. We both do. Sarah does her part as well. So you see there is no need to worry about us.

The important thing, my dear children, is not to lose hope. This cannot go on forever, or even much longer. We will be together again soon. I am certain of that. You must trust and believe it too. Your dear mama and little sister send their love.

With love from your loving papa.

Only after she read it through a third time did she notice the date at the top. January 10, 1939.

She looked over at Russ Bennett, who'd been lingering a little distance away while she read, stood, and led him out of the reading room into the cloisters.

"This was written four months ago," she said.

"These are unsettled times," he explained. "I'm amazed it got through at all."

"Do you think they're still all right?"

He took a moment to answer. "Four months is not such a long time."

"Did you tell David?"

"It's addressed to the two of you. I didn't want to open it. And there's no return address so I couldn't be sure. I'll call him as soon as I get home."

"Read it to him." She started to hand him the letter, then thought better of it. "Can you wait for a minute?"

"Of course."

She went back into the library, returned to her carrel, and tore out a blank page from her notebook. Then she copied her father's letter onto it, put the original in the pocket of her skirt, and went back to the cloisters. Russ was leaning on a balustrade, smoking a cigarette. She handed him the piece of paper from her notebook.

"Here's a copy for you to read to David. I had to keep the original."

"Of course," he said again. Then he did something he never should have. He reached an arm around her shoulders for comfort. The dam broke. She began to cry. Not a silent shedding of tears in the spring darkness but a series of wrenching sobs that convulsed her body and echoed out over the campus. The few girls who'd come out to the cloisters for a breath of air or a cigarette hurried back inside. No one came over to ask if she was all right. They knew she wasn't. Part of her was embarrassed. Part of her didn't give a damn. They were alive.

She'd been sure she'd flunk the anthropology exam. She came through with flying colors. The letter crackling in her pocket every time she moved was a shot of pure adrenaline. They were alive.

When Millie had started school the previous fall, Lydia Bennett had predicted that her German education overqualified her for an American college. "But if you find you're bored," she'd said, "you can petition to sign up for advanced courses." Lydia hadn't been entirely wrong. Millie had done more reading, amassed more facts, and knew more languages than most of her classmates. But in another sense, she was totally unprepared. In Germany, she'd sat taking dutiful notes while great men droned on, force-feeding anointed truths and outright prejudices. Here professors questioned and girls answered and questioned back, everyone debated and no one was afraid. Occasionally, when opinions clashed, she remembered the day at the *Lyzeum* when the teacher had passed out single-edged razors and the class had cut the beating Jewish heart out of German history. This school was not a killing ground of truth. It was a hothouse of learning, protected by a bubble of privilege, nurtured by a bevy of professorial gardeners. She respected most of them; she adored Miss Albright.

Miss Albright wasn't really a Miss. She was married to Professor Rouget, who taught modern European history. Though she would never say as much to anyone, Millie had noticed something about the male professors on campus. They strode the walkways and taught their classes and accepted invitations to tea at the Deanery and meals in the dorms with a certain arrogance. How could they not have felt superior with all those scrubbed young faces, some quite lovely even to a middle-aged professor, especially to a middle-aged professor, turned up to them in eagerness. But the other side of that coin of haughtiness was an aura of shame. They couldn't quite understand how they'd ended up teaching in a women's college, no matter how excellent a women's college, when their colleagues were opening the minds and shaping the characters of the future leaders of the world at Harvard, Yale, and Princeton. Professor Rouget wasn't as bad as most of them. Millie thought that was Miss Albright's fault, or achievement.

Miss Albright had refused to take Professor Rouget's name when they married. That, some of the girls whispered, was the least of it. Before they'd come to Bryn Mawr, Miss Albright and Professor Rouget had lived together. Without benefit of clergy, the fastidious whispered. In sin, the bolder girls declared. They'd had to marry, not for the usual reason—they had no children—but because the college had made it a condition of hiring them. Nonetheless a few girls on campus refused to take Miss Albright's courses, despite the fact that she was now an honest woman, as the phrase went. The parents of one student who had signed up for her seminar on the Victorian novel forced their daughter to take Mr. Collins's course in Romantic poetry instead.

Millie had no fear of contamination by Miss Albright. She had only admiration for her quick mind, crinkly red-haired beauty, and irreverence. Miss Albright seemed to return a certain regard. Perhaps it was Millie's European background. Sometimes at tea with three or four girls, Miss Albright would hold forth on Sinclair Lewis and his view of small-town America. The day the seminar discussed *Middlemarch*, Miss Albright went on talking to Millie afterward all the way across campus, and when they arrived at Rhoads, she seemed surprised. "I guess I got carried away," she said as she turned to retrace her steps toward the off-campus apartment she shared with Professor Rouget. Millie walked on air for weeks.

Miss Albright encouraged Millie to go out for *The College News*, and when at the end of her junior year she was made editor in chief, Miss Albright took her to dinner at the College Inn to celebrate, no other students, no Professor Rouget, just the two of them. They sat across the starched white tablecloth from each other in the flickering candlelight and talked about books and Millie's future and Miss Albright's past. The rumors about her and Professor Rouget before they married were true, and Millie was both shocked and intrigued. The women she looked up to were admirable. Her chic, gracious mother, of course, but her mother had always made it clear how important it was to play by the rules. Lydia Bennett had gone to jail for breaking rules, but that was for a cause. Miss Albright had flouted convention for her own convictions and pleasures, not society's betterment.

"I told you about my past for a reason," Miss Albright said when they'd finished their sweetbreads, the waiter had taken away their plates, and the candles had burnt low, though the light still made Miss Albright's fiery hair, which insisted on escaping from her chignon, spark in the softly lit room. "Do you remember the line in *Middlemarch*, near the beginning, where Sir James says to Celia, 'your sister is given to self-mortification'?"

Millie nodded.

"Sometimes I see a bit of Dorothea in you, Millie, and that worries me. She's wonderful on the page, but that's partly because her blindness and self-sacrifice make us want to scream at her. Open your eyes, Dorothea. Stop punishing yourself. Stop pushing pleasure away."

Millie was stunned. "I'm not punishing myself. If anything, I have more pleasure than I deserve."

Miss Albright smiled and shook her head. "That's what I mean. In this world, there is no such thing as more pleasure than anyone deserves."

That night back in her room Millie opened her journal and began to write.

Friday, May 9, 1941

Tonight Miss Albright took me to dinner at the College Inn to celebrate my being made editor in chief of *The College News* . . .

The entry took her half an hour to finish. She wanted to get down everything, what Miss Albright said and what she said in return, even what each of them wore and ate. The only detail she left out was Miss Albright's line about punishing herself. Once her parents and Sarah were here, nobody would want to bring that up.

Thirteen

DAVID HAD A MORE DIFFICULT TIME ADJUSTING TO LIFE in America. His classmates and even some of the teachers and coaches saw to that. The anti-Semitism Millie encountered was veiled and fastidious. Good manners forbade rudeness. High ideals prohibited vulgar bigotry. The prejudice David met was as muscular and aggressive as the contact sports the boys were required to play. Occasionally, when David and Millie were together, they debated which was worse, the outright insults or the subtle snubs. They never could make up their minds.

Then, just as David was getting used to the situation, the Third Reich declared war on England, conquered most of Europe, and began rattling sabers at America. In no time at all, he went from being a dirty Jew to being a filthy German. It was no use arguing that he was an enemy of the Germans. Adolescent bodies and minds grow too rapidly for subtle distinctions. There was only one way to prove himself. He made up his mind that as soon as he turned eighteen he'd enlist.

Millie pleaded with him not to. She reminded him that they'd sworn to stay together. He assured her they would, as soon as he finished defeating Hitler. Mr. Bennett tried to reason with him. When war came, of course David would fight. Mr. Bennett understood how personal the battle would be for him. But there was no hurry. Russ Bennett, who'd served in the last war, believed he had some knowledge of the military. The more education David had, the more use he'd be to the Army. Later David would learn just how wrong Russ Bennett had been. A seasoned private or noncommissioned officer was likely to be twice as valuable as a well-educated junior officer. But that would be later. For the moment he allowed himself to be persuaded. He enrolled at Haverford. At least he and Millie would be close to each other.

The venture was not a success. His mind was on other matters. He wasn't the only one. At the end of the first semester, two of his classmates left to join the Canadian Air Force. In June, three left to join the U.S. Navy. This time he didn't discuss the plan with anyone. He simply turned up one morning first in line at the Army Air Corps recruiting office. He remembered his father's instruction about being early and eager. The officer in charge was surprised when David said he didn't want to be a pilot. Every boy who walked through that door dreamed of being a pilot.

"Bombardier," David told him. "That way I can drop bombs on German targets."

The officer was listening closely, not something he often did, but the bombardier request had made him sit up and take notice. He thought he detected a faint German accent. He asked for David's birth certificate. David took it from the breast pocket of his coat and handed it over. The recruiter couldn't make out most of it, but he could recognize the language. He began to laugh.

"You're an enemy alien. You're not going to get near a plane in this man's army, let alone in the bombardier's seat. No telling which side you'd drop them things on."

A month later, he ended up at Camp Blanding in Florida,

a private in the 79th Infantry Division. That was all right. He'd kill Nazis on the ground instead of from the air. That was even better. He'd see their faces as they fell. He was young enough to think he'd enjoy that, but then so was everyone else in his unit.

As it turned out, a Jew was no more welcome in the barracks than in the dormitory of a good Christian boarding school, though now there was a new twist. Many of the men who taunted and tried to fight him had never seen a Jew before. But enmity does not demand familiarity. It's more likely to flourish without it. A joke went through the barracks, though the first time David heard it, the soldier who asked it made it sound like a serious question. "Tell me something, Mosbach, is it true a Jew is just a nigger turned inside out?"

Halfway through basic training he was transferred to another division. He was surprised. So were the other men and even the noncoms in his unit. Men didn't get transferred in the middle of basic training. It didn't take long for him to figure out what was going on. His new unit was made up of men of foreign descent, German, German-Jewish, and Italian. As soon as they fell into formation that first morning, the sergeant ordered them to turn in their weapons and dress uniforms.

"We got weekend passes coming up, Sergeant. You want us going into town in fatigues?" one of the men argued.

"There ain't going to be no weekend passes," the sergeant snarled as he marched them to a muddy field and ordered them to start pitching the tents they'd been issued. "Barracks is too good for the likes of you Nazi and I-talian spies."

For the next five months David and the other men lived in a muddy field in those tents, worn relics of the last war, and performed the most menial and unpleasant duties the

Army could come up with. The joke among them was that in this unit KP was a reward for good behavior.

Then one day, for a reason the Army never explained and David never learned, a new sergeant showed up—the last one had had a southern drawl; this one barked with a Brooklyn accent—and told them to break camp and reclaim their uniforms. The next morning David received his orders and a train ticket to Maryland. He didn't have a chance to find out where the others were posted, though months later he would come across some of them.

He spent the next forty-eight hours sitting and standing on trains crowded with men in uniform and wives and girlfriends and children going to meet other men in uniform, waiting for hours in rural junctions for connections to other trains that were invariably late and just as crowded, and bouncing over unpaved country roads in a military bus. Finally, the bus came to a stop, the doors opened, and he swung his duffel over his shoulder and climbed down to the dusty road. Ahead of him, the sun was just rising behind a distant mountain. He put his hand up to shade his eyes. In front of him was a stone wall with an iron gate. A sentry box stood on one side of the gate, a sign on the other. The sign was the only indication of where he was. It said STOP. Great, he thought, I've been posted to Camp Stop.

He squinted into the slanting rays of early morning sun, made out the silhouette of an MP in the guard box, approached, and saluted. The MP returned his salute and asked for his orders. At first David thought he had misheard. The MP seemed to be speaking German. Obviously the past forty-eight hours spent on crowded unreliable trains and buses, drinking cold, bitter coffee, and eating stale sandwiches and greasy doughnuts had monkeyed with his senses. Then it got

worse. He glanced past the MP into the camp. A platoon of soldiers was marching down the street. They were wearing Wehrmacht uniforms. He blinked. They were still wearing those
gray-green uniforms. And now he could hear them chanting
in cadence. They were counting off in German. He knew he
wasn't dreaming, and yet . . .

He looked from the parade ground to the MP. The man
was grinning. "Welcome to Camp Ritchie, Private Mosbach.
I'm from Dortmund. How about you?"

"Berlin," David answered. He was still incredulous but beginning to catch on.

"Uncle Sam finally realized we weren't enemy aliens but
a goddamn gold mine he was sitting on. We speak the language. We got the customs on wires. We know the country,
or at least our particular corner of it. And we have firsthand
experience of the fucked-up German mind. Hell, the prisoner
you end up grilling—if you don't wash out—might be the
kid who called you a dirty Jew back in the good old days.
You're going to feel right at home here, Mosbach."

The MP was on the mark. For the first time since he and
Meike had boarded the train in Anhalter Bahnhof—and even
before that, he realized when he thought of all the events
leading up to that day—he felt as if he'd come home.

Not that life at the camp was easy. The physical training,
including the course in close combat, commonly dubbed Kill
or Be Killed, was brutal. The classes in photo interpretation
and terrain and aerial intelligence were grueling. The course
in Order of Battle entailed endless hours memorizing every
unit in the Wehrmacht, its chain of command, arsenal of
weapons, terms, abbreviations, personnel, and every fragment
of information the military possessed about the enemy army.
The idea was that if an interrogator mentioned names, places,

and details known only to those involved while questioning a prisoner, the prisoner would conclude that someone had already spilled the beans and pour out some more.

Many weren't up to the task. The washout rate, as the MP had warned, was high. David kept making new buddies and losing them. Every week men were sent back to their original units. But David had made up his mind. He was not going back.

It wasn't all harsh physical training and endless study and memorization. A Hitler impersonator held mock rallies where they practiced swearing allegiance to the Fatherland and the Fuhrer. The replica of a German village for instruction in house raids was straight off a Hollywood set. Ava Gardner could be just around the corner, they joked when the practice was over. The chow was, those from camps across the country agreed, the best in the Army. That was because the chief cook had worked at the Waldorf Astoria in New York, or so rumor said.

Not everyone at the camp was of German descent. French, Italian, Spanish, Dutch, and others who had fled to America or been born there to immigrant parents went through similar training. As time went on, there were Japanese. And here and there was an American whose family had been in the country for generations but who had a facility for languages. One man was fluent in eleven different tongues and understood four more. But David trained and lived, ate and slept with German Jews. For the first time in years he was not taunted as a dirty Jew or a yid or a kike, or left alone in the dorm as others went off to a party or dance at a nearby girls' school—there were no parties or dances in this training—or waylaid in a hallway by someone looking for a fight. And for the first time he could put his experience in context. When he heard about other escapes from Germany or Hungary or the Netherlands, he knew he'd gotten off easy. He swore he'd never tell Millie that. It would only make her feel worse.

The training was, as the MP had warned, punishing, but instead of drifting through his studies as he had at Haverford, he excelled—with the exception of one course. Prisoner Interrogation was not the most demanding class. He didn't come away from it bloodied and bruised as he did from Kill or Be Killed. He didn't fall asleep over the manual as he did over the memorization charts of Order of Battle. In fact, he looked forward to the practice sessions in questioning POWs. He enjoyed sizing up people, trying to spot their weaknesses, figuring out how to exploit their vulnerabilities. The instructor, Captain Baum, said David was so good at it that after the war he ought to train to become a psychiatrist. His buddies Sam and Danny razzed him about that. Herr Doktor Mosbach, they started calling him. Then Baum was promoted, and Captain Krantz replaced him.

"The first order of business," Krantz announced the day he took over, "is to forget all the crap that's been drilled into you. The training films are bullshit. In those fairy tales, you offer a Kraut a cigarette, and after the first puff he's telling you where his unit is stationed. You tell him you'll make sure his family knows he's alive and well, and he's drawing you maps of fortifications. Bullshit," he repeated. "No food, drink, or cigarettes until after the interrogation. And if you don't get anything out of them that first time, no food, drink, or cigarettes until you do. No whispering sweet nothings in their lousy Kraut ears. You shout. You threaten. You bully. You make them think you have the same tricks up your sleeve as their Gestapo bastards use. You can't lay a finger on them, thanks to the goddamn Geneva Conventions, but anything short of that is A-OK with me. Anything that gets them shitting in their pants and willing to turn in their own mothers to save their skin is more than A-OK. I don't give a fuck how you play the game, as long as you win it. Any questions?"

No one had a question. They were, for the most part, highly intelligent men, and because they were, they couldn't believe Krantz meant what he said. It was one thing for a sergeant to scare men into becoming soldiers in basic training. They'd all been through that. It was something else to believe you could verbally beat information out of a prisoner. You didn't have to have training in psychology to know you get more flies with honey than vinegar, as David's mother was fond of saying. Krantz just wanted to show them he was the tough guy in the room.

David knew what was up the minute he came out of the barracks and saw the bus with the blacked-out windows. According to scuttlebutt, close to half a million German POWs were imprisoned on American soil. Some of them worked on farms and in factories to compensate for the manpower shortage now that so many men were fighting overseas. Occasionally a handful of them were trucked into the camp to be interrogated. The Army wasn't looking for information. The prisoners had been questioned as soon as they'd been captured. Now they were merely useful as guinea pigs for training.

David was third in line for a practice session that morning. "How'd it go?" he asked when Sam came out of the room where he'd grilled a prisoner under Krantz's eye.

"I blew it."

"How?"

"When I told the prisoner to sit, he pulled the old I'm-a-German-officer-and-prefer-to-stand gambit. But according to his record, he'd been busted up pretty bad when he was captured, so I said, suit yourself, but since you got that wound saving another man, it seems to me you've earned a seat. You could see the wheels spinning in his tiny Kraut brain. Was I pulling his wounded leg or did I really think he was a hero. I said his comrade had told us how he'd saved his life. He sat in the chair. I offered him a cigarette. He looked like he wanted to kiss me. Krantz could barely wait till the session was over to tell me if I ever did that again, he'd bust my ass out of here so fast my head would spin. I said no cigarettes, he howled. I told him I thought he meant before the interrogation. No means no. I was sure he was going to blow a gasket."

"Do me a favor," David said. "Hang on to these while I'm in there." He held out a pack of Lucky Strikes. "I'm not taking any chances on reaching for them out of habit."

Sam laughed, but he took the cigarettes.

David's interrogation went well enough, at first. He didn't shout or bully, but he did remain distant and correct, almost disdainful. Nonetheless, he managed to pick up on the prisoner's sullenness. This wasn't an arrogant Wehrmacht soldier; this was a disgruntled boy. He opened the prisoner's folder and pretended to study it again. Finally he closed it and looked up.

"You were with the KG 76."

"I never said that."

"You didn't have to. We know these things. Fine unit."

The prisoner didn't answer.

"Hogg is a good commander."

The prisoner shifted in his seat.

"You must be proud of serving in that unit under him."

The prisoner's mouth curled in disdain, but he said nothing.

"What I don't understand is why a man with your record is still a corporal. How come you weren't promoted long ago?"

Still no answer, but another shift of position.

"It wouldn't have anything to do with the fact that Hogg is Prussian and you're Bavarian?"

The man looked at David, then away, but his mouth twitched as if he was fighting to keep the words from spilling out.

"They're all alike, those Prussians. Good soldiers. I'll give you that. But so are a lot of men from other areas. Brandenburg. Saxony. Bavaria. But try telling that to a Prussian."

The prisoner couldn't stand the injustice any longer. "Do you know how many Prussians were promoted over me? Not one of them with my record." He began listing them.

"What exactly did that achieve, Mosbach?" Krantz asked when the interrogation was over. "We're looking for information, not a grudge list."

"I'm sorry, sir, I was getting to that, but you didn't give me time."

"Time! You think the Krauts are going to give you time before they start firing?"

"I think a few minutes spent establishing rapport with the prisoner will pay off."

"Rapport! Rapport doesn't save lives, Mosbach. Information saves lives. Troop location, troop strength, troop movement saves lives. If I catch you establishing fucking rapport again, I'll bust your ass out of here so fast your head will spin."

"How'd it go?" Sam asked as he handed the pack of Luckies back to David.

"He threatened to bust my ass out of here so fast my head will spin."

Sam managed a laugh, then frowned. "You think he means it?"

"Nah. Like we said that first day, he just likes to play tough guy."

Nonetheless, Krantz continued to ride him. He rode them all, but he rode David the hardest. The same traits that had made him a star interrogator under Baum made him a failure under Krantz.

One morning toward the end of his training period, he was told to report not to his usual class but to camp headquarters. His heart was in his throat as he made his way past the barracks and classroom buildings. Maybe he'd been wrong. Maybe Krantz really meant what he said, though the timing was strange. He'd finished the prisoner interrogation course two weeks earlier.

A truck stood, engine idling, outside the building. An officer asked him his name, checked his clipboard, and told him to get aboard. Most of the seats were already taken. If he was washing out, so were a lot of other men. He found a seat toward the back. No one was sure what was going on, but there were rumors. They couldn't be washing out, some of the men said. They hadn't gotten orders. So it had to be the other thing. A couple of men told them to shut up and stop tempting fate.

They bounced along over deep ruts in an unpaved road for almost an hour. Finally the truck came to a stop in front of an unimpressive frame structure behind a patch of weedy brown grass. The only indication that the building was up to anything official was an American flag on a tall pole in the scruffy yard. It whipped and snapped overhead as they filed out of the bus, up a path, and into the lobby, which was small, with a stained linoleum floor, peeling green paint, and several spittoons. A man in a shabby green suit that matched the walls and a battered hat told them to wait until their names were called. There were no benches or chairs in the lobby. A few of the men leaned against the walls or squatted on their haunches, but most of them stood, not at attention but erect. They weren't that far from their German boyhoods. They knew, or suspected, what was ahead. You didn't slouch or squat on an occasion like this.

Only four of them were left when David heard his name called. He went through the door the other men had entered and exited by. A clerk in an Army uniform sat behind a desk piled with papers. Without rising, the man handed David a card and told him to read it. "Loud and clear, soldier. I want to hear every word."

David began to read. "I hereby declare under oath . . . renounce any allegiance . . ." His voice grew louder. ". . . to any foreign state . . . that I will support and defend the Constitution . . ." And so on to the end.

The clerk took the card back, stamped a piece of paper on his desk, and handed it to David. "Congratulations, soldier. You are now a citizen of the United States of America."

All the way back to camp, as the truck bumped over the rutted road, he tried to figure out what he felt. Relief, certainly. Pride, yes. Maybe a childish gleeful thumbing of his nose at his former country or at least at the people who had taken it over. But some small, ineffable sadness kept tugging at his consciousness. He felt as if a part of him was gone forever. Good riddance, he told himself and whistled an American song under his breath. Nothing patriotic and corny like "The Star-Spangled Banner," which was too hard to whistle

anyway, or "America the Beautiful," just some popular mel-
ody the way Artie Shaw and his band played it. The music
wouldn't sound the same anywhere else in the world.

He graduated from the camp with flying colors and then
some. He didn't tell Millie about the *then some*. He knew
she'd never forgive him. He couldn't even tell her about Camp
Ritchie. The top secret designation of the camp was drilled
into everyone who passed through it. After the war, he'd learn
the only installation that had been more hush-hush was the
Manhattan Project.

In no time at all he managed to forget Captain Krantz,
though eighteen months later, when interrogating a prisoner
whom he remembered from the days when they were both
at *Gymnasium*—the man, who'd been two years ahead, didn't
recognize David—he thought of Krantz again and just how
wrong he'd been. With talk of rugby, offers of cigarettes, and
other friendly overtures, he managed to extract some useful
information about enemy positions that the prisoner didn't
even realize he was giving.

At Camp Ritchie, David had been trained in intelligence
work, schooled in secrecy, and conditioned never to let down
his guard. But in one regard, he allowed his wariness to flag.
Living among Jews, he'd forgotten what it was like to be a
Jew in the outside world. The incident at the ski lodge on
his last and only weekend leave before he was to ship out reminded him.

Millie, who'd graduated from Bryn Mawr the previous June,
gone to work as a fact-checker at Russ Bennett's magazine, and

was living in an apartment with two girls from school who'd also gotten jobs in Philadelphia, had assumed she and David would spend his weekend leave at the Bennetts' house in Ardmore, but Russ Bennett came up with another idea. He suggested a ski lodge in Vermont. He wasn't being irresponsible, he said. He hadn't forgotten about gas rationing. But since he had to take a swing through New England on business, and since four in the car didn't consume more fuel than one, it was almost their patriotic duty to send their soldier off with a bang.

They were in luck. When they arrived Friday evening, the snow, which had fallen all day, was just tapering off. There would be fresh powder for the weekend.

David and Millie were out early the next morning. As she followed him down the slope, much as she used to follow her cousin Anna on family holidays in Austria and Switzerland, she was grateful once again to Russ Bennett. At first, she'd thought his suggestion of a ski weekend strange, almost frivolous. Now she realized it was wise. They couldn't escape the specter of David's imminent departure, but with the wind stinging their faces, the powdery slopes racing up to meet them, and their minds focused on controlling their bodies, they could outrun the dread for moments at a time.

The incident occurred as they were heading back to the lodge late in the afternoon. At first neither of them made anything of it. It had taken David a moment even to recognize the boy getting off the lift ahead of them who said hello. Then he remembered he'd been in the form behind him in boarding school. David hadn't thought much of him one way or another. Boys rarely did of younger boys unless they were pests or admirers. And he'd had enough to worry about with the boys in his own form. He returned the boy's greeting and kept going.

He and Millie were slow taking off their skis and boots. They kept groaning about muscles they hadn't used in years, teasing each other about who'd done better on the slopes, and trying to hang on to the moment they both sensed slipping through their fingers. As they made their way through the lobby, David noticed the boy from school and a man who looked enough like him to suggest a family relationship in a huddle with the manager. A little while later, when they were sitting with the Bennetts in the lounge with the huge stone fireplace, the manager came over, bent close to Russ, and asked if he could speak to him for a moment. Russ followed him out of the lounge. He was back in minutes, his face red, whether from the effects of the sun on the slopes or the warmth of the fire or anger was hard to tell.

"How soon can everyone be packed?" He was speaking to the three of them but loud enough for his voice to carry. He wanted the other guests to hear, though as he said later, he knew they wouldn't care. They'd probably be relieved.

"I blame myself," Russ said when they were in the car on the way to a hotel where they'd spend the night before heading home the next day. "I should have known the damn place was restricted."

"How could you?" Millie asked. "You never had to think about it."

"That's just the point," Lydia said, her long upper lip growing longer with indignation. "We should have thought about it. Not paying attention is no excuse. Not paying attention just encourages the practice."

"You could have stayed," David said, though they all knew

that was the last thing they would have done. "Millie and I could have gone to the hotel and met you tomorrow."

"We all could have stayed," Russ said. "That's the beautiful irony of it. The bastard, excuse me, ladies, the manager said the lodge did not permit Jewish guests, but since you were with us, and since, get this, you didn't seem typical, he'd make an exception just this once. Didn't seem typical! What the hell did he expect, horns?"

"And a tail," David said, but he was thinking that in preparing him for new tests, Camp Ritchie had undermined his old vigilance.

The following Monday, Millie went to the 30th Street Station to see David off. She'd known saying goodbye would be agony. She hadn't expected the other pain, the one that came flooding back. The sunshine streaming through the tall windows was the same heartless light that had poured into the Anhalter Bahnhof that day. The tattoo of her heels on the marble floor as they made their way across the vast art deco waiting room echoed the sound of her mother's high heels.

He hadn't wanted her to come to the station with him. "It'll be crowded with people saying goodbye," he warned.

"Then we'll be in good company," she answered.

"You have to promise you won't cry."

You have to promise you'll come back, she wanted to say but managed not to. "No tears," she swore, "or maybe only a few so you don't think I'm hard-hearted."

A disembodied voice announcing the train and track number boomed out over the waiting room and bounced off the travertine marble walls and red and gold coffered ceiling. He hefted his duffel. She tightened her jaw against the tears she'd promised not to shed. A flood of men in uniform and wives and girlfriends and parents and children began flowing down the steps to the track.

They stood facing each other on the drafty platform waiting for the train to come in.

"Take care of yourself, Mil."

"I'm supposed to take care of myself? Is that what passes for humor these days?"

Over his shoulder, she could see the train approaching.

"I wish to hell you weren't going." She hadn't meant to say it, though she'd known she would.

"We've been through this."

They had, again and again and again. He'd told her that it was his fight, and if he didn't do it, who would. He'd catalogued the insanity and cruelty and injustice that had to be stopped. He'd explained that he was fighting for her too, and for their mother and father and Sarah. The sooner they beat Hitler, the sooner the family would be reunited. There was only one thing he neglected to tell her. It was the *then some* of his record at Camp Ritchie. He'd done so well, despite Captain Krantz, that they'd asked him to stay on as an instructor. He could have fought Hitler from the safety of a Maryland training camp. There were even those who insisted he'd be more effective there. What was one soldier with an axe to grind against the hundreds he could arm with useful skills? Only he couldn't have fought Hitler from the safety of a stateside camp. Not really. Not the way he wanted to. But he knew he could never persuade her of that.

Fourteen

"Do you mind if I ask you something?" Millie said on her way out of Harry Sutton's office. She'd been thinking about it since their drink in the officers' club.

"I'm an open book."

"How did Hans Sutheim end up in the States rather than England? In view of his English mother."

"No English family. That's why she became a nanny. I suppose she would have preferred a Brit Kindertransport, but we couldn't afford to be choosy."

"When was that?"

"Early. Thirty-four. Right after they murdered my father. There were no official Kindertransports yet, but she saw the bloody writing on the wall. She'd seen it before, but my father had refused to read it. Or maybe he read it and was determined to stay and fight it."

She thought of her parents' discussions that she'd eavesdropped on through the heat register.

"What happened when you got to the States?" She was thinking of Theo standing all spit and polish in front of his carefully made bed being passed over again and again.

"You really want to hear the saga of little Hans Sutheim?"

She crossed his office and sat in one of the chairs on the other side of his desk. "That's why I asked."

He leaned back, put his feet up, and looked at her over them. "The usual for kids who were brought over without their parents by charity groups. I was taken in by a family in New Jersey."

So he'd been almost as lucky as she had.

"Newark, to be exact. They had four daughters and wanted a son, or at least a boy on the premises. Two months after they took me in, the father lost his job. He was a bookkeeper, though I don't remember where. Funny how much I've forgotten. Or repressed. Anyway, there were those four girls to feed, not to mention mom and pop. The money they got for me helped, but not enough, so they had to return me, so to speak. You can't blame them. I don't. Even then, I didn't. Besides, I was lucky. The agency found another family for me right away."

She was glad Theo hadn't heard this story.

"This time I was the one who got fired—with cause I hasten to add. The father was a rabbi. Orthodox. It wasn't easy following all the rules—hell, I didn't even know most of them when I got there—but I learned pretty quickly. Every morning I prayed with the father and the two sons and thanked God for not making me a woman."

"What?"

He grinned. "I see you don't know the drill, either. That's the way an observant Jewish man begins his day. 'Blessed art thou, Lord, our God, ruler of the universe, who has not created me a woman.'"

She shook her head, not in surprise but in recognition. "I suppose the sentiment is common to most faiths, but trust our coreligionists to codify it in daily prayer."

"I also went to synagogue with them and sat downstairs with those fortunate men," he went on. "When I put the bottle of milk back in the refrigerator, it never got near the meat shelf. I was good as bloody gold on their turf, but when I wasn't on their turf, I figured I could live by my own rules. That was what got me in trouble. One day on the way home from school, I heard the siren call of a White Castle. While I was sitting at the counter enjoying a forbidden cheeseburger, bought, I might add, with the money I earned as a delivery boy for a drugstore, one of the sons I prayed with every morning walked past and, since the place was off-limits to him too, couldn't resist looking through the window. By the time I got back to the house, my bag was standing outside the front door. They wouldn't even let me in. Didn't want me sullying the premises, I imagine. After that I kicked around with another family for almost a year. Then I turned eighteen and got really lucky. I'm not being ironic. The Depression was still around, but somehow I managed to find enough jobs to work my way through City College."

"City College? Theo said you went to Harvard."

He laughed. "That's the accent. Wallach tends to jump to conclusions. Witness the beating up of the guard."

"He didn't jump to conclusions. The man had been a camp guard. Anna spotted him."

"You're right. He had been. But a few weeks earlier a bunch of DPs beat the hell out of another man in another black market. That incident turned out to be a case of mistaken identity. Wallach was just lucky his wasn't."

He took his feet off the desk and sat up in the swivel chair. "Now get back to work, Captain. If you don't have enough *Fragebogen*, I can have Fraulein Schmidt find you some more."

She stood, gave him a mock salute, and managed not to smile until she was out of his office. She'd never seen him embarrassed before.

There was another aspect of Harry Sutton's past she wondered about, but you didn't go around asking a man how he'd lost a couple of fingers. It wasn't an arm or a leg, but you still didn't inquire. Asking nothing was the unwritten rule around men who had seen action. And if someone was foolish or insensitive enough to pry, the men never answered. Like David when she'd questioned him about the two buddies in the snapshot he kept in his mirror. The men might talk among themselves, but never to people who hadn't gone through it. Never to outsiders. More than once she'd wandered into an office where Theo or Werner or Jack or some of the other officers were talking, and they'd suddenly fallen silent. At first she'd taken it personally. Then she'd realized it had nothing to do with her. Or rather in a way it did. It had to do with their own nightmares, but it had to do also with protecting her and all the others who hadn't been there. Mary Jo, the nurse she'd met in the PX with whom she occasionally had dinner or went to a movie, had told her about a patient for whom she wrote letters. His hands had been badly burned and he was undergoing skin grafts. His wife had asked in a letter if he'd ever killed a German. "No," he'd dictated to Mary Jo as she wrote. "I always aimed above their heads."

The idea was to keep the innocents innocent. She never would have learned about the two buddies in the snapshot with David if the officer from the Judge Advocate General's Corps hadn't come to the apartment to question him. She wasn't exactly eavesdropping. She'd left them alone in the parlor and taken the letters she'd been writing into the dining room to finish. But they hadn't pulled the doors closed, and she couldn't help hearing. The JAG officer had a loud voice.

Once or twice, when David's voice dropped to a hush, the officer asked him to repeat his answer.

"I see from your file," the JAG officer began, "that you were the man who brought in that I.G. Farben director at gunpoint."

"I wasn't playing cops and robbers. The man seemed to think we were paying a social call. Sat there in his damn library, puffing on a cigar, drinking brandy, and dropping the names of his friends in high places in American business. He even offered us brandy. When I told him we were there to escort him to headquarters, he said he preferred not to go. I said he didn't have a choice. He insisted he was an old man and couldn't possibly leave his house at that hour in the rain. My service pistol seemed the only way to persuade him he could."

She heard the JAG officer laugh.

"That's not what you came here to question me about," David said.

"No. I just thought it was a good story."

"Or a way to oil the interrogation wheels."

"I'm not the enemy, Captain."

David didn't say anything to that.

"You interrogated a Corporal Heinrich Kropp when he was taken prisoner. Is that correct?"

"You've got the report there," David said.

"I'm corroborating it, as I'm sure you understand."

"I interrogated Kropp," David admitted.

"The first time he was taken prisoner or the second?"

"The second."

"Do you know who interviewed him the first time he was taken prisoner?"

"Lieutenants Blau and Meyer. We were all lieutenants then."

"Didn't you often work as a team?"

"Yes."

"But not for that interrogation?"

"I wasn't there that night."

"Where were you?"

"I'm sure that's in your report too." There was a moment's pause. "Sorry. I was in a village about twenty clicks away."

"Wasn't that unusual?"

"Do you know anything that's usual in a war?"

"What were you doing in the village?" the JAG officer asked.

"Walking around in a Wehrmacht uniform trying to make contact with some Germans we'd heard were trying to set up a resistance cell."

"So Lieutenants Blau and Meyer interrogated Kropp without you."

"I told you, I wasn't there."

"But you did interrogate Kropp the second time he was taken prisoner?"

"Yes."

"Was he a difficult prisoner?"

"What do you mean by difficult?"

"Was he hard to break?"

"I didn't try to 'break' prisoners. I tried to extract useful information from them. In my experience you get more flies with honey than vinegar."

Millie had to smile. It was their mother's expression.

"Was he cooperative?"

"He was a former communist who'd been interned in a

concentration camp for being unworthy to bear arms. But when the losses started piling up, they decided he was worthy to die for the Fuhrer after all. So yes, as you can imagine, he was a cooperative prisoner."

"What did he tell you?"

"That he wanted to report a war crime."

"Is that the way he phrased it?"

"He said it in German." There was another pause. "Sorry."

"I know this is difficult, Captain. How did he describe the war crime?"

"He said he had been taken prisoner by the Americans with about twenty-five or thirty others in his unit on November 16, 1944. They were questioned that night by two German-speaking interrogators."

"Lieutenants Blau and Meyer?"

"He didn't know their names, though I did from the reports. He said the interrogators had no accents. They spoke perfect German. So the prisoners decided they were German. And since they were in the American Army, they must be German Jews. Ironic really."

"Why?"

"It was drilled into us at Ritchie never to let an interrogee know we were German, let alone German Jews. We all had cover stories for why we spoke the language so well. Mine was that I'd spent summers in Germany with my grandparents. The fear was that if we got captured, being German Jews would make it worse for us. Like the Jewish GIs who threw away their dog tags before they went into battle. And given what happened to Danny and Sam, I guess the warnings were on the money."

"Did he tell you what happened after he was questioned the first time?"

"He was held in a pen with the rest of the prisoners. A few days later the Germans retook the area. The German prisoners were repatriated, and the Americans became the prisoners. Some of the repatriated Germans pointed out the two Americans who had interrogated them. They told the commanding officer they were German Jews."

"Did the prisoner tell you who the commanding officer was?"

"Hauptmann Franz Hoffmann."

"What did Hauptmann Hoffmann do then?"

Again there was another silence.

"I'm sorry, Captain," the JAG officer said. "I didn't hear you."

"He ordered a detail of his men to take the two interrogators who'd been pointed out as Jews down the road and shoot them."

"Did anyone protest?"

"You know a German soldier who's going to contradict his commanding officer?"

"What about Lieutenants Blau and Meyer?"

"According to Kropp, Lieutenant Blau reminded Hoffmann of the Geneva protocols regarding prisoners of war."

"What did Hoffmann say to that?"

"He said the Geneva protocols didn't apply because they weren't captured soldiers. They were Jews. And Jews had no right to live in Germany. Then he repeated his order to take them down the road and shoot them."

"Did Kropp witness the shooting?"

"He said he did."

"Did you ask him how the men were shot?"

This silence went on for longer. "I'm sorry, could you repeat that, Captain?"

"In the back," David said.

"One more thing, Captain. I want to make sure I have this absolutely right. You deemed this prisoner reliable?"

"I listed him as 'highly reliable.'"

There was another silence, then she heard the sound of clasps on a briefcase being snapped shut and floorboards creaking as David walked the officer to the door. She couldn't hear what they were saying until suddenly David raised his voice. "Do me a favor," he said.

"If I can."

"Make sure the bastard gets the firing squad."

"I'll do my best, Captain."

During the next few days Millie kept turning over the conversation in her mind. She even went into David's room and stood staring at the snapshot of the three GIs in a jeep, and as she did, something David had said in the interview came back to her. It wasn't relevant to the war crimes case but it was to her. She couldn't believe she hadn't thought of it before. He'd said he hadn't been there the first time the German POW had been questioned because he was in a village twenty kilometers away walking around in a Wehrmacht uniform trying to make contact with members of a nascent resistance cell. Suddenly she knew what David was up to all those nights he disappeared. He wasn't with a Fraulein. He wasn't even with a girl. He was still working in intelligence. She was sure of it.

Fifteen

❧

FRAU KNEFF'S VISIT THAT FIRST NIGHT BECAME A ROU-
tine. Every Wednesday, Friday, and Sunday, she came for
dinner. No weather, no time of day, no marauders in the
Russian sector could stop her.

Frau Kneff made the effort, but Millie knew how much
the invitations cost Anna. No, not the invitations, Frau Kneff's
presence. Once Millie complimented Anna on her generosity.

"I hate her," Anna burst out, then stopped, shocked at the
violence in her voice. "No, hate is the wrong word. She saved
Elke's life. I'm jealous of her."

"Elke just needs time."

The words had become familiar, and like all familiar re-
frains, they were beginning to lose their meaning.

"It's not time," Anna said, "it's me. I don't know how to
be a mother."

"What do you mean you don't know how to be a mother?
You are a mother," Millie insisted, but she understood what
Anna was saying. The war had taken its toll on Frau Kneff,
but the camps had broken Anna. She'd become fearful and
suspicious. Walking the streets, she gave a wide berth not only
to those in uniform, but to civilians as well. In shops and even
at home, a sudden movement made her flinch. She kept the
world at arm's length. She gave Elke no breathing space. She

couldn't keep her hands off her daughter, always hugging her, smoothing her hair, reaching for her hand. She couldn't tear her eyes away from the sight of her. When she spoke to her, her tone was a wheedling plea for affection. Like any attempt to coerce love, the harder she tried, the more unlovable she became. And the more Elke punished her for it. Sometimes Millie wanted to slap her cruel little face. Then she'd catch Elke's expression in an unguarded moment—what child should have only moments of unguardedness?—and she didn't know which of them she felt more sorry for, except that pity is not a competition.

One night after Anna finished putting Elke to bed, she came into the parlor where Millie was sitting with a copy of *Der Weg* and took one of the chairs opposite her. Her hair had stopped falling out, and she'd put on a few pounds, but the improvements were only cosmetic. Pain brimmed like tears in her eyes. The full mouth that used to look as if she was about to take a bite of life was now a gaping wound in her face.

"I've made up my mind," she said.

"About what?"

"King Solomon."

"What are you talking about?"

"I'm talking about being a mother. About what Elke needs, not what I want. She's miserable with me. Time isn't going to change that. Maybe she'll get used to me, but she'll never forgive me."

"That's ridiculous."

"It's true, and you know it. She's happier with Frau Kneff."

"So what are you going to do, give her back to Frau Kneff?"

"I have my name down for a flat."

"I thought you had your name down to immigrate to the States."

"I do, but I've changed my mind."

Millie was incredulous. "You're going to stay in Germany? You're going to give up your daughter but stay in the grave-yard of the Jews to be near her?"

"I'm going to stay where Elke can be happy. When the flat comes through, Frau Kneff can come live with us."

"And you'll be Aunt Anna?"

"Better a loved aunt than a hated mother."

"You're not making any sense," Millie said, but she was, in a way. "You realize you're sacrificing yourself for a child's whim?"

"It's not a whim. It's the only world Elke has ever known. It's five years of love and care and a thousand little things I'll never be part of. It's the foundation of her life. I can't knock that out from under her. You call it a sacrifice. I say it's what parents do for children. That's what I did when I gave her away in the first place. That's what thousands of parents did when they sent their children off on Kindertransports. That's what your parents did when they let you and David go."

It hadn't happened quite that way, though that was the way Millie had made it sound to Anna. The only consolation for Anna's decision was that the flat wasn't likely to come through quickly, and Millie would make sure that Anna's name stayed on the list for immigration to the States. Anna was bound to change her mind. And Elke was bound to come around. The scars of childhood remain, but the convictions and prejudices are less steadfast. It would just take time, Millie told herself again. But what, it suddenly occurred to her, if they went back in time rather than forward? She was still toying with the thought when she saw the display of picture frames in the PX.

Years earlier when the visas had come through, her mother had divided among the five suitcases more than the Leica lenses, the remaining jewelry, and the little money left. She'd also divvied up the family photographs. The lenses, jewels, and money would be valuable. The pictures would be priceless. These days the photograph of her parents on the beach at Wannsee stood propped up on the mantelpiece in the parlor, the picture of her father in his uniform wearing the Iron Cross Second Class on the dresser in David's room, and the snapshot of her and David and Sarah again on the beach at Wannsee on the childish chest of drawers in the small room she'd moved to. Sarah's hand puppet was there too, but tucked in a drawer rather than on display.

Her mother had packed other photographs as well. She'd gone through album after album choosing pictures of family celebrations and holidays and rites of passage. One snapshot that had ended up in Millie's suitcase had been taken at the lake the summer she had perfected her dive and Anna had met Sigmund. In it, Meike and Anna are standing side by side in their one-piece woolen suits, all the rage that year, with their arms around each other's waists and their mouths so happy you could almost hear the laughter bubbling out of them. Sleek bobs curl forward on both their cheeks, and even in black and white, the radiant richness of Anna's hair comes through. Millie had never put that picture out in the States. There wasn't space. And how much misery could she court? But after she placed the other three photos in the new frames from the PX, she took the one of her and Anna, slipped it into a small silver-plated frame, centered it on the break-front in the parlor, and stood staring at it. The photograph was beginning to yellow with age. The world it captured had faded completely. It seemed impossible that they'd ever been so happy. It seemed impossible they'd ever been so blind.

The photograph stood there unnoticed by anyone except her for a few days. If Anna did spot it, she didn't say anything. Perhaps all that joy was too painful for her. Or perhaps she was willfully blind.

Then, one night Elke came into the parlor to say good night. Anna insisted on the ritual, though Millie wished she wouldn't. Forced gratitude is worse than ingratitude. At least she no longer curtsied. That had been a holdover from Frau Kneff, not as bad as a Nazi salute, but an expression, Millie couldn't help thinking, of the same instincts. She was wearing pink cotton pajamas and a pink flannel robe, again from the PX, and Anna had braided her hair into two long plaits tied with pink grosgrain ribbon. She was a beautiful girl with the saddest mouth Millie had ever seen on a child. Even the street urchins who scuffled over cigarette butts didn't look so lost. They were too busy fighting for survival.

Elke said good night and was about to turn to leave when something caught her eye. Instead of heading out of the room, she walked to the space between the windows where the breakfront stood and leaned closer to get a better look at the photograph. She turned back to Millie. "Who's that?"

"You don't recognize us?"

"I know that one is you." She pointed to Millie in the snapshot. "But who's the other lady?"

Millie stood and crossed to stand behind Elke. She put her hand on the birdlike shoulder. "Look closely, Elke."

Elke looked but said nothing.

Millie picked up the frame and bent until her head was beside Elke's. "Doesn't she look familiar to you?"

Elke still didn't speak.

"It's your mama."

"No." She started to pull away, but Millie kept a hand on her shoulder.

"Yes. Look again."

Elke stood with her face averted, as if she were afraid to look again. Millie took her chin in her hand and gently turned her back to the photograph.

"Don't you recognize her?"

Elke stood staring at the snapshot.

"I'm the one on the left and your mama's the one on the right. It was taken a long time ago, before you were born."

"She's pretty." Elke didn't so much speak the words as breathe them.

"Would you like to put the picture on the mantel in your room?"

Elke pulled away. "No."

Millie grinned. "Good. I was only being nice. I prefer it here. That way I can look at it as much as I want."

As Elke started out of the room, she glanced back at the photograph. Millie had the feeling she was having second thoughts about not wanting it, but that might have been wishful thinking.

❧

The photograph didn't change anything, not really. Elke remained sullen and angry. She went on periodic and focused food strikes. Some nights she closed her mouth against soup, others potatoes, still others meat. Her tantrums continued. But then, a week or two after the night she'd spotted the photograph, Anna reached for her hand, and she didn't pull it away. A few days after that, she reached for Anna's hand.

When she did, she looked up at Anna with an expression Millie couldn't quite read. It wasn't love. Millie wouldn't go that far. All she knew was that it didn't look like hatred either.

❧

Perhaps Millie's displaying the snapshot helped, but David was the one who saved the day. That hadn't been his intention. He wasn't thinking of Elke. He certainly wasn't concerned about Frau Kneff. He was trying to help the Zelinskys, a young couple he'd worked with in the DP camp who were now living in a flat on the outside, as the expression went. The rest was an unintended consequence.

David didn't talk about his war experience, and of course he didn't even hint at whatever he was doing in intelligence now, but he didn't mince words about the misery of the sick, lonely, and abandoned displaced persons, or the licentiousness of those who'd gone so numb to pain and death that only a moment of pleasure, or at least gratification, could light a spark of life. Occasionally, however, in moments of optimism, he admitted that wasn't the whole story. As the bar mitzvah in the desecrated cemetery had shown, hope refused to die. In German town halls, Jewish men and women were registering their marriages, though sometimes they had to compensate for their lack of proper papers with their rations of American cigarettes. In German hospitals, Jewish women were giving birth to Jewish babies. On German streets, Jewish mothers were parading their offspring in carriages and strollers. And not only was hope rearing its head; happiness was beginning to show its face. But as Harry Sutton might have put it, the situation wasn't all beer and skittles.

Many of these proud new mothers had been weakened and broken by years in concentration camps. The problems weren't only physical. They knew nothing about caring for newborns or infants or toddlers. They had no mothers or grandmothers or aunts to teach them. But what they, or the Occupation, did have was a surfeit of hungry German women, many of them widowed by the war and made child-less by the bombing. Only a recalcitrant fool, David said when Millie protested that she didn't like entrusting Jewish babies to German women, would resist the obvious solu-tion. Suddenly it was not unusual to see those proud Jewish mothers, and sometimes fathers, who had no more experi-ence in being a spouse or a parent than their wives, parad-ing those carriages and strollers accompanied by a German woman, all three of them fussing over a small beribboned miracle, the future of the world.

In this particular case, Mr. Zelinsky had come to David's office. He was, he apologized, at his wit's end. For months he and his wife, who had met right after the liberation of Buchen-wald, had done nothing but talk about the coming baby, plan its future, speculate on its likely characteristics, debate its name. Aaron after his late father, if it was a boy; Miriam after his wife's late mother, if it was a girl. Though he wanted to honor his father, he confided to David that he loved the idea of having a little girl called Mimi.

Everything had gone splendidly. Mimi had arrived on time. The delivery had not been too difficult, though, the young father blushed, who was he to talk of difficult or easy? He wasn't the one who had given birth. She was a gorgeous baby with ten wondrous fingers, ten wondrous toes, and a head full of dark ringlets that hadn't fallen out. And his wife, the baby's mother, was terrified of her.

When she tried to nurse, Mimi pushed the breast away and howled. Her mother wept. She was afraid to carry the baby from one point to another for fear of dropping her. Baths were a nightmare of a small body slipping out of control, imagined drownings, and other mayhem.

"I try to help," Mr. Zelinsky told David, "but what do I know about caring for a baby? To tell you the truth, I'm afraid of hurting her too."

David had a list of German women who had been approved by the displaced persons' camp, which paid them, to serve as nannies. He started to take the directory from his desk drawer, then a remembered image stopped him. Frau Kneff was sitting on the sofa in the parlor and Elke was curled against her as Frau Kneff read her a story. Twenty-four hours later, Frau Kneff had a job. Then came the unintended consequences.

Among Jewish displaced persons, and there were millions of wandering gentiles as well, marriage was a chance at happiness and babies were hope, but getting out of Germany was salvation. They didn't have to hear Harry Sutton's predictions of how similar the new Germany was going to be to the old to know that truth. America was, of course, the promised land. England was desirable. Cuba or Latin America would not be so bad. They were Jews. They knew how to survive anywhere. But they had to get out of Europe, the graveyard of the Jews, as Millie had described it to Anna, as the few Jews who'd survived called it. The Western democracies, like France and Holland, had shown their true colors during the war. No Jew in his right mind would agree to return to Poland. Rumors of resurgent anti-Semitism were already filtering back. Firsthand memories of it were still fresh. Like most displaced Polish Jews, the Zelinskys were determined not to return, though one United Nations Relief and Rehabilitation Agency worker had suggested they might want to be near their parents' graves. Mr. Zelinsky hadn't bothered to answer that one. The day of the incident they had an appointment at the Colombian consulate. They didn't usually go out together and leave Mimi alone with Frau Kneff, but today it couldn't be helped. The Colombian consulate demanded the presence of both of them.

Frau Kneff had hoped to take Mimi to the park. She was looking forward to pretending, even for a few hours, that she was a mother again. She was not an ungenerous woman. She didn't intend to show off to other lonely German women. She merely wanted to act out a fantasy for herself. She loved this new baby. How could you not love a baby? But she missed Elke. Elke had been hers. Until she wasn't. But a low, gray cloud, spitting cold rain, hung over the city, as it had done for the past several days. All morning, Frau Kneff kept carrying Mimi to the window and peering out, looking for a break in the clouds. The day was still gloomy when she put the baby down for her afternoon nap. Then God smiled. That was the way Frau Kneff thought of it. By the time the first whimperings indicated that Mimi was awake, Berlin had changed seasons, as it often does in March and April. The sun had broken through. A breeze was herding the clouds away. The sky had been scrubbed clean. She lifted Mimi out of the crib, changed her diaper, dressed her in her best coat and leggings, and tucked her into the carriage under several blankets. The sky looked like spring, but the trees were bare and winter still snapped in the air.

She was sitting on a bench—imagine, a bench in a Berlin park again; say what you want about the Amis, they got things done—with Mimi on her lap, thinking about Elke. She was always thinking about Elke. It would be the most logical thing in the world. Elke had always loved babies. And now that Frau Kneff had another baby to look after, even if it wasn't the same as looking after her own Elke, Anna wouldn't mind. Frau Kneff knew how painful to Anna her visits had been. The fact that this baby, too, was Jewish made it even better. It proved Frau Kneff really did not have an ounce of prejudice.

She'd lost her wristwatch in a bombing long ago, but she could tell from the angle of the sun in the newly laundered sky and the lengthening shadows of the trees that it must be close to three. Riemeisterstrasse wasn't far, perhaps a fifteen-minute walk. Elke would just be coming home from school. She lifted Mimi off her lap, tucked her into the carriage, and started out of the park.

The timing was, as she'd hoped, perfect. Anna was just putting the key in the lock of the outside door when Frau Kneff pushed the carriage onto Riemeisterstrasse. She called out. Anna turned, saw her, and stood waiting. Even at this distance, Frau Kneff could see the wary frown on her face. But Elke started running toward her, her skinny legs in their gray woolen stockings and brown oxfords flying over the still-muddy street, her braids streaming behind her, her breath getting shorter as she got closer to her other mama, her true mama, her mama who had brought her a present, for what else could she be pushing than a new doll in a new carriage? It was as big as life-size. Elke ran faster.

She reached Frau Kneff and bent to peer into the carriage. She reared back. This was no doll. This was a real baby. Her mama had given her away and gotten herself a new baby. She wanted to punch its little face. Instead, she turned and started walking fast back to her other mama, who wasn't her real mama, though everyone said she was. Maybe she didn't have any mama at all.

Between them Anna and Frau Kneff managed to get the carriage up the stairs to the flat.

"Like old times," Frau Kneff said as they maneuvered it. "We used to do this with your carriage," she said to Elke, but Elke had already clattered up the steps ahead of them.

Anna opened the door. Frau Kneff wheeled in the carriage, bent, and lifted Mimi out. "This is my new baby, *Schatzi*. Isn't she cute? Just like you when you were little, only her curls are black, not red like yours. Do you want to hold my new baby?"

"I'm not sure that's a good idea," Anna said, but she didn't have to worry. Elke had already started down the hall away from them.

"Take Frau Kneff into the parlor," Anna called after her.

Names had always been a dicey business among them. At first Elke had insisted on calling Frau Kneff Mama and refused to call Anna anything. Gradually Frau Kneff had become Aunt Teresa, but Anna still didn't have a name. Now Anna decided it was time Frau Kneff became Frau Kneff.

Anna continued down the hall to the kitchen, put on the water for tea, poured a glass of milk for Elke, sliced a cake and arranged the pieces on a plate, and carried a tray with everything back to the parlor. Frau Kneff was sitting on the sofa with the baby on her lap. Elke was perched on the edge of a cushion, her eyes on the faded carpet, her mouth a thin line of rage. The baby was turning her big black eyes from Frau Kneff to Elke and back.

"Would you like to hold baby?" Frau Kneff asked Elke again as Anna put down the tray.

Elke didn't answer.

Frau Kneff lifted Mimi's chubby arms—when was the last

time either woman had seen a chubby baby?—toward Elke. "See, she wants to go to you."

"Why don't you let her have her milk first?" Anna said. "And you have some tea."

She took a cup and saucer, poured tea, put it on the table within reach of Frau Kneff, took a plate, put a slice of cake on it, and placed it beside the cup and saucer. Then she leaned toward Frau Kneff. "I'll hold the baby while you eat."

"Let Elke hold her," Frau Kneff insisted and began lifting the baby out of her lap toward Elke. The baby waved her arms as if she were swimming through the air. As she got closer, she reached out, grabbed Elke's braid, and tugged.

Elke screamed and sprang off the sofa. Mimi tumbled to the floor, hitting the table as she went. The cup followed.

Both women were on their feet in a flash. Frau Kneff scooped up Mimi. Anna bent over both of them. The baby was howling, and Frau Kneff was trying to quiet her while she examined the small body for burns and injuries, and Anna kept insisting that everything was all right and hoping that was true.

Finally the baby's cries subsided into hiccups, and the women reassured each other that she wasn't hurt.

"No thanks to you," Frau Kneff said to Elke, who lingered, wide-eyed, in the doorway. "You're a naughty girl, *Schatzi*. A naughty, naughty girl."

The words followed Elke as she ran down the hall to the bedroom. Now that the baby had stopped crying, they could hear the door slamming.

Anna managed to get Frau Kneff out of the flat as quickly as possible, then went down the hall to the room she and Elke shared and opened the door quietly. Elke was lying across the big bed with her face buried in a pillow. Anna sat beside her and put her hand on her back. Despite all the food from the PX, it still felt dangerously fragile.

"You're not a naughty girl, Elke. It wasn't your fault. You didn't mean to hurt the baby. Frau Kneff never should have tried to make you hold her."

Elke didn't move. Anna thought of repeating the reassurance, then decided against it. Instead, she sat with her hand on her daughter's back, waiting. Finally Elke turned her head so half her face was visible. One eye looked up at Anna.

"Are you going to get a new baby too?"

"What?"

"When you get tired of me, are you going to give me away and get a new baby too?"

"Never," Anna said. "Never. Never. Never. You and I, Mama and Elke, are together forever."

Even as she spoke the words, she had the feeling she was tempting fate, but they seemed to reassure Elke, a little.

Sixteen

꩜

MILLIE HAD BEEN HEARING ABOUT THE FILM FOR WEEKS now. The first time was on an evening before the incident in Alexanderplatz when she and Theo had gone for dinner to Die Möwe. The Seagull, as it was known among the Americans and Brits, was a café on Neue Wilhelmstrasse in the Russian sector where Allied cultural and denazification officers and German artists and intelligentsia, many only recently returned from exile in Russia, gathered to argue art and politics, hunt for sex, and hope for love over cheap borscht and sausage, beer and vodka—especially vodka. No ice, no mixers, no frou-frou cherries or slices of citrus to turn the alcohol into a cocktail, merely tiny glasses of clear liquid guaranteed to defang the Berlin winter, blunt memories, and assuage the guilt of living almost well in the midst of so much misery. The German population of Berlin was starving, and the Russian occupiers weren't eating much better, despite the fact that unlike the Americans and Brits, who imported supplies from home, the Russkies subsisted off the German land, with the exception of vodka and caviar, which they shipped from Mother Russia to fuel the obscenely elaborate receptions they threw to impress the other occupying forces. That night in Die Möwe everyone had been talking about the fact that the Russians had lost no time reactivating an old Nazi film studio near Potsdam. They were already shooting movies in the rubble. Somehow the ugly uninhabitable ruins took on a haunting dreamy aura on celluloid, those who had seen early rushes said. The movie all the talk was about that night, however, had been shot not in Berlin but in Auschwitz.

No one was looking forward to seeing the film, but they all agreed they had to. She and Theo had planned to go. Then he was confined to quarters, and she was on her own. She thought of asking the nurse from the 279th Station Hospital, then decided Mary Jo witnessed enough horror in the wards and didn't need to bear any more witness in her off hours. Besides, she was probably busy. She'd fallen for a doctor at the hospital and was spending most of her time off with him. Millie asked David if he wanted to go to the film with her.

"How many ways can you find to torture yourself?" he answered. "At least tell me you're not foolish enough to go wandering the Russian sector or any sector of the city alone at night."

"I won't go alone. If you're not interested, I can tag along with Werner Kahn and his group."

She managed to stay with Werner and two other officers on the U-Bahn and the short walk to the half-bombed-out building that was serving as a theater, but once inside she lost them in the crowd of Allied personnel jostling and jockeying for seats. The air was thick with the haze of smoke from Chesterfields and Players, Gauloises and Belomorkanal, and the babel of American and English, French and Russian officers waiting for the film to begin. A handful of women, most of them American or British, but a few Frauleins, or so they looked, sat among them. The French and the Russians had no rules against fraternization. It wasn't only that they were more broad-minded but also that the issue was less of a problem for them. The French and Russian troops didn't have as much to offer the Frauleins as the Americans or even the Brits. Nonetheless, she couldn't help thinking the movie was a strange choice for a date with a Fraulein.

Most of the seats were already taken, but she managed to find one in the middle of a row toward the back. The lights were beginning to go down as she struggled toward it, stepping on shoes and boots, getting tangled in scarves and coats, apologizing.

The din of conversation died in fits and starts. A projector scraped noisily into action. The credits began to roll. They got as far as the name and logo of the studio and the title of the film before a loud snap jolted the room, followed by the flapping of torn film spinning on the reel.

An officer in a Russian uniform sprang out of his seat, ran shouting to the back of the theater, and disappeared through the door to the makeshift projection room. Waves of nervous laughter rolled across the room. She could swear it was the sound of relief. No one, including her, wanted to see this film. They were here out of obligation or guilt or hopeful disbelief. Surely the things they'd heard couldn't be true.

The curses of the Russian officer were growing louder, and as the lights came up she saw him. She'd been too busy finding a seat and making her way to it to notice him before. Harry Sutton was sitting in the middle of the second row. There was nothing out of the ordinary about that. The only surprise was the girl sitting beside him. Her blond hair streamed over her shoulders, which were covered with a silk scarf that screamed PX. Perhaps the two of them weren't together. The girl might be with the officer on her other side. Then Harry leaned over and said something in her ear. At least

Millie thought he did. She couldn't be sure because the lights were already going down.

This time the celluloid held through the credits and kept going. It was all Millie could do not to cover her eyes. Others were more squeamish. The American officer sitting in front of her was bent over with his elbows on his knees and his head in his hands. Every now and then he sat up, watched for a moment or two, then resumed his hunched position. Off to the right someone groaned. As the film wound on, others echoed the sound. Most of the audience, however, sat silent and stiff as corpses.

Suddenly there was a commotion in the front rows. For a moment she thought a fight had broken out. Then she realized someone was struggling across the row of seats to get to the aisle. People were muttering, and someone was sobbing, and the figure broke free and stumbled up the aisle toward the door. Through the darkness, she made out the girl who'd been sitting beside Harry Sutton. She recognized her because the light from the screen where a tractor was shoveling a mountain of bones into a hole in the ground glinted off her silky blond hair. She turned from the girl to the front rows to see if Harry was going to follow her. He was still in his seat.

The film ground on. She had no idea for how long. Horror distorts time. Finally the lights came up. The entire audience seemed to be holding its breath. No one spoke. This was a world for which there were no words. Heads didn't even turn. Who could look at another human being after witnessing the acts human beings were capable of?

Slowly, still silent, still not meeting one another's eyes, they began to stand. The only sound was the shuffling of shoes and boots on the cement floor as they made their way out of the theater.

She moved with them, but alone. Danger brings individuals together. Neighbors pitching in to fight fires and floods, people singing in bomb shelters, strangers sending care packages halfway around the globe. Shame isolates. She stepped into the Berlin night as if it were the blackness of the human heart she'd just glimpsed.

Suddenly she was aware of someone walking beside her. She turned her head. Harry Sutton had fallen in step. Neither of them spoke. They made their way in silence, following the twin beams of their flashlights. The Russian sector was even darker than the American and British. Nonetheless, despite the murkiness, as they got closer to the U-Bahn entrance she made out two GIs standing in front of it with two Frauleins, talking and laughing and carrying on as if the world were a benign place. What was wrong with these men? You didn't have to see the film to recognize the horror. You didn't have to have a rule against fraternization to know that a year ago those girls were sitting in movie theaters with other soldiers, cheering at newsreels of your buddies being blown up and shot down and caged behind barbed wire. You didn't have to be Jewish to rage and ache at the atrocities.

Determined to give them a wide berth, she took a step off the broken sidewalk, tripped on a piece of rubble, and stumbled forward. Harry grabbed her arm to steady her. As he did, the beam of her flashlight careened through the night and illuminated the group at the entrance to the U-Bahn. They were in the spotlight for only a moment, but that was all it took. One of the GIs was wearing David's face.

At first David hadn't seen her. He'd been blinded by the beam of light. But when she got control of the flashlight and began walking again, he recognized the silhouette immediately. He supposed there was a certain irony to that. Only after he'd been trained to identify the shapes of aircraft and other military equipment had he realized he'd been doing that with human beings all his life. The ability wasn't unusual. The world distinguishes friend from foe and everyone between by bearing and gait and a myriad of physical quirks that are identifiable without ever seeing a face. Certainly, he'd have known Millie by the straightness of her spine and the lift of her chin—their mother had been a stickler for posture—and the way she walked with her feet slightly turned out like a ballet dancer. He would have known even if he hadn't gotten a glimpse of her profile as she turned the corner.

It wasn't the first time he'd flirted with the idea of telling her. She'd worry, of course. And she'd try to talk him out of it. He remembered the weekend he'd come home from school and said he was going to enlist. She'd tried reason and tears and marshalled every argument in the book, but when he'd finally joined up a year later, she'd come around. She wasn't unreasonable, at least about anyone except herself. But he knew he wouldn't tell her. He was sworn not to. The vow hadn't been hard to keep. For one thing, he wasn't the only one involved. For another, Camp Ritchie had trained him in the habit of secrecy. According to one of his instructors, he hadn't needed much training. He was a natural.

❧

She knew something was wrong before she opened her eyes the next morning. More wrong than the uneasy feeling that she'd had a little too much to drink the night before. It was one of those vague premonitions that take shape slowly as the mind moves from sleep to wakefulness. The sense of doom is amorphous—a dire medical diagnosis, a broken love affair, a foolish act to be regretted without end—but harrowing. Then it came to her. She opened her eyes. Sure enough, beside her Harry Sutton slept the sleep of the innocent, or the sexually spent.

She was a fool. Worse than that, she was a pathetic text book case. It wasn't only the reaction to the film, though that was bad enough. Sex is a common howl of life against death. Eros and Thanatos, as he'd teased her when she'd mistaken the publisher of a pornographic magazine for a Nazi martyr. But why did she have to choose him? If only she'd gone to the film with Theo. The thought of Theo made her feel worse. Even a stranger would have been preferable. She could have forgotten a stranger. She could have pretended the incident had never happened. But Harry Sutton would be a daily reminder.

The worst part was that it wasn't only the film that had driven her to him. It was her sense of betrayal. That was where the text book case came into it. Abandoned by one man, she'd fallen into the arms of another. The fact that the first man was her brother and the faithlessness wasn't romantic or sexual didn't change matters. He'd let her down. He'd betrayed her. She'd thought he was off on intelligence missions, but he'd been sleeping with the enemy after all. He'd been committing the one act she'd persuaded herself he was incapable of. So she'd turned to the first man who'd come along. It hadn't even been lust. She could have forgiven herself that, almost. Unvarnished physical hankering would have meant she was normal, just like everyone else in this damn Occupation. No, this had been something more shameful. Need, as naked as their bodies. She'd needed to be connected to another human being. She'd needed to obliterate the feeling of being abandoned, cut loose, let down by the one person in the world to whom she was inextricably attached.

She turned over so that her back was to him. The rough Army blanket exacerbated the beard burn on her shoulder and breast. She had to get out of here. She started to sit up. If she didn't jostle the mattress, if she didn't wake him, she could get into her clothes and away from the apartment without having to face him. It would be bad enough in the office, when they were both fully dressed, when they were both in uniform, when he couldn't see the rough red patches on her skin.

She sat on the edge of the bed and leaned forward, hoping she could ease off the mattress without his sensing her movement. Behind her cellophane crackled, then a lighter snapped open and closed.

"Good morning."

She didn't turn around.

"You don't have to salute, but a civil good morning wouldn't be out of order."

Dragging the scratchy Army blanket off the bed and wrapping it around her, she stood and took a step toward the one chair in the room. The move made the beard burn on her thighs sting. The man couldn't even shave properly. She had to push the two uniforms tossed over it aside to sit. Like the rest of the apartment, the bedroom was sparsely furnished and impersonal. The only signs of its inhabitant were the books and magazines on the floor next to the bed, and on the night table his military-issue eyeglasses, a full ashtray, a pack of Lucky Strikes, and—oh, God, no—a wrapper from Army-issue condoms. She couldn't read the print from across the room, but she knew what it said. *Put it on before you put it in.* She had to get out of here.

"I take it you don't think it's a good morning," he said.

"What I think is that last night was a mistake. It never should have happened. It never would have if—" She stopped.

"If what?"

"If your Fraulein hadn't run out—" She stopped again. That wasn't what she'd meant to say. She'd forgotten the Fraulein until now. At least, she'd forgotten that Fraulein. She'd been too distraught about David's.

He propped himself up against the headboard.

"If I didn't know your hostility to the entire German population, I'd think you were jealous. But just for the record, she wasn't my Fraulein. She was with the officer on her other side."

"Why on earth did he take her to that film?"

"He thought she might find it instructive."

"Did she?"

"You were sitting behind us. You saw for yourself."

"And I bet now she's going to say she never had an inkling."

"You think that's impossible?"

"The first morning I came to work here you told me that the day a German walked into your office and admitted he was a card-carrying Nazi, the entire department would get snookered on your dime."

"Maybe she didn't want to know so she managed not to. I'm not saying that's admirable, merely possible. Would you have wanted to know in her place?"

She tugged the blanket closer around her as if the physical sting could take away the shame. "Why, every time this subject comes up, do we get into a discussion of my behavior?"

"Maybe because part of this job is putting yourself in someone else's shoes."

"Or Nazi boots."

"Pretty small boots in this case. She must have been all of seven or eight when Hitler came to power, barely fourteen when the war started."

"You know what the trouble with this Occupation is?"

"I have a feeling you're going to tell me."

"It's not an attempt at denazification or building democracy or anything like that. It's an orgy." Still holding the blanket with one hand, she gestured around the room with the other. "I'm as bad as the rest of you. But at least I'm not fraternizing with the enemy."

"Is this the way you treat a friend?"

"You think it's funny. You all do. Jack, who probably studied German at Yale with visions of Frauleins dancing in his head. My brother, David."

He sat looking at her for a moment, his eyes strangely naked without his glasses. "So that's the problem."

"What do you mean?"

"Your brother, David."

She was silent for a moment. "Did you see those two men having a grand old time with the Frauleins at the U-Bahn station last night?"

"When you almost fell?"

"One of them was David."

"For Pete's sake, Millie. It was pitch-black. For all you know, that was Uncle Joe Stalin lurking in the night."

"I saw his face when the flashlight swerved. All those nights when he didn't come home, I persuaded myself he was doing some kind of intelligence work. Now I know better."

"You don't know better. Even if it was David, and I'm not saying it was, I wouldn't be too quick to jump to conclusions."

"What other conclusion is there?"

"Ask him."

"I can't."

"Why not?"

She thought of the bitter abandoned woman she was determined not to become. She stood, picked her uniform up off the chair, and started for the door. "I just can't."

"At least now I understand what happened last night. I had a feeling it wasn't only the whisky that made me suddenly so irresistible. You didn't have enough to drink for that. Neither of us did."

She stopped and turned back. "Can we not talk about last night?"

"I don't mean the sex. I mean the rest of it."

"There was no rest of it."

"Don't you believe it. There was a lot more going on last night than the sex. Which, if you don't mind my saying, and I'm sure you do, I enjoyed thoroughly. But if you hadn't stumbled and seen your brother with that girl, you never would have ended up here. But you did see him, or you think you did, and suddenly you were, shall we say, amenable. Don't misunderstand me. I'm glad I could be of service in your hour of need. But now I understand that's all it was. Last night had to do with you and your brother. What that's about I don't pretend to know. What I do know is that it had nothing to do with me."

She pulled the blanket tighter, though it was like a hair shirt against her bare skin.

"Wuzza, wuzza, did I hurt the major's feelings?"

He took a deep drag on his cigarette and sat staring at her for a long moment. Then he picked his glasses up off the night table, slipped them on, and went on staring.

"You know, Millie, for a nice girl, sometimes you can be such a bloody bitch."

❧

When she arrived at work later that morning, the door to his office was closed. She made it to her own without having to see him and stayed holed up there with interrogations until lunch. Then she slipped out quickly and walked to a mess some distance away. She didn't want to take a chance of running into him at the one closer by. When she returned, his door was still closed. As she headed for her own office, she heard Fraulein Schmidt telling someone on the phone that Major Sutton wasn't in today. She felt a flash of satisfaction. At least she'd had the guts to face him. Then Schmidt went on. "He's at headquarters in Frankfurt."

He didn't show up in the office until the following afternoon. His door was open when she went by on her way out that evening, but he didn't look up. At least she didn't think he did. She couldn't be sure, because she didn't look in.

A few days later, Fraulein Schmidt stuck her head into Millie's office to say Major Sutton wanted to see her. She reached for the compact in her handbag. It had nothing to do with that night in his apartment. What girl didn't check her lipstick before a meeting? Then she told herself she'd be damned if she would and started for his office. Werner and Jack were already there. Harry had called the three of them in to meet Theo's replacement, a man named Bill Shirley. Shirley, Harry explained, had learned his German at Stanford. He didn't even glance at Millie as he said it. Those confidences in the officers' club had never happened.

Seventeen

SHE WAS QUIET LETTING HERSELF INTO THE FLAT THAT night. She and Werner had taken their new colleague, Bill Shirley, to the Russian sector for a production of *Uncle Vanya*, and she didn't want to wake Anna and Elke. Then she realized it wasn't as late as she'd thought. The Russian sector ran on Moscow time, and she was always temporally disoriented when she came back from the future.

A lamp was still on in the parlor. Anna must have forgotten to turn it off. Years without electricity could do that to a person.

She started into the room, then stopped. David was sprawled on the ugly red sofa.

"I didn't expect you home," she said.

He turned toward her and grinned. As he did, his lip, which was crusted with a red scab, started to bleed. He raised a handkerchief to it. "Don't worry, Mil. It only hurts when I laugh."

She crossed to the sofa, sat beside him, and took his hand with the handkerchief away from his mouth. "What happened?"

"Nothing. Really. Just a fat lip. Or it will be tomorrow."

"Do you mind if I'm indelicate enough to ask how you got it?"

"I walked into a door."

"David!"

"Okay, someone took a swing at me."

"A few weeks ago I wouldn't have asked why. I thought I knew what you were up to. Now I'm not so sure."

"What made you change your mind about whatever it was you thought I was up to?"

"I saw you on the street in the Russian sector. You were with another GI and two Frauleins."

"Must have been a case of mistaken identity. The Russian sector is pretty dark."

"I had my flashlight. I was upset about the Frauleins. But I figured okay, you're my brother, not to mention a grown man, and I'm not about to sit in judgment on you. But now you're brawling in the streets too. Or did it happen in a bar?"

"The open air."

"What I don't understand is how you can spend your days doing so much good and your nights getting up to so much trouble."

"Maybe because I'm not doing so much good. I'm not doing any good. No one is. The job's too big. The problem's insoluble. Millions of homeless, stateless people no one will take in. Hunger. Sickness. Old people giving up. Babies dying. Or being killed."

This was better. This was the David she knew.

"Did I tell you the latest?" he went on. "One of the workers was on garbage duty. Guess what he found in the trash?"

"I'm not sure I want to know."

"A baby."

Her eyes widened.

"Wait, there's more. There was a mark on its throat, a pale lavender smudge that looked a lot like a thumbprint."

"That's inhuman."

"Now you get it."

"What did you do?"

"We couldn't do much for the baby, obviously. The mother was another story. It didn't take long to find her. DP camps are hotbeds of rumors." She noticed that he, like everyone else, had started abbreviating the expression, turning those miserable souls into a convenient shorthand. "Some of them are even true."

"What will happen to her?"

"What do you think should happen to a fourteen-year-old kid who gives birth all alone in a field behind the camp? Seems the father decided not to take her back to the States after all. But I bet he took the story. I can hear him now. Boy, did I have me a hot Jew babe in Berlin. A hot Jew babe. She didn't even know how babies were made, let alone what to do with the one she had. She was terrified she'd get tossed out of the camp. No parents. Not even a distant relative. No wonder she took up with that bastard. But there's a happy ending. We managed to keep her out of jail or even court. We told the officials she was mentally deranged from her experience in the camps. Not the DP camps, the concentration camps. And who's to say she wasn't? So now she's just locked up in a mental ward. Do you still want to talk about how much good I'm doing?"

"It would be worse without you."

"I doubt it."

"You think the answer is nights of debauchery?"

"Debauchery." He started to laugh again. The blood dripped down his chin onto his shirt. "Jesus, when did you turn into such a prig?"

"When you started screwing Frauleins."

"I prefer to think of it as emergency love."

"Is that supposed to be funny?"

"As a matter of fact, it was. It wouldn't kill you to let go occasionally."

She thought of Harry Sutton. Only she wasn't going to think of him. "Let go of what? Humanity? Decency! A sense of right and wrong? The memory of what happened?" She stopped.

"You think I don't remember what happened?"

"You don't behave as if you do."

Again, he thought of telling her the truth. But of course he couldn't. And then suddenly he didn't want to. He was tired of her self-flagellation. He was exhausted by her need for constant reassurance. He was fed up with her stubborn refusal of the very comfort she kept demanding.

"We didn't do anything," he said quietly.

"All right. What I did."

"That's not what I meant, and you know it. We got out. That's it. End of story." He sat staring at her for a long moment. "Did you ever think, Mil, that forgiveness, like charity, begins at home?"

"I'm supposed to forgive you for screwing the enemy?"

"I wasn't talking about forgiving me. There are two people in this conversation."

The morning after they had words about forgiveness beginning at home, David walked Millie to work. It was his way of apologizing, though he wasn't sure what he was apologizing for.

After they said goodbye in front of the building, he stood for a moment, watching her make her way up the steps and through the massive doors. Her back was straight. No, not straight, rigid. Her stride was long and purposeful, as if to deny the girlishness of those long legs and the second-position tendency of her feet. Her eyes were focused directly ahead. She thought she had herself under control. People always did when they were about to unravel.

At first Berlin had seemed like a good idea, for both of them. They'd navigate the past together. They'd rely on each other, as they always had, to lay it to rest. He should have known better. The minute she'd led him to that damn break-front in the flat and stood waiting for him to say something, he should have known better. She hadn't come back to Berlin to lay the past to rest. She'd come to wreak vengeance for it. More important, and more grievous for her, she'd come back to resurrect it. That was why she chased little girls down the street and combed the columns of *Der Weg* for survivors. More than resurrect it. She'd come back to rewrite it. If they could all be together again, her action would be undone.

※

The camp guard from Sachsenhausen recovered, fortunately for Theo, and, as Harry had predicted, would go on trial. In certain circles Theo was something of a hero. The Army was of a different opinion. They wanted him out of Germany. He wasn't sure where he was being sent—he'd find that out when he got his orders in Frankfurt—but he knew he wasn't headed anywhere desirable. "Do we have a base in the Antarctic?" he joked with Millie that afternoon on the way to the Anhalter Bahnhof.

She'd been dreading seeing him off. Not because she was sorry he was going. If anything, she was relieved. The newsreel of his boot connecting with the man's head while he counted off family dead was still playing in her mind. It got uglier each time. She wanted to stop seeing it. She wanted to stop seeing him. That was the problem. She was afraid her eagerness to say goodbye would wound him. She was even more afraid saying goodbye in the Anhalter Bahnhof would undo her.

She'd managed to avoid the station since she'd returned to Berlin. It hadn't been difficult. The building was in ruins, much of it still flooded, and no trains had been running until recently. Now, as she and Theo made their way through the exposed girders of what used to be an impressive public building, a cold drizzle fell on the rubble. She'd steeled herself for the tattoo of her heels on the marble floor, the echo of her mother's years ago. Her footsteps made no sound in the dirt. She'd girded herself against the ghosts of the crowd rushing beneath the soaring roof, but there was neither roof nor crowd beneath, only a handful of travelers and several beggars, some of them missing arms or legs. That part was unchanged. There had been beggars then too, maimed and wounded in a different war.

She and Theo stood on the platform, uneasy in each other's presence and their own skins. He'd sensed the change in her. But neither of them could admit it. They promised to write. They made vague plans to meet. They tried to hide their discomfort at the long goodbye and their eagerness for it to be over.

Then suddenly it was. She turned and started back down the platform, moving at a brisk clip. She refused to be intimidated. She stepped through the charred remains of what used to be the door to the interior of the station. Her breath caught in her throat. She stopped, inhaled, exhaled, a second time, a third. That was better. She began walking again. That was when she noticed the people, first only a handful, then a crowd, then an onslaught bearing down on her. She stopped, leaned against a girder, and closed her eyes. She must be imagining things. Fifteen minutes earlier the station had been almost empty. She opened her eyes. The crowds were still coming. Men were pushing, and women were rushing, and children were struggling to keep up. She was trying to dodge them, but each time she moved one way to avoid collision, she managed to crash into someone else. She was running now, the charred ruins swirling around her, the broken floor shifting beneath her feet. Suddenly the ground came up to meet her, and her head shuddered with the blow.

An air of hysteria hung over the waiting room, shrill and ugly as the black swastikas on red and white buntings that snapped in the wind whipping through the station. People raced for trains, trailed by porters laden with luggage. Others hurried in the opposite direction toward the throbbing city that beckoned beyond the exits. Men in fedoras and homburgs marched to the beat of a new Germany, scrubbed clean by Hitler and his henchmen of the shame of defeat. Women in calf-grazing skirts and slouch-brimmed hats hurried toward shops and cafés and assignations. Soldiers strutted in their uniforms, demilitarization a bad joke they could laugh at now. Boys in short-panted imitations of the uniforms danced in their wake. There were beggars, there are always beggars, war-wounded veterans dragging maimed bodies and hopping on crutches and propelling themselves on wagons, every one of them with an old field cap held out for contributions. Announcements of arrivals and departures boosted the noise to cacophony.

"*Schnell*," her father called above the noise. "Hurry," he added in the language he was rushing toward. He was careful to avert his eyes from the soldiers who strode by, though the Iron Cross was heavy in his breast pocket. They had no need for porters. Each of them carried a single suitcase, or rather three of them did. Her father clutched two, his own and Sarah's. They held their own passports too, each stamped with a large J for *Juden* and the words *Gut nur für Auswanderung*. This dividing up of things was unprecedented. On family holidays, their father always carried everything, passports, money, even maps. He'd never trusted anyone else with them.

They made their way, fought their way really, through the crowd, her father leading the way with the two suitcases, her mother holding Sarah's hand, Meike and David keeping close behind them. Every now and then, her mother turned to make sure they were there. Once when two soldiers came between her parents and Sarah in front and David and her behind and their mother lost sight of them, she stopped dead. "*Schnell*," her father barked, and Meike and David snaked around the soldiers and caught up with them.

The long wooden benches in the waiting room were crowded with travelers. Her father found space at one end for her mother and Sarah. After a few minutes, another train was announced and the man sitting beside her mother stood, picked up his suitcase, and headed toward the platform. Their father gestured to Meike to take the seat. She shook her head. She could see the mustache of perspiration on her father's face, despite the cold air blowing through the entrances to the station.

"You take it, Papa. David and I are fine here."

They went on standing against the wall, their suitcases at their feet. A few minutes later, another train was announced.

The man beside her father remained where he was, but the couple on the other side of the man stood and moved off. Some people would have noticed they were a family and slid down to let them sit together, but this man didn't seem to. He was too engrossed in his newspaper. It was the *Völkischer Beobachter.*

"Should I ask him to move?" David whispered.

"Don't look for trouble," Meike said, and they took the two seats at one remove from Mama and Papa and Sarah.

Eighteen

⁓

THE MPs ON DUTY IN THE ANHALTER BAHNHOF took her to the 279th Station Hospital on the Unter den Eichen. A year ago the beds had been filled with the wounded heroes of the Thousand-Year Reich, the Waffen-SS. Now American doctors and nurses like her friend Mary Jo were treating American GIs and German civilians. She insisted she didn't need medical care. She certainly didn't need a hospital. She'd tripped over some rubble. The most serious wound was to a new pair of nylons. She showed the MPs the holes in her stockings. She was hoping her legs, not in a class with Betty Grable's but passable all the same, would do the trick. The MPs took in her legs but were adamant. The doctor was too.

"I'm fine," she told him after he'd examined her.

"Have you ever heard the word *concussion*?" he asked and told her he was sorry, but those were the rules. He couldn't release her on her own. Someone had to come for her.

Her first thought was Anna, but the week before, she and Elke had moved into a small flat of their own, without Frau Kneff. They'd been lucky to get the apartment. A telephone was out of the question.

She called David's office. The woman who answered the phone said he was at Schlachtensee.

"You see what I mean," Millie told the nurse. "Schlachtensee is handling the arrival, medical examinations, and delousing of two hundred displaced persons a day," she quoted David's figures, "and you won't let a woman with holes in her stockings leave on her own reconnaissance."

"Those are the rules," the nurse echoed the doctor.

"I have a friend, a nurse here, Mary Jo Johnson."

"I know Mary Jo," the nurse said. "She's on duty in the wards now."

Millie had the feeling the mention of being on duty in the wards was intended to shame her. It succeeded. She had no choice but to call her office. Fraulein Weber answered the phone. At least it wasn't Schmidt. Sullenness was preferable to gloating. She asked to talk to Captain Kahn, Captain Craig, or even Captain Shirley. Fraulein Weber said they were all in interviews and managed to sound as if Millie had some nerve asking. She explained that she was calling from the 279th Station Hospital on the Unter den Eichen. Weber didn't say anything to that.

"I need someone to sign me out," Millie went on. "I'm really fine, but apparently that's Army regulations." Another silence from Fraulein Weber. "Please tell Captain Kahn or Captain Craig or Captain Shirley when they finish their interviews."

Harry Sutton turned up twenty minutes later.

"I'm sorry," she said as soon as he walked through the door, "but the doctor wouldn't release me on my own."

"What happened?"

"Nothing. That's why all this is so silly. I tripped in the Anhalter Bahnhof."

"Are you all right?"

"I'm absolutely fine. The only casualty is a new pair of nylons." This time she didn't demonstrate the damage.

He raised his eyebrows. "I grant you the Occupation is a bureaucratic mess, but people don't usually get taken to the hospital for a simple fall and torn stockings." He turned to the nurse and held out his hand for the papers. "I'm the commanding officer."

The nurse gave him the papers. He stood looking down at them, then lifted his eyes to her. "This says you fainted. There's also something about a possible concussion."

"I did not faint," she insisted. "I tripped."

"If that's your story you stick to it." He put the file down on the desk, bent over the release, and began to sign it. Suddenly his head snapped up. "Are you sure? No other symptoms?"

It took her a moment to catch on. She wished the floor would open up and swallow her. No, she wished it would swallow him. "Damn it, Harry, it's been twelve days. Symptoms, as you so delicately call them, do not turn up in twelve days." At least she didn't think they did. She had no firsthand experience. But his insinuation infuriated her.

He went back to signing the release papers, but now he was smiling. "Nice to know you found the night so memorable that you're measuring time by it," he said under his breath.

He really was a bastard.

She didn't look at him as they went down the steps of the hospital and past the bullet-pocked façade to the street where Private Meer was waiting in the jeep, but she could tell he was still smiling.

When they pulled up in front of the building on Riemeisterstrasse, he glanced at his watch, then told Meer not to wait.

"I'm fine," Millie insisted.

"The order was to see you home. Besides, it's too late to go back to the office." He followed her up the stairs and into the apartment.

"I'm home now. Thank you."

"You're welcome." He walked past her into the parlor and sat on the sofa, staring at the breakfront. "That's quite a piece."

"Confiscated goods."

"What makes you so sure?"

"My mother—" She stopped. "Look around you. The place reeks of *kleinbürgerlich* stolidity. Except for that. It stands out like a sore, or rather a gorgeous, thumb."

"Maybe it's a fake."

"That's what the woman tried to tell me when I requisitioned the place. It's the real thing."

"You're sure?"

"Absolutely."

"Bryn Mawr art history?"

"Something like that."

He leaned back and looked from the breakfront to her. "Do you want to tell me what happened to make you faint in the station? I'm not asking for personal reasons. We've established that. But I'm supposed to be concerned about the physical and mental health of my staff."

"I told you. I keep telling everyone. I stumbled on a piece of rubble. For all I know, some *Trümmerfrau* left it there intentionally to trip up an unsuspecting Jew."

He went on staring at her for a moment. "The fall may not have hurt you, but you've contracted the disease."

"What disease?"

"Hatred."

She looked away, then back. "I'm sorry I can't be as forgiving as you."

"I'm not forgiving."

"Then what do you call it?"

"Uncertain."

"Of which Germans deserve clearance and which don't?"

"Of myself. Of what I would have done under the circumstances." He hesitated. "Of what I did under the circumstances."

The statement surprised her. "What did you do?"

"Nothing. That's the point. That's what most of us, Jews as well as Germans, were guilty of. Turning away. Averting our eyes. And each time we did, the next time became easier. The other side of the coin of the Nazi laws. They persecuted in increments. First Jews couldn't intermarry, then they couldn't go to school, then they couldn't own anything. And each time we said, oh, this isn't so bad. We can live with this. We can wait it out. We're accustomed to waiting it out. We're Jews. Just be patient and mind your own business. For me it started in the schoolyard. My third year at the *Gymnasium*. That just happened to coincide with Hitler's first year in power. One of the boys had got sick. Shades of the incident with you and the soap. The teacher on duty in the yard that day taught racial history. I can still see him stomping around in that bloody Nazi uniform as if he was on parade. There was one other Jewish boy in the class. A sad kid really. He'd had polio and wore a brace on one leg. I wasn't particularly nice to him. It was hard enough being a Jew. I didn't want to be the Jew who was the only friend of the crippled Jew. The Nazi told him to clean up the mess, though he'd had nothing to do with causing it. I drifted to the other side of the yard. I didn't want to be anywhere near what I knew had to end badly. What was already ugly. But that didn't stop me from keeping an eye on it. I can still see the boy, his bad leg dragging behind him, as the teacher hauled him to the spot. Another boy followed them. Unlike me, he had a spine. He started to help the crippled boy. The teacher was a big bruiser. The slap to the back of the boy's head sent him sprawling into the vomit. Then he did the same to the boy with the brace. 'I ordered the Jew to clean it up,' he barked, 'and the Jew will clean it up.'"

"None of that was your fault. You didn't do anything."

"Exactly my point. All that was necessary was not doing anything. That's what a lot of the people we interrogate are guilty of."

"What of the ones who did do something? The ones who committed crimes or at least offenses?"

"I have a feeling we're not talking about the people we interrogate."

She didn't say anything.

"Come on, Millie. What did you do? Turn in Jews? Cavort with Nazis?"

She still didn't answer.

"I don't know what made you faint in the station this afternoon—"

"I keep telling you, I didn't faint."

He held up his right hand, palm toward her. "Okay, what you were running away from so fast that you fell, but I'll put money on the fact that it was more than Nazi ghosts."

"Thank you, Dr. Freud."

"Why are you really here, Millie? And don't give me that song and dance about all those *Fragebogen* that need to be translated or how grateful you are to Uncle Sam for taking in you and your brother."

She was silent again.

"I haven't given you a copy of *Der Weg* in weeks, but I keep seeing it on your desk."

"You can't blame someone for hoping."

"You're right, you can't. But I have a feeling it's more than that."

"Your feeling is wrong." She stood. "But thanks for springing me from the hospital all the same." She started for the door.

He stood and followed her. When they reached it, she turned and held out her hand. "I mean that. Really. I'm grateful."

He took her hand. "The world hasn't seen this much comity since Elbe Day." He went on holding her hand. "Except if I remember correctly, in the photograph of the American captain and his Russian counterpart meeting beside the Elbe, the two soldiers had their arms around each other."

"Everyone knows that picture was staged for the press. And the last thing we need is a replay of that night in your apartment." She withdrew her hand. "All the same, I'm grateful."

A few days later, Mary Jo stopped by Millie's office and asked if she'd like to have lunch. Mary Jo didn't go on duty until that evening. They walked a few blocks to a large mess with a smaller lounge that was so thoroughly Americanized Millie felt as if she were stepping into Schrafft's back in Philadelphia.

"I hear you fainted in the Anhalter Bahnhof."

"What did the MPs do, send out an all-points alert? I didn't faint. I tripped on some debris."

"Are you okay?"

"I'm fine. But how did you find out about it?"

"You mentioned my name to the nurse."

She'd forgotten that. "I'm sorry."

"Don't be. I wish I could have helped."

"Thanks. But I'm fine now," Millie repeated.

"Dr. Pinsky said he was concerned about a concussion."

"Who's Dr. Pinsky?"

"The doctor who examined you."

"I know this is the Army, but is my medical record an open book?"

"After the nurse said you'd asked for me, I told him we were friends."

"And that was all it took?"

Mary Jo's smile gave her away. That and the deepening of the freckles on her nose and cheeks.

"Dr. Pinsky is the doctor you've been seeing?"

The freckles flared more brightly. "Did you like him?"

"I'm sure he's very nice, though I suspect I didn't see him at his best. Or maybe it was only that he didn't see me at my best. Can I ask how serious this is?"

"He's talking about marriage."

"Wow. Dr. Pinsky is a fast worker."

"Only I'm not sure."

"Judging from that blush, you look pretty sure to me."

"Oh, I'm sure of the way I feel. And I think I'm sure of the way he feels."

"Then what's the problem?" Millie asked, though she was beginning to have an inkling.

"My family."

"I take it there are few if any Pinskys in Friendship, Indiana."

"When I told my mother about him, she wrote back

asking what kind of a name was Pinsky. My father thought it sounded Jewish, but she told him it couldn't be. Our Mary Jo would never do that to us was the way she put it."

"So are you going to do that to them?"

"I don't know."

"What does Dr. Pinsky say? I can't go on calling him Dr. Pinsky. What's his first name?"

"Phil. Philip. Isn't that lovely. He says it means lover of horses."

"What does Lover-of-Horses have to say?"

Mary Jo dropped her eyes. "I don't know. I haven't had the nerve to tell him. I don't want him to think my family is . . ." Her voice drifted off.

"Anti-Semitic?"

"They're not. Not really." She looked at Millie pleadingly. "What do you think I should do?"

"I don't know, but I do know one thing. When you get around to telling Phil, he isn't going to be surprised."

Mary Jo was the one who looked surprised. "You think he knew all along how they'd feel?"

"I'd put money on the fact that he's been fighting this battle all his life."

A German waitress in a pale blue uniform with a white apron came to take away their plates, then returned with the check. "Look on the bright side," Millie went on as they put their American money on the table. "You wanted to see the world."

"That's what my mother's going to say," Mary Jo answered as they stood. "And she'll remind me she always predicted it would end in disaster."

Nineteen

❦

AT FIRST SHE THOUGHT SHE WAS DREAMING THE BANG-
ing on the door. It had never happened to her, but she'd
heard enough stories from others to have it seared into her
unconscious. Fists hammering in the middle of the night.
Doors being broken in at dawn. Catch them when they're
home. Get them in their nightclothes. Round them up
when they're most vulnerable. Even when they were dressed,
packed, and waiting, having been informed of the day and
even the hour, the brutes liked to bash their way in, shouting
and smashing and using their rifles to prod grandmothers
and three year olds and everyone between. But this was no
dream. She was fully awake, and the pounding on the door
was still going on.

She swung her feet to the floor, grabbed her robe, and
started down the hall. The door was vibrating from the blows.
She pulled it open.

Three men stood on the landing, David in the center with
his arms around the shoulders of the other two, propped up
by the other two. She didn't recognize the man on the right,
but Harry Sutton was on the left. David hung between them,
his head down, his hair falling over his eyes, his tie looped
around one leg, a dark stain on the front of his trousers. In

the dim light of the outside landing she couldn't tell if it was vomit or urine.

"It must have been some party," she said, then turned to Harry. "Somehow I expected better of you."

"Would you have preferred we left him for the MPs to bring home? Which way to his bedroom?"

She stepped aside and pointed down the hall. "Past the parlor and kitchen," she said. "The door on the right."

Still propping him up between them, they started down the hall. He wasn't so much moving his feet as letting them drag behind him. That was when she saw it. The toes of his shoes were spreading the trail. It wasn't vomit or urine. She switched on the light to make sure. It was blood. And his tie wasn't hanging from his leg. It was tied tightly, like a tourniquet.

She caught up with them. "What happened?"

"I'll explain later," Harry said as they maneuvered David through the door to his room. "Do you have a scissors?"

"Why?"

"For Christ sake, Millie, just get the scissors!"

She went to the kitchen, rattled through a drawer, and carried the scissors back to the bedroom. They'd managed to get David onto the bed. He was muttering curses under his breath; and the other man was murmuring to him to take it easy, breathe deep, just take it easy; and Harry was grabbing the scissors from her. Starting at the ankle, he cut a line up David's trouser leg to the point where the tie was cinched, then peeled back the fabric. The entire thigh was covered with blood.

"It's not as bad as it looks," Harry said.

"He's right, Mil," David gasped.

"We need a doctor." She wasn't shouting, but she came close. "We have to get him to a hospital."

"No hospital," David muttered. "Too many other people."

"There's a doctor on the way," Harry said. "Stopping at the hospital first to get what's necessary."

"What's necessary for what?" Now she was shouting. "Would someone please tell me what's going on?"

"To remove the bullet," Harry said. "It's just a flesh wound. It didn't hit bone or anything."

She whirled on him. "Where did you get your medical training, Major?"

"He's right," the other man said without looking up. He was too busy tightening the tie around David's thigh.

This time David's gasp was sharper.

"Sorry, old buddy, but it has to be tight to do any good."

"And before you ask Sergeant Roth where he got his medical training," Harry said over the knocking on the door to the flat, "he was a medic in the war."

He left the room and was back in a moment with a man in an Army uniform carrying a black leather doctor's bag.

She was never able to put the events of the next hour, or was it longer, in any kind of sequence. The smell of alcohol and the glint of the light from the bedside lamp bouncing off the forceps; the whiteness of the gauze against the red blood; David's eyes wide with pain in his dirt-smeared face as the doctor bent over him; his sharp intake of breath and the sound of metal against metal as the bullet dropped into the bowl. Then the sergeant was winding a bandage, and the doctor was snapping closed his bag, and Harry was following him out of the room. She caught up with them in the hall and started firing questions at the doctor.

"He's going to be fine," the doctor said. "He'll barely have a scar. I gave him something to sleep now. He'll be up and around before you know it."

"You don't have to write this up, do you, doc?" Harry asked as he walked the doctor to the door.

"Write what up?" the doctor answered. Then he and the sergeant were gone, and she and Harry were standing face-to-face in front of the closed door.

"Somehow I expected better of you," she said again. "I'm not sure why, but I did."

"Better than what?"

"Whatever happened tonight."

"What do you think happened tonight?"

"Whatever it was, I'm pretty sure it involved Frauleins and something else illegal or you wouldn't have asked the doctor not to report it."

He shook his head and grinned, but he wasn't smiling. "Talk about jumping to conclusions. Maybe you and Wallach deserve each other."

"What am I supposed to think?" she said, but he was already on his way to the parlor.

"I'll tell you if you give me a chance, but do you mind if I sit down while I do it? It's been one bloody hell of a night."

She followed him. He sat on the sofa, leaned back, took off his glasses, rubbed his eyes with his thumb and forefinger, then put them on again.

She was still standing.

"You're right about one thing," he said. "What went on tonight was illegal, but not in the way you think. Tonight, and all those nights you thought David was out romancing Frauleins, he wasn't, though I suppose there was some romance involved. There always is with cloak-and-dagger stuff."

"Is this your idea of explaining things?"

"David is part of a network of Jewish GIs. They weren't happy with all the bureaucratic red tape and international squabbling. The Brits are determined to stop illegal immigration to Palestine. The French are more sympathetic but have no money. The Russkies, on the other hand, are eager to get rid of as many Jewish DPs as possible, both in their sector and on the Polish side of the border. And with the threat of repatriation of more Polish DPs, the Jews are desperate to get out of Europe. Talk about euphemisms. The Occupation calls it repatriation. The Polish government says it's harassment of the Polish people. That's the term they use when Jews try to reclaim stolen property. The penalty is a fine of twenty thousand *zloty* to be paid in ten days—under threat of execution. Not to mention the less official pogroms that are beginning to break out again. So David and the sergeant who was here tonight and a handful of other men set up a smuggling ring."

"I don't understand how smuggling cigarettes is going to save Polish Jews."

"They're not smuggling cigarettes. They're using the cigarettes to bribe the guards. Three hundred cartons per trip. Every few nights several 'liberated' army trucks filled with siphoned gas leave Berlin for Stettin in the Soviet zone. By the time they arrive there six or seven hours later, a few hundred or more Jews are lined up on both sides of the German-Polish border. Then all hell breaks loose. Jews rush the border. Guards collect their cigarettes. People pile into trucks. Each one is supposed to carry fifty people. Twice that number usually manage to crowd in."

"I still don't understand how David got shot."

"Apparently tonight some guards who weren't in on the

deal showed up as the trucks were about to pull out. They started shooting. David was just swinging up into the driver's cab."

"You saw all this?"

He shook his head. "I'm not part of the operation, but the men who run it keep some of us more or less informed so we can cover their backs in cases like this. When word does leak up to the brass, it's our job to persuade them that a controlled flow of refugees through the American zone and on to Italy and Palestine is preferable to the chaos of thousands of DPs trying to get there on their own."

"That still doesn't explain those Frauleins he was with that night after the film."

"For Christ sake, Millie, you have Frauleins on the brain. Maybe they were Poles he met on one of his smuggling ventures. Not every girl with blond hair is German."

"Why didn't you tell me this before?"

He shrugged. "It wasn't my place to."

"Why didn't David?"

He stood. "I think that's something you should ask him." He started for the door. "Or better still, yourself."

She was sitting beside his bed when he opened his eyes the next morning.

"I'm sorry."

"One more thing to blame yourself for? You didn't fire the gun, Mil. And before you start beating your breast in mea culpas, don't you want to ask how I feel?"

"I'm sorry. Again. How do you feel?"

"Fine. Hungry."

"Are you allowed to eat?"

"It's a flesh wound. No damage to body organs. I can eat. I can drink. I can smoke. I can still get up to the trouble you were sure I was getting into nightly."

"I never should have doubted you."

"Let's just say you tend to be a little hard on people. But not nearly as hard as you are on yourself."

She stood and asked him what he wanted for breakfast.

"Whatever you're making, and lots of it."

Twenty

⁓

HE WASN'T SPRAWLED WITH HIS FEET ON THE DESK OR
even leaning back in the swivel chair. He was hunched over
with his head resting on his hand studying what looked like
photographs. She knocked on the open door. He looked up
at the sound and, when he saw her, pulled open the center
drawer and swept the pictures or whatever they were into it.

"I didn't mean to interrupt," she said.

"You're not," he answered as he closed the drawer.

"I just wanted to thank you again. For last night."

"You're welcome. But for the record, it's not again. You
never thanked me last night."

"I'm sorry. I was distraught."

"That's one way to put it."

"But I am grateful."

"Think nothing of it. Taking care of Mosbach medical
emergencies has become part of the job. Who knows? If I play
my cards right, it may even boost me up a notch in pay grade."

She managed a smile.

"How's David?"

"Fine. Back at work in a few days. For all I know he'll be
making those night drives to Stettin again too, but he's still
playing his cards pretty close to his vest about that."

"He has to. He's not the only one involved."

"Gee, I didn't know that."

"I thought you came in here to thank me."

"I did, but it's hard to thank a man who's so damn patronizing."

He smiled. "So I've occasionally been told."

She was surprised. "You mean I'm not the only one?"

"Are you disappointed?"

Damn him. "Of course I am, Major. I was hoping for a special place in your heart."

She started to leave, then turned toward him again. "And now you can go back to those top secret photographs you shoved into the drawer when you saw me."

The smile slid from his face.

"That was supposed to be a joke," she said, but on the way back to her office she remembered the photo of Dachau that the German interrogee had insisted was a picture of Dresden. Whatever he'd been looking at was either highly classified or even grimmer than those photographs of camp dead, though she couldn't imagine anything could be grimmer than that.

❧

A few days later he walked into her office carrying what looked like several photographs, but she was more surprised by his presence than what was in his hand. Except for the instance when he'd brought the Persil letter from Anna, he usually sent Fraulein Schmidt or Weber to summon her to his office. He closed the door behind him, stood for a moment looking uncomfortable, then sat in the chair on the other side of her desk.

"How are things going in your neck of the denazification woods?"

The question made her wary. He hadn't come to her office

and closed the door behind him to ask her how things were going.

"Fine."

"No one giving you trouble?"

"No more than usual."

"I did tell you about that buzzer in the well of your desk. The one that rings in the guard room."

"You told me the first morning I came to work."

"Just wanted to make sure."

He looked at the photographs he was still holding, though they were facedown, and he couldn't see them any more than she could. Then he unbuttoned the breast pocket of his uniform jacket, slid them in, and buttoned the pocket.

"Anything else?" she asked.

"Do you remember that day we went to the center where they store the Nazi Party records?"

"I'm not likely to forget it. It made my blood run cold. But it led to Elke."

"How are they doing?"

"Fine. Or at least as well as can be expected."

He started to unbutton his pocket again, then changed his mind. She'd never seen him so nervous.

"You asked that day if all the Kraut records were as good as the ones for party membership." He hesitated.

"And you told me never to go into intelligence work."

He tried for a smile but didn't quite make it.

"And you were probably right," she went on, "because I seem to be having quite a time getting whatever you came in here for out of you."

"That's because I'm not sure if it's a good idea."

"I won't know unless you tell me what it is."

"An old buddy of mine has a pretty nasty assignment."

"Is there any other kind in this Occupation?"

"This is worse than most." He hesitated again. "Concentration camp records."

The sound of her own intake of breath startled her.

"He found my mother," he went on. "He even found my father, though I didn't need that. I knew it before I left. My mother lasted until '42."

"I'm sorry." The inadequacy of the words made her feel worse every time she uttered them.

"I asked him to keep an eye out for some other names. Uncles, aunts, cousins." He hesitated again. "And Mosbach."

Once more the sharp intake of breath didn't seem to come from her.

"I hope you don't mind."

It took her what felt like forever to get the words out. "I'm grateful."

His hand went to his pocket again. She watched his fingers undo the button. He took out the photographs. She didn't understand. She wanted to know, but she wasn't sure she wanted to see. No, she was sure. She couldn't face that.

He leaned across the desk and held them out to her. "I could have asked him just to write down the information, but I had a feeling you'd want to see the actual entries. These are photos of them."

She sat looking at him, paralyzed. She'd wanted to know. She had to know. But suddenly on the verge of knowing, she wasn't so sure. As long as she didn't have certainty, she had hope. More than hope. Stolen moments.

She remembered an autumn dusk at school. It must have been six or seven months after the letter from her father arrived. She'd been heading one way through Pembroke Arch, and a man had been coming toward her from the other direction. The arch was dim even on sunny days. Now it was shrouded in shadows. But she didn't need light to make out the form. She recognized the tilt of head under the fedora, the forward thrust of body, and the quick impatient step. It would be just like him to surprise her. She began to run to meet him. She was almost upon him when a girl burst out of Pembroke West and threw her arms around the man. "Daddy," she cried.

Harry was still leaning toward her holding out the photographs. Somehow she managed to lift her arm to take them from him.

"Do you want me to stay or would you rather be alone?"

She didn't answer. That was when he realized she was already alone. He decided to stay.

She put the photographs down on her desk but didn't look at them immediately. She couldn't. She didn't know how long she sat that way, staring not at the photographs but at Harry Sutton, though she wasn't seeing him. He knew that but went on sitting there.

Finally she looked down. The photograph on top was of a few lines from a ledger. The picture was a little blurry, but she could make out the writing. It was in a legible record keeper's hand.

The Jew Max Israel Mosbach died of heart failure July 8, 1943.

She sat staring at it. Heart failure. Wouldn't that be swift? Perhaps even painless? She knew she was clutching at straws, but what else did she have to hang on to?

She lifted the top picture off and sat staring at the one beneath it.

The Jew Gerda Sarah Mosbach died of heart failure June 29, 1943.

Heart failure. The coincidence was too much. Still, didn't that mean her mother hadn't suffered either?

She slid the photograph to the side and sat staring at the last one.

The Jew Sarah Mosbach died of heart failure May 9, 1941.

Heart failure? She calculated the years. At eleven?

Somehow he knew what she was thinking. "The cause doesn't mean anything," he said.

She looked up. She'd forgotten he was there.

"What?"

"The Krauts kept meticulous records, all right. Pages and pages, ledgers and ledgers of accurate names and dates. But the causes are pure fiction. That was their idea of shielding themselves from history's judgment. They weren't about to admit the real causes. They're not in the record. And who knows, maybe it's better they're not."

"What?" she said again. She was having trouble making sense of any of it.

"Or maybe it's worse. The human imagination can be more terrible than reality. Though I doubt that's the case here." He stood. "I'm sorry," he said.

She didn't answer.

"But I thought you wanted to know."

She still didn't say anything.

He started for the door, then stopped and turned back. "Was I wrong?"

She went on looking at him.

"No," she said finally. "I wanted to know."

❧

After he left, she sat staring at the photographs spread out on her desk. The names were accurate, he said, and the dates.

Where had she been in the summer of 1943? Working at the
magazine, living in that tiny apartment with two roommates.
What had she been doing in June and July? No weekends on
Long Beach Island, not with gas rationing. There had been a
victory garden on 17th Street. Sometimes she and her roommates had pitched in on weekends. Every Thursday evening
she'd volunteered at the hospital. And there had been other
girls' brothers and cousins and friends of friends, officers and
enlisted men, coming through town. It was a patriotic duty
to sit across a table from them hanging on every word, and
foxtrot and rhumba and jitterbug with them, and go just far
enough, as the saying went, to cheer them up, because who
knew if they'd come back, but not give them the wrong idea.
The days and weeks of that early summer merged into a single memory, shadowed by the constant hunger for mail. For
weeks she didn't hear a word from David, then she'd come
home from work and pry open the mailbox in the vestibule
of the building to have two or five or six letters spill out. But
try as she might, she couldn't attach a specific memory to June
29th or July 8th.

She looked at the third photograph. May 9, 1941. More
than two years earlier. Why had Sarah been the first to go?
But maybe that was better. At least she hadn't been left alone.
She'd had her mother to the end. Or had she? There was no
reason to assume they'd been together.

She looked at the date again. 1941. She was still in school.
More than a year away from graduation. The beginning of
May. The campus greening. Classes moving outdoors. Groups
of girls sprawled on the grass beneath the blooming cherry
trees, blushing with the promise of the season and the reflected color of the blossoms, while a professor lectured on
Tintoretto or the French Revolution or George Eliot. The

memory stopped her. She looked at the date again. May 9, 1941. That was the night Miss Albright had taken her to dinner at the College Inn to celebrate. While Sarah had been filing naked and terrified into a gas chamber, or inhaling her last diseased breaths, or counting off in a sadistic game of shoot the tenth or fifth or second person in line, she'd been preening in her paltry little triumph. This was worse than the moment so many years ago in the Anhalter Bahnhof. No, nothing was worse than that. This compounded it.

❧

She didn't know what she was doing in the station. She had no reason to be here. She wasn't going anywhere. She wasn't seeing anyone off. She didn't even know how she'd gotten here.

This time it wasn't raining as it had the afternoon she'd said goodbye to Theo. The sky was a scrim of fast-moving clouds racing over the bombed-out walls and exposed girders. There were more people, though it still wasn't crowded. Not like the mob she'd imagined that day she'd tripped, or fainted. Nowhere near like that other day almost eight years earlier. The day she'd been so quick thinking.

❧

She leaned forward to see past the man reading the *Völkischer Beobachter*. Sarah was resting against their mother's shoulder. Their father was pretending to read a newspaper. She knew it was a pretense because he kept raising his eyes from the big broadsheet to track the people coming and going. He took his watch from his vest pocket, studied it, looked up at the station clock as if his own might be wrong, then returned it to his vest pocket and went back to pretending to read the paper.

The man between her and her father turned a page of the *Völkischer Beobachter* noisily. She averted her eyes from it. She didn't want him to think she was reading over his shoulder. She didn't want him to notice her at all. And she couldn't bear to look at the paper. The hate-filled headlines in the ugly Gothic script terrified her. SWEEP OUT THE JEWISH VERMIN WITH AN IRON BROOM. JEW AS-SASSIN MURDERS NAZI OFFICIAL IN PARIS. *EIN VOLK, EIN REICH, EIN FUHRER.*

A voice came over the loudspeaker announcing another train departure. The man between her and her father folded his paper and tucked it under his arm. She took David's hand in preparation for sliding over to sit beside her parents and Sarah. As she did, she noticed two SS officers approaching. Their eyes raked the waiting passengers; the older one's cruel and dark and beady, the younger's the color that she imagined the Aegean Sea to be. Somehow the beauty of those eyes made it worse. She held her breath waiting for them to go by. Her father was still pretending to read the newspaper, but it was trembling in his grip. The officers walked slowly up the row, then turned and started down it again, studying faces as they went. The man beside her picked up his suitcase, stood, and started off. She began to slide into his place. The SS officer with the cruel eyes stopped in front of her father. She slid into the seat she'd been about to leave and nudged David back into place.

The officer demanded her father's papers. Her father reached into the breast pocket of his coat and drew out his and Sarah's passports. The officer with the Aegean Sea eyes stood behind his colleague, both of them examining the pass-ports. The first officer pivoted to her mother and demanded her papers. She took them from her handbag and held them out to him. Again, the second officer stood reading over the first's shoulder, then moved a few steps until he was standing in front of Meike and David. They looked up at him. His eyes weren't the color of the Aegean Sea. They were the icy blue of snow on a frigid day.

"Are you with the Jews?" he asked.

David went on staring from under his shock of blond hair. Meike dug her nails into her palms.

"Are you with the Jews?" the officer repeated.

"The Jews?" she said as if she didn't understand the word.

"The Jews you're sitting with."

She went on looking up at the officer. She didn't turn her head to look at her parents and Sarah. Her mind was racing. Be smart, Meike. Think quick. Answer fast.

"We're not sitting with those people. We never saw them before in our lives."

Twenty-One

୰

THIS TIME SHE FOUGHT THE MPs. OF COURSE SHE didn't know they were MPs. All she saw were two men in uniform. All she felt were four hands grabbing her. She tried to pull away. They held her in place. She flailed and kicked and pummeled. They pinned her arms and cuffed her hands. She screamed. A large sweaty hand covered her mouth. She tried to bite it. It clamped her jaw closed. They hustled her across the rubble of the waiting room, out of the station, and into a jeep. One kept her pinioned in the back while the other drove.

By the time they pulled up in front of the hospital, she'd realized they were MPs. She tried to apologize. She tried to explain. They sat straight-faced and uninterested.

She had trouble climbing out of the back seat and held her cuffed hands out to one of the MPs to be freed. He merely helped her out of the jeep.

"I'm fine, really. It was just a momentary scare."

The MP who'd refused to remove her cuffs put his hand on her elbow. His grip was not rough but firm enough to hold her. She let him lead her past the bullet-pocked walls up the hospital steps.

She recognized the doctor. He was the same one who'd seen her last time, Mary Jo's Phil. She wondered if they'd called him specially or if he just happened to be on duty.

"Hi, Dr. Pinsky," she said jauntily as he led her down the hall. "Long time, no see."

He managed a wan smile. "Hello, Captain."

She'd expected an examining room again. He held open the door to an office, indicated a chair for her, walked around the desk, and sat behind it.

"Do you want to tell me what happened?" he began.

"Why don't you tell me? One minute I was walking through the station, the next two MPs were roughing me up."

"Apparently you weren't just walking through the station. You were stopping people and shouting at them."

"That's ridiculous." She hesitated. "What was I shouting?"

"The MPs don't speak German." He sat staring at her. "Did you ever hear of battle fatigue, Millie? Do you mind if I call you Millie?"

"As Mary Jo's friend, I insist on it."

His blush wasn't as flattering as Mary Jo's. "Or shell shock?" he went on. "That's what they called it in the last war. The names change, but not the condition."

"I haven't dodged any shells or fought any battles."

"You haven't fired a gun or dropped a bomb, if that's what you mean, but according to your commanding officer—"

"What does he have to do with it?"

"I called Major Sutton. He was the one who signed for your release last time. It seemed the logical thing to do."

"Logical!" she shouted, then caught herself. It was bad enough she'd fought the MPs. She couldn't afford to make a scene in the hospital. She managed to force a laugh. "Forget Major Sutton. Maybe what I need is General Patton to slap my face and order me back into action."

This time he didn't even try to smile. "That's up to Major Sutton, but I'm going to recommend that you give up this

denazification business. If it were up to me, I'd send you back
to the States. But that's his call, not mine."

Harry was waiting for her at the nurse's desk.

"Maybe you ought to stay out of Anhalter Bahnhof." His
tone was joking, but he didn't look as if he found it a laughing matter.

She didn't answer.

He led her down the gravel path to his jeep and started
to climb in.

She stood watching him. "Where's Private Meer?"

"I know how to drive."

"That sounds ominous."

"Just get in."

"Where are we going?"

"Back to the office."

Good. He wasn't going to blow this out of proportion after all. She climbed into the jeep.

"To clear out your things," he went on. "Your denazification days are over."

Of course, David found out about the incident. The fact that
he found out so quickly meant that Harry had called him.

"I hear you had a brush with some MPs this afternoon,"
he said as he walked into the kitchen, where she was peeling
potatoes.

"Apparently you and Harry Sutton have no secrets from
each other."

He put his hand over his heart. "I owe him my life. Or at
least my leg. Not to mention getting me out, or keeping me

out of a scrape with the United States Army. What were you doing in the station?"

"I still have those lamb chops from the PX. Do you want dinner?"

He put both hands in his pockets and leaned against the counter. "Scene of the crime?"

"How many do you want? Two or three?"

"Except there was no crime."

She didn't answer.

"You did what you had to do, Mil. We both did."

She turned to face him, still holding the knife. "Not both of us. I was the one who spoke up. I was the one who denied knowing them. 'We never saw them before in our lives,'" she said in a high-pitched imitation of her younger self.

"Okay, you're right. You were the one who said it. You were the one who had the guts to say it."

"Guts. Next thing I know you'll be quoting Hemingway. Watch Meike Mosbach show grace under pressure as she denies ever knowing her own flesh and blood. Watch her run like hell for the exits."

"I ran with you."

She turned back to the counter and began chopping. "All I know is the last thing Mama and Papa and Sarah, because she was young but not so young that she couldn't understand, heard me do was betray them."

Twenty-Two

SHE HADN'T ARGUED WITH HARRY WHEN HE'D TOLD her that her denazification days were over. She'd even felt a flash of relief. She could stop reserving judgment. She could stop sitting across a desk from the scum of the earth pretending to believe equivocations and evasions and lies. But something still felt unresolved. She'd come to Berlin to find certainty. She'd found it, and buried hope. Now she had to find a way to go on without hope. She had to find a way to step into the Anhalter Bahnhof or pass a group of girls on their way to school without fainting or fighting or falling apart, and for that she had to stay on. Maybe if she found a German who really did have clean hands, if she kept as open a mind as Harry did, she could pull it off. Maybe she could learn to forgive. She decided to tell him she was ready to go back to work.

She found him in the officers' mess where he usually went for lunch, a long cavernous room in a former Wehrmacht drill hall. At one end, a stone eagle holding a laurel-wreathed swastika looked down over the rows of tables. At the other, doors to a kitchen swung open and closed as German waitresses carried trays of hamburgers and French fries and corned beef hash to the few men—it was almost two o'clock—who sat eating and smoking and watching the Frauleins come and go. Harry was sitting alone at one end of a long table. He wasn't watching the waitresses come and go. He was reading what looked like a bound official report. One hand held the pages open, the other a cigarette.

She approached the table and stood for a moment. It took him another moment to look up.

"Whatever it is, it must be riveting."

He closed the report. She glanced at the cover page. "Report on the Nazi Judiciary" was typed across it.

"Don't you ever take time off?"

"This isn't denazification. These chaps are too far gone for redemption."

She thought of asking why, in that case, he was torturing himself, but she had other matters on her mind. She pulled out the chair and sat across from him. "I've had a week off. I haven't gone near the Anhalter Bahnhof. I'm ready to go back to work."

He ground out his cigarette. "You know I can't let you do that."

"Why not? I wasn't overly zealous, no matter what you think. I tried to be fair."

"It doesn't matter what I think. It matters what General Clay thinks. Besides, you may be fair to the Germans, but you're bloody hell on yourself."

"What is all this bloody this and bloody that? I'm sure that's not the English your mother taught you."

He shook his head. "You really are impossible. You turn up here asking me to do something for you, then begin insulting me. But in this case you're right. It's an affectation. To make people like Wallach think I'm pure Oxbridge. Now you know the worst about me."

"Surely that's not the worst."

"See what I mean."

"That was supposed to be a joke."

"Go home, Millie."

"Where exactly is that?"

"I thought you were so grateful to Uncle Sam for taking you in. You and David both."

"I am. But David's here."

"He's a big boy. He can take care of himself."

"I'm aware of that."

"Boy, do I love it when you get that tone in your voice."

"All I meant was he's the only family I have."

"More than some of us."

"I'm aware of that too," she said, and this time he didn't complain about her tone of voice.

"Fine. Stay in Berlin. But get out of the revenge business. Try doing something useful."

"Such as?"

"You're the one with the Bryn Mawr degree. You figure it out."

"Thanks."

"You didn't do a bad job in the denazification office."

"Talk about damning with faint praise."

"You managed to find some decent needles in the haystack. And wasn't it your idea to team up a Social Democrat, a left-wing Catholic, and an anti-Nazi conservative to run one paper?"

"I figured they'd cancel one another out."

"That's exactly what they seem to be doing. We're either going to have an impartial newspaper or a totally nonfunctioning one."

"Does that mean I can come back?"

"It means you're not such a lousy judge of character after all, though sometimes the process damn near kills you. How would you like to go to work finding people to translate American books into German?"

"Another attempt at persuading Germans that all Americans are not barbarians?"

"It seems American literature is not as well-known to Germans as the government would like. In Munich the powers that be hired Erich Kästner to run *Neue Zeitung*. I assume you know the name."

"*Emil and the Detectives*, not to mention a lot of other novels and poetry the Nazis burned."

"Despite that, he stayed in Germany, but let's not go into that again. It turns out he'd never heard of John Steinbeck. Then again he was shocked to hear that New York City had a permanent symphony orchestra."

"He probably would have fainted if anyone told him about the Philadelphia Orchestra."

He smiled. "So you have a home after all, or at least some civic pride. The point is the government wants to start bringing out German editions of American books. It's not my purview, but Colonel Coffin asked me for some suggestions. He's setting up a team to find translators. They would have already been cleared, so you wouldn't have to get mixed up in that. Only in finding the right fit for a particular book. Hell, you might even try your hand at it yourself. Didn't you write a couple of pieces for that swanky magazine before you were dispossessed of your job?"

"While the men were away, we girls got to play."

"There's that tone again. Anyway, if you're interested I'll set up an interview with Colonel Coffin for you."

She said she was interested.

A week later she went to work in a cubby in a makeshift office on the second floor of the building where she'd worked in the denazification department. There was no crowd of Germans waiting to be interrogated. There were no Frauleins Schmidt and Weber. There were no secretaries at all, only stacks of American books, piles of German books and magazines and journals, files on the authors and translators of the latter, and two male colleagues, one of whom she'd swear was working for the Office of Strategic Services, but then again she'd been wrong about David's intelligence work.

The job was a relief. The printed word was easier to deal with than human beings. *Dodsworth* and *Babbitt* were better company than toadying or combative German petitioners. *Dodsworth* and *Babbitt* took her back to those days at Bryn Mawr when Miss Albright had held forth on Sinclair Lewis's view of small-town America. *The Jungle*, *The Brass Check*, and *The Flivver King* gave her hope that society might be capable of reforming itself after all, if someone like Upton Sinclair appeared on the scene at the right moment. She was especially eager to find the right translator for *The Flivver King* with its portrayal of the Henry Ford–inspired character's virulent anti-Semitism.

She'd been working in her new job for a few weeks when Harry Sutton turned up one Friday afternoon just as she was about to leave. She hadn't seen him since the day she'd tracked him down in the officers' mess. He asked how things were going, and she said they were going just fine. He went on looking at her for a moment, as if he didn't believe her. She hated when he did that.

"Since you're flourishing here, since we're no longer at loggerheads over collective guilt and other major policy matters of the Occupation, how would you like to drive out to Wannsee tomorrow afternoon? No arguments, no *Fragebogen*, just an afternoon in the open air. We can bury a metaphorical hatchet in the sand."

The invitation caught her off guard. Her acceptance surprised her even more. Then she remembered the night in his flat. She was getting better at keeping that at bay.

"Only an afternoon in the fresh air," he said, and she wondered if her expression had given her away.

The next day they set out under a cloudless sky through a city that was finally greening. Here and there a gritty wisteria vine, lilac bush, and even an undaunted wild rose fought its way through the rubble, insisting, in the face of all evidence to the contrary, on hope. They were both out of uniform, though he was still in khakis, and no one would mistake the yellow sundress she'd found at the PX for the pricey outfits from Nan Duskin in Philadelphia that the Bennetts used to give her for birthdays, Christmas, and no occasion other than their innate generosity. Still, the effect felt odd, as if they were masquerading as normal people in normal times.

They had no trouble finding a space to park the jeep. Except for military vehicles, Berlin was still empty of traffic. The beach, however, was crowded with GIs strolling arm in arm with Fräuleins, sprawled on blankets with Fräuleins, and tangled in embraces that stopped just short of fornication with Fräuleins. The war, the camps, even the Wannsee Conference to hammer out the final solution to the Jewish problem that had taken place in one of the nearby buildings might never have happened.

They started walking, but the sand made it difficult. She stopped to take off one of her shoes and shake it out, then a few steps later repeated the gesture with the other. He bent, unlaced his oxfords, and pulled them off. The big toe of his left foot poked through a hole in his sock. "No cracks," he said when he saw her look at it.

"I know a Frau who will darn that for three cigarettes, two if they're Pall Malls."

"And have you turn me in for employing a German? Not on your life."

She kicked off her own shoes, then instinctively turned her back to him as she unhooked her stockings from her garter belt. When she turned back, she couldn't see his eyes behind his dark glasses, but he was smiling.

"What's so amusing?"

"Your modesty."

She waited for him to make a comment about its being a little after the fact. He didn't.

They started walking again. The farther they got from the long, low pavilion, the thinner the crowd on the sand grew, though they had to swerve their course to avoid a GI and a Fraulein on a blanket. He had one hand up her skirt and the other down her blouse.

"I have a feeling this wasn't a good idea," Harry said, "in view of your feelings about fraternization."

"I can't help wondering what's going to happen in nine months, or sooner, depending on when these romances started."

"I don't think there are going to be a lot of half-German babies going back to the States, if that's what you mean. The Army makes it hard enough for the men to marry. They're not going to encourage them to take the kids home, even if they want to, which is unlikely. And I'm talking about the white soldiers. They're already making it impossible for the Negroes. The white GIs are mad as hell that they're with the Frauleins in the first place. The brass isn't about to let them sully the country they fought for with miscegenation."

"So the Frauleins will have to raise the babies on their own."

"That's the first time I heard you use the word without wrapping it in venom. Is it possible Millie Mosbach is going soft on Germans?"

"Possible, but not bloody likely, as you would say."

They walked on in silence for a while until they reached a grassy area beyond the beach with a small, pastel-painted pavilion. She stopped and stood staring at it.

It was Sarah's fifth birthday. Their mother had packed a picnic basket complete with a cake from Kranzler's. She could still see Sarah's eyes as their mother lifted it out of the hamper. The strains of "Hoch Sollst du Leben" floated over the water. Happy birthday, dear Sarah.

She sat down hard on the steps.

He sat beside her and took off his dark glasses to look at her. "Are you all right?"

She closed her eyes. The image faded. The music died. She opened them. The sun beat down through the newly leafed trees, dappling the wide expanse of lawn, bouncing off the surface of the lake, and splintering into blinding facets.

"I'm fine."

"You keep saying that. You also keep saying you don't want to go home. But maybe you should try London or Paris or Timbuktu, because I know one thing for sure. Berlin isn't doing you any good."

She didn't say anything to that.

"In the beginning, when you first showed up, I thought you were here for vengeance."

She hugged her knees and went on staring out at the water. "You weren't entirely wrong."

"Then I realized that was only part of it."

She didn't answer.

"You were searching."

"I've stopped that. Thanks to you." She swiveled to face him. "I didn't mean that the way it sounded. I'm grateful." She turned back to the lake. "In a way."

He waited, and when she didn't say anything else, he went on. "Now I think it's more than both those things." He hesitated. "Now I think it has to do with penance."

She glanced at him briefly. "I thought we came out here for a day in the fresh air, not another session with Major Freud of the U.S. Army Medical Corps."

"I ran into David at the officers' club the other night. We had a drink. He told me what happened in the station."

"The doctor told you what happened in the station. Both times."

"I mean what happened in the station originally."

She started to stand. He put his hand on her arm to stop her.

She sat again and turned back to the lake. "He shouldn't have."

"I asked him."

"He didn't have to answer."

"He's worried about you. He may be a wiz at enemy interrogation and aerial interpretation, but when it comes to the human condition, he's in over his head and he knows it."

It was what she'd thought that first night when she'd

gone through the apartment looking for him, but that was different.

"Whereas you're an expert."

"Maybe I'm worried about you too."

"He still shouldn't have told you."

"You mean he let the cat out of the bag? Revealed your deep, dark secret."

"It's not exactly something to be proud of."

"I'm not so sure."

"Okay, I'm proud of myself for quick thinking. Being so fast on my feet. Now can we drop it?"

"I don't think you were so fast on your feet."

"You're wrong. I didn't hesitate for a moment."

"How did you manage to get to the Netherlands after the incident in the station?"

She whirled from the lake to him. "The incident! Talk about euphemisms."

"The tragedy, the crisis, the crime, whatever you want to call it."

"The betrayal."

"Okay, have it your way. How did you manage to get to the Netherlands after it?"

"Didn't David tell you that too? While he was recounting the story of my life?"

"He said you took the train and crossed the border into the Netherlands."

She turned back to the lake, its surface broken into shimmering pieces by the glare of the sun. "We did. End of story."

"Didn't you have to show your passports when you got to the border?"

"Only on the Netherlands side."

"Not on the German? Isn't that a little unusual? It's not my point, but still."

"Something happened on the train. With a man in our compartment. He was a Jew. The guards decided he was smuggling something. He probably was. We all were. But when they couldn't find anything, they got angry. Hustled him off the train and beat the living daylights out of him for outsmarting them."

"But they didn't hustle you and David off? Despite the tell-tale J on your passports?"

"They never bothered to check our passports. They were too busy saving face by beating up the man. Once again, another Jew's misfortune was our good luck."

"But you had your passports. You were ready to hand them over."

"We didn't exactly have a choice."

"What I mean is you and David were each carrying your own papers as well as your own suitcases."

"We all were, except my sister, Sarah. She was too little."

"Was that usual?"

"Was what usual?"

"When you went on family holidays, did you each carry your own papers?"

"Of course not. We'd have our own luggage, but my father would carry all the papers. Even the maps." She shook her head at the memory. It almost made her smile. "He was very orderly. And we were only kids. He didn't trust us not to lose things."

"Exactly. But this was a special instance."

"That's one way to put it."

"According to David, when your father gave the two of you your papers, he also gave you instructions."

She was silent.

"Didn't he?"

"I know what you're driving at. David's been saying it for years. But he's wrong. I don't remember any instructions."

"Talk about selective memory. Come on, Millie. You just said he was very careful. Very orderly. He wouldn't have just handed you your passports without giving you instructions about them, and I don't mean only warning you not to lose them. According to David, he told you that if any of you was stopped, the others must pretend not to know him and keep going. According to David, he told you that again and again."

"He wouldn't have denied us. My mother wouldn't have either."

"That's different."

She was still staring out over the water, but she shook her head. "No, it's not."

"As you said, you and David were kids. The future. His and your mother's hope."

"What about our sister? Wasn't she the future? Wasn't she their hope?"

"I'm sure that broke his heart. Just as it's breaking yours. But better to save two of you than none. All I'm trying to say is I wouldn't take too much credit for being so fast on your feet. You're a quick thinker, but not that quick. It wasn't your idea. It was your father's. You were only following his orders, like any good German daughter. If anything, he'd be proud of you."

"You want me to take a bow for betraying them?"

"I want you to stop wallowing in self-pity. We're all ashamed. It's a condition of our survival."

"What do you have to be ashamed of? And don't tell me

about that incident in the schoolyard when you didn't stand up for the crippled boy. That was omission, not commission."

He was silent for a moment, and she turned to look at him just as he slipped his dark glasses back on and turned away from her to the lake. She looked away again too. She'd gotten only a glimpse of his expression, but it seemed indecent to go on watching him.

"There's no point in each of us having dinner alone," he said on the way back.

"You're not exactly alone in an officers' mess or club."

"Don't you believe it. Loneliest place in the world. Come on, I'll make you dinner."

"You know how to cook?"

"Don't sound so surprised. One of the jobs that got me through college was in a diner. I started out as a dishwasher and worked my way up to the lofty position of short order cook. I turn out a mean eggs over easy with bacon. But I can do better than that tonight. I just happen to have a couple of steaks from the PX languishing in my refrigerator. And before you say anything, yes, that was forethought. I was counting on the combination of a day at Wannsee and my innate charm to lure you up for dinner."

"It's the word *lure* that worries me."

"Okay, how do you feel about just letting me make you dinner?"

"I think I can handle that."

The impersonality of the flat struck her again. She didn't expect a domestic touch, but most men, even men in the military, would leave some imprint, if only a mess. He wasn't particularly neat—magazines and books were strewn around, opened packs of cigarettes lay on tables, ashtrays looked as if they hadn't been emptied since the last time the Fraulein or Frau he wasn't supposed to employ had come through—but the impression was of an apartment that could be vacated in half an hour. For the first time it occurred to her that he wasn't as easygoing about the situation as he pretended. He couldn't wait to say goodbye to Berlin.

The last rays of the afternoon sun spilled through the tall windows and cast an unforgiving light on bare walls hung with a few insipid prints of German landscapes inhabited by rosy-faced boys and girls—he couldn't possibly have chosen those—a couple of chairs, an upholstery-sprung sofa, and two cheap wood veneer end tables. The only personal effect besides the books and magazines, packs of cigarettes, and overflowing ashtrays was a tennis racket in a wooden press leaning against one wall. He watched her taking it in.

"Not exactly Biedermeier elegance," he said.

"At least there are no stolen goods."

"You're sure the piece in your flat is a confiscated real Mc-Coy, not a reproduction?"

"Absolutely."

"I take my hat off to Bryn Mawr's art history department."

She hesitated. "It's a bit more than that," she said finally. "We had a piece like that, exactly like that, in our apartment. I don't know how it ended up in the one we're in now, but I can guess."

"Have you thought of trying to reclaim it?"

"More impeccable German records?"

"They exist."

"I'm not sure I have the stomach for them."

"That sounds promising. In fact, I'll drink to it. Gin and tonics or martinis?"

"Whatever you're making."

"Gin and tonics. First of summer." He started out of the room, and as she wandered the space picking up the books he'd left around and paging through them, she heard the sound of him chipping ice in the kitchen. She was still leafing through one of the volumes when she looked up and saw him standing in the doorway watching her.

"Do you realize this is the first time I've seen you out of uniform?"

"Actually, the second."

He shook his head and smiled. "You're the one who brought it up."

"I thought I ought to clear the air."

He crossed the room and handed her one of the drinks. "Anyway, you look nice."

"Thank you."

They went on standing that way for a moment. Beyond the window, a truck rumbled by, then the room went silent again. He lifted his right hand and ran an index finger over her shoulder where the strap of her dress had slipped off.

"You got burnt."

She stood waiting. A group of boys went by, shouting in German. Then a single English sentence floated to the window. "So's your old man."

They both laughed. "Forget translations of Steinbeck. We're spreading plenty of American culture." He took his hand from her shoulder. "And I promised you dinner."

She was relieved. Really, she was. The last thing she wanted was a replay of that embarrassing night. But later, after they'd had dinner and he'd driven her home through the Berlin night that somehow didn't seem quite so forbidding in warm weather, she stood in front of the bathroom mirror, tooth-

brush in one hand, glass of purified water in the other, looking at the pale marks the straps of her dress had left and
thinking about the evening. She hadn't realized she'd gotten
sunburnt until he'd run his finger over her shoulder. The
burnt skin had felt hot and tender under the pressure. He'd
used his right hand, his undamaged hand, as she thought of
it. But who was she to talk of damage?

That was why nothing had happened this evening. Maybe
it was self-protection after that first disastrous night in his
apartment, or maybe it was simply lack of attraction to the
walking wounded. Whatever his motives, he obviously had
no intention of getting mixed up with a girl who was so hope-
lessly mixed up herself.

Twenty-Three

⤻

LATER SHE'D THINK IT ODD THAT THE THREE INCI-
dents occurred in a single day. Or maybe it wasn't odd.
Maybe she was just ready to notice.

The first took place in her office that morning when she
interviewed a potential translator. She'd been surprised to
find the woman's name on the list. According to the file, the
woman had worked translating British and American children's books into German during the first five years the Nazis
were in power. Millie was curious but decided the woman's
culpability, or lack of it, was no longer her purview. Instead
she asked the woman whether she'd ever translated anything
besides juveniles.

The woman sat very straight in the chair beside Millie's
desk—the space was too small for them to sit across from
each other—her gray-streaked hair pulled back in a tight
bun beneath an obviously prewar cloche, her hands in neatly
patched cotton gloves folded in her lap, her eyes holding Millie's steadily. She was so self-possessed Millie felt as if she
were the one auditioning.

"I started out translating scientific articles," the woman began, "then turned to children's books for my son. I wanted
him to be able to read as many different kinds of books as
possible. He was not permitted to go to school. They said he

was mentally infirm. He was not mentally infirm. He was different. He did not function well in a classroom with many other children, but he was very bright. By the time he was six, he had memorized the entire Berlin transportation system, every tram, U-Bahn, and S-Bahn, their designations, their routes, everything."

Millie looked at the file again. She'd sworn she wasn't going to inquire into the woman's political past—that wasn't her job—but old habits, old obsessions, die hard. She asked the woman why she hadn't worked after 1938.

"There was no need to translate children's books after that. My son was gone. They took him to the House of Shutters." The woman hesitated. "You have heard of it? The official name was the Hadamar Euthanasia Center."

Somehow Millie managed the futile words again. "I'm sorry."

"That is why I am applying for a job as a translator," the woman went on. "For years this country has read nothing but propaganda. Perhaps you think I am naïve to believe that a few books, a handful of words, can change the world. Can prevent more Houses of Shutters in Germany. But I have to have hope. How can you live without hope?"

Millie knew the use of the word *you* in the sentence was colloquial. Perhaps the woman was trying to demonstrate her familiarity with English idiom. The question had not been directed at her. She'd meant *one*, not Millie. How can one live without hope?

She glanced at the stack of books piled on the floor beside her desk. She'd intended to give the woman *The Call of the Wild*, but some rumor of Jack London's flirtation with eugenics came back to her. So many Progressives of that era had indulged in similar flirtations, and she was sure it didn't intrude in this particular book of his, but she didn't want to take the chance. She pulled *Main Street* from the stack of books. "The author was the first American to win the Nobel Prize for literature," she explained as she handed the woman the volume.

"You see," the woman said as she took it. "I had hope for this job, and now it has come through."

She was still thinking about the question, or the hope, of hope on her way to the Anhalter Bahnhof that afternoon. It was her third trip to the station, and she'd made up her mind that this time there would be no hysterics or mishaps. She was seeing someone off again, but this was a happy parting. Anna and Elke were leaving for Hamburg, where they would board a ship to the States. And this time she had David with her.

They were milling around the station platform, the four of them and a man named Emil Kohn. Anna had tried to discourage him from coming to see her off. She'd given half a dozen reasons, but not the real one. She was embarrassed, or perhaps only afraid. It had been a long time since anyone had fallen in love with her. And she had Elke to think of now, though that was scarcely an argument against his seeing them off. Elke was crazy about Emil. She may have had a surfeit of mothers, but she'd never known a father. Emil had promised her she would have one before long. It was only a matter of time until his papers came through, he followed them to the States, and they were a family.

Millie was happy for Anna, but surprised. She didn't understand how the damaged woman Anna had become could join this riotous orgy of marriage and hope. There was that word again. But the more she thought about it, the more logical it became. Millie would never put it into words. She would never give even an inkling of what she was thinking to David. But her reasoning made sense. Anna, and Emil because he'd been in the camps too, had earned the right to happiness. They'd paid for it with unimaginable suffering. Those who'd had it easy, who'd stood by while others suffered, who'd been responsible for others' suffering, had no such right.

She and David stood on the platform waving until they knew Anna and Elke could no longer see them, then said goodbye to Emil, who couldn't seem to tear himself away, and started back to the station.

"You sure you're going to be all right?" David asked her as they stepped into the rubble. A light drizzle was falling through the ruins of the roof.

"I'm fine," she answered, but didn't speak again until they'd made their way across the space. She was working too hard at keeping the ghosts at bay. "Are you coming home?" she asked when they were out on the street. "No pressure, I swear. I just want to know if I should make dinner."

"No need to bother."

"Another night drive to Stettin?"

He stood looking down at her. "More dangerous than that," he answered, but he was grinning. "I have a date. Not a Fraulein, in case you were worried, and I know you were. She's a Brit aid worker."

"That doesn't sound so dangerous."

"You haven't seen her. She's a knockout," he tossed over his shoulder as he started away from her.

She stood watching him go, shouldering his way through the crowd with that long, loping gait, dragging a part of her in his wake. He kept moving until only his head was visible above the throng, then turned a corner and disappeared. She felt the familiar flash of loss. But she was getting better at tamping it down. Really, she was.

He didn't turn around, though he knew she was watching him. That was why he didn't turn around. He didn't want to see her standing there outside that damn station, trapped in the memory of that damn station.

The realization had come to him early one morning as the sun inched up behind them on the long ride back from Stettin. Maybe Stettin had something to do with it. Helping others survive was a kind of justification for his own survival. But she couldn't seem to find the same vindication. And he couldn't find it for her. He could love her. He could try to be there when she needed him. But in the war against herself, he was raising the white flag. From now on, she was the lone combatant.

There was no reason for Millie to stop in Harry's office on her way out of her own that evening, except to tell him that Anna and Elke were on their way and to thank him again. It was after five, but he rarely left promptly.

She pushed open the door. The outer office was empty. The doors to the inner offices were closed. The place was silent. She was about to leave when she heard the murmur of voices. It was coming from the closet where they stored office supplies, care packages, and various items no one knew what to do with. She started in that direction. She wasn't sure why. Neither voice was deep enough to be Harry's. She was halfway down the hall when she realized the voices belonged to Fraulein Schmidt and Fraulein Weber. They were speaking in German, which they were careful not to do when others were in the office. The door to the closet was open, and Fraulein Schmidt was standing in front of the small mirror she'd had one of the men put up, her hand, holding a tube of lipstick, going back and forth over her mouth. Millie couldn't see Fraulein Weber because of the angle of the door, but she could hear her.

"I told you, Bertha, I didn't go out with Nazis, and I won't go out with Amis."

"I don't see how you're going to have any fun if you don't. Besides, the Amis are nice."

"That's what you said about the Waffen-SS. 'Oh, they're really sweet boys, Annelise.'"

"Well, they were, and so are these boys. The difference is the Amis are generous. What good is having legs like yours if you're plodding around in patched cotton stockings instead of nylons?"

"You make me sick."

"Everyone makes you sick. The Waffen-SS. The Amis. The Ivans. I know you've had some hard times . . ."

"Everyone's had hard times. I'm not asking for sympathy."

"But you can't—" Fraulein Schmidt must have glimpsed Millie out of the corner of her eye, because she stopped in mid-sentence and whirled to face her. "Did you want something, Captain Mosbach?"

"Nothing you can help with, thank you."

Fraulein Schmidt stood staring at her for a moment, then closed her tube of lipstick, dropped it into her handbag, and pushed past Millie down the hall and out the door.

Fraulein Weber came out of the closet carrying one of the

care packages and made her way to her desk. "If you want to report me, you can."

"For what?"

"The package of food."

Millie stood staring at her. "I'm not going to report you."

"If you expect me to say thank you, I won't."

"I didn't ask you to." Millie started to leave, then turned back. "You really do hate us, don't you?"

"No more than you hate Germans."

"That's different."

"Why? Because you're all good, and we're all bad. Oh, you feel so sorry for yourself. Well, look around you, Captain. You're not the only one who suffered."

"Please, Fraulein Weber, I sat in this office for five months listening to what Germany endured at the hands of the Allies. But the Allies didn't overrun all of Europe, or set up the concentration camps, or murder millions of innocent people."

"Including my father and brother."

It took a moment for the words to sink in before Millie could utter the familiar response. "I'm sorry."

"Save your pity. Just stop being so damn holier than thou. You lost family to the Nazis. I lost family to both sides. My father was a communist. My brother was too, and something else just as bad according to the Nazis. How do you say it? He preferred boys to girls. They took them away together."

"I'm sorry." The inadequate words again.

"Wait, there's more. My little brother died in the Diersfordt Forest. Who knows whether it was an Ami or Tommie bullet? He was thirteen. They gave him a gun and said protect the Fatherland. My mother and I managed to survive. Then the Red Army marched in. My father and brothers were victims. We were just stupid."

"I don't understand."

"That's right, you don't. You understand nothing. Everyone knew the first thing the Ivans did was rape. It didn't matter how old or young, ugly or infirm, feeble grannies or little girls, as long as you had a vagina they could stick themselves into. Of course, we tried to hide. That was where the stupidity came in. My mother and I went down to the cellar. Later we found out our neighbor who went up to the top floor of the building had better luck. I don't know how she got so smart. Most of the Ivans had never seen a building of more than one or two stories. They were afraid to go any higher. But they knew about cellars. I don't know how many that first day. My mother passed out after six. That didn't stop them. I was conscious throughout. Eleven, but that doesn't count two who took second turns. So don't get into a competition with me, Captain. While you were sitting behind your desk hating me and Fraulein Schmidt and every German who walked through the door, I was behind my desk hating everyone."

Millie wasn't sure where she was headed when she came out of the building. All she knew was that she had to get away from Fraulein Weber. She thought of going to the hospital to see when Mary Jo went off duty. They could go to a movie. They could go to dinner and she could listen to Mary Jo's problems. At least those could be solved one way or another.

It took her a minute to realize the drizzle from earlier in the day had turned into a steady rain. She opened her umbrella and started for the U-Bahn, then changed her mind. The thought of going underground was suddenly oppressive. Maybe it was Fraulein Weber's story of the cellar. She had to walk it off, though she wasn't sure what *it* was. The translator this morning whose son had been murdered in the House of Shutters but who still had hope. Fraulein Weber's devastation that had left her with nothing but hatred. Or the visit to the station between the two incidents. Always the station.

She started walking. The rain was coming down harder now. She stood for a moment, debating whether to go down into the U-Bahn after all. Through the mist she spotted a streetcar approaching.

She found a seat near the rear of the car and slid into it. The city was starving, but somehow even emaciated men managed to take up too much room. The man on her right reeked of sweat, the one on her left of sweat and sour, wet clothing. Across the aisle, another man pushed open a window. The woman beside him complained he was letting in the rain. The man on her other side closed the window. The first man opened it again. The streetcar stopped, a passenger closer to the front got off, and she made a dash for the seat. Another man who was slower gave her a dirty look. She turned away from him and as she did, she noticed the woman sitting across from her. She was one of those girls Millie saw all over the city these days, not a Fraulein with nyloned legs and a crimson lipsticked mouth, but her sadder sister, another Fraulein Weber, in a shabby dress that hung on her as if on a hanger and made her look twice her age, though, Millie realized as she went on staring, the girl couldn't have been much older than she was. Her exhaustion and defeat and something else—Millie went on staring—her misery, made her look older. She sat rigid and still, absolutely apart from the jostling, hostile crowd. Her face was as lifeless as a mask. Her glazed, unseeing eyes reminded Millie of a doll Sarah had loved. When it was laid on its back, tiny eyelids with thick lashes closed over its eyes, but when it was upright, the lids popped up and it stared into space with a blind demonic intensity. Millie looked away from the woman. She couldn't bear the eyes. And she'd be damned if she'd feel sorry for her. Just because she wasn't a nylon-stockinged, lipsticked Fraulein didn't mean she was another Fraulein Weber, broken by suffering, crushed by loss. For all Millie knew, she was having a hard time under the Occupation not because of the pain of what she'd been through or scruples about swapping her body for food, cigarettes, and a good time, but because she was an unrepentant Nazi, a she-werewolf waiting for the Reich to rise again.

The streetcar stopped abruptly, tossing people and bundles together. The girl clutched a box on her lap to keep it from sliding off. Millie hadn't noticed the box before. She'd been too busy looking at those unnerving eyes. It was the size and shape of a florist's box. Had someone given this sad creature flowers? Was she giving them to someone or perhaps on her way to a cemetery? She remembered the swastika on the headstone the day David had taken her to the bar mitzvah and steeled herself again against the pity. Besides, people didn't take flowers to graves in boxes. And this box was made of wood, so it couldn't be for flowers after all. From the way the girl was clutching it, it contained something more valuable. It could only be a family heirloom. She was on her way to a black market. Millie was sure of it.

She went on staring at the box, trying to fathom what was in it. Her mother's silver chest had been similar, though that hadn't been as long. Perhaps the girl came from a more affluent or aristocratic family who'd had need of fish knives and marrow spoons and other specialized utensils. A service like that would make quite a gift for an officer to send home to his wife. She could see him sitting at the head of a dining table in some small town in years to come. "I picked it up for a song when I was stationed in Berlin."

The girl readjusted the box so it sat more securely on her lap. A decorative design was carved into the lid. Her mother's chest had had a fleur-de-lis. This one had a cross. Religious relics were one more commodity for sale on the black market. She looked from the box to the girl's face. It was still, expressionless as a mask. The car lurched to a sudden stop. This time she caught the box just before it hit the floor, and as she did, her face came startlingly alive, her eyes wide with horror, her mouth open in a silent howl of pain. She was, for a moment, a living reproduction of *The Scream*.

As if she were a mirror, Millie's own face froze in revulsion. She remembered Mary Jo's stories of the dead children. The box wasn't a silver chest or a case for a religious relic. It was a coffin. The woman was carrying a child's body. She was carrying her child's body. On a streetcar.

The car came to a halt. Millie stumbled out of her seat. She wasn't sure which stop it was, and she didn't care. She had to get off that streetcar. Just as she'd fled Fraulein Weber, she had to get away from that woman and her dead child.

The doors opened. She lurched down, staggered into the rubble, caught her balance, lost it again, and crashed to her knees. As she did, she reached out to break her fall. Later, she'd realize she'd been lucky not to break her hand or wrist. Still, something had shattered.

❧

She stood on the street, bleeding from her palms and knees, watching the streetcar move off into the fog. She'd never felt so lost. The signposts she'd once used to navigate the city were no longer clear. It didn't matter whether they were in German or English. She couldn't make them out. She started walking. She'd thought she was heading for her apartment. Somehow she ended up at his.

She lifted her hand to ring the bell and managed to get blood on the doorframe. She was trying to wipe it off with her handkerchief when he opened the door. He stood for a moment in khaki uniform trousers, a tee shirt, and bare feet, looking surprised. Then he noticed the blood on her hands and running down her shins.

"Don't tell me. Let me guess. You've been to the Anhalter Bahnhof."

"I was seeing Anna and Elke off earlier, but that's not where it happened."

He opened the door wider, stepped aside for her to come in, and closed it behind her.

"Then where?"

"Getting off a streetcar."

He looked down at her legs again and carefully lifted her skirt a couple of inches to see her knees.

"From the looks of it, you flung yourself from a speeding train. Come on." He let go of her skirt, straightened, and led her down the hall to the bathroom. "Sit."

"Next you're going to tell me to roll over and play dead." She was trying to joke, but they both heard the hysteria in her voice.

"I'll settle for your paws." He turned on the water, reached out to take her hands, and looked at the palms.

"I can do it," she said.

"You can't even get off a streetcar." He held one of her

hands under the faucet, soaped it, repeated the action with the other hand, then toweled them dry. Funny how adept he was even without two fingers, and gentle.

"I'm getting blood all over your towel," she said.

"If you look around, you'll see what a fastidious house-keeper I am." He moved on to her knees. "Jesus, you must have gone down in a pile of rubble. The ruins of half of Berlin are in here. Take off your stockings."

She unhooked them from her garter belt. There was no need for her to turn away from him. He was too busy taking methylate and bandages from the medicine cabinet. She sat on the closed toilet seat watching him work and remembering her mother washing and bandaging David the day his schoolmates had cornered him in the alley.

He finished her knees, straightened, and stood looking down at her. "Accident-prone doesn't begin to describe you, Mosbach. It's just lucky I'm around to take care of the damage. Again.

"Do you feel like telling me what happened?" he asked when they were back in the living room. "And don't give me that song and dance about tripping getting off the streetcar."

She told him about the girl with the coffin on her lap. "At first I thought she was on her way to the black market. I was trying to guess what was in the box. Then I realized."

He sat looking at her across the expanse of sofa between them. "Do you think that dead baby brought it on itself? That's our usual excuse, isn't it? They built the camps. They started the war. They asked for it."

"That's what I told Fraulein Weber."

"What does she have to do with it?"

She told him about the conversation in his office. Then about the translator whose son had been murdered.

He shook his head. "When you about-face, you do it with a vengeance."

"I haven't done an about-face."

He waited. When she didn't say anything else, he went on. "Just seeing that things are a bit more complicated than you thought?"

She still didn't say anything.

He continued looking at her for a moment, then leaned forward, picked up the pack of cigarettes on the table, and held it out to her. She shook her head. He went through the rituals of lighting it, inhaling, exhaling, then leaned back again.

"I've been thinking about that day in the Anhalter Bahnhof," he said.

"Which one? I seem to have spent quite a bit of time there lately."

"I wasn't thinking of lately. I was thinking of the day that started it all."

"You're going to tell me again that I wasn't such a quick thinker. I was just following instructions."

"A bit more than that. I was thinking of David."

"He wasn't the one who spoke up. He wasn't the one who denied knowing his own family."

"No, that was your job. You were older. He followed your lead."

"Exactly. It's my fault, not his."

"Your fault? You saved his life, Millie. You can't forgive yourself for what you did to save your life, but what if you'd done what you, in your bottomless shame, think would have been the honorable thing and told those SS bastards, sure, we're with the Jews. We're the Mosbach family. We stick together. Not only would you not be here. David wouldn't either. And you don't have to know the Talmud, which I don't, and I'm willing to bet you don't either, to know the line. He, or in this case she, who saves one life saves the world."

❦

They didn't speak in the jeep on the way back to her apartment. You can't speak in a jeep, only shout. He was still silent as he walked her to the door of the building, but when they reached it, he stood looking down at her.

"Do you ever think, Millie, why your father gave you those instructions?"

"To save me."

"To save you for what?"

She didn't answer.

"A lifetime of self-flagellation?"

She was still silent.

"He gave you life. He'd want you to grab it."

"Easier said than done."

He turned and started back to the jeep. "Tell me about it," he said without turning around.

He'd spoken so quietly she wasn't sure she'd heard him correctly.

Twenty-Four

❧

SHE NEVER DID GET TO THE HOSPITAL THAT NIGHT, but a few days later Mary Jo showed up at her apartment. Her eyes were red, the freckles on her cheeks inflamed, and the twin trails of mascara that ran down both cheeks made her look like a tragic clown.

"What's wrong?" Millie asked as she led her down the hall to the parlor.

"You won't believe it."

"Try me."

"Phil's family. They're worse than mine. They said they'll disown him if he marries me. They said they'll sit . . . what's the word when someone dies?"

"Shiva."

"They'll sit shiva for him." Mary Jo widened her eyes. "Can you imagine anything so awful?"

"Unfortunately, I can."

"You're not surprised."

"You think your family has cornered the market on narrowmindedness?"

"But how can they object to me? I don't mean me in particular. They don't even know me. But how can they object to a Christian?"

Millie sat looking at her for a moment, trying not to smile.

She didn't want to hurt Mary Jo's feelings. "Maybe you'd better not marry him after all."

"But I love him."

"As in some of my best friends are Jews."

"What?"

"It's what people say when they're trying to prove they're not anti-Semitic. I couldn't possibly be an anti-Semite. Some of my best friends are Jewish."

"You think I'm an anti-Semite?"

"I didn't until you asked that question about how Phil's family could possibly object to you, a Christian."

"I didn't mean it the way it sounded."

"Nobody ever means it, but if they didn't, they wouldn't say it. What does Phil think about all this?"

"He says he still wants to marry me."

"And what do you think? You do realize that if you marry him, your children will be half Jewish?"

"I know that," she said, but there was a sullen undertone in her voice, as if she wasn't quite ready to yield the point.

"Maybe you better slow things down a little."

"You mean break it off?"

"I mean slow it down. A few weeks ago, I got a letter from a college friend who's already filing for divorce from the Air Force officer she married on his way to the Pacific."

"What does that have to do with Phil and me?"

"It has to do with the war and its aftermath. Yesterday, bombs were falling, cities were going up in flames, millions were dying, and people were going crazy. Falling in love too easily. Falling into bed too fast. Falling for the wrong people. Then the war was over, they went home, and reaction set in. The problem is we're still living in a war zone here, and the same crazy rules or lack of them apply. But you'll be going

home soon, and once you're there you might see things differently."

"You think so?"

"I don't know. I've never been in Friendship. I've never
met your parents. But it seems to me that if you can't see the
equivalence between Phil's family's objections and yours, you
might not be ready to fight this particular religious war."

❦

The realization came to her out of nowhere, except, of course,
epiphanies only seem sudden. A slow, secret, even from ourselves, especially from ourselves, gestation period precedes the
thunderclap. When she thought about it later, she'd trace the
incubation period back to the morning the translator told
her about hope, and the afternoon Fraulein Weber taunted
her about hate, and the dead child on the tram that evening,
and maybe even to Mary Jo's glimpse of her own image in
the mirror.

She was sitting on the sofa, reading a book she'd taken out
of the library of Amerika Haus. Like the books she was as-
signing for translation, the centers being set up in various cities were supposed to introduce Germans to the finer aspects
of American culture, but it was turning out that Germans,
especially young Germans, preferred Rita Hayworth films
to Eugene O'Neill plays and "Chattanooga Choo Choo"
to "Fanfare for the Common Man." She'd had no trouble getting her hands on the library's copy of Richard Wright's *Black
Boy*, though it had been sold out in the PX. It was a favorite
among the Negro GIs, but had little appeal for former Hitler
Youth.

She looked up from the page. Later, she wouldn't be able
to remember why. Nothing had moved in the room, but

something must have shifted in her. She put the book down on the sofa, stood, and crossed to the breakfront. Now she knew why David hadn't commented on it when she'd first led him through the flat. It was nothing like their family piece, or at least it wasn't that piece. The inlays in that breakfront had been swans. How had she forgotten? Sarah had named the swans. These insets were sphinxes. You'd have to be blind to mistake one for the other. Willfully blind. She crouched down to look at the legs. These were straight. The legs of the piece she'd grown up with had been gently curved. She stood and went on looking down at the piece. *Fälschung*, the woman had said. *Authentisch*, Millie had insisted. She had no idea whether this was a reproduction or the real thing—her knowledge of antique furniture wasn't nearly as good as she'd pretended to Harry—but she did know that it was not the piece she'd thought, not the one that had stood in the parlor of their house. She couldn't imagine how she had confused them. Only suddenly she could.

She had to tell David. She looked at her watch. It was after nine. He might be on another mission to Stettin or on his way to the British sector to see the knockout aid worker. She had no intention of trying to track him down in either case. And there was only one other person who would be interested.

He was in his uniform khakis, a tee shirt, and bare feet again.

"I owe you an apology," she said before she even stepped into the apartment.

"Probably more than one, but for what in this specific instance?"

"That Biedermeier breakfront."

"You mean Art History 101 let you down? It's a reproduction?"

"I don't know if it's fake or authentic, but it's not the one I thought it was."

"What made you change your mind?"

She didn't answer.

"Okay, I won't gloat. But as long as you're here, you might as well come in."

He stepped back. She stepped into the apartment. He closed the door behind her.

She reached up and put her hand against his cheek. "I hope you've shaved recently."

"What?"

"Just a private joke."

"Want to let me in on it?"

"Maybe. Eventually."

It went on from there. She supposed she'd known it would. That was why she'd had to tell him. Even if she'd been able to find David, she would have had to tell him.

Nothing had prepared her for making love with Harry. Not the weekend back in the States with the medical officer who was shipping out. That had been a desperate end run around the specter of death. Not the times with Theo when they'd thrashed and panted in that overcrowded bed and tried to pleasure themselves into amnesia. Certainly not the one-night stand with Harry when even locked together, hungry and breathless and desperate on her part, she'd managed to keep him, and herself, at arm's length. Nothing had prepared her for making love with Harry except the last months with Harry. Somehow all the disagreements and misunderstandings, the times they'd snapped at each other and the times they'd declared uneasy truces, the shared horror of damp basements festering with evil and photographs of murderous lies had bred that most elusive human connection, trust. It was a powerful aphrodisiac. It electrified touch and heightened sensation. Mouth to mouth, skin to skin, it inflamed. It made them laugh at the wonder of their coming together after all this time and hushed them into wide-eyed silence as they put a few inches between their sweat-slicked, shocked-with-joy faces to measure each other's desire. She took his maimed hand and licked the wound. He moved his other hand. Does this please you? it asked. His tongue. Does this? And this? And this? Does this excite you? her mouth taunted in return. And this? And this? Until finally the watchfulness gave way to abandon. He was above her, and she locked her legs around his hips and hung on for dear life. She straddled him, and he bucked with bliss. Little by little, then faster and faster, they yielded to each other and themselves. A moment, or a lifetime, later, her world exploded in a galaxy of light. When her vision cleared, she looked down at him in time to see his face contort with the agony of pleasure and hear his howl split the Berlin night.

He woke her twice in the darkness, once intentionally to make love, a second time inadvertently when his cry split the night again, though this time not in passion, at least not that kind of passion. She couldn't make sense of what he was saying, or rather there was no sense, only a string of curses alternating between English and German. "Bastards," he cried. "*Drecksack*. Sons of bitches. *Schweinehunde*."

Mary Jo had told her about the wards at night with men howling curses and shouting warnings to buddies and begging for their mothers. But beside her now the curses turned

to moans, and these were not battle cries but pleas for forgiveness. "*Verzeihung*," he begged. "*Verzeihung*," he sobbed.

She shook him gently, enough to startle him out of the
nightmare but not to wake him completely. He murmured
something and wound himself around her. It took her a little
longer to fall back to sleep. She kept wondering what he'd
done to be forgiven for.

Neither of them mentioned the incident in the morning.
There was nothing odd about that. People frequently didn't
remember being saved from themselves in their sleep. But she
had a feeling he did and didn't want to talk about it. She
didn't blame him. Trust doesn't demand full disclosure any
more than family ties do.

Twenty-Five

∞

THE THING ABOUT HARRY, SHE'D THINK AT ODD MO-
ments when she was sitting in her office or standing under
the shower or lying next to him while he slept during the
long days of summer that gradually began to shorten, was
that he had an uncanny sense of her interior weather. It never
occurred to her to ask how he'd come by that exquisite sympathy. No, not sympathy, empathy. All she knew was that he
sensed when her furies were circling. And he knew that at
those times she was beyond his reach. But at other moments
when she emerged from the blackness, he tried. God, did he
try. She wondered how she'd gotten so lucky. She knew she
didn't deserve to be.

They spent afternoons lying on the sand at Wannsee or
walking the shady paths there; evenings alone in his flat or
out in the raw, pulsing city that was already rising from the
ruins; a weekend in Cologne, where they passed hours wandering the cathedral; another in the Bavarian countryside,
where it rained the entire time and they'd gotten out of bed
only to go down for meals. Even then they'd skipped lunch
one day and made do with the cold coffee and rolls from
breakfast. That was the afternoon she let him in on her joke
with herself about the beard burn. At first, she'd been afraid
to mention that night. She didn't want to ruin what they

had now. He hadn't mentioned it either. She hadn't believed it at the time, but she knew now that he really had been hurt.

Then everything began to change. She'd known it would once they started going home. David was supposed to be the first to leave. As she kept reminding him, if he wanted to return to Haverford on the GI Bill, he had to be back in the States for the start of the academic year.

"Now, don't get upset," he said to her one morning when they were alone in the flat, sitting at the massive carved table, drinking coffee, and eating good German pumpernickel spread with PX butter.

"That's a disheartening start to a conversation if ever I heard one. What am I not supposed to get upset about?"

"I can't go back to Haverford."

"Fine. Go someplace else. The States are full of colleges and universities."

"What I mean is I can't go back to school. Not after all this."

She should have known it was coming. She had known. "I understand what you mean. I really do. The idea of sitting in lectures, studying, writing papers must seem pretty tame to you after what you've been through. But did you ever think it might give more meaning to what you've been through?"

"You think History 101 is going to explain Hitler or the war or anything?"

"I think it might give you some perspective. Others seem to think so. You aren't going to be the only GI in those classes. The one thing I do know is that willful ignorance isn't the answer."

"No one's talking about willful ignorance. Maybe I'll go back eventually. But not yet. Not until the job is finished."

"The war is over. Haven't you heard?"

"Not for all those survivors desperate to get to Palestine."

"So you're going to stay here to go on smuggling them out?"

"I'm not going to stay here. I want to work at the other end of the operation."

This was worse than she'd expected. He wasn't just putting off going back to school. He was running away. From her.

"You're going to Palestine?"

"It's not the end of the earth."

"I thought we were going to stay together."

"We will. After I finish this. Besides, you have Harry now."

She wanted to slap him for that. Harry hadn't been with her that afternoon in the Anhalter Bahnhof. Harry hadn't sat beside her sweating and trembling in the crowded fear-stalked compartment as the train alternately hurtled and crept toward the border. Harry hadn't shared all those years, first of desperate hope, then of the shameful realization that there was none. Instead, she pushed her heavy chair back, stood, and left the room. She had turned into that unloved familyless woman after all.

❧

She couldn't change his mind, though after that first painful morning when she walked away in silence, she tried. Oh, did she try. But two of his old Ritchie buddies succeeded, though one of them, Heinrich Kauffman, had to die to do it.

Among the Ritchie boys, attitudes to the country of their birth varied. Some went back to search for family. A handful returned to live. Many, perhaps most, swore never to set foot on German soil again. Heinrich Kauffman belonged to the last group. He made his way to Palestine, where he had a brother. When Heinrich had been fourteen and his brother twelve, their parents had managed to get their older son to the States and the younger to Palestine. Their parents had perished in the camps, but now, finally, the brothers were together again, living in a settlement. They were also possibly, probably, fighting British rule. In August of 1946, British soldiers shot and killed both Kauffman brothers.

"British soldiers!" David raged when he got the news. He had friends among the English military who worked with DPs. "Our fucking allies!"

Millie was sure that was the last straw. Now nothing could keep him from going to Palestine to continue the fight. And putting himself in danger again. But she hadn't counted on Peter Gruenbaum. That and the fact that her line about willful ignorance hadn't gone entirely unheard.

Peter Gruenbaum, one of the oldest of the Ritchie "boys," had been teaching German at a small Midwestern college when he'd enlisted and been posted to the camp. Now that the war was over, he was teaching again, but at Columbia. He was the one who'd written David of Heinrich Kauffman's death. Now he wrote again for another reason. He'd won a grant to set up a program to study the writings of survivors and those who had perished in the camps and was looking for an assistant. If David was interested, the university would admit him as a sophomore on full scholarship.

"I told them that between your work with survivors," Peter wrote, "and your record at Ritchie, you're uniquely qualified. There weren't many men there who were tapped to stay on as instructors. In fact, you're the only one I know. You refused the offer then. I thought you were foolish, but I understood your motives. You had to prove yourself. Kill Nazis. Beat Hitler. You did. Now it's time to move on. It's time to understand not only what happened but why and how it happened. To make others understand. Thinking is better than killing, David. Knowledge is better than anger. Understanding is better than revenge. Come work with me. I don't know if we'll make the world a better place, but perhaps we can make it just a little more tolerant."

"You never told me they asked you to stay on at the camp as an instructor," she said when he showed her Peter Gruenbaum's letter.

"I couldn't do it. I had to get into the fight."

"Apparently," she answered, but there was no anger in her voice. She knew he wouldn't have shown her the letter if he wasn't going to take Peter Gruenbaum up on his offer.

❧

Ten days after she saw David off from the Anhalter Bahnhof, without any dire side effects, she accompanied Harry to the station. He had his own academic plans. That day she'd tracked him down in the officers' mess, he hadn't been reading the report on the Nazi judiciary for pleasure. The road to the Third Reich, he'd decided, had been paved by the negligence and betrayal of judges and lawyers. He'd taken to quoting John Locke on the subject. Where the law ends, tyranny begins. It stood to reason that if the judges and lawyers had been at fault in the past, they could save the future. He'd applied to two law schools, been accepted by both, and decided on the University of Pennsylvania in Philadelphia. That way he and Millie could be together. She'd be going back to work at the magazine, as a fact-checker again. A returning vet, Russ

Bennett had written, sat in her old office in the editorial department.

Harry hadn't wanted her to come to the station to see him off. She knew what he was afraid of, but she assured him she could handle it. And she was handling it. She heard no echo of her heels as they crossed the rubble of the station. She imagined no Nazi banners snapping above her in the September breeze that blew through the open roof. The MPs were just American boys in uniforms, not kindhearted or well-intentioned perhaps, but not out to get her. She was fine. He was the one in trouble. No, he wasn't in trouble. He simply wasn't there. He was already back in the States, a civilian, sprung from Berlin's dangerous madness. She told herself she'd be following him in two months, but still, his distraction frightened her. Maybe they wouldn't make it after all. As she'd warned Mary Jo, you couldn't rely on love you'd found in a war zone. Mary Jo hadn't. A month after she'd returned to Friendship, she'd written that she was engaged to, literally, the boy next door. They'd played together as children. She said the wedding would be in November and added that she'd love to have Millie there but doubted she'd be home by then. And even if she were, Mary Jo went on, Millie probably wouldn't want to come all the way to Indiana just for her wedding. Besides, it was going to be a very small wedding. Millie wanted to tell her that one excuse was always better than two or three.

Now she and Harry stood on the platform beside his compartment, facing each other, except that he couldn't meet her eyes. He kept lighting cigarettes in that singlehanded way, taking a few puffs, then flicking them away. Every time he did, a swarm of kids lunged for the butt.

"Why don't you just give them the pack?" she joked.

He didn't even smile.

Beneath the brim of his officer's cap, dark smudges underlined his eyes. He'd been up half the night. She knew because she'd been up, listening to the click of his lighter, watching the ember of his cigarette, feeling the mattress shift as he turned one way, then the other. As far as she knew he'd had no nightmares, except the waking ones, whatever they were.

She asked for the second or was it the third time when the train was supposed to get into Bremerhaven.

He went on staring over her head without answering.

She asked the name of the troop ship he'd be sailing on, though she already knew it.

He unbuttoned the flap of his uniform jacket, took another cigarette from the pack, and lit it.

She gave up. "Maybe I shouldn't wait for the train to leave after all."

He still didn't answer her.

She was angry. She admitted it. But the gesture didn't show her exasperation. She was sure of that. She took a step toward him, put her hands on his shoulders, and leaned toward him for a farewell kiss. His body went rigid. He might as well have slapped her face. She dropped her hands and took a step back.

Now he was looking at her.

"I'm sorry," he said.

She shrugged.

"It has nothing to do with you."

She made a show of looking around. "I don't see anyone else at this going-away party."

He closed his eyes, then opened them. "Don't you believe it."

She stood looking up at him, and suddenly she saw him.

She saw him as clearly as she had the breakfront after all those months. And she understood his exquisite sensitivity to her internal weather.

"You left from here the last time?"

"And I've managed not to come back since."

"I'm sorry. I'm so sorry."

"I can still see her standing on the platform. I can still hear her voice. 'Soon,' she kept saying. 'We'll be together soon.' She knew she was lying. But I believed her. At least I pretended to believe her. How else could I get away? Hell, I didn't even cry."

"You were being brave."

"That's what I told myself. But I wasn't being brave. I was glad. I was getting out of this rotten country where I'd become a dirty Jew. I was getting away from her. Don't misunderstand me. I loved her. But after my father was killed she circled the wagons around the two of us. I was all she had, and she hung on for dear life. I was amazed she was letting me go. And let's remember, I wasn't just going away. I was going to America. The land of big, sleek motor-cars, and jazz music, and gangster movies. Hell, standing on the platform, I was too excited to cry."

"That was normal."

"Maybe, but what I did next wasn't. When it was time to board the train, she reached out to hug me. Just the way you did now. Some boys were standing near us on the platform. Bastards from my *Gymnasium*, from what used to be my *Gymnasium* before Jews were forbidden to study there. Hitler Youth bastards. God knows where they were going. Not fleeing the country, that's for sure. They were on their own. No mother on the verge of tears. No Mama trying to hug them, to hold on to them, to embarrass them. When she stepped in to hold me, I didn't only stiffen the way I just did with you. I took a step back, away from her, out of her reach. I can still see her face. She looked as if I'd slapped her. That was the last I saw of her." He took a drag of his cigarette, then flipped it away. "Or to put it another way, that was the last she saw of me. A boy pulling away from his mother. A boy ashamed of his mother."

"Normal behavior for a boy that age," she said again.

"Normal behavior for a callous little prick."

She didn't argue with him. He knew every word she could say. He'd said them all to her. They were two of a kind after all. His hand was the minor injury. The truly debilitating one was invisible, just as hers was. The city and the way they'd left it would always be a festering wound eating at them from within. It was a bond. It was also a barrier. Loss can be consoled. Pain can be solaced. But there is no comfort for shame. Because shame is not the result of a wrong suffered but of a wrong committed. Nothing can breech the isolation of that. Not sympathy. Not sex. Not even love.

The whistle sounded. All up and down the train, people were climbing into compartments and slamming doors and leaning out of windows. He bent to kiss her, quick and a little angry, then took the two steps up in a single stride, settled into his seat, and sat staring through the window at her. But she knew he wasn't seeing her. He was seeing his dead mother. And she was looking at the girl who, years ago, had flung herself into the compartment, breathless, terrified, stunned at her treachery. They were each other's ghosts.

The train started to move. As it did, the angle of the light striking it changed, and she recognized her own reflection in the window. Not the image of the scared, scarred girl she'd been but the likeness of the woman she was becoming. It was superimposed on him. Maybe she was wrong about love being no balm for the shame. Maybe they could make it after all.

Twenty-Six

EVERYONE WAS HAVING BABIES. THE HALLS OF THE apartment building in West Philadelphia where they lived among other students on the GI Bill and their wives were an obstacle course of carriages and strollers. Men who'd thought nothing of dropping a few hundred or even a thousand dollars in a high-stakes poker game because who knew if they'd be alive tomorrow were saving nickels and dimes for the once-a-month babysitter and movie. Their wives were giving one another hand-me-down maternity dresses, then reclaiming them a year later. The world was hell-bent on repopulating itself. Millie's Jewish friends were especially determined. They had so many murdered to make up for. Her old suitemate Barbara already had twin toddlers and an infant.

Millie didn't know what was wrong with her. Not that she couldn't conceive, but that she was reluctant to. Two weeks after they were married in the living room of the Bennetts' house in Ardmore—David had refused to give her away; he said he didn't like the terminology, but he did walk her down the short makeshift aisle between the rented chairs—ten days after they returned from a weekend honeymoon in the Bennetts' house on Martha's Vineyard, she told Harry that she'd made an appointment at a clinic on Walnut and 20th Street. They were having dinner at the small table in the corner of the living room nearest the kitchen, beside a window overlooking Baltimore Avenue. During the day the view, if you could call it that, was unlovely and treeless. In the evening, she drew the heavy curtains he'd hung to keep out the glare from the streetlamp. The apartment was on the second floor.

"What kind of a clinic?" he asked, and she knew from the even tone of his voice and the careful expression on his face that he was thinking of her two episodes in the Anhalter Bahnhof, though he never mentioned them.

"Not that kind of clinic," she said. "The Psychiatric Institute is on 48th Street."

"How do you know something like that?"

"You forget how much I walk the city."

"Then what kind of clinic?"

"Birth control."

She waited for him to say something. When they'd first moved into the apartment, he'd found her in the bedroom one day, sitting on the side of the bed holding the hand puppet she'd smuggled out of Germany for Sarah. She'd expected him to ask what it was. He hadn't. There was no reason to think he associated her decision now with the incident. She hadn't made the connection until recently. Her dread of pregnancy was the dark underbelly of the dream of a world filled with the sweetness of her Sarah and eventually David's. Bringing another Sarah into the world wouldn't bring back Sarah. It would only exacerbate the betrayal. It would be saying I'm still here, alive and well, with a new Sarah to love. It would be dancing on Sarah's grave. Only Sarah didn't have a grave.

"What are you thinking?" she asked finally.

"That I married a frugal woman."

"What does that have to do with anything?"

"Do you have any idea how much money we squandered buying out the entire stock of condoms in that little drugstore on the Vineyard?"

"Now you're bragging."

"Not in the least. Every last one. We were the scandal of the island. Why do you think everyone was staring at us when we left on the ferry?"

"Because we're such a devastatingly attractive couple?"

"That too." He grinned. That was when she knew she'd been wrong. He'd understood her brooding on Sarah's puppet that day. He'd intuited her dread of dancing on Sarah's grave. That was why he was making a joke of it.

They made love that night. There was nothing unusual about that. They'd been together less than a year, married only a month. But she sensed a difference this time, a certain gravity in him, a recognition that this was serious business they were up to, more serious than pleasure or even procreation. It had to do with a fierce unspoken pact between them.

Afterward she turned on her side for sleep, and he molded himself against her. She was just drifting off when he spoke. "I kind of like the idea."

"What idea?"

"Of its being just the two of us for a while."

She kept her appointment at the clinic and left with a small package containing a diaphragm and a set of instructions. Nonetheless, she felt guilty. She was in a bind of guilt. Getting pregnant would be a betrayal of Sarah. Avoiding pregnancy meant letting down Harry, no matter what he said, no matter how good a front he put up. He was the one who had no family at all, except for her. That was the point. He was doing this for her.

In an absurd attempt at compensation, she became the perfect housewife, a paragon of the misguided virtues she'd never admired. The apartment was, if not spotless—the ugly linoleum of the kitchen floor and the stained bathroom tiles made that impossible—then clean and fiercely neat. Harry's shirts went to and returned from the laundry with a military regularity. And she cooked. Each evening she returned from the magazine, took off her high heels and suit, changed into slacks and one of his old Army shirts, and went into the tiny kitchen, where she managed to turn out elaborate dinners based on recipes clipped from magazines and newspapers, though it didn't escape her that the same publications that were promoting complicated dishes designed to keep women in the kitchen for the shank of the day had competed to print shortcuts for getting dinner on the table in twenty minutes during the war. And she walked. As she'd told Harry, she spent hours walking the streets, trying to adjust to them, trying to believe they were the new reality.

Yesterday, she'd been living in a rubble-strewn world where black markets flourished, Soviet spies and re-emergent Nazis lurked, and homeless, stateless people languished in despair. Today, she paced block after block of intact buildings, among people drunk on postwar optimism, in a turbocharged economy that felt like one huge overstocked PX. Everyone was happy, or at least hopeful. No one wanted to hear about the hunger, deprivation, and desolation that still stalked Europe. But she couldn't shut it out. She was brooding about it that afternoon on her way home from the supermarket carrying two bags of groceries. The bags filled with crisp apples and freshly baked bread and a chicken she planned to stuff as well as a variety of canned and boxed goods were more evidence of how easy life was here and how harsh it still was in Europe, as if more evidence were needed.

As she let herself into the building, a cacophony of reedy children's voices screeching with unrestrained excitement rushed down the stairs to meet her. She hoped Harry had gone to the library. It was Saturday, and he'd planned to study at home, but she doubted anyone could with this din. The noise grew louder as she climbed to the second floor. She turned the corner into the hall and saw what must have been half a dozen strollers and carriages. What seemed like twice that many children chased one another through the obstacle course. Some of them had helium balloons that said happy birthday tied to their wrists. Two little girls were competing to see who could scream her joy louder. Another was sobbing. A couple of boys were hooting as they traded punches. Two women standing in the open door to an apartment, neither of whom was her neighbor, added to the noise by shouting at various children to calm down.

Clutching her grocery bags, she began to thread her way through the maze of children and their paraphernalia. She didn't see the piece of birthday cake, but she felt it under her shoe. As she did, her legs went out from under her, and she was toppling back onto a warren of strollers and carriages, her grocery bags tumbling from her arms, their contents spilling out and rolling in every direction. The crash silenced the children, for a moment. Then the crying and screaming and hilarity started up again.

The two women who'd been in the doorway and a third, her neighbor, were trying to help her up and gathering her groceries and asking if she was all right. She told them, through gritted teeth as she struggled to stand, that she was fine and didn't need help, though when she managed to get to her feet, the shoe with the birthday cake on the sole slid again and she had to make an effort to regain her balance. By that time Harry, who'd been trying without success to shut out the birthday party racket, but who'd heard the crash and thought, he told her later, that this time the little bastards had gone too far, was in the hall. Somehow he managed to get rid of the women and maneuver Millie and the grocery bags into the apartment. She carried her shoe. She'd be damned if she'd get icing all over the rug.

He took the grocery bags into the kitchen. She limped after him, wearing one shoe, carrying the other. When she reached for the paper towels to clean it, she noticed that her arm was bleeding. They both stood looking down at it.

"If there's any justice in the world, I broke the stroller that inflicted this wound."

"Forget justice. You're just lucky I'm on the scene to pick up the pieces. Again."

It took her a moment to recognize the song he was humming as he led her down the hall to the bathroom and opened the medicine cabinet. "Seems Like Old Times."

❧

The fact-checking job at the magazine wasn't entirely stulti-fying. Occasionally, she enjoyed the challenge of tracking down verification of an arcane piece of information. Now and then, she delighted in coming across an esoteric fact. But when she passed her old office in the editorial department, she couldn't help resenting the vet sitting there. She knew the reasoning. He was a man supporting a family. She was merely a wife, supplementing Harry's government stipend while he studied for his career. But the rationale didn't blunt the bitterness. Sometimes her anger was fanned by others. That was what happened the day she had lunch with her old friend Rosalind Diamond.

Rosalind was back at Bryn Mawr, still in the classics department, but teaching. Occasionally, on Saturdays when Harry was studying, Millie took the Paoli Local out to the school and they had lunch. Sometimes, Rosalind took it in and came to the apartment for one of Millie's extravagant dinners. Rosalind and Harry liked each other.

That day Millie took the Paoli Local out to Bryn Mawr, and they went to the Deanery for lunch. They talked about the still slow recovery of Europe, the bill to let more displaced persons into the United States, and the Marshall Plan, then toward the end of lunch the conversation turned, as it always did, to lighter, or at least more personal, issues. Rosalind had come back from an academic conference smitten. She and a classics professor from Dartmouth had fallen in love over Ovid.

"Your mother must be over the moon," Millie said, "as Harry would put it."

"Would that she were."

"What's wrong?"

"He's not tall. My mother has an obsession with height. She says no self-respecting girl would marry a man who's shorter than she is. He's not dashing. Her word, in case you couldn't guess. And he teaches college, which means he's poor. She keeps reminding me of how I've been brought up. As if that's an argument in favor of growing up with money."

"What does your father say?"

"'As long as you're happy, Princess.'"

They both laughed.

"He also offered to buy us a house."

"This time your mother is going to have to cry uncle for good."

"You don't know my mother. She'll probably try to get him to wear lifts in his shoes to stand next to me for the ceremony."

Miss Albright was there that day too, with another faculty member. Once, she'd joined Millie and Rosalind for lunch, but it hadn't been a success. At least it hadn't been a success for Millie. In the old days, she'd been Miss Albright's protégée and Rosalind's champion. Now she was an outsider. It wasn't only that they were fellow faculty members. It was that they had careers; she had a job.

Miss Albright stopped at their table on the way out and asked how things were going at the magazine. Millie said they were fine.

"I keep looking for your byline. If not there, then in other magazines or papers. You know I admired the pieces you published during the war."

"Exactly. During the war," Millie said. "Before the men came home."

"That makes it harder, Millie, not impossible. The Dorothea syndrome can rear its ugly head in many aspects of life."

"What's the Dorothea syndrome?" Rosalind asked when Miss Albright had moved on.

"She thinks I have a flair for self-mortification."

"I wouldn't call it a flair," Rosalind said. "Maybe only a tendency."

❧

She began submitting ideas for articles. She was careful not to send them to Russ. He was the publisher, not an editor. And this time she didn't want to pull strings. The editors, who

were men and knew her place, were not receptive. Nonetheless, she kept at it and finally one of them assigned her a brief
interview with a man who'd written a book about the relationship between the economy and the length of women's
hemlines and, after that, another with Bess Myerson about
what she was doing two years after she'd become the first Jewish girl to win the Miss America Pageant.

"You're a good interviewer," the editor said.

She wanted to tell him not to sound so surprised. She settled for explaining that she'd honed her skills weeding out
ex-Nazis. He must not have been impressed, because he
turned down three more of her ideas. Harry encouraged her
to take them to other magazines and Sunday supplements.
She had no more success there.

Then at the end of Harry's second year of law school, the
Soviets closed all road, rail, and sea traffic to Berlin. Two days
later, the Allies began an airlift. The British, French, and
Americans, especially the Americans, would fly in enough
food, medicine, coal, and all other necessities to keep two
and a half million Berliners alive for as long as necessary, they
said.

This time Millie went straight to the editor in chief. She
walked into his office before he could assign a man to the
story and listed her credentials. She was fluent in German.
She knew the city. She'd lived there during the Occupation.
And, she added after a moment, as a child. She'd proved her
interviewing skills.

He still hesitated.

"I spent five months interrogating Germans in the denazification program. I know how to talk to Germans. I know
the German mind." The editor went on considering her. "I'm
almost one of them."

She got the assignment.

She'd known Harry wouldn't try to stop her, but she hadn't expected him to be so enthusiastic.

"It'll be good for you."

"It's an assignment, not therapy," she said, but even as she spoke, she was wondering why, if she didn't view it the same way, she was so eager to go back.

"All the same, it'll give you a chance to see a different side of Berlin or at least Berliners. Remember those stories we had to sit through about how much they'd all suffered under Allied bombings? What was the name of that customer with the pinned-up sleeve?"

"The one who insisted the picture of Dachau was really of Dresden?"

"That's the one. He and all the rest will have to change their tune now that we're dropping supplies instead of bombs. We got used to living with hate, theirs as well as our own. It'll be interesting to see what it's like living with gratitude. Maybe it'll produce a different reaction."

"I wouldn't bet on it," she said.

The last time she'd traveled by ship. Now she was flying. These days everyone seemed to be. According to one statistic she'd tracked down checking an article on future trends, in less than a decade more people would be crossing the Atlantic by plane than by ship. High above the ocean, with engines droning, the plane vibrating, and sleep elusive, she didn't believe it for a minute.

In Wiesbaden she transferred to a C-47. Once again she was attached to the military, though this time she was wearing a press pass rather than a uniform. She strapped herself into one of the few seats. Most of them had been removed to make room for cargo. Unlike the seats on her flight over, this one was hard and faced the interior of the cabin. She had to twist around to look out the window. Once they started taxiing, she didn't want to. They were almost at the end of the runway by the time the pilot managed to lift off. The plane shuddered into the air. It was that weighed down with supplies. The descent into Tempelhof an hour later was worse. It wasn't even a descent, it was a plunge. Her ears throbbed. She twisted around to look out the window again. The ground was coming up to meet them too fast. The plane skidded to a stop what seemed only inches from the end of the runway. The officer across from her noticed her white-knuckled grip of the seat and told her this was nothing compared to flying formation.

She climbed down from the plane onto the tarmac. She might have been stepping back into the Occupation. The group of women spreading sand on the runway could have been the *Trümmerfrauen* picking up and passing along the rubble of the bombed-out buildings. The men in dyed or camouflaged Luftwaffe uniforms rushing out to service the planes could have been the stream of disgruntled customers who'd passed through her office. And of course there were Frauleins. They stood at wagons parked along the side of the runways, passing out coffee and doughnuts and smiles to the American air crews.

"So much for non-fraternization."

She'd thought she was muttering to herself, but the officer walking beside her heard the words.

"Non-fraternization is a thing of the past, if it ever was," he said. "But this is different. They're bait. If the military wants planes taking off and landing every sixty-three seconds, and that's the goal, they have to keep the crews on the tarmac. Frauleins are the only way to do it."

She left the airport and took a taxi into town. The first thing she noticed was the change. The city was still in ruins and rubble, but more buildings had been restored and here and there a new one was going up. The second was the lack of it. Black markets still flourished, though now the haggling for food and medicine was even more cutthroat. And now instead of scrounging for cigarette butts, children lifted their faces to the sky, waiting for the handkerchief parachutes filled with candy and chewing gum that the pilots rained down on them.

For the next forty-eight hours, she walked the streets where harried-looking Berliners smiled at her and occasionally said *danke* and the parks where they were already cutting down trees for the coming winter, visited homes and shelters, talked to strangers, and tracked down people she'd known.

Frau Kneff was working in a nursery for *Besatzungskinder*, Occupation children, whom the GIs hadn't wanted to take home and the Germans preferred not to think about. She grabbed Millie's hand and kissed it. "As long as you keep flying, the children eat. Mostly dehydrated food, but still nourishing. Once we got Spam. It was like Christmas, the *Zahnfee*, and every child's birthday rolled into one." Millie didn't like the hand kissing, but she was glad for the children and thought again, as she often did, of the woman carrying the dead body of her child on the tram.

She found the woman who'd translated children's books. She was working on a manuscript of her own now, about the House of Shutters and other institutions like it. "Did you know you had hospitals like that in America?" she asked.

Millie said she hadn't known.

"Hitler talked about them. He said America was ahead of us, but we were going to catch up and surpass them." She stopped and thought for a moment. "I don't suppose any country is blameless. But now your pilots drop parachutes of candy for the children."

She had a drink with Jack Craig, who was still there, though in a new office. He was the only one of the old group who had stayed on, the only one who'd been permitted to stay on. General Clay's directive that Harry had told her about that night in the officers' club had finally come down. Anyone who'd been naturalized after 1933 was not permitted to work in the military government. And Jack was still with his Fraulein.

"Why don't you marry her?" Millie asked.

He grinned. "She's working on it."

General Clay's directive wasn't the only sign of the return of the old order. She interviewed a German lawyer, a liaison with the American officials, who grumbled about the advantage Jewish lawyers enjoyed because so many of their Aryan colleagues were disqualified due to their Nazi pasts. "Of course, that can't go on much longer," he assured her.

She spoke to a Social Democratic politician who complained of Jews who'd fled Germany for easier lives rather than return home to help rebuild the Fatherland. She didn't point out that the few Jews left to flee were the relatives of the multitude who had been expelled or murdered.

By the time she headed out to Tempelhof for the flight back to Wiesbaden, she'd filled several notebooks.

She wasn't surprised when she saw the crowds milling around outside the wire fence that surrounded the airfield. She'd witnessed the same crush when she'd arrived two days earlier. Men and women were curious. Children were hoping for candy or gum. Inside the airport building, however, the scene had changed. When she'd arrived, there had been a scattering of military personnel and German officials. Now the place was packed with people carrying suitcases and bundles and small children. She asked one of the Army officers who was trying to keep order what was going on.

"DP evacuation. No point sending all those planes back to Wiesbaden empty. We fly in supplies and fly out the poor beggars."

She flashed her press pass and moved past him to go out onto the field.

The Germans outside the fence had been curious but still suspicious. Could they count on the Amis to keep this up? The displaced persons in the airport building had been hopeful but still wary. Could they really be getting out? The atmosphere on the airfield was more lighthearted. Frauleins in short skirts and silk stockings or bobby socks passed coffee and doughnuts to boys in well-worn flight jackets with their caps pushed back on their heads, the better to smile and laugh and flirt. One particular officer caught her attention. At first she spotted him because he was tall and his head bobbed above the others. He didn't have his cap pushed back on his head, and he wasn't laughing or flirting, though he did smile and say thanks as he took the container of coffee and two doughnuts from the Fraulein. Then, unlike the other men who lingered around the truck, he moved a little distance away and leaned against the wire fence, drinking and eating.

She wandered over. "You're not Fraulein inclined?"

"They're nice enough gals."

"I hear a but."

He moved his coffee to the hand that was holding the doughnut, reached into his pocket with his free hand, drew out a picture, and handed it to her.

She took it from him and studied it for a moment. "Your wife and son?"

He grinned and nodded.

He wasn't a kid, and something about him said he'd been flying for some time. He didn't have to be here. "In that case, why aren't you back there with them?"

He shrugged.

She waited. He obviously wasn't much of a talker, but she had a feeling he wanted to say something about this.

He took a bite of doughnut and chewed, then drained the coffee container and crumpled it. "It's funny," he said finally. "I got everything I ever wanted. The two of them." He took the picture she was still holding and put it back in his pocket. "I even got a house, thanks to Uncle Sam. Think of that, me owning a house."

He stopped. She waited.

"But something didn't sit right. I kept having these dreams about being back in the cockpit."

"You mean you missed flying?"

He shook his head. "Nah. I like it. When I make some money, maybe I'll do it again, like a hobby. But that's not what I mean."

Again she waited.

"I kept dreaming about being over the target and watching the bombs fall. I liked making the target, but I didn't like the bombs. I mean it wasn't like I was bombing Hitler or Göring or those guys. I was killing women and children. It was my job, but that didn't mean I liked it. So now I'm doing this. Don't get me wrong. I know this doesn't make up for it." He hesitated. "But it's gotta count for something."

She hadn't taken a single note. She didn't want him to stop talking. But she knew she'd remember every word.

She'd planned to fly home from Wiesbaden the following day, but when she reached her hotel, she found a wire from Jeanette Wolff, a Jewish survivor who'd lost two daughters in the camps and was now a West Berlin city councilor. Frau Wolff, who had recently been beaten up by Communist protestors in the municipal assembly, would be happy to grant Millie the interview she'd requested. There was nothing she could do but postpone her flight to the States and hitch a ride back to Berlin on another cargo plane the next morning.

She came out of her hotel into an overcast summer morning. It was Friday. In the annals of the Berlin Airlift, it would become known as Black Friday.

By the time she reached the airport, it was raining. This time she boarded a C-50. It was larger than the C-47 and could carry more cargo. Nonetheless, the takeoff wasn't much worse than the one three days earlier, though it certainly wasn't any better. They were near the end of the runway when the plane finally shuddered aloft.

She was hoping they'd get above the clouds, but they never managed to. Her heart seemed to leap into her throat with every plunge of the plane. She clutched the seat with each roll. She tried not to think of how bumpy the descent would be. This was terrifying enough. She didn't care what those predictions about the future said. She'd never get used to flying.

Once again, the descent was sharp and terrifying. Her ears

were throbbing, but this time she couldn't see the ground coming up to meet them. She told herself that was better.

"Jesus," the officer strapped in across from her said, "the cloud cover goes right down to the roofs."

She heard muffled sounds coming from the cockpit.

"Fuck! Fuck! Fuck!"

"The rain is messing with the radar," another voice shouted.

They were suddenly out of the clouds, but too low. Through the window across from her, she saw buildings speeding past. The plane was bouncing over the tarmac, veering wildly from side to side. The buildings gave way to trees. The plane lurched onto its side. She heard a thunderous crack. They came to a stop.

She struggled to undo her seat belt. The metal fastening was stuck. She finally pried it open and tried to scramble out of her seat, but the plane had thrown her on her back. She reached for the overhead. It was too far above her. She tried to leverage herself out of the seat. Gravity held her in place. She flailed her arms and churned her legs. Another noise was crackling through the plane. It sounded like the end of the world. The window across from her flamed red. Then everything went black.

❦

The face looming over her was familiar, but it took her a moment to place it. Dr. Pinsky. She hadn't thought of him in years. She must be dreaming. Or dead. Except she couldn't be dead because she hurt too much.

"We have to stop meeting like this," the face said. "I'm Dr. Pinsky. Do you remember?"

She nodded. That hurt too. "What are you doing here?" she asked.

"I might ask you the same question."

"I'm not sure."

"The plane overshot the runway and crashed. Then two others piled up after it. No fatalities, fortunately, but a couple of you are in here. Here is the 279th Station Hospital. Again. You're going to be fine. Nothing life threatening. Just one broken arm, two broken ribs, and—"

"A partridge in a pear tree."

"And a lot of bruises and contusions. You're going to feel pretty sore for a while. And I'd stay away from mirrors. But keep up the good spirits."

"Can I wire my husband?"

"We already did."

"Thanks," she said and was asleep by the end of the word.

❧

Harry spent the next several days calling, wiring, and pleading with everyone he still knew in the Army. He was a retired major. He had connections. He ought to have some clout. They could get him anywhere, they assured him, except Berlin. He'd heard about the airlift, hadn't he?

❧

"What are you doing still here?" she asked Dr. Pinsky again the next time she saw him.

"Avna, that's my wife, got pregnant two months before I was supposed to be discharged. I wasn't about to leave her here alone until we could get her out. She's Polish. So I re-upped, and we're still here." He hesitated. "Do you ever hear from Mary Jo?"

"She married the boy next door. Literally. I wasn't invited to the wedding."

"Funny how these things turn out."

"At the risk of sounding like a Pollyanna, from the way your voice caresses the name Avna, I'd say for the best."

He smiled as he went on percussing her chest—he was worried, he said, about one of the broken ribs piercing her lung—and as he did, she went on thinking about Mary Jo. She'd left Friendship to see the world and returned to it when the world became too discomfiting. Millie couldn't help wondering whether, as the years went by, the experience would make Mary Jo a better or at least more tolerant person, or if she'd come to regard it as a youthful folly and, finally, a shameful interlude that must never be mentioned in front of the children. Mustn't let them know that Mommy had almost married a Jew.

He kept her in the hospital for four days. He said he was worried about injuries they couldn't see. She didn't know if he was talking about physical or mental wounds and didn't ask. Neither did she try to talk her way out. At night, in her dreams, she was back in the burning plane. Once a young nurse shook her awake.

"It's all right," the nurse said. "You're safe."

During the day, other images and sounds assaulted her. The conversations with David ran in her head. You were just following instructions, he said. Harry's words came back to her. She who saves one life saves the world. And one other exchange echoed again and again.

Your father gave you life, Millie. He'd want you to grab it.

She had no trouble hitching a ride back to Wiesbaden once she was discharged from the hospital, though they were flying out more DPs, and the stripped-down cabin was crowded with men and women and children, lots of children. Like the black market, the orgy of hope, marriage, and procreation was still going strong.

It took another two days to get a flight back to the States. This one went to New York. Harry was waiting at the gate at Idlewild. She ran toward him through the long fingers of the setting sun. When she reached him, she threw her good arm, the one that wasn't in a cast, around his neck. He held her more gingerly.

"Are you all right?" he asked.

"I won't break, if that's what you mean." She tightened her grip on him.

"Really all right?"

"Really."

They were talking about her injuries from the plane crash, but they were talking about more than that. They were talking about Berlin. Still.

They didn't return to the subject until they were in the depths of New Jersey. She began to tell him about her stay in the hospital, not the nightmares that the nurse had awakened her from, but the days of turning things over in her mind.

"Funny how a near-death experience focuses your thinking," he said.

"I made some decisions."

"Want to let me in on any of them?"

"The diaphragm is on the way out."

"You won't get an argument from me about that. Anything else?"

She hesitated. "It occurred to me that I might not feel so guilty, so cruel, so heartless . . ." She stopped again.

"Running out of self-indictments?"

"No, it's just hard to say. I might have an easier time if I didn't think of a child as a replacement for Sarah. Sarah's gone. Naming a child after her won't bring her back. It will just make me more, I don't know, more afraid, more clingy. Like Anna when she first got Elke back."

"Did it ever occur to you we could have a boy?"

"That's the funny thing. Of course I know we could, but whenever I think about having a baby, I think about a girl. The Sarah syndrome again. It'll make me crazy, and it won't be any good for the child. That's why I've decided if we do have a girl, I don't want to name her Sarah."

"Whatever you say." He switched on the headlights, and the twin beams pierced the shadows of the dying day.

They were silent for a few miles, and when he spoke again, she could tell from his voice that the serious part of the discussion was over, for the moment.

"At the risk of being premature, what are we going to name this soon-to-be-conceived baby girl? If I know you, you already have a list."

"No list. Just a name."

"I'm all ears."

"Victoria."

The car veered toward the shoulder of the road, and in the light from the oncoming traffic she saw him wince. He wrenched the wheel to get them back into the lane, and by the time the headlights of another oncoming car illuminated his face, he'd got his expression under control.

"If it's all right with you."

He took a while to answer. "It's a good name," he said finally.

She supposed that was the way it would always be between them, bumps and swerves and close calls, as they moved forward into the past.

Sources and Acknowledgments

AMONG THE SCORES OF EXCELLENT BOOKS ON THE ALLIED Occupation of Berlin and the part that Jewish GIs played in it and in the war, three were especially useful: *Sons and Soldiers* by Bruce Henderson, *Jews, Germans, and Allies* by Atina Grossmann, and *Exorcising Hitler* by Frederick Taylor.

In addition to books and memoirs, many people provided professional and personal support. I am grateful to Carolyn Waters and the entire staff of the New York Society Library for their expert help and unfailing humor; to the Fredrick Lewis Allen Room of the New York Public Library, which provides a safe haven for research and writing; and to Eric Pumroy, the archivist at Bryn Mawr College. I am also indebted to Noah Reibel for introducing me to Kay Boyle's accounts of the Occupation; Christine Smith for sharing her memories of the Berlin Airlift; Helga Warren for her expertise in the nuances of the German language; Stacy Schiff and Laurie Blackburn for listening and suggesting and listening some more; and Elizabeth Church and Ed Gallagher. Fred Allen and Richard Snow once again kept me on the historical and literary straight and narrow, and whether she knows it or not, Liza Bennett's fingerprints are all over this book. My special thanks go to Gail Hochman, an extraordinary agent and valued friend whom I was so lucky to find again after too many years apart; her terrific sidekick, the indefatigable Marianne Merola; Jennifer Fernandez, Olga Grlic, and the entire team at St. Martin's Press; and to Elisabeth Dyssegaard, whom I cannot thank enough for her light but sure editorial touch and the kid gloves with which she wields it.

Laura Mozes

ELLEN FELDMAN, a 2009 Guggenheim fellow, is the author of *Paris Never Leaves You* (published in over twelve countries), *The Unwitting, Next to Love, Scottsboro* (shortlisted for the Orange Prize), *The Boy Who Loved Anne Frank* (translated into nine languages), and *Lucy.* Her novel *Terrible Virtue* was optioned by Black Bicycle for a feature film.

THE LIVING AND THE LOST
by Ellen Feldman

Keep On Reading
- Reading Group Questions
- Movies & Books

Get to Know the Author
- A Conversation with Ellen Feldman

Also available as an audiobook
from Macmillan Audio

For more reading group suggestions
visit www.readinggroupgold.com.

 ST. MARTIN'S GRIFFIN

Reading Group Gold

Reading Group Questions

1. As children in Germany, Millie, David, Harry, and Theo suffered similar persecution. How can you explain their widely different attitudes to the Occupation and the German people?

2. Do you think their treatment when they arrived in the U.S. further shaped and hardened their reactions?

3. Early in the novel, a near riot occurs over a dollhouse, which, like the Biedermeier breakfront in Millie's apartment, may or may not have been appropriated from the homes of Jews who were sent to the camps. How do we, who were not there, sort out guilt, complicity, and innocence? Do we have a right to condemn or to forgive?

4. Determining guilt, innocence, and the degrees of complicity between them are dicey matters. How do you deal with someone like the German who was probably a Nazi sympathizer but now claims a clearly imaginary Jewish fiancée? The woman whose autistic son was murdered in an institution? Fraulein Weber, whose father and older brother were killed by the Nazis and whose younger brother was killed by the Americans or British in battle and who, along with her mother, was raped by the Russians?

5. Frau Kneff was obviously wrong to "kidnap" Elke, but she had saved her during the war and she loved her. Do you think it was in Elke's best interest to be torn away from the only mother she'd ever known?

6. While she's at Bryn Mawr, Millie goes home on two separate weekends with two friends whose families are very different. She finds both experiences unsettling. Discuss the differences between the families and the diverse effects they have on Millie.

7. Fleeing Nazi persecution, Millie and David encounter Jewish prejudice against Blacks on the ship, anti-Semitism in America, and after the war, rules preventing Jews from serving in the Occupation. Were American policies and beliefs hypocritical? Do you think they have changed?

8. Millie's friend Mary Jo believes that neither she nor her parents are anti-Semitic. She has even fallen in love with a Jewish man. Yet she is shocked that his family would be as offended by his marrying her—a Christian— as hers is by her marrying him. Discuss the subtleties and blindness of her assumptions.

9. After Millie discovers Harry is Jewish, she sees him differently. Is this another form of prejudice? And what of Harry's insistence that though he's not a believer, as long as there are disadvantages to being a Jew he'll be one?

10. David talks about how the Occupation forces prefer dealing with the nice clean, blond, blue-eyed Germans rather than the survivors of the camps, who are plagued by lice, TB, and other diseases and have been turned almost feral by brutality. What does this say about human nature and the ability to feel compassion?

11. What makes Millie suddenly see the Biedermeier breakfront with new eyes?

12. The GIs and the Frauleins who took up with them were young. The men had lived through a war; the girls had never known a world without it. Do you sympathize with them for grasping at pleasure?

13. Millie is consumed by survivor guilt which, due to her actions in the railroad station, takes the form of shame. Late in the novel she muses on this:

> "Loss can be consoled. Pain can be solaced. But there is no comfort for shame. Because shame is not the result of a wrong suffered but of a wrong committed. Nothing can breech the isolation of that. Not sympathy. Not sex. Not even love."

Do you think the love she found with Harry will breech the shame? Do you think the fact that he too is haunted by survivor guilt will make overcoming the shame easier or more difficult for each of them?

Movies & Books

The Allied Occupation in Film and on the Page

While scores of movies have been made and
novels and memoirs written about World War
II, the Allied Occupation that followed it has
attracted less attention. We abhor war, but are
clearly fascinated by it. Nonetheless, many of the
films and books that do exist provide a riveting
glimpse, sometimes grim, occasionally hilarious,
into that postwar world.

Perhaps the best-known movie—or one of the two
best-known (see below for the second)—about the
Occupation is *Judgment at Nuremburg*. If nothing
else, and there's a great deal else, the cast of this
film about the trial of Nazi war criminals is huge
and stunning. Spencer Tracy, Burt Lancaster, and
Marlene Dietrich headline, but no matter how
many times I've seen the movie, and I've seen it
often, Judy Garland and Montgomery Clift as survivors testifying during the trials are the ones who
break my heart. Dietrich is wonderfully cynical as
a Nazi officer's widow, and a scene at the end between Tracy and Lancaster never fails to strike me
with a beautiful if overly simplified moral clarity.

I also have a small personal anecdote about
another star of the movie who is no longer well
known. Richard Widmark was a member of an
arts club to which I belong. One evening some
years ago, a friend, who was also a huge fan, and
I decided to break club tradition—privacy was to
be respected at all costs—by approaching Widmark while he was sitting comfortably in a corner
of the club with a drink, reading. We knew we
were interrupting him, but who would mind being
disturbed by two members of a younger generation telling him how much they admired his work?

*Keep On
Reading*

We screwed up our courage, approached him, and began to sing his praises. He looked up, smiled that smile we knew so well, and said he was sorry but he didn't have his hearing aids in and couldn't hear a word we were saying. My fandom remained unacknowledged but undiminished.

The other well-known, perhaps even better-known, film is *The Third Man*, which turns out to be better than the book on which I thought it was based. The reason the film is superior is explained by Graham Greene himself in an introduction to one edition. "*The Third Man* was never written to be read but only to be seen." In other words, it started as an idea for a film, but for his own creative purposes, Greene tells us, he had to write the story, which was subsequently published. Of course, both the film and novella are set in Vienna, but the ambiance, with its rampant crime and perilous black market, its shortages of goods and abundance of spies, is so close to Berlin at the time that the two cities might be interchangeable.

Another favorite film is *The Big Lift*, which can't hold a candle to *The Third Man*, few movies can, but which has Montgomery Clift, again, this time as a GI in Berlin during the Airlift. There are two wonderful scenes. In one, Clift suspects that an elderly German is spying for the Soviets. The man admits he is counting the number of planes the Americans are flying in for Russian intelligence. Clift, confused, replies that the Americans print that information publicly every day. Yes, the spy agrees, but because it is printed, the Russians don't believe it.

In another scene, Clift's GI buddy is bullying and belittling his Fraulein girlfriend, as men of all

nations have been known to do throughout history. The Fraulein tells him he sounds just like a Nazi, which stops the buddy in his tracks. It also turns him into a more sensitive man, a rapid transformation I applaud but doubt.

One, Two, Three is set in Berlin before the Wall was built but as the Cold War was heating up. Featuring thrilling shots of two young actors, Pamela Tiffin and Horst Buchholz, speeding between East and West Berlin on a motorcycle with carefree abandon, and an over-the-top performance by James Cagney, the movie is a hilarious take on both Soviet and American foibles. The sad irony of the political and cultural spoof is that shooting began before the Wall went up, but by the time the film was released in 1961 the Wall not only divided the city but was a symbol of brutality and oppression around the world. As a result, the movie did badly at the box office in both the U.S. and Germany, but when it was re-released in 1985, it became a success, especially in West Berlin.

*Keep On
Reading*

A more realistic movie about Germany under the Allied Occupation is *Town Without Pity*, a grim tale of rape, suicide, and community cruelty. One of the most interesting aspects of the film to me is the light it sheds not on the Occupation of Germany but on postwar America. Based on a book by a German writing under the name of Manfred Gregor, the screenplay was written by Dalton Trumbo, who, due to the blacklist, didn't get credit for that film or for so many other gems until years later. The aftermath of a war does not always reflect what it was fought for.

Books set in the Occupation are even more rare than films. One fascinating and almost unknown novel is *Last of the Conquerors* by William Gardner Smith, a Black GI who served in Germany after the war. The book is a clear indictment of a segregated Army and country pretending to spread democracy and equality to a nation that treats Blacks perhaps not well, but better. The book's portrait of American bigotry is honest, painful, and relevant to our moment. One scene reveals not only the depth but the breadth of American prejudice. During a drunken evening on the town, the protagonist's white commanding officer (all Black units had white officers) boasts, patronizingly and hypocritically, that he'd match his Black soldiers against any in the Army, but he has to admit the Germans did get it right about Jews. The novel, while polemic, is well written with a clearly Hemingwayesque touch. An interesting footnote to the book is the difficulty of obtaining a copy these days. The one I read came from the New York Public Library, but a quick check of used books online reveals an old paperback that was originally 75 cents now selling for $35 and a hardcover priced at $475.

A lighter and later take on the Occupation is David Lodge's first novel, *Out of the Shelter*. This autobiographical coming-of-age story, which Lodge had trouble getting published, is the tale of a young British boy's summer-long visit to his sister, who's working for the Americans in Germany during the Occupation. His awakening from a cosseted English childhood of rigid rules and postwar scarcity to a wider world of less certain moralities and astonishing American abundance is at once touching, funny, and written with Lodge's usual grace and wit.

Deutschland by Margaret Bourke-White paints a raw and wrenching portrait of Germany in the

immediate aftermath of the war. The photographs of the suffering and destruction are shocking. The firsthand observations are immediate, occasionally wry, and cover everything from the black market, to the relative appeal of American, British, and French soldiers to German girls, to social dancing classes.

Meyer Levin's memoir, *In Search*, ranges over the years before and after the Occupation as well as the period itself. His observations are personal, often searing, and deeply affecting. He tells of Jewish GIs who, forbidden to fraternize with Germans, leave matzos on doorsteps of German Jewish organizations on the eve of Passover, of being snubbed by a German Jewish woman with whom he felt an instinctive connection but who found him socially inferior, and of his darkest thoughts about retribution and revenge. As the title of his memoir indicates, Levin was in search of the meaning of his Jewish identity. A few years later, his French wife gave him a copy of the French edition of *The Diary of Anne Frank*. Deeply moved, he was instrumental in its publication and success in the U.S.

Perhaps the most sweeping view of the Occupation can be found in *The Smoking Mountain* by Kay Boyle. An editor at *The New Yorker* asked Boyle, who was in Germany under the Occupation, for a fictional account. One of the interesting aspects of this gripping collection is that while most of the short stories—except for the first, which is clearly reportorial—work as fiction, they are grounded in Boyle's experiences in a fraught world where victors and vanquished, Germans and Americans, military and civilians, all struggle to find a way to coexist. In Boyle's gimlet eye, few come out blameless.

Keep On Reading

A Conversation with Ellen Feldman

What was the inspiration for The Living and the Lost?

Often I'm not sure about the origins of a novel, but in this case I can say the central theme was inspired by an anecdote I read while researching my last book, *Paris Never Leaves You*. I won't repeat the story because that would be a spoiler. At the time, I knew I couldn't use the incident in *Paris*, but I could not stop thinking about it. Gradually it began to take form in my imagination as a completely different novel.

So the story of Americans in Berlin during the Allied Occupation came from earlier research?

Only partly; their emotional and moral plight came from that anecdote, but I wasn't sure how to work their dilemma out in a novel until my stepson, a bibliophile who deals in old and sometimes rare books, gave me a copy of *The Smoking Mountain* by Kay Boyle. She was in Germany during the Occupation, and her account of it set me thinking and researching. The more I learned, the more I knew this was Millie's milieu.

Did other research lead you in new directions?

That's the fun of research. I always discover new worlds and new stories that lead me deeper into the characters and their lives. This time I stumbled across the story of the Ritchie Boys, young men and boys who fled Nazi regimes in Europe, came to America, were originally regarded as suspect or downright dangerous, and ended up fighting courageously for their adopted country. They were an inspiring group with a variety of fascinating individual stories.

Judging from what you've said so far, the research sounds as if it was exhaustive, but not especially personal.

The original idea for the book was personal. I am always interested in guilt, forgiveness, and how we move forward into the future without being crippled by our past. But I did stumble across a more personal connection to the material while researching the book. In a memoir of the period, I learned that in the wake of Kristallnacht, Bryn Mawr College took up a collection to establish two scholarships for non-Aryan German girls. Since I'm a graduate of Bryn Mawr, this discovery made me especially happy and proud. I did some digging and found an oral history of the college that painted a vivid picture of campus life before and during the war. It also inspired Millie's experiences with the two friends who took her home for weekends and their very different families. The more I read, the more vividly I remembered my own time at Bryn Mawr and drew on it to create the ambiance and physical settings of those scenes. Some of the faculty and my fellow students also inspired some of the characters who inhabit the book.

Berlin is almost a character, perhaps one of the main characters, in the novel. Have you been there, and what are your feelings about the city?

My feelings about the city have evolved over the years. As a teenager, I was on a student tour of Europe, and I still remember one boy leaving the group as we entered Germany and rejoining us when we left. His parents were Holocaust survivors. The experience affected me deeply.

Many years later, when I published *The Boy Who Loved Anne Frank*, I returned to Germany several times on publicity tours. My initial reaction was fear and discomfort. Those feelings dissipated quickly. I found a country that has worked hard to deal with its past, as my characters in this novel must. And I found Berlin a vital and exciting city changing literally by the day. An interesting footnote was that when I was there the first time, the second language of East Berliners was Russian, of West Berliners English, which reflected the conditions of the Occupation and Cold War, a subject I explore to some extent in the book.

Your last novel, Paris Never Leaves You, *was set in France during World War II and in New York ten years later.* The Living and the Lost *is set in Germany and America before the war and Berlin under the Occupation. You've also published two other books about America during and after the war,* Next to Love *and* The Boy Who Loved Anne Frank. *Would you say this period and these issues are your special field of interest?*

In a sense the era is not an interest but an obsession. I was born into an America still shadowed by World War II and in the throes of its prosperous aftermath. All of my characters are haunted by their pasts. Perhaps writing these novels is my form of being preoccupied with my own past and my pre-past as it came down to me through the stories of my parents and various relatives and family friends. But I have written on other subjects as well and am currently at work on a novel inspired by four real-life immigrant women who went on to great success. It's set mostly in

Hollywood during the early days of the moving
picture industry and hasn't a thing to do with
World War II or its aftermath. I have to admit,
living in the glamorous unreal world of Jazz Age
movie studios is a pleasant respite from the horrors
of war and its aftermath, though that doesn't mean
my characters don't face difficult decisions and
daily disappointments or that I don't anguish over
their setbacks and heartbreak.

*Get to
Know the
Author*